Praise For L. R. Braden

Winner of:

Eric Hoffer Book Award—SciFi/Fantasy category

First Horizon Award for Debut Authors

Next Generation Indie Book Award—Paranormal category

Imadjinn Award—Best Urban Fantasy

Colorado Authors League Award for Writing Excellence—
Fantasy and Paranormal categories

Finalist: *Colorado Book Award*—SciFi/Fantasy category

"A fast-paced, engrossing, unexpected, and tension-filled magical work. . . . A great read for every female-lead Urban Fantasy enthusiast."
—The Queen of Swords, NetGalley reviewer on
Demon Riding Shotgun

"Think of 'Venom' but a girl and a demon, and even more attitude and sarcasm, and consuming evil demons, and thwarting those wanting to take over the Earth! . . . loved it and when it ended definitely wanted more!"
—Bonita S., NetGalley reviewer on
Demon Riding Shotgun

"Holy Wow!!! I absolutely loved this book!!! I'm dying for more of this world; it is incredibly compelling with vivid world-building and fascinating well-developed characters! This is a must read!"
—Witch-at-Heart, Amazon reviewer on
Demon Riding Shotgun

"L.R. Braden's Magicsmith series contains the best of all worlds—murder, mayhem, and magic. How can you go wrong?"
—Jeanne Stein, Bestselling author of
The Anna Strong Vampire Chronicles

"A delightfully tormented anti-heroine with the mother of all inner conflicts. Braden delivers an expertly paced plot brimming with magic, gale-force fight scenes, and delicious romance. This character will get under the reader's skin, muscle, and bone."

—Hunter J. Skye, Author of the award-winning
Hell Gate Series on *Demon Riding Shotgun*

"This is one of my favorite fictional worlds to visit. . . . I devoured this like a reader starved for every word, gulping yet somehow managing to savor the delightful taste of the story."

—Lucretia, Goodreads Review on *Of Mettle & Magic*

"Once I started this book, I didn't want to put it down. . . . If you aren't reading this great urban fantasy series, you are definitely missing out."

—Penny N, NetGalley Reviewer on *Chaos Song*

Other Titles
by L. R. Braden

The Magicsmith Series

A Drop of Magic, Book 1
Courting Darkness, Book 2
Faerie Forged, Book 3
Casting Shadows, Book 4
Of Mettle and Magic, Book 5
Chaos Song, Book 6
Lies and Illusion, Book 7

The Rifter Series
(set in the Magicsmith Universe)

Demon Riding Shotgun, Book 1
Personal Demons, Book 2
A Demon Faerie Tale, Book 3
Dancing with a Demon, Book 4

Personal Demons

The Rifter Series – Book 2

by

L. R. Braden

Magical Realms Press

Magical Realms Press
PO Box 24
Broomfield, CO 80038

Print ISBN: 978-1-968414-17-7
Ebook ISBN: 978-1-968414-16-0

We love to hear from readers!
Contact us at:
MagicalRealmsPress.com
LRBraden.com

Cover design: Debra Dixon
Interior design: Hank Smith & Jim Brown
Photo/Art credits:
Woman (manipulated) © Artzzz | Dreamstime.com

Dedication

For David and Jeannette.
Thanks for welcoming me into your family.

Chapter 1

MIRA

WIND WHISTLED through gaps in the rusted siding of the defunct train car. Metal groaned as Mira stepped inside and the old car settled under her weight. She squinted into the dark corners, searching for any indication of the creature who'd left a string of mutilated corpses across Atlanta. Her magically enhanced vision drifted over the graffiti that covered every inch of the interior space, colors muted in the last glint of fading twilight.

<Pretty paintings.> The voice could almost have been an effect of the whispering wind, except that it spoke within Mira's own head, and only Mira could hear it.

She traced her fingers over the chaotic spray-paint designs, picking up a layer of dust. The jumble of overlapping images would certainly speak to the aesthetic tastes of a demon—even a demon as unusual as the one who shared her body. She rubbed the dust between her fingertips. "No one's been in here for a while."

She brushed her hand against the dark fabric of her jeans and turned toward the entrance.

A metallic *clang* echoed through the night, faint except that Mira had used magic to amplify her senses.

She froze halfway out of the train car and scanned the decaying buildings and vehicles of the abandoned rail yard. She and Ty—the Paranatural Task Force agent she'd recently agreed to work with on the sly—had come here based on reports of mangled bodies found in and around the area. The reports also mentioned an elderly man with strange marks like cracks in his skin. "Puppet lines," as Mira called them, were a manifestation of the strain a demon put on its physical host and a sure indication they were dealing with a rifter. Unlike Mira, most rifters wrought a month or two of chaos and death before burning themselves up. This one had to be nearing its expiration date, but it could still do plenty of harm before it popped.

Mira squinted toward a large building on the far side of the yard.

More graffiti coated the dark bricks and the lower-level windows. "It came from over there."

<That's Ty's side. Maybe it was him?> The demon's tone matched Mira's skepticism that Mr. Just-So would be clumsy enough to knock over a broom while searching for something that could easily kill him if he lost the element of surprise.

"I still can't believe we're working with a PTF agent," Mira muttered to the night.

<Seeing as how most would collar or kill you as soon as shake your hand, yeah, I wouldn't have bet on that either. But Ty's all right.>

"At least he doesn't seem inclined to report me," she agreed. "But his methods are gonna take some getting used to."

Before coming to the train yard, Ty had insisted on marking out a grid over a map of the area and assigning each of them a search pattern to ensure nothing got overlooked. Mira had been all for sniffing around until she found a track worth following, as she always had, but she'd agreed to give this partnership thing an honest try.

She stepped down onto the weed-covered dirt. She *was* trying, but the way Ty seemed to need to control every aspect of an operation, to control *her*, chafed. She'd been on her own since she was eleven . . . if you didn't count her demon. Human relationships had gone out the window after her possession. Too messy. Too many difficult, dangerous questions in a world that barely tolerated the fae and treated human practitioners as tools. Someone like her . . . well, there weren't any others like her. Once Mira and her demon had come to an understanding about whose body and life they were sharing, Mira had grown used to calling the day-to-day shots, doing things her own way. With Ty in the mix, it felt like everything was in flux again.

<You knew we'd have to compromise when you agreed to this arrangement.>

"Whose side are you on?"

<Mine.>

Mira nodded, lips pursed, still staring at the distant building. A gust of wind stirred her hair and tickled her nose with dust, rust, and the smell of old oil. "Let's check it out."

The demon shrugged, lifting Mira's shoulders.

Mira crouched low and jogged across the open space in the direction the noise had come from, carefully avoiding the rusted steel beams of broken tracks that littered the ground. She crossed the invisible line that marked the boundary of her search area and entered Ty's.

Let's just hope he doesn't shoot me by mistake.

The doors to the central hub had been reinforced with plywood, chained, and padlocked against trespassers. Mira frowned and ran her hand over the metal links. If the rifter was inside, he hadn't come through here.

She looked along the sides of the building in either direction. She could circle around, find another door or a broken window maybe. She sighed. *We could be chasing a stray cat for all we know.*

<Do you want to go back, finish our assigned search pattern?>

Mira bristled. She couldn't tell if the mocking she heard in the comment came from the demon or her own imagination.

She gripped the steel chain in both hands and called on her magic. The demon stirred as Mira pulled energy out of the Rift—the incorporeal plane of energy that overlapped the mortal world and all the realms connected to it. Demons lived in the Rift, when not hitchhiking in human meat puppets. They were made of the same chaotic energy human practitioners used to cast magic. In that way, Mira supposed, humans did as much damage to demons as demons did to humans.

Mira exhaled and focused the swirling eddies of energy into shape, giving them order and purpose. The metal between her hands turned red, then yellow, then white. The center link melted, dripping a handful of steaming impact craters into the dirt. Mira waited until the glowing ends of the chain faded to gray, then gently slid the links through the door handle and set them on the ground without so much as a rustle.

She flexed her fingers and shook her tingling hands, then eased open the door. The hinges scraped. She froze, straining her senses. Nothing moved. The only sound was the wind and the distant traffic of the city. A wisp of cloud passed in front of the swollen moon. The world flickered as the shadows took over for a moment, then they were chased back by the silver glow.

Mira exhaled. She wrapped a thread of magic around the hinges to dampen the sound and widened the gap enough to slip through.

Moonlight streamed in from the building's skylights, casting long shadows from the crisscross of scaffolding onto the concrete floor. Several large bay doors that would once have allowed trains to pull in were boarded over, each sporting the tag of a local artist. Steel tracks set flush to the floor created a ladder effect across the pitted, dirt-crusted surface.

A figure crept along the far edge of the building. Long, matted, white hair draped their shoulders and obscured their face save for the profile of a beak-like nose. Pale, wiry limbs moved amid tattered strips of soiled fabric, fingers nearly scraping the floor as the hunched form slunk from shadow to shadow between patches of moonlight. One bony hand clutched something. Mira squinted, then nearly gagged as she realized the man—he had to be the rifter—was dragging an extra appendage. A dark smear snaked across the pale-gray floor in his wake.

<Looks like dinner.>

Mira scowled, but since the demon was inside her, the expression didn't have much effect. Not that the demon tended to care about Mira's disapproval in any case.

There but for the grace of God. . . . She sent a silent, grateful prayer for the miracle that had allowed her to strike a balance with her possessor all those years ago and saved her from becoming one of the creatures she now hunted.

The rifter shuffled from pillar to pillar, dragging its gory meal toward a break in the south wall—a section of empty window frame partially covered by a loosely propped piece of plywood. At the pace he was moving, she had maybe a minute before he reached the opening.

She glanced around the rest of the interior. *Plenty of open space, good solid supports, no one nearby* . . . *couldn't really ask for a better space to fight in.*

<Are you going to call Ty?>

She fingered the cell phone clipped to her belt. Carrying the device—basically a tiny tracker—made her uncomfortable, but she had eventually given in to the practicality of being able to quickly communicate with Ty. Yet another concession to this whole partnership thing. The plan had been to locate the rifter, text the location, then trail it at a discrete distance until they could take it down together. It had seemed logical enough when she'd agreed to it. Now, watching her target move slowly away, she wasn't so sure.

She worried her lower lip between her teeth, then shifted her hand to the sheathed kukri knife also attached to her belt. *By the time Ty gets here, the rifter will have moved on, and the next place we catch up to it might not be so accommodating.* She slid the long, curved blade free. *We can handle this ourselves.*

Mira felt the demon grin. <Just like the old days.>

Her lips twitched up to match. The "old days" were barely two weeks gone, hardly any time at all, but Mira couldn't deny the thrill of acting without the need for debate or consent. The single hunt she'd worked with Ty—not including the unofficial case on which they'd met—had gone smoothly enough, but she'd chafed at his slow pace and meticulous planning. Right now there was a rifter in front of her, and she was going to kill it. Simple.

She stalked forward, keeping to the shadows, relying on her experience, rather than her magic, to keep her hidden. At this distance, the moment she drew any significant amount of energy from the Rift, the demon in that rifter would know.

She scooted around the edge of the building opposite the rifter, darting from pillar to pillar and shadow to shadow, just as it was. But she was moving faster, closing the distance. She'd reach the opening first.

The rifter scurried through a patch of moonlight. Puppet lines ran like frozen arcs of black lightning across the skin around the old man's eyes. Beyond those charred lines, his wrinkled, mottled flesh sagged like cellophane off his bones. He gripped his prize with fingers turned black and rotting from long exposure to the Rift. The pale glow of the moon glinted wetly off the red end of the severed limb he carried. His victim's skin had been a shade darker than his own, and male, judging by the amount of hair and the thickness of the lifeless fingers.

<This guy looks almost gone,> said Mira's demon.

Mira nodded and continued to creep toward the broken window. Demons rode their hosts hard. In all the years since she'd been inducted into this shadowy existence, Mira had only met one other rifter who'd been able to balance the power between demon and host as she had. Now they, too, were gone.

Mira crouched behind the final pillar before the opening. She inhaled, tightened her grip on the forward-heavy blade in her hand, and waited for the rifter to take the last few steps that would bring him into range.

<Now.>

She opened herself up to the energy of the Rift, wrapped it around herself, and charged the startled rifter.

TY

TY'S FLASHLIGHT beam drifted over the mess in the corner. He gagged and covered his nose and mouth to block the smell. It didn't work. He was inside a long, narrow building that had once been used to store and maintain engines and passenger cars. One such relic sat on rusted rails like a steel Twinkie layered in dust, rot, and multicolored spray paint. Several of the bay doors were missing, so the chill breeze of the spring night had followed him inside. Unfortunately, the wind did more to stir up rather than dissipate the smells of decay and mildew wafting off the pile of shredded cloth, glistening bones, and chunky globs of what looked like chili con carne he'd discovered in the corner.

This must be the rifter's nest. He backed up a step, sweeping his flashlight side to side and peering into the deeper shadows of the long room, searching for the slightest sign of movement. He reached for the cell phone clipped to his waist. If this was its nest, the rifter would be back. He and Mira could set an ambush. That would be safer than stumbling around in the dark.

As his fingers closed on the hard plastic of his phone case, a crash like a train wreck shattered the silence of the night.

In one smooth motion, he dropped to a crouch and drew his sidearm, aiming down the center of his beam as it swung across the room. It took a second for him to register that the noise had come from farther away than he'd initially thought, near the center of the train yard. A moment more and his pulse returned to normal as the sudden burst of adrenaline faded.

He straightened and turned toward the source of the sound, straining. Fainter noises drifted from that direction.

Mira. Panic and dread surged through him, squeezing his chest like a vise. His palms started to sweat. *She wasn't supposed to engage until I was there to back her up!*

He clicked off his flashlight and holstered his sidearm. It had been instinct rather than thought that made him draw the weapon, since a regular bullet would do little against a rifter. He'd learned that the hard way, when the first one he'd fought had walked away after taking four to the chest and doing a swan dive off a high-rise. Instead he pulled the short-barrel shotgun, loaded with rock salt rounds that Mira had given him, from the holster strapped across his back.

He took a deep breath and waited another moment for his eyes to adjust to the darkness, reminding himself that charging in would likely get them both killed.

I won't lose another one.

He licked his lips and slipped outside, stalking through the shadows toward the source of the sounds. The sun had set before they'd even started their search, and the last strips of twilight were fading in the west. Lamp posts were spaced around the lot, but piles of broken glass at their bases were all that remained of the bulbs. He squinted, wishing he could see as well in darkness as Mira seemed to.

Another loud crash and a flash of light drew him to one of the large central depot buildings. He frowned. *That building is in my section of the search grid. What was Mira even doing there?*

The flash of light had illuminated a broken-out window nearby. The back of his jacket snagged on rough bricks as he slid along the side of the building and peeked inside.

Dust drifted out through the hole. He stifled a cough. Several small fires burned around the room—mostly ignited trash and debris, though one flame danced on the dark surface of what looked like an old oil stain.

Mira was climbing to her feet on Ty's right. She dusted off her dark jeans and leather jacket. She coughed and waved a hand to clear the air in front of her face. Her shoulder-length hair—mostly brown except for a wide swath of snowy white near her left temple—hung loose, framing her hungry expression. Mira's right eye was nearly invisible in the flickering shadows of the firelight; her left eye was a golden beacon shining through the darkness.

Ty followed her gaze across the room. The rifter was also climbing to his feet. Apparently, the flash Ty had seen had knocked them both sprawling.

Ty barely recognized the man from his driver's license photo. Tufts of unruly white hair and a jaw of pale stubble surrounded a sharply hooked nose and high cheekbones draped with papery, age-spotted skin. Jagged lines of darkness seemed to ooze from deeply recessed eyes that shone with a metallic tint similar to the gold in Mira's. His fingertips were blackened as though he'd held them in a fire. He hunched, moving more like an orangutan than a man, his arms swinging low as he lumbered toward Mira.

Mira raised her hands. The hairs on Ty's neck and arms stood to attention. The air filled with the sound of crackling. Electricity snapped and arced over Mira's body, then shot from her fingers in a cascade of blue-tinged lightning that reminded Ty of the evil emperor from *Star Wars*.

The rifter knocked the lightning aside with apelike movements. Arcs of energy shot in every direction, singeing metal and concrete, shattering glass, and igniting wood.

Ty cringed and ducked as a stray bolt ricocheted in his direction and blew off the sheet of plywood that had half covered his hiding place. Ozone and ash tickled Ty's nose.

He opened his eyes and cautiously peered over the lip of the windowsill.

The rifter had closed the distance to Mira and was now swinging a piece of rusted steel rail as long as Ty's leg. Mira dodged and circled, knife in hand, but wasn't able to get inside the guard of the longer weapon. She was losing ground, drawing the fight deeper into the building.

Ty took a steadying breath. His shotgun didn't have the range or accuracy to risk a shot from that distance. Not with Mira standing so close. He climbed through the open window, scraping his broad shoulders on the frame, and stepped onto the battlefield . . . only to trip over something under the window. He stumbled, froze, and glanced down.

Is that a— Ty lifted his gaze away from the severed limb he'd stepped on and swallowed the bile threatening at the back of his throat.

The rifter's weapon swung toward Mira as she reversed direction from the previous attack. She didn't have time to dodge. She raised both arms and tucked her chin. Steel connected with flesh and bone. Mira grunted and flew off her feet. She slammed into one of the steel pillars supporting the room. The metal dented. More dust sifted down from the beams above. Mira collapsed to the concrete. The rifter raised his weapon.

Ty watched the scene unfold in slow motion. The image of a young man with dark-brown skin and buzzed hair flickered over Mira for a moment.

Jamal.

Ty's previous partner looked at him, eyes accusing.

I won't lose another.

Ty charged forward, shouting a battle cry of rage, grief, and guilt.

The rifter jerked and spun. Its eyes were dark pits flecked with copper.

Ty planted his feet, raised his shotgun, and pulled the trigger.

The rifter swung its hand as it had to deflect Mira's lightning, but the rock salt spread wide. The rifter couldn't track the tiny particles. It howled as the salt burrowed dozens of stinging craters in its flesh. Mira had made it clear when giving Ty the gun that salt alone wasn't going to stop a demon, or even slow it down by much, but it would hurt like hell and make it flinch.

The rifter flailed.

Mira, halfway to her feet, shouted and slid across the room.

Something invisible slammed into Ty's side and sent him tumbling. He felt ribs crack. The shotgun dropped from his fingers. The invisible force vanished as the other side of him made all-too-real contact with a pile of half-rotted wooden crates stacked near a wall. Splintered wood cascaded around him.

Ty coughed and winced. *Maybe not broken but definitely bruised.*

He tried to shift, but debris covered him, pinning him down. His breath came faster, making him cough again.

No. He shook his head and reminded himself it was only wood, only boxes, but the feeling of concrete and steel beams, of several tons of collapsed building, weighed down on him, choking off his air and crushing his will to move. Blood pounded in his ears and sparks danced in his vision. He squeezed his eyes closed, but a thin layer of flesh was no protection from the images of the past that swarmed him. The scars on his waist and leg ached with remembered pain.

Old scars, he reminded himself. *Focus on the present.*

He thrust one hand into the pocket of his pants and clenched his fingers around the familiar shape of a smooth stone with one groove scratched in the side just wide enough to fit his thumbnail into.

Focus on the present. His breathing slowed. He could feel splinters of wood digging into his side, smell the oil soaked into the train yard floor, taste the dust at the back of his throat. A noise filtered through the muffling wood. His thoughts jumped to Mira and a vision of her being knocked clear across the wide room by the rifter.

Again her features were overlaid with the ghost of Ty's childhood friend, the partner he'd failed to save, but as Mira went sprawling, Jamal stood up and walked over to Ty in the cinema of his mind. He crouched down and rested one hand on Ty's shoulder.

The strong should protect the weak.

Ty almost laughed, but the twinge in his ribs made him think better of it. "Mira isn't weak."

Jamal squeezed. The sensation seemed as real as if he were flesh and blood.

But this monster's victims were.

The severed limb he'd tripped over near the window floated in his imagination, and he gagged anew. *The strong should protect the weak. Mira and me . . . together, we're strong.*

That was why he'd agreed to this partnership in the first place, despite his misgivings. He wasn't strong enough to fight these kinds of monsters on his own. Maybe she was—she'd been doing it for years, after all—but from what he'd seen, she could use someone to watch her back . . . and sometimes to keep her in check. Together they could protect the weak, if they could just get their shit together.

Fingers gripped Ty's ankle and pulled him out of his thoughts in a clatter of broken boxes. He scrabbled at the concrete, but continued to slide, then to lift, until he was dangling upside down. His jacket bunched up around his shoulders. The tips of his buzzed, black hair skimmed the ground as his fingers struggled for purchase. He looked toward his trapped foot. The arm that held him looked thin enough to snap. Lines of sinew stood out beneath the rifter's eerily translucent skin. Copper shone from the dark pits of its eyes as it looked him over. Pale lips pulled back in a growl that exposed black gums and gray, decaying teeth. A strand of yellowish drool leaked from the corner of its mouth. Ty cringed. From this close, the rifter smelled almost as bad as the rotting remains Ty had found in its lair.

The rifter raised its free hand, fingers curled like claws.

Ty kicked out with his loose foot and flailed with his hands. He wasn't a practitioner; he couldn't see magic until it took shape in some corporeal form, but he got the feeling he'd be done for if that prepped hand hit him.

The rifter tensed to strike, then it jerked straight. The inky caverns of its eyes went wide.

The vise on Ty's ankle released, and he crumpled to the floor, curling at the last moment to protect his neck and roll away. He came up to his hands and knees on the dusty ground and stared at the stiff rifter.

Mira stood behind it, the wide belly of her blade buried in the rifter's back. Her other hand was on the rifter's neck, fingers digging into flesh. She stood barely as tall as the rifter's shoulder, but a shell of white steam flecked with darker patches and golden sparks swirled around her, encasing her, making her look nearly twice her actual size. Black mist rose off the rifter like toxic gas. The wisps drifted toward Mira and spiraled up her arms. A face began to form in the mist, overlaying the old man. The demon was being drawn out.

Ty exhaled and bit his lower lip. This was part of the deal of their partnership, this was how Mira exterminated demons. She devoured them, absorbing their energy to make her own demon stronger and to stave off the physical deterioration that would otherwise kill her. He fought the urge to look away. What she was doing was important. As far as he knew, she was the only one who could end a demon. Others could kill a host and send a demon back to the Rift, sure, but actually end it? He shook his head. He would keep her safe, no matter what.

The rifter began to thrash and scream as thicker streams of the dark mist were drawn out of him and pulled toward Mira. Her tiny body was obscured by the swirling cloud encasing her, but Ty could see the white patch in her hair had spread, and her eyes—one gold and one brown when she and her demon were in balance—were both a molten yellow. A second set of features formed in the mist over the soft curves of Mira's face.

Ty winced. Even knowing full well what she was, knowing she used her paranatural abilities to protect the helpless humans of the mortal realm, he found it difficult to look at the truth of her. He usually found it easy to forget that there was a demon riding around inside Mira's body. But now? He could barely see the small woman with wavy hair, soft brown skin, and a sharp tongue he'd come to admire, or even the powerful practitioner he'd chosen to partner with. She was not just a woman, not just a partner. She was a rifter, and the demon was taking over.

Chapter 2

MIRA

ENERGY SURGED through Mira. The old man's blood trickled over her fingers where they gripped the knife hilt. She dared not remove the blade even now, with the demon sufficiently entangled. He'd surprised her with his power. Most demons grew stronger the longer they were in the mortal realm, kind of like the buildup to one last, grand finale before they burned out their host and were pulled back to the Rift to wait for another likely target. This one must have been within a day or two of its end, and pretty damned strong to start with.

As the dark, copper-tinged tendrils of the demon's essence were pulled from the old man's body and absorbed into hers, she felt the demon within her swell beyond the boundaries of their usual arrangement. Mira's consciousness was pushed further back, to a corner of her mind where she would remain while the demon was in the driver's seat. She imagined this was how most rifter hosts lived while possessed, a passenger in their own body. She only had to deal with it after a feeding, when the demon's energy was too much to contain, or when they needed to call directly on the demon's powers.

The demon continued to drain the screaming rifter. Even if the old man wasn't aware of what was happening, he'd regain consciousness the moment the last of the Rift energy was extracted. He'd be himself for a moment, just long enough to realize what was happening. Then he'd die. They always died.

Mira looked away from the twitching, flailing, soon-to-be corpse in her hands. She still had enough physical control for that.

Ty was watching her from a crouched position on the floor. The rich brown of his irises seem almost black in his narrowed eyes. A deep frown pursed his thick lips, masked slightly by his short goatee. The sepia tones of his skin blended with the shadows of the room as the small fires caused by her fight with the rifter died down. He seemed to be studying her, examining the way the old man's demon was pulled out of his body and into hers. His expression flickered between fear and admiration. His gaze met hers for an instant, then he turned away.

He's freaked out to be working with a monster.

<Relax. He probably just doesn't want to watch this guy die.>

Mira gave herself a mental hug. Her body was now being controlled entirely by the demon. *He's been a soldier, a PTF agent, and a cop. He's seen plenty of people die.*

<Doesn't mean he enjoys it.>

But he wasn't looking at the rifter when he got disgusted, Mira insisted. *He was looking at us.*

<Fine, so maybe watching us eat another demon freaks him out. So what?>

Yeah, thought Mira. *So what? Why should I care what he thinks about me anyway? Everyone else is afraid of me. Why would Ty be any different? I am a monster after all.*

Mira's demon pulled the knife free of the old man's back. She released his neck. The man dropped heavily to his knees, gave one gurgled groan, and glanced over his shoulder at her. His hazel eyes clouded over. He toppled forward and landed with a meaty smack against the concrete floor.

"That's better." Mira's voice carried a purr when the demon spoke through her mouth. It had been unsettling at first, hearing another person's words leave her lips, but Mira had had years to get used to her situation. She no longer struggled when she was in the passenger seat. Fighting for control just made the whole experience harder. No, better to relax and enjoy the ride as best she could. In a few hours, once they'd burned off the excess energy of the feeding, Mira would be back in the driver's seat, for better or worse.

Ty stood up and dusted off his clothes. He winced and gingerly touched the side of his rib cage.

"Are you hurt?"

He glanced up, then away. He didn't meet her gaze.

Mira curled a little tighter in the corner of her mind. *Definitely freaked out by us.*

He shook his head. When he looked up again, it wasn't fear or disgust she found on his face. It was anger. "What the hell were you even doing here?"

"What?" The demon's confusion mirrored Mira's own.

"The plan. The search grid." His voice rose to a near yell. "You shouldn't have been anywhere near this building."

"We heard a noise." The demon shrugged. "We came to investigate."

"Alone?"

She shrugged again. "It might have just been a cat, or rats, or some random vagrant."

Ty set his hands on his hips and started pacing, traveling to the edge of the firelight and back. The trash fires were burning low. They'd be out completely in a few more minutes. He exhaled and pinched the bridge of his nose between his thumb and forefinger. "You were supposed to text when you made visual contact."

Mira was getting angry herself now, though she couldn't do much about it in her current situation.

"We made a judgment call."

"You nearly got yourself killed," he shouted. "I can't protect you if I don't know what you're doing. The plan was there to protect you."

Protect me? Who the hell does he think he is? You and I have been on our own for most of my life. We don't need some chivalrous asshole swooping in on a white horse just to—

<It's kind of sweet.>

Mira choked on her tirade. *Sweet? Seriously?*

<Admit it. You like that he was worried about you.>

Mira pushed aside the treacherous flutter of emotions she didn't want to acknowledge. *Just tell him we don't need his protection.*

<But we kinda did. Or his help, at least.>

Whose side are you on?

The demon laughed, and the sound trickled out Mira's mouth.

Ty stiffened. "You think this is funny?"

"Humor is one of the main perks of this realm." She licked her lips and sauntered toward him, swinging her hips way more than Mira did when she walked.

What are you doing?

Ty backed up a step. "What are you doing?"

"Humor isn't the only perk."

No, no, no. We agreed Ty was off-limits.

<You said. I never agreed.>

This situation is complicated enough without adding sex.

<It's not like we haven't slept with him before.> She lifted her hands and set them against the solid muscle of Ty's chest. His eyes went wide. He took another step back and bumped against a pillar. She closed the distance.

That was before we knew him. Before we agreed to work with him. Before we had to see him every day. Mira pounded against the demon's control. It did no good.

<But you like him. I know you like him. And he likes you.>

Ha! Shows what you know about humans. He's disgusted by me. By us. By what we are.

"What are you doing, Mira?"

Mira winced when Ty said her name. It wasn't that he couldn't tell the difference when the demon was driving . . . probably . . . but Mira hadn't been able to give him anything else to call her. Her demon had steadfastly refused to choose a name. Even Mira didn't have a separate name to call it. She'd tried assigning it random names in the hopes one would stick, but that just made it surly and uncooperative. Finally she'd had to accept that, just as demons didn't have bodies or genders beyond those of their hosts, they didn't have names.

The demon trailed one finger over Ty's cheek, along his jaw, and over the scratchy beard on his chin. She traced the line of his lower lip.

Were his lips always this soft? Mira pushed the thought away.

"I've had a big meal," the demon crooned. "I've got energy to share." She raised her other hand to his side, where he'd winced earlier. "Enough to make you feel all kinds of better."

Ty grabbed both her wrists, squeezing just beyond what was comfortable. His expression was stony, closed. He pushed her away. "Don't."

Mira, who'd been figuratively leaning onto the balls of her feet, settled back, withdrawing further into the background of her mind. She wrapped herself in layers of numbing distance, glad she didn't have to school her features to hide the sting of his rejection. *See. No one wants to make love to a monster.*

<Maybe if *you* didn't see yourself that way—>

There's no other way to see it.

The demon pulled her hands free of Ty's grip, stepped back, and smiled. "Your loss." She turned around and started walking.

"Where are you going?" he called.

She waved a hand without looking back. "To find someone more fun to spend the night with."

MIRA

MIRA STROKED ONE finger down the shea butter skin of her companion's bare back, brushing aside a strand of dark-brown hair. The blue-and-black figure of a dragon snaked along the woman's ribs and over her shoulder blade, dancing among glistening droplets of sweat. Her long eyelashes fluttered, but her silver-glittered eyelids stayed closed. Her chest rose and fell in deep even breaths. The spell Mira had cast would keep the woman asleep for an hour or so. Plenty of time for her to gather her things and be gone.

She rolled over and planted her feet on the shaggy, yellow rug beside the metal-frame bed. She stretched, sighed, and glanced at the clock. Well after midnight. She rose and walked to the bathroom, feet slapping against the cheap beige tiles of the motel room floor. The lighted sign of the pool hall across the street, where she'd found her companion, glared through the room's open curtains.

She bent over the sink, turned the tap, and splashed a handful of icy water into her face. Shutting off the faucet, she braced her hands and stared into the mirror. Her left iris was liquid gold, but her right was the earthy color of healthy soil. The white stripe in her hair was only about two fingers wide. The demon lay contentedly inside her. The excess energy from gorging on the rifter had been funneled into the woman on the bed during their marathon lovemaking session. When Mira's sleep spell wore off, her companion would become the Energizer Bunny until the energy dissipated naturally.

Mira checked each of the magical anchors that pinned the demon to her soul, noting the balance of energy. Each time the demon fed, it grew a little stronger, like a person's stomach stretching after a series of large meals. Trying to keep all the new energy would blow out the anchors and rip Mira's body apart, but as long as they were careful to keep only what they could balance, their reservoir grew deeper with every feeding. The rest of the energy had to be expelled, and the quickest way to do that was to transfer it to another living being.

Mira often preferred to dispel excess energy by releasing it through a series of spells, or by bolstering herself and engaging in some physically strenuous activity, but that took longer, and after the sting of Ty's rejection she'd needed to feel a human connection, even a shallow one. Sex had the benefit of exercise *and* a living target, plus the energy could be put to use by the recipient—the rifter version of recycling.

Satisfied that she and her demon were still in balance, Mira wiped her face on the threadbare, blue towel hanging by the shower and collected her clothes from the motel floor. The woman on the bed let out a soft snore and rolled over. Mira smiled. Sandi-with-an-I had made the first move, waving Mira over nearly as soon as she'd entered the pool hall. Mira normally avoided learning the names of her one-night stands, but Sandi was an over-sharer. It turned out Sandi was a stressed-out dental hygienist looking for a no-strings release. They'd moved to the motel after two games of pool, twice that many drinks, and a good deal of laughter. Mira got the feeling she and Sandi could have been friends in another life.

She zipped her pants, tied her sneakers, and pulled on her shirt and jacket. She opened the motel door and cast one last look at the figure sleeping on the bed. The scene morphed in her imagination until Sandi became Ty. His broad shoulders and the curve of his hips were a dark mountain range that vanished beneath the stark contrast of his white sheets. The flat planes of his abs were marked by pale scars on one side. His face was peaceful as he rested in the dreamless sleep of Mira's spell—the only time Mira had seen that expression. She'd left him like that the night they first met. She hadn't known his name then, and she'd never expected to see him again.

"So much for that plan," she muttered. She pulled the door closed behind her as she stepped out into the night and headed for another motel across town where Ty would be sleeping.

She walked along the nighttime streets of Atlanta, heading toward the brighter lights of the city's center. The spring air was warm and heavy with the promise of rain. Crickets, freshly emerged from winter, chirped in the darkness. She forced herself to keep an even pace as cars rumbled past, their headlights momentarily washing out the world. She could have called a cab or jumped on a bus, but she hated the loss of control that came with being a passenger. She got quite enough of that with her demon. Besides, she still had plenty of energy, even after sharing with Sandi, and she enjoyed the peace and freedom that came with walking at night.

It took nearly an hour to reach the beige-walled, brown-roofed, motel building where Ty had taken a room. The renovated U-Haul that had served as Mira's home for the better part of six years was parked beside Ty's silver pickup truck in the motel parking lot. The exterior of the truck was currently painted with an illusion that made it look like an orange moving van with green lettering and a phone number that called a deli in Kentucky.

Mira unlatched the back of the truck and stepped up on the bumper. Most of the interior space was taken up with her black Ducati. Thick gray straps held the motorcycle in place between the cabinet-lined walls, and Mira had to play Twister just to reach the far side. She patted the leather seat as she passed and whispered, "Soon, baby. I promise." She hadn't had much chance to ride the bike since teaming up with Ty. She'd offered to let him perch behind her, but he'd insisted the truck was a more practical two-person vehicle. She'd conceded the point, but she missed the feeling of riding free.

Mira opened a drawer and pulled out an X-Acto blade, a sterile pad, and two small band-aids.

The demon stirred within her. <You should get some sleep.>

"When I'm done."

<I know Ty got a room with two beds, but I think we should crawl in with him.>

"You're trying to distract me." She unzipped her jeans and tugged them down to her knees.

<You could say you didn't see him in the dark.>

"It's not going to work." Mira measured from the raised scar at the bottom of the ladder on her thigh and pressed the blade against her flesh.

<Why must you torture yourself like this?>

"Why must you keep asking?" She made a swift incision, hissing at the sting. "Hail Mary, full of grace. Blessed art thou among women, and blessed is the fruit of thy womb. Pray for us poor sinners, now and at the hour of our death."

<That host was nearly used up. He wouldn't have lasted more than a day or two anyway.>

"I still killed him. The circumstances don't change the truth."

The demon made a *tsk* sound inside her head. <You're always asking these saints of yours for forgiveness. Has it ever occurred to you that maybe you should try forgiving yourself?>

Mira cleaned and covered the fresh cut. Then she tugged on the silver chain around her neck, pulling a small medallion cast with the figure of Saint Jude from under her shirt. She kissed the image, squeezed it tight, then let it fall back against her chest.

<Seriously, would it kill you to treat yourself a little better?>

Mira pursed her lips, wiped the blood off her blade, and put her ritual supplies away. "I don't expect you to understand."

<Oh, I understand all right. I understand that you've convinced yourself you're irredeemable, but that's just you projecting your own—>

She slammed the drawer closed. "Just drop it, all right?"

<Fine, fine. What do I know? I'm just stuck in here with your thoughts is all.>

Mira pulled up her pants, then yanked open an overhead cabinet and grabbed a scratched black laptop.

<I thought we were going to bed.>

"Yeah, well, I changed my mind." She crossed her legs and plopped down on her butt. Her knee bumped the motorcycle tire. Her back was pressed to the textured metal of the wall separating the back of the truck from the cab.

<You're sulking.>

Mira ground her teeth. "I just don't feel like going to bed yet." She sighed. The truth was she didn't even know why she was avoiding going to Ty's room. He was probably already asleep. And even if he wasn't, it's not like he'd mention what happened earlier. The look of disgust on his face when he saw her feeding flashed through her mind. She bit her bottom lip. The demon was wrong; she wasn't just projecting. She shook her head. "It's never too early to think about your next meal. This rifter was the last one we traced from those who escaped that necromancer mess at Arlington. That means we're back to looking for leads that might point to random possessions."

<Maybe look for something in California. We haven't been there in a while.>

Mira lifted the lid of her laptop and pressed the power button. The ancient device hummed to life. A small icon pulsed at the bottom of the desktop, indicating she had a new email. She opened the browser and found a message from Father Bembe, a priest she'd known as a child. She'd helped him with a demon that had targeted his congregation. Her hand dropped to her thigh. One of those lines, the very first one in fact, was for a blue-eyed girl who'd killed eleven churchgoers before Mira put her down. She shuddered. That one still gave her nightmares. Not the demon, or the eleven victims, but the eyes of that little girl staring up at her as she drained her life. The girl had been almost the same age Mira was when the demon first possessed her—a vision of what she might have become had her demon followed the usual pattern.

She cleared the lump from her throat and opened the email.

Mira,

   I hope this message finds you. I got this address from your abuela, though she says you don't respond. I fear the problem you helped me with before may be back. There is no one else to ask. Please come.

—Bembe

Mira stared at the handful of words on her screen. Her mouth had gone dry. It wasn't impossible for a demon to pop up where she'd already taken one out, but natural rifters—those not created through necromantic interference—were relatively rare. What were the odds a second one would turn up not just in her hometown, but in her childhood church?

<Looks like we found our lead. That's got to be some kind of record.>

Mira licked her lips and forced a laugh. "I thought you wanted to go to California."

<Florida's okay. At least there's a beach.>

Mira took a shaky breath and exhaled. *Florida.* She hadn't been back there in years. She hadn't intended ever to go back. Not after what had happened the last time.

"Do you really think he's found another?"

The demon gave the mental equivalent of a shrug. <We could ask for more details, see if he's jumping at shadows.>

Mira closed the laptop then tipped her head back so her skull rested against the metal wall. She closed her eyes. Swirls of anxiety twisted like a thunderstorm inside her, threatening to break loose and drown her in a torrent of memories she'd done her best to forget. "Why did it have to be Florida?"

<We don't have to go.>

"Father Bembe isn't a fool. He saw what happened to the child we weeded out last time, and he knows about my past. He wouldn't have contacted me without good reason."

There is no one else to ask. The words floated against the darkness of her eyelids.

<So you want to go?>

"Of course I don't want to go," Mira shouted at the ceiling. "What are the odds I can investigate a rifter in my old neighborhood without stumbling across anyone I know? And if *abuela* finds out. . . ." She shook her head, trying to rein in her rampant emotions.

<So you *don't* want to go.>

Mira pressed her fingertips to her temples. "I can't just ignore him. Even if it isn't a rifter, he's clearly in some kind of trouble."

<Okay, how about you just tell me when you make up your mind.>

Shoving her laptop aside, Mira stood up and paced the tiny space, barely two steps in either direction. She worried at her lower lip and thought of all the reasons she'd avoided visiting Florida for nearly a decade. Could she slip in and talk to Father Bembe without anyone else finding out? Did she have a choice? If there really was a rifter loose in her old neighborhood. . . . It was a vision of her abuela—her grandmother—becoming some rifter's victim, like the poor souls decomposing at the train yard, that finally decided her.

She stopped her pacing and blew out a deep breath. "This is going to suck."

<At least you'll have Ty to back you up. Maybe he can run interference.>

"*¡Ay, coño!*" She brought her hands to her mouth with a gasp as another surge of anxiety tore through her. "I hadn't even thought about him being there."

<What's the big deal? I think he's proven himself quite useful.>

"What's the big deal about a guy who makes my heart race but looks at me like dog vomit following me around my hometown, where he might learn all kinds of things about my past that I'd rather pretend never happened? Yeah, why would that bother me at all?"

<He doesn't look at you like dog vomit.>

Mira snorted.

<Unless he's got a *very* weird relationship with dog vomit.>

She tucked her laptop back in its cubby. "Maybe we should do this one on our own."

<Fine with me, but you did promise to give this whole partner thing an honest try.>

"We can still be partners even if we don't work *every* case together."

<Mmmm, not so sure about that. If he ran off in the middle of the night to fight a rifter without you, would you still feel like his partner?>

Mira drummed her fingers against the countertop. "I really hate it when you make sense."

<Hey, I'm not saying don't leave him if that's what you want to do, although I personally think you'd be making a huge mistake. I'm just saying don't expect him to be waiting here when you get back.>

She pressed her palms flat on the cool surface of the counter and hissed, "Fine," through clenched teeth. "Let's just get this over with."

As she got out of the truck, Bembe's words echoed in her mind. *Please come.*

"We need to hurry. If Bembe really has found a rifter. . . ."

<Time means bodies,> the demon finished.

Chapter 3

TY

TY JERKED AWAKE thrashing. The sheets tangled around his body felt like steel beams and shattered concrete pinning him down. His heart was racing. Sweat coated his skin, and the night air made him shiver. Hands pawed at him, gripping his shoulders, shaking him, bouncing him against the bed. In his nightmare they'd been the hands of the rescuers who'd pulled him from the collapsed building, except they'd been pushing him further down into the dark rather than pulling him free. He knocked the hands away and took a shuddering breath, blinking in the harsh glare of the bedside lamp. Gray ceiling tiles met beige walls decorated with generic abstract prints. The blank screen of a television perched in the corner like a black hole.

Motel room. He licked his lips and took a steadier breath.

"Are you awake?"

He turned his head slightly to squint at the owner of the hands. Mira was leaning over him, kneeling on the edge of his bed. The cheap mattress sank under her knees. His body rolled toward her. His ribs bumped her knee. The hair that framed her face as she looked down at him was mostly brown, with only the thin strip of white that was always present. Her left eye still contained a metallic sheen, but her right was a deep, warm brown that he felt he could fall into. Her lips, a perfect pink bow, were turned down at the corners, and a small frown creased the space between her eyebrows. His hand twitched with the desire to reach up and smooth that skin, to erase the worry carried there. His gaze drifted back to her mouth. His groggy mind raced with the memories of those lips, the feel of her skin, her hands on his body.

No. We're partners now. I can't think of her that way. But the remembered sensations persisted. His heart started racing for a different reason. Ty scooted sideways, creating some distance between them, and rubbed a hand over his face to break the visual contact.

"Finally." Mira pulled back, safely out of reach. "You're a really heavy sleeper."

"What—"

"Come on." Mira's slim fingers clamped around Ty's wrist, pulling his hand away from his face. Her hand was so small it only half circled his thick wrist, but her grip was like steel. She stood up, and Ty found himself being dragged out of the bed.

He scrambled to get his legs beneath him. The blankets dropped to the floor, leaving him in only his blue-plaid boxers and bare skin. He shivered. "What's going on?"

She glanced back at him, down, then up. Spots of pink bloomed on her cheeks. "We've got a job."

He pulled his arm back, bringing her to a halt. She stopped but didn't let go. He glanced at the drawn curtains, then at the clock. "It's the middle of the night."

"Excellent observation, Detective." She released his wrist and moved to his suitcase, which rested at the bottom of the closet. She opened the lid and started pulling out clothes.

"What are you doing?" he demanded as a red sweatshirt hit him in the face, followed by jeans, a bundle of socks, and a fresh pair of boxers. She seemed irritated, though at what he had no idea. The new job maybe? Or the fact that he'd been asleep—as any sane person would be at that hour. Or was she still mad that he'd turned down her earlier invitation?

"I'm trying to get you moving." She circled around behind him and shoved him, stumbling, toward the bathroom. "Geez, you really are thick in the morning, aren't you?"

Heat flooded him until he realized the meaning behind her words. "Why such a rush?"

"Just get dressed. I'll explain on the way." She flicked on the bathroom light and pulled the door closed, then shouted, "And hurry."

Ty stared at the closed door in stunned silence for a moment, then he looked down at the bundle of clothes in his arms. *What the hell?* An overwhelming urge to throw open the door and demand an explanation filled him, until Mira's agitation filtered through the confusion and sleep clouding his mind. She always had a sharp tongue, but she'd seemed . . . unsettled.

He took a deep breath and pushed his frustration aside. Part of having a partner was trusting them without question. He and Mira weren't there yet, but trust had to start somewhere. He'd follow her lead for now and trust there was a reason for her actions and attitude.

He dropped the clothes, turned on the sink faucet, and splashed some water in his face. He took several more deep breaths, trying to shake off the lingering effects of his nightmare. He wished he had his anchor stone, but that was currently in the pocket of his jacket in the other room. He closed his fist anyway, picturing the stone, imagining its weight, remembering the feel of the gouge across its surface. He exhaled and opened his eyes, feeling a bit calmer.

He glanced longingly at the shower, but Mira's impatience made him turn away. He splashed one more handful of cold water in his face, then picked up the clothes she'd thrown at him and, folding them, made a neat pile on the edge of the tub. He returned to the sink and lifted his toothbrush, first in the row of neatly arranged toiletries lined up like soldiers on the counter. Mira's wakeup call had started him off on the wrong foot, but he'd salvage as much of his morning routine as he could. He squeezed a pea-sized dollop of toothpaste onto the brush.

By the time he opened the bathroom door again he was clean—as clean as he could get without a proper shower—shaved, minty-fresh, fully dressed, and felt much more like himself. Mira was pacing the motel room wall to wall. She stopped when he entered.

"Finally." She darted past him and scooped all his bathroom essentials into a small bag, then she planted a hand at the small of his back and ushered him toward the front door.

Ty planted his feet. His suitcase was missing. All of the personal belongings he'd unpacked were gone as well, except a small pile at the end of the bed. "Where's all my stuff?"

"In the truck."

Ty clenched his jaw and counted to ten in his head. He didn't like people touching his things. Everything in his life had a place. Mira was generally a pretty tidy person, except when her demon was calling the shots, but she didn't know his methods, his order. He shuddered to think what the inside of his suitcase might look like when he opened it.

Mira flapped her hands in exasperation. "I don't know."

Ty frowned, then realized Mira hadn't been speaking to him. She did that sometimes, responded to something the demon conveyed in the privacy of her thoughts as though they were a separate person standing in the room. It was disconcerting, like a great many things about his new partner, but he was getting used to it.

She tapped her foot on the compressed, blue carpet. "Are you going to stand there all day?"

He reminded himself to breath. Fighting with her now wouldn't accomplish anything. He did a final walk-through of the motel room to ensure Mira hadn't left anything behind, then grabbed his holstered gun, wallet, PTF badge, keys, and jacket off the bed. He stuffed yesterday's boxers into a pocket so he didn't have to carry them across the parking lot and checked the other pocket to ensure his stone was still in place. Then he stepped into his shoes and faced Mira, who was practically vibrating with impatience. "Okay, let's go."

Night lay heavily across the city when he stepped out of the motel room. Moisture hung in the air, not quite falling but enough to dampen his skin when he moved through it. Hazy halos circled streetlights and the flickering vacancy sign at the motel entrance.

Mira headed for the back of her souped-up U-Haul and lifted a tow bar. "Help me get your truck hitched."

It took only a few moments to get the trucks lined up for towing, but by the time Ty hopped out of his pickup to help tether them, the moisture had turned into proper rain. Fat drops exploded on the dark pavement as he and Mira scrambled to anchor the chains.

Ty yawned and fumbled one of the connections. The heavy links clattered to the asphalt.

"Clumsy much?" Mira chided as she reached for the chain.

"Well excuse me for being not quite awake yet. *Someone* yanked me out of bed in the middle of the night."

"If you'd taken my offer earlier, you'd have enough energy to run a marathon right now."

Heat swarmed Ty's system as memories of their single sexual encounter filled his thoughts. It was true he'd felt like a million bucks when he'd woken up alone the morning after. He'd chalked that up to endorphins at the time, but now he knew it was because she'd funneled the life essence of the rifter she'd just killed into him during their lovemaking in order to rebalance her own weirdly delicate energy needs.

He shuddered and focused on tightening the final chain. "That should do it."

Mira trotted to the cab of the lead vehicle and climbed in. Ty took a moment to check that the doors on his truck were locked, then followed.

Mira's hands were white on the wheel. She turned the key in the ignition as soon as Ty's door was closed. Damp air blew through the vents in the dash. Wipers squeaked across the windshield, smearing the rain and mixing it with dried bird shit and fuzzy tufts that had fallen from blooming trees during the three days the truck had been parked at the motel. The headlights cut a swath through the dark as she pulled onto the road.

Ty settled back against his seat and crossed his arms. "Now that we're moving, care to fill me in on what's got you barking orders like a drill sergeant this morning?"

She glanced at him, then returned her eyes to the road. "I got a message from an old acquaintance in Florida, someone I did a job for a few years back. He thinks there's a demon in town."

"Florida, huh?" He kept his voice carefully neutral. He knew from the files he'd found after running her prints that Mira was originally from Miami, though she hadn't lived there since she was a kid. He also knew she'd left family behind there. Family she steadfastly refused to talk about. "Whereabouts in Florida?"

The plastic steering wheel creaked in her grip. "Miami."

Ty pursed his lips and nodded. *No wonder she's stressed. Putting down rifters is one thing. Facing personal demons. . . .* He turned his attention to the front, suddenly picturing the street in Boston where he and Jamal had grown up. *That's another story entirely.* He cleared his throat. "This acquaintance of yours . . . you trust them?"

"We wouldn't be driving right now if I didn't."

"What's the situation?"

"I don't know."

He raised an eyebrow and cast her a sidelong glance. He wasn't surprised to find her going off half-cocked—from what he'd seen, she seemed to function on instinct more than discipline—but he'd assumed she had *some* idea what they were walking into. "How are we supposed to make a battle plan when we've got no idea what we're facing?"

"We'll get the details from Father Bembe. We can plan after that."

Ty's second eyebrow rose, wrinkling his forehead. "Father? As in priest?"

Her focus drifted in his direction but darted back to the road as soon as their eyes met. She gave a stiff, stone-faced nod.

Ty's gaze slid to the silver chain around Mira's neck. He knew she was religious, despite the fact that most churchgoers would be lining up to burn her at the stake if they found out what she was. Now they were going to her hometown, to meet with a priest from her past. Did this Bembe fellow know what she was? He had to, right? Why else would he call her about a demon problem?

Mira was as silent about her past as he was about his, which usually suited him just fine. He didn't want anyone poking and prodding the still-healing wounds of his personal trauma. But if they were walking into the middle of some shit from Mira's past, he needed to know. "Does this case have anything to do with your family?"

If she'd been stone before, now she turned to ice, cold and brittle. "No."

"Because if—"

"I said no," she snapped. "We're not going to see them, or talk to them, or go anywhere near them. We'll get this job wrapped up as fast as possible and be gone. They'll never even know I was there."

Ty got the impression those assertions were more for herself, or maybe her demon, than for him. In fact it seemed as if she'd almost forgotten he was there by the time she stopped speaking. Despite his itching need to be prepared, he let the matter drop. He could imagine how she must be feeling, or at least how he'd be feeling if they were headed to Boston instead of Miami. He hadn't visited his own hometown since Jamal's funeral. Too many ghosts.

She pulled onto the highway heading south. He wished he could do something to ease the strain in her expression, the tension in her rigid body, but he knew the signs of a person lost in their own memories. Pressing her now would only frustrate them both. With Florida hours away, he might as well rest so at least one of them was thinking clearly when they arrived. He settled lower in his seat and tucked his chin to his chest. "Wake me when it's my turn to drive."

TY

TY HISSED AS the coffee from one of the two Styrofoam cups he'd just purchased from the gas station convenience store scalded his tongue. He stomped his foot and shook his head, then continued across the asphalt to the pumps. The clouds had cleared as they drove south to reveal pale-blue sky. While the rain had let up, the humidity had increased, so even though nothing was falling, Ty still felt damp. They were maybe an hour outside of Miami.

Ty peeked through the windshield at Mira, curled in the passenger seat with her head pressed to the window and Ty's jacket draped over her like a blanket. Ty had woken up and taken the wheel shortly after sunrise. Mira had relinquished the driver's seat easily enough, but she'd sat in tense silence, staring out the window, for most of the four or so hours he'd been driving. It had only been in the last hour that she'd finally dozed off, and he hated the thought of waking her. He would have driven straight through, except for the fact that he didn't know the specifics of their destination and the equally pressing matter of the gas light coming on. Still, he entered the cab like a burglar sneaking into an occupied bedroom. He set the drinks in their cup holders, set the packaged muffins he'd bought on the bench, and gently tugged the door closed with the latch lifted until it clicked softly into place, blocking out the sounds of the bustling station.

He twisted toward Mira and studied the contours of her face. Dark circles deepened the shadows beneath her eyelashes. Her eyelids twitched in R.E.M. He hoped it was a good dream. At least the crease that had puckered her brow all last night had finally smoothed. He brushed a strand of white hair off her forehead and tucked his jacket tighter under her chin where it had started to slip. *We made good time. Maybe I should pull around back and let her sleep for a bit. Goodness knows she won't get much rest if we jump straight in on another case.*

He sighed and leaned back in his seat, wrists crossed over the steering wheel. Mira was as tough as they came. He'd seen her throw fireballs and break through walls. He'd even seen her freeze time. She'd survived alone on the streets since she was a kid. The idea that she needed anyone to look after her—least of all a guy who'd gotten his last partner killed—was ridiculous. His gaze rolled to the side. But he couldn't shake the impulse. For all her magical abilities and demonic sidekick, despite his own shortcomings, he still wanted to keep her safe. Maybe he was seeking redemption. Maybe he just didn't want any more ghosts following him around. *Or maybe. . . .* He pushed the thought away before the persistent voice at the back of his mind could complete it.

Twisting the keys in the ignition, he pulled the truck around behind the gas station to park in the shade of a shedding cottonwood.

Mira murmured and shifted. Her eyes fluttered open, one brown, one gold.

So much for letting her rest.

"Where are we?" She mumbled as she wiped her eyes and blinked in the daylight.

"A gas station in Fort Lauderdale." He held up one of the packaged muffins. "Hungry?"

"Thanks." She took the offering, opened the bag, tore off a piece, and popped it into her mouth.

"There's coffee, too, but it's hot."

She nodded and grabbed one of the throwaway cups, lifting it to her lips.

Ty thrust his hand over the top of the cup. Hot coffee splashed against his palm. He winced but was distracted an instant later as soft lips pressed to the back of his hand.

Mira pulled back and looked at him as though she'd suddenly encountered an alien species.

"I told you," he said. "It's hot." He plucked the cup from her fingers and returned it to its holder.

She continued to stare as though he were a madman as she popped another chunk of muffin into her mouth. Her lips curved up slightly as she chewed.

He cleared his throat and set his hands back on the wheel. "So, where exactly is this priest we're going to see?"

Mira directed him to get back on the highway.

After about fifteen minutes of silence, Ty cleared his throat. "How long since you were last in Florida?"

Mira continued to stare out the window.

Ty sighed. "I'm not prying. I just want to know how current your information is."

"Not very." Mira's words were quiet, subdued. She reached for her coffee and took a sip, then wrinkled her nose and glared at the cup in her hand.

"Still too hot?" he asked.

"What is this?"

Ty frowned. "It's coffee."

"It's nasty." She put the drink back in its holder and went back to watching the scenery slide by.

Ty hazarded a sip from his own cup. The liquid had cooled enough not to scald him. The drink carried a waxy flavor from the cup and a slightly burnt aftertaste. "It's gas station coffee. What did you expect?"

She sank a little lower in her seat and rubbed her temples. "Sorry, I'm just. . . ." She made an exasperated "argh" sound and shifted her gaze to the ceiling. "I don't even know right now."

After a moment of silence he asked, "This priest we're going to see. How exactly do you know him?"

Mira opened her mouth, closed it. Her expression twisted into something close to pain.

"Never mind," he said, wondering if Mira had *any* clear-cut relationships. "As long as you trust him, that's good enough for now."

The tension around her eyes eased. "Thank you."

He nodded and shifted his focus back to the road, recalling the easy companionship and laughter he'd shared with Jamal. But he'd known Jamal his whole life. Mira was practically a stranger. True partnerships took time . . . and trust.

Mira turned on the radio and flipped through stations until she found one she liked. Then she settled back, fingers tapping her thighs along to the rhythm.

Ty watched her from the corner of his eye. *Maybe someday.*

One song ended and another began, then the DJ invited people to call in with opinions about the new paranatural alliance experiment in Colorado and rumors that the Unified Church was going to open negotiations for a revised treaty with the fae. Ty cut his gaze to Mira. The crease between her eyebrows had returned, and her lips were pressed to thin lines.

Human relations with the fae had been on everyone's mind recently, since a rampaging siren had nearly pushed the mortal realm to all-out war. It had been a group of paranaturals—humans with nonhuman abilities, along with some fae allies—who'd put an end to the threat, saving a lot of lives and earning a decent amount of goodwill in the process. The Church was claiming they'd sanctioned the action, which Ty didn't believe for a second. But Church support for the alliance would go a long way toward legitimizing it, so he figured the real heroes were willing to share credit. With enough backing, maybe paranatural inclusion in the PTF would spread.

Ty wondered what Mira thought of the situation. If magic practitioners could carry PTF badges, would she stop hiding who she was? But she wasn't just a practitioner. Even if the world accepted sorcerers and werewolves, even if they made a new deal with the fae, getting anyone to accept a demon. . . . He shook his head. He was still struggling with that one himself.

A caller on the radio started spouting a litany of Purity propaganda. Mira turned off the tirade and hugged herself as though the words had been directed at her.

Ty wracked his brain for something to say, but everything sounded like a platitude.

"Take the next exit." Mira straightened and pointed to a green sign marking the off-ramp with icons for gas, food, and lodging, then glanced at him and added a belated, "Please."

Ty got into the right lane, crossed a bridge over a river, and dropped into the city. Murals decorated the buildings, the fences, even the trash cans. Ty stared as he passed not one but three six-foot, rainbow-painted, chicken sculptures. He glanced at Mira, wondering if she'd answer if he asked what was up with the roosters, but the way her narrowed eyes tracked the scenery as though she were under attack made him press his lips and keep driving.

Locals strolled the wide sidewalks in colorful shirts and shorts. People of all ages sat at tables in paved plazas playing chess or dominoes. The architecture was simple and blocky, with few buildings climbing higher than three stories and most settling with only one. Palm trees grew from tiny patches of dirt built into the brick sidewalks. Awnings and umbrellas struggled to shade the people crammed around metal tables in front of restaurants or crowded around food carts.

After rolling along for a few minutes, Mira said, "Turn left at the next intersection."

Ty took the corner wide, turning into a residential neighborhood.

Single-story homes with plaster walls in shades of blue, yellow, pink, or white lined the street. Short fences of matching plaster or painted iron wrapped the properties. Some had lawns, some were paved with concrete or cobblestone, some were patterned with decorative rocks, but all were clean and precise, with not a pebble or blade of grass out of place. Palm trees dotted the median between street and sidewalk, casting dappled shade across the road.

Halfway up the second block sat a medium-sized church with yellow adobe walls, three arched doorways, and a central tower capped with a red dome. Above the center door sat a circular window of colored glass, and above that was a clock. As Ty pulled around to the parking lot next to the building, he wondered if there was a bell in the tower that would toll the hour.

He glanced at Mira, who was staring at the building as though it were haunted. He cut the engine. She didn't move. He opened his door and stepped onto the rough pavement of the little lot. He stretched his arms high, reached down to touch his toes, then twisted to relieve the tension in his lower back. He took a deep breath. The air was salty and thick. He looked back into the cab. "Shall we?"

Mira finally slid out of her seat.

Ty closed his door and headed toward the front of the church. It wasn't a large building, barely wider than the houses that surrounded it, but it was well kept. Thick grass ringed the property. Palm trees swayed in the gentle breeze along a wide walkway that led from the street to the main entrance. Nearer the building, stone planters held neatly trimmed bushes. An old man with leathery, liver-spotted skin the color of molasses and short silver-white hair seemed to be maintaining the grounds at that very moment. A pale-blue, button-up T-shirt draped his broad but slightly hunched shoulders, and his black slacks defied the blazing afternoon sun. He held a pair of gardening shears in one hand, with which he sculpted the bushes near the front door, mercilessly snipping any twig that dared to grow out of place.

Rather than walk all the way to the sidewalk and back down the main path, Ty strode across the manicured lawn.

The gardener glanced over his shoulder, scowled, and stomped toward Ty with his clippers raised. "You're in such a hurry you can't stay on the path?" His words were marked by a thick Spanish accent. A white rectangle showed at the center of the man's collar.

Ty stumbled to a stop. He was already halfway across the lawn. He wouldn't do any more damage moving forward than going back, yet the disapproval in the old man's stare held him in place. He cleared his throat, mumbled an apology, and started to backtrack.

The man's hard gaze shifted to the space behind Ty. A grin stretched his lips, revealing a wide gap between his front teeth and transforming his expression from irritation to joy. He raised his hands in welcome, his clippers seemingly forgotten. "You came."

Ty twisted to find Mira standing at the edge of the grass, hands wrung together. Her mismatched gaze darted over and away from the old man as though afraid to come to rest. "Hello, Father Bembe."

Chapter 4

MIRA

"COME, COME." FATHER Bembe waved Mira and Ty forward, but Mira took the time to skirt around the lawn and follow the walkway to the front of the church.

She'd been growing more and more tense as the landmarks around her became more familiar, more steeped in memory, but despite her sour mood, a smile tugged at her lips when she saw Ty follow her the long way around. Bembe's disapproval was a powerful thing.

"Let me look at you." Father Bembe gripped Mira's shoulders, holding her at arm's length. His hands, though wrinkled and swollen with arthritis, were strong. He was more stooped than she remembered but still a whole head taller than her.

Mira cast a sideways glance at the pruning shears, now dangerously close to her face, but dutifully held still for inspection.

"You've grown." Father Bembe's eyes twinkled. "Not just older and taller." He poked one finger of his empty hand against her sternum. "Inside as well."

<Does he mean me?> asked the demon. <Can he tell I'm stronger?>

Mira pressed her lips tight and studied the bushes behind Bembe. There were only a handful of people who knew what she was, and part of her hated every one of them for carrying that knowledge, even when they seemed accepting of it. After all, who could truly accept a monster? Tolerate? Sure. Use? Absolutely. But truly accept? Embrace? Love? She gave herself a small shake and stepped out of Bembe's grip.

The old man frowned, then shifted his gaze to Ty, who'd stopped a few paces behind Mira. "And who is this?" His eyes flicked to Mira. "A boyfriend?"

Mira choked and sputtered. "No. He's. . . ." She looked over her shoulder. Ty was staring at her with a stony expression. "He's. . . ." She looked away from both men, searching the sky for the words that eluded her.

"I'm her partner." Ty stepped forward and offered his hand. "Her non-romantic, totally professional partner."

Father Bembe wrapped his gnarled fingers around Ty's outstretched hand and narrowed his eyes. "You work with her?" Again he shifted his gaze to Mira, searching. "He works with you?"

Mira exhaled. "Yes."

Father Bembe lifted one eyebrow. "He is—"

"A PTF agent," Mira finished, cutting off what she assumed Bembe was about to say. "He's a totally normal human who hunts dangerous magical creatures."

Bembe turned his gaze back to Ty, all softness gone from his expression.

Ty tugged his hand, but Bembe didn't release it.

<Should we tell him . . . them . . . that the other one knows?>

Let them think what they want. Mira cleared her throat. "How about we go inside and you tell us why you called."

Father Bembe blinked as though waking up. He released Ty's hand, and his smile sprang back into place. "Of course. If Mira has brought you to help, you are most welcome here. Come, we will speak in my office." Father Bembe led the way up the few steps to the front of the church. He pulled open the door and stepped aside to let them enter. "Welcome to Our Lady of Mercy."

The temperature dropped by ten degrees when Mira stepped through the narthex and into the nave, instantly cooling the sweat on her neck and making her shiver.

<This sure brings back memories.>

Yeah. Mira let her gaze drift over the interior, taking in the altar, the pulpit, the narrow pews. They'd all been replaced since the last time she was there, when her fight with the rifter girl who'd infiltrated the congregation had splintered wood and scattered furniture. When Mira had used the carved wooden crucifix hanging on the wall to bash the young woman across the face after being thrown into the sanctuary. She stared at the space in front of the altar and wondered how Father Bembe had managed to clean up all that blood, or if the tiles were also new.

Father Bembe touched her arm, making her twitch. His shaggy eyebrows drew together, and a deep frown curved his lips. "Come."

Ty followed Father Bembe along the side aisle to a door near the back of the church. Mira trailed after, weighed down by her memories.

<I could take over for a bit if this is too hard for you.>

Mira choked on a laugh.

Ty glanced over his shoulder.

Mira waved away his unspoken question.

He pressed his lips tight and continued after the priest.

<I could totally be in charge for a few days.> The demon's tone was sulky. <You wouldn't even get puppet lines in that amount of time . . . if I was careful.>

I'm trying to fly under the radar here. Low profile is not exactly your M.O.

<I can be discreet.>

Yeah, right. You probably just want another crack at getting Ty to sleep with you.

<Who wouldn't want to hit that? And don't say you, because we both know that's a lie. Anyway, I was only offering because I know how stressed you get about your family.>

Since we're not going to see my family, that won't be an issue. Right? Mira paused as the demon's silence stretched. "Right?"

Ty and Father Bembe both turned to look at her. Her cheeks warmed. She tucked her chin, pushed past them into Father Bembe's office, and dropped into one of the chairs in front of the small wooden desk.

I need to know we're on the same page about this. Mira was careful to keep her lips pressed tight as she prompted the demon.

<Sure, whatever. I just live here. Your family dysfunction is your business.>

Mira rolled her eyes and tried to even out her breathing. As Ty took the seat next to her, Father Bembe closed the door and circled to a chair on the other side of the desk. His office was small but felt cozy rather than cramped. A stand draped with Father Bembe's vestments for Mass occupied one corner. Just looking at the long, green robes made Mira start sweating. Well-ordered bookshelves lined one wall. Papers scribbled with notes covered the desk. One small window looked out over the side yard, and a second door, which Mira knew from past experience led to the rectory Father Bembe called home, stood beside the one through which they'd entered. A brass cross hung between the two doors.

Father Bembe shuffled aside some of the papers on his desk, clearing a space to rest his hands, which he placed palms down against the wood. He leaned forward and leveled his gaze at Mira. "I believe there is a demon in this city."

"What makes you think that?" asked Ty.

Bembe's gaze shifted to him and narrowed, as though assessing whether Ty was mocking him. "It has taken one of my flock."

Mira stiffened. "You think it's possessed a parishioner?" The face of the girl she'd killed flashed in her mind. *Not again.*

Bembe shook his head and straightened in his seat. "Not possessed. Taken. Maybe killed." His eyelids drooped and his gaze grew distant. "Probably killed." He jerked and refocused on Mira. "But maybe not yet. God willing, he may have a chance . . . now that you're here."

<If it really is a rifter, that kid's dead.>

Ssh, I'm trying to have a conversation.

<Just callin' it like it is.>

"You haven't answered my question." Ty leaned forward, bracing his elbows against his knees. "What makes you think there's a demon involved?"

"Ramon went missing two days ago, and he's not the only one. Three other children have gone missing from his school in the past two weeks."

<Definitely dead.>

Mira frowned. "You think a demon is in his school?"

"The police have made no progress. They say the children may have simply run away, but Ramon would not run away. His mother is sick. He helps take care of his two younger siblings. He is a good boy. He would not run away."

"So you jump to demon?" Ty's expression was twisted with skepticism. "Even if the kids didn't run away, they could as easily have been taken by a human serial killer as a demon. Much *more* easily, in fact."

"So said your PTF, when I called them and they refused to help." Father Bembe shook his head. "The spirits are restless. I have felt an evil in this city, even here in this church. I do not yet know the source, but it is real, and it is growing."

Ty opened his mouth, but Mira raised a hand to forestall his next question, or criticism, or whatever it was going to be. She hadn't known Ty long, but she'd worked with him enough to know he liked things to be tidy. Things like evidence and explanations. Unfortunately, he wasn't likely to get that with Bembe. Mira hadn't revealed herself to Father Bembe all those years ago when abuela had brought her to Our Lady of Mercy for Mass. He'd sniffed her out. Just like he'd sniffed out that rifter that Mira helped dispose of. He seemed to be sensitive to the currents of the Rift as few non-practitioners were. In another life, one where he didn't answer the call to priesthood, he might have made his living as a psychic. Mira had learned to trust his instincts.

She pursed her lips then said to Father Bembe, "Give us what you've got and we'll look into it."

He nodded and pulled open a drawer in his desk. He reached down.

When he straightened, he handed a stack of folders over to Mira. "This is everything I've been able to discover about the missing children."

Ty was looking back and forth between Mira and Father Bembe, disbelief etched on his face.

The demon's chuckle echoed through Mira's head. <I don't think Ty's got much faith in the father.>

Mira rolled her eyes and turned to Ty. "Even if it isn't a demon, someone is taking kids, and we're already here. There's no harm in checking. If it turns out to be a regular human psycho, we'll turn it over to the police."

Ty raised his hands in an *I give up* motion. "Fine. We'll check it out." He stood and opened the office door.

Mira rose to follow.

"Wait a moment, Mira. I'd like to speak with you in private."

Ty frowned.

"Go on," Mira said. "I'll be right there."

Ty nodded, stepped outside, and pulled the door shut.

Mira settled back in her seat and looked at Father Bembe.

He nodded toward the silver chain around her neck. "Do you still consider yourself a lost cause?"

Mira's hand moved without thought. Her fingers came to rest on the small bulge of the medallion hidden beneath her shirt.

"I want to show you something." Again Bembe reached into the drawer of his desk. This time when he straightened, he was holding a thin plastic binder. He turned it toward her and flipped it open on the desk.

Mira leaned forward. The three-ring binder held sleeves with newspaper clippings. She narrowed her eyes. She recognized some of those headlines.

Father Bembe tapped his finger against the first article. "Thirteen people dead in a series of strange subway accidents that abruptly stopped after workers reported seeing the ghost of a woman on the tracks." He moved to the next clipping. "Three children who claim a glowing woman saved them from the monster who killed their parents during a camping trip." He turned the page. "A serial killer who mutilated his victims vanished from the room where local law enforcement had him surrounded, but the killings stopped." He turned another page. "A schoolteacher who locked her students in the classroom after setting her desk on fire. The students claim to have been saved by a woman with white hair. The teacher was never found."

He turned page after page, flipping through the events like a scrapbook of Mira's life. He set his hand next to the image on the final page—a petite woman seen from behind. Her arms were raised, and a glowing white mist shot through with black and gold spread like wings around her. The headline above the article read, *An Angel in Baltimore.*

Father Bembe met and held her gaze. "Hundreds of people saved when an angel stopped five buildings from collapsing long enough for them to be evacuated."

Mira looked away. "I'm no angel."

He closed the binder, resting his hand on top. "I'm sure I haven't found them all, but I've seen enough to tell me the sort of person you've grown into."

<That is a very creepy book. It's like he's been stalking us since you left.>

He was watching to see if I went bad. Mira cringed as the realization hit her like a punch to the gut. *If he hadn't liked what he'd found in those articles . . . would he have told the PTF about me?*

"We all struggle with the darkness inside us. None of us are perfect." He set a hand against his chest. "I struggle with little Maritza's death every day. I was the one who brought her to your attention, who asked you to end her. I wish every day, for all our sakes, that that hadn't been the case, but I know in my heart that what we did was necessary. What you have done since, the path you've chosen to walk . . . you have done good work, necessary work, but it has cost you. I see the weight you carry, and I would like to lift some of that burden, if I can."

Mira frowned, wondering where this conversation was going.

Father Bembe folded his hands together on top of the binder. "How long has it been since your last confession?"

Mira burst out laughing. She couldn't help it.

Bembe continued to watch her with a kindly expression until her giggles petered out.

Mira wiped her eyes. "I'm sorry, Father, but you know better than I the rules of confession. Contrition I've got in spades, but to be truly repentant I must sincerely intend not to commit the act again. I can't do that. I hunt people down with every intention of killing them."

"You do not wantonly murder. You seek out those who have been tainted by evil. You are doing God's work."

<Finally. Someone who doesn't think *all* death is a bad thing.>

"I still kill people."

"So does a police officer acting in the line of duty. Does that officer not deserve salvation?"

"Not if that cop intends to shoot someone else the next week."

"As you said yourself, I know the rules of confession. The loss of innocent lives when you destroy the demon within is tragic, but those lives were taken by the evil that possessed them, not by you."

<That's what I've been saying! Tell him I agree.>

Mira shook her head. Her hand drifted to her thigh. She stroked the fabric that covered her raised scars. "The circumstance doesn't erase the sin. I still took those lives."

Bembe followed the motion of her hand and frowned. He looked into Mira's face. "God will forgive your sins. Can you?"

Mira sighed and stood. "I appreciate the gesture, I do, but I can't do this right now. Like you said, there's a chance your boy could still be alive."

<Yeah, right. You don't believe that.>

"And I've got enough sins to keep you busy for a week."

Bembe exhaled and lowered his gaze. His shoulders drooped. He held the pose for only a moment, then he puffed his chest and straightened. "I will always be available to you. Even if you do not wish to make a formal confession, it may help to have someone you can talk to. Someone who knows the truth." He hesitated. "Speaking of which. Is it wise for you to be working with a PTF agent?"

"Ty's okay." She gestured to Father Bembe's scrapbook. "He was there at the angel thing in Baltimore. That's where we met."

"So he knows."

Mira sighed and turned to study the cross hanging on the wall. She nodded.

Father Bembe leaned back in his chair, watching her. "And you trust him?"

She hesitated.

<Yes. The answer is yes. Say it. Y-E-S.>

She shrugged, then nodded again.

<Ugh. You're so stubborn.>

Father Bembe stood, circled the desk, and rested a gnarled hand on Mira's shoulder. "It warms my heart to know you've finally been able to open up to someone."

She shook off his grip and took a step toward the exit. "We're just partners, not soulmates. He happened to be useful when I needed a hand, and it turns out we've got similar goals. That's all."

"But he knows what you are, and you haven't run away." He smiled. "That's progress."

"Right. Good chat." Mira took another step toward the door.

"Will you visit your grandmother while you're in town?"

Mira froze as though suddenly encased in ice. She licked her lips. "I don't want her to know I'm here."

Father Bembe's eyebrows drew together. "She misses you. She's worried about you."

"She's better off without me."

"She doesn't believe that, and neither do I."

"Believe what you want, but if you drag her into this, so help me—"

"Fine." He raised his hands just as Ty had done when she'd snapped at him. "If you're not going to your grandmother's, where will you stay?"

Mira shrugged.

Bembe nodded and turned to his desk. He scribbled something on a piece of paper, tore it off, and handed it to her. "The address for a motel in Sweetwater. The owner is a friend, but no one who will recognize you from your old life."

She took the note, hesitated, then jotted down a number on Bembe's notepad. "This is Ty's." Despite agreeing to carry a cell phone for the sake of her new partnership, she wasn't keen on anyone else finding out she had it. Avoiding people was difficult enough without them being able to contact her directly. "He always has his phone on him, so use that if you think of anything else that might help. Otherwise, I'll stop by when I have something to report."

She stepped out of the office and closed the door behind her. Leaning against the solid wood, she took a deep breath. A faint smell of incense hung in the air. The church was empty of parishioners, but her memories filled the space. She'd spent a lot of time in this building, looking for answers.

Father Bembe had listened to her confessions when she attended church as a teenager, during the short time she'd fooled herself into thinking that having a demon inside her didn't matter. That she could return to a normal life. He'd poked and prodded, ferreting out the truth behind the fire in Detroit and the "accident" at her school. After that, she'd told him everything. The thefts, the murders, the lies—everything she'd done to survive alone on the streets of an unfriendly world. She'd thought he would condemn her, if not to the mortal authorities, then as an abomination in the eyes of God . . . but he hadn't. He'd said she had a gift, if she could find a way to use it. He'd told her about the deaths in their community, his suspicion that a young girl was involved. He'd sent her on her first true hunt.

They hadn't intended to kill the girl. Not at first. They'd hoped Mira could help her, balance her the way she'd balanced herself. That had been a foolish hope, but even as Father Bembe prayed for that dead girl's soul, he'd praised Mira and called her a servant of God.

Mira had left home that very night. Not because of what she'd done, but because of what she realized she was going to do. What she was meant to do. Ever since her possession, she'd been cursed with a terrible hunger that forced her to feed, lest the demon within tear her physical body to shreds. She'd survived those first terrible years on the deaths of other lost souls—humans unlucky enough to cross her path when she was in need. But no more. Father Bembe and that first rifter had shown her another way. A better way. She would feed on evil. She was not just a servant of God, she was His soldier.

She took another deep breath and blew it out, clearing away the feelings that speaking with Father Bembe had stirred up. *I'm not a child anymore. I don't need to tell myself stories about righteousness to make myself feel better.*

<Instead you tell stories about monsters to make yourself feel like crap.>

"I am what I am. Maybe God approves. Maybe He doesn't. There's no way to know for sure." She pushed away from the door and headed for the exit, but she couldn't help casting one last glance over her shoulder at the polished tiles in front of the altar.

I've chosen my path. All I can do now is walk it.

Chapter 5

MIRA

THE AIR WAS THICK and warm as they followed the path from the cracked parking lot, past the fenced-in swimming pool with a single brown sunbather, to the room they'd rented in Sweetwater. A black plastic number eight hung just above the peephole. Mira hiked the go-bag with her essentials higher on her shoulder and scanned the area as Ty opened the door.

The motel Father Bembe had directed them to was small but clean, with pastel-teal walls and navy carpet. Two queen-size beds sat against one wall with a nightstand between them. Opposite the beds was a wide dresser with six drawers and a cabinet hiding a mini fridge. A forty-two-inch flat screen TV sat on top. A small round table and two wooden chairs filled most of the remaining floor space. An alcove at the far end of the room led to the bathroom and a narrow closet hiding a small safe. The caustic smell of industrial-strength cleaner made her nose itch. All in all it was just like a million other rooms she'd slept in.

Mira unslung her bag and flopped into one of the chairs. She set the file Father Bembe had given her on the table, then pulled out and plugged in her laptop. The bulky old device had seen better days. The case was dented, the screen cracked, and it couldn't hold a charge for shit, but even if she'd had the money to replace it, she wouldn't. Her tech guru ViVi had set this monster up to be untraceable. Ty sat down opposite her and pulled his shiny, sleek computer from a padded bag. He'd been quiet on the drive over, almost as if he were afraid of her.

<You can hardly blame him after the way you've been snapping and sulking since we got that message from Bembe.>

Heat seared Mira's cheeks. It wasn't as if she didn't realize she was being snappish, but she couldn't seem to stop herself. *It's this place. Coming here makes me feel like a scared kid all over again. And having him see me like that. . . .* She cleared her throat. *Let's just focus on the task at hand.*

She brought up a browser tab. "Where do you want to start?"

"I'll dig a little deeper into the four kids your priest gave us." He dragged the folder toward himself. "You see if there are any other disappearances or strange deaths in the area."

He kept his eyes on his work, never looking at her. The line of his jaw was tight, as though his teeth were clenched.

Mira chewed her lip. *I should apologize for being so grumpy today.*

<When are you *not* grumpy? He may as well get used to it.>

The reasonable part of her brain said she should make amends, but the louder part objected to exposing her vulnerability any more than she already had. She sighed and turned her attention to her computer screen. Her browser window opened to its default page, Merriam-Webster's word of the day.

Fidelity. The quality or state of being faithful to a person, cause, or belief. She glanced across the table.

The demon gave her a mental nudge. <Feeling fidelitish, err, fidel. . . . How do you turn this one into an adjective?>

She scrolled down the page. *Fidelitous.*

<Ugh. That's gonna be a hard one to use.>

Mira switched to her search tab. A quick scan of the local news revealed articles about the four missing high school students. Mira's finger itched to open the links, but Ty was handling that end. She had to trust he'd be thorough, otherwise what was the point of dividing the work? She scrolled past. Aside from stories about the missing children, Mira found the usual assortment of human horror—two car accident victims, one suicide, one stabbing, a domestic beating that ended with a bang, and a middle-aged man who'd apparently been eaten by an alligator. She clicked on that last one.

It seemed a local man had taken his daughter on a bird-watching expedition in the Everglades. According to the daughter, her father had left the path to take a picture of a nest of anhinga—devil birds—while she scouted ahead with the binoculars. When she returned to the place she'd left him, her father was gone. The girl searched the nearby area, then called the police when she couldn't find him. Search teams later found a mangled arm half a mile away that was identified as belonging to the father, both from the ring on his finger and a DNA test. The rest of his body was never recovered.

<Freaky.>

"Remind me never to hike in the Everglades."

Ty looked up. "You find something?"

She shook her head, took one last look at a picture of the eaten man standing alive and well with the wife and daughter who'd survived him, and moved on.

"So we're looking at four missing teens." Ty sighed and rubbed his goatee. "That's a lot, but still not outside the realm of possibility for runaways or a serial killer. Especially in that age range."

"Father Bembe seemed convinced that Ramon wouldn't run away."

"And I'm inclined to agree with him." He pushed one of the papers from Bembe's file over to her. The picture on top was of a boy with freckled cheeks, light-brown hair, and dark-brown eyes. "Straight-A student, vice president of the school's environmental club, and a member of his church choir. He even waited tables part time at a local café to help pay his mom's medical bills. The kid was golden. If he ran away, it wasn't because of any trouble I can find."

"A clean record doesn't mean there was no trouble," Mira pointed out. She'd been a PI for a long time. She knew even demons could look like saints sometimes. "What about the others?"

"No strong links except the high school. One was a cheerleader. Another was a track star. The last doesn't seem to have left much of a footprint. We've got guys and girls, a senior, two juniors, and a sopho-more." He shook his head. "If they all knew each other beyond passing in the halls, I'm not sure how."

<Maybe the alligators got them.>

Mira chuckled. "Doubtful."

Ty raised an eyebrow.

She cleared her throat. "Sounds like we should visit the school."

Ty folded his arms. "You still think this is our kind of case?"

"I'm going to treat it like it is until I see proof that it's not."

"All right." Ty stood with a sigh. "Let's check out the high school."

MIRA

MIRA STEPPED ONTO the curb in front of the high school—a col-lection of whitewashed buildings with terra-cotta tile roofs, arched windows, and a gated perimeter. One side of the parking lot was a wide field of manicured grass bordered by walkways and shaded by mature trees planted perfectly in a line. The main entrance was four stories of classic architecture with a modern twist. Columns and arches accented brickwork and stucco. Decorative crenelations capped the top. The property looked more like Mira's mental image of a university campus than a simple high school.

<Is this where you would have gone? You know, if you'd stayed in school.>

Maybe. Mira pictured herself as a teenager, walking the lawns and entering the classrooms alongside other students. She'd wanted that once. Imagined she might actually manage it even. Until, of course, reality had kicked in.

She shook her head. "Doesn't matter."

"What doesn't matter?" Ty rounded the front of his pickup and joined her on the sidewalk.

"Nothing." Mira shook her head again. "Let's just get this over with."

The two of them circled the main building, meandered through breezeways, peeked in windows, and wandered toward the athletic fields. Since it was well after school let out, only those students with extra-curricular activities remained on campus.

Mira called up her magic as she walked. Not just her magic but the demon's magic as well. Mira might be able to conjure a fireball or shoot lightning from her fingers, but tracing energy was a delicate matter—one more suited to her copilot. She loosened her grip on the reins and let her demon swell to fill the space until it felt as though they each had one hand on the wheel.

"What are you doing?"

Mira blinked and glanced at Ty. He was staring at the top of her head, and she could just imagine the widening of the white stripe there that must have drawn his attention.

"Relax. No one will notice a thing." She looked him up and down. "Unless it's how nervous you are."

"This is a school," he said. "There are kids here."

He's afraid of me . . . afraid I'll hurt someone. Mira tried to ignore the knot that constricted her chest.

"We're testing the grounds," said her demon before Mira could frame a response. With the control levels shifted, the demon's words were no longer restricted to Mira's head. "It's a passive spell. No fireworks. I'm just going to see if there are any pockets of malicious intent."

Ty frowned. "I didn't know you could do that."

"Baby, I can do all sorts of things you haven't even imagined."

Mira cleared her throat and said in a tone lacking the sultry flare of the demon, "You know how all living things have energy, right?"

Ty nodded.

"When people are twisted up about something—like they're angry enough to murder someone or feeling really guilty—those energies get so knotted that it leaves behind a tangle in the ambient energy of the Rift, at least for a while."

"So you can track a killer through their bad vibes?"

"Sometimes. Not everyone gets emotional about evil acts. Psychopaths, for example. People who don't lose any sleep about what they're doing."

Mira exhaled and let her vision shift. She kept her eyes open, so the people and buildings were still there, but everything was overlaid by the world as the demon saw it—a world of roiling energies. Color drained from the landscape as a cold fog seemed to roll in around her. The people walking by became ghosts, pockets of denser energy in the shapes of humans. Where they passed, the currents of the Rift rippled. Seeing both the shadow of the physical world and the overlay of the Rift made Mira's stomach clench as her eyes tried and failed to focus on anything stable. She shuffled forward, fingers splayed as her vision swam.

Ty gripped her elbow. "You okay?"

His features wavered as though seen through the surface of a pool. The Rift swirled around him in an aura of agitation.

<He's anxious.>

The currents of Ty's energy swirled faster than average, churning inside him.

No more than most people with a worry on their mind.

<I don't think worry is the only thing on his mind.>

Mira made a closer study of the areas where Ty's energy clumped together—his chest, his groin, the hand touching her.

<I told you he was attracted to you.>

"What do you see?" Ty asked.

Heat flared in Mira's cheeks. She jerked her gaze away from Ty. "Just give me a second."

She stumbled along the path between two buildings, each lined with windows looking into empty classrooms. Those classrooms were like spider nests, so tangled with threads of malcontent it was a miracle anyone could walk through them, except of course that the strands had all the physical presence of a gust of wind.

Two girls walked by, one carrying a pile of books, the other holding some kind of instrument case—probably a flute, judging by the size. The musician was babbling about some party as she strutted along the pavement, ponytail swinging in time to her hips. Her energy was bubbling like a shaken soda. By comparison, the girl with the books was a day-old cola with the fizz gone flat. The flow of her energy was wrapped so tightly in her throat that Mira wondered whether she'd be able to speak even if the other girl paused long enough to allow it. The currents of the Rift snagged on the quiet girl as she passed, twisting into loose cables that trailed behind her like streaming ribbons.

Other ribbons crisscrossed the path, wrapped the trees, and tangled together in little clusters all around the campus.

<Talk about a needle in a haystack.>

Ty and Mira circled around a third building and followed a path toward the open fields near the back of the property.

"You sensing anything useful?"

Mira stopped, wrapped her hands around the top bar of the chain-link fence that blocked the field, sighed, and let the magic go. The demon's presence shifted to the background. "That was a waste."

"No murderous impulses?"

"Just the opposite. There are so many knots of anger, guilt, and anxiety here that walking around is like cutting a path through dense jungle vines."

Ty pursed his lips. "Well, it *is* a high school."

She sighed and leaned forward, bracing her elbows against the fence. Teens dotted the grass on the other side. A group of girls in cheerleader uniforms practiced flips and lifts that made their short skirts flutter. Two boys in pants and T-shirts of matching colors made up the bottom of a human pyramid. Farther afield, another group of students sprinted over a line of thigh-high hurdles.

"The first two kids who went missing were a track runner and a cheerleader." Ty joined her at the fence, his gaze sweeping the field. "You think that's a connection? After-school practice? It would be easier to grab someone with the campus empty. Hell, we walked right in here."

Mira could easily picture a few more kids on that field, running or cartwheeling with their classmates. "Except Ramon didn't stay after school. He had to get to his job."

Ty nodded. "Let's have a chat with the principal. Maybe there's some connection we're not seeing yet."

Mira let her gaze drift over the practicing kids. A few glanced in her direction. Her attention lingered on one of the cheerleaders. She was a little on the tall side and lanky, as if she'd just had a growth spurt and her weight hadn't had time to catch up. Her long, dark hair was pulled into a high ponytail that whipped around her head as she danced. Mira squinted. *Does she look familiar to you?*

The demon took a moment to consider. Mira could feel that other awareness focusing on the girl. <Nope.>

The cheerleader Mira was staring at turned to look in her direction, as though feeling Mira's gaze. Her facial features, like the rest of her body, were a bit on the gaunt side. She looked like a piece of stretched taffy right before it snapped.

Hmm. Mira turned away, but the nagging sense of familiarity continued to prickle at the back of her mind. "Let's move on before someone decides we're a couple of perverts."

The two of them headed toward one of the back doors to the main building. Ty tugged the handle. It didn't budge. "Guess they don't want just anybody wandering the halls."

"Allow me." Mira nudged Ty out of her way. She set one hand against the warm metal door. Tugging at the energy she could no longer see, she funneled a thin stream of magic into the lock. She fumbled the tumblers, but for each she set in place another fell. Heat blossomed in her chest as she felt Ty's eyes on her, waiting for results, watching her fail. She grew more flustered, and the magic surged.

Coño!

The lock grew warm under her palm as her magic lost focus.

The demon shouldered Mira's consciousness aside and grabbed the wheel, pulling back the magic just before the lock exploded. <Allow *me*. You stick to fireballs and earthquakes.>

Mira pouted in a corner of her mind as the demon knocked the tumblers and turned the lock, just as Mira had been intending before she lost control.

<That's what you get for trying to show off. You know delicate work isn't your strong suit.> The demon sank back into the passenger seat, and Mira pulled the door open.

Ty nodded. "Impressive."

She looked away, studying her sneakers. *If you hadn't stepped in, I would have blown the whole wall apart.*

<That would have been impressive, too.>

Yeah right.

<Whatever. Go ahead and take the credit.>

Mira kept her lips pressed tight as Ty passed her, then followed him inside.

Music filtered through the empty halls of the school building. Drums, flutes, trumpets, and trombones broke the silence as band members practiced merging their individual sounds into some semblance of order.

Ty took a deep breath and turned in a slow circle. A smile tugged at his lips. "This is familiar."

<I bet Ty was in marching band. I can just picture him strutting around the field in a uniform, all in a line with the others. Ask him what he played.>

No.

<Ask him, or I will.>

Mira sighed. The last thing she needed was to get into a power struggle with her demon when she was already feeling off-balance. *Fine.* She put her hands on her hips and looked at the ceiling. "Did you play an instrument?"

He looked at her and shook his head. "It's not the music that's familiar, it's the hallway. The lockers. Just the feel of this place." He grinned.

Mira frowned. "You must have really liked school."

"My dad was a teacher—still is—so I spent a lot of time in halls like this even when I wasn't in class. Plus I did football, basketball, and JROTC."

<Quite the joiner.>

"Your parents must have been proud." The words came out strained, and Mira realized she was clenching her teeth.

Ty's smile faltered as he studied her face. "Sorry. I guess this must be a sore subject for you."

She pushed past him, annoyed that she'd let her emotions get the better of her . . . again. *It's this place,* she fumed. *This town. I can't think straight here. And having an audience isn't helping.*

<Especially an audience you're trying to impress.>

Mira wanted to wrap her hands around the demon's neck and shake the laughter out of it. *Can you be on my side for once? I feel as if someone peeled off my skin and all my nerves are showing.*

<You want my advice?>

Only if it doesn't suck.

<Humans care too much about too much.>

What's that supposed to mean?

<It means you need to relax. Don't take everything so seriously. Keep stressing out like you are and your head is going to explode.>

Mira sighed and continued down the hall, peeking through the narrow windows set into the classroom doors. Ty trailed a step behind. She paused in front of the third door as her mind snagged on what she saw through the glass.

Countertop benches with inset sinks divided the room. Glass beakers, graduated cylinders, trivets, pipettes, Petri dishes, and Bunsen burners were arranged on the shelves against the far wall. Mira licked her lips. She closed her eyes.

She was a wiry youth with short-cropped hair she'd cut herself and loose-fitting clothes abuela had gotten from a cousin who was two years younger but had already outgrown them. She'd tried three times to dye the white stripe out of her hair, but all she'd managed was to turn her natural brown a shade of mud. She'd briefly tried wearing color-changing lenses to hide her mismatched eyes, but they hadn't been worth the cost. Instead she just kept her gaze down as much as possible.

Five other children joined her in the memory. Tony, Carlos, Luz, Gianna, and Jennifer. The tools and containers needed for that day's chemistry experiment were set out on the tables in neat rows. She and Jennifer had spent their recess arranging them for Mr. Schoeff. It gave the girls an excuse to avoid the crowded field where the other kids played.

Like Mira, Jennifer was a little odd. She was tall, one of the tallest in their grade, and looked like a giant next to Mira. She had pale, white skin and lank yellow hair that hung to her waist. Despite being hard to overlook physically, Jennifer was quiet and withdrawn. She rarely spoke due to a pronounced stutter. She was the first friend Mira had made in years.

Mira and Jennifer stood side by side as the other kids cornered them in the chemistry room. These weren't the popular kids—those barely registered that Jennifer or Mira existed. These were kids at the bottom of the social food chain. Kids with broken homes and absent parents, hand-me-down clothes and bad attitudes. You'd think they would have welcomed two more outcasts, but instead they saw the girls as an opportunity to feel big in their tiny lives.

Carlos was the leader. Second string on the football team, he was big and mean. The others walked in his shadow, as though his bulk might protect them from the judgment of their peers.

Jennifer shriveled as insults rained down, words made into daggers and thrown with painful accuracy. Mira balled her fists. Her eyes stung. Her chest burned. Jennifer started to cry. Their tormentors laughed. The room exploded.

"Hey." A hand tugged Mira's shoulder. "I asked you a question."

Mira opened her eyes and turned toward the somewhat squeaky voice that had spoken. A woman was standing next to her. She had light-brown hair pulled into twin braids that brushed her shoulders and stretched the sun-kissed skin across her forehead. Her mascara-crusted eyes were brown, and the bow of her pink lips shimmered with gloss.

Mira blinked a couple of times, struggling to bring herself back to the moment. "Who are you?"

"That's my line." The woman released her grip and took a step back.

Mira took in the woman's uniform—brown slacks and a beige polo that hugged her curves in all the right places. There was a silver badge pinned to her chest and a patch on her sleeve. A belt of black leather pouches circled her slender waist, and a small walkie-talkie perched on her shoulder.

"You want to explain to me why you're walking around this campus?"

Ty stepped forward, one palm raised in a placating manner while he reached for his badge with the other hand. "I'm PTF Agent Ty Williams. We're looking into the recent disappearances from this school." He flipped his badge open and let her inspect it.

The cop grunted and gave a stiff nod.

Ty tucked his badge away.

"I got a complaint about a suspicious couple watching the kids on campus. You should have called ahead. It would have saved a lot of trouble."

"Sorry," Ty said. "We didn't mean to disturb anyone. We just wanted to get a feel for the place."

She nodded again. "So the PTF thinks these teens going missing is unnatural?"

"We don't know yet. We were just on our way to speak with the principal. Perhaps you could direct us to his office?"

The cop glanced down the hallway behind her. When she turned, Mira's attention caught on a collection of pale scars that ran like jagged lightning over her cheek and jaw.

Does she look familiar to you?

<I dunno. You meat bags all kinda look alike, although this one's pretty sexy.>

The cop turned back to face them. "I'll lead you there, give you a proper introduction. Agents Williams and . . .?" She raised an eyebrow at Mira.

"Fuentes," Ty said.

Mira cringed at his easy use of her real name.

The cop's expression changed in the blink of an eye, flitting from confusion, to fear, to disbelief. "Mira?" She leaned forward, squinting into Mira's face like a nearsighted old lady. "Mira Fuentes?"

Butterflies erupted in a queasy hurricane inside Mira's stomach.

<How does she know your name?>

Mira shook her head. "Do I know you?"

The cop took two staggering steps back and raised her hand to cover the scars on her cheek. "You don't recognize me?" She gave a soft laugh and lowered her hand. "Why would you? It's been, what, ten years?" She met Mira's gaze. "Gianna Lopez."

Mira's gaze settled on the scars on the woman's face—a woman who knew her real name. Ten years ago, Gianna's hair had been lighter, her nose had been softer, her cheeks had been fuller, but the underlying structure was there. Her brown eyes had watched Mira and Jennifer from the safety of Carlos's shadow. She'd laughed . . . until the laughter turned to screams.

Mira couldn't pull her attention away from the scars on Gianna's face as memories of exploding glass streaked with blood flooded her mind. Five children rolled out on gurneys, taken away in ambulances. That was the last time Mira had set foot in school, too ashamed even to find out if her victims were all right. A week later, she and Father Bembe had killed a girl, and Mira had never looked back.

<It was the right choice.> Her demon's voice was sure and strong. <If we'd stuck around, someone would have put two and two together. You would have been shipped to the Church for sorcerer training, and the first paladin who set eyes on us would have chopped off your head.>

Mira shuddered. For someone like her, paladins—the Church's puppet practitioners who watched for demon possession in the sorcerer troops—were the stuff of nightmares.

A growing pressure in Mira's chest, throat, and behind her eyes threatened to turn to tears as memories of her past failures continued to surge, but she smashed it all down and lifted her chin. She gestured to the woman's uniform. "You're a cop now. I wouldn't have guessed that."

Gianna folded her arms. "And you're with the PTF? Yeah, I wouldn't have guessed that either."

Ty looked from Mira to Gianna and back again as the two women stared at each other in assessing silence. "I take it you know each other?"

Mira said, "Not really," at the same time that Gianna said, "Kind of."

"Right." Ty braced his hands on his hips. He studied Mira for a long moment, then shifted his focus to Gianna. "Shall we go talk to the principal?"

"Just point us in the right direction." Mira tried to hold Gianna's gaze, but her eyes kept drifting to those scars. Were the other kids she'd hurt marked like that? Was Jennifer?

Gianna pursed her lips. She shook her head. "Visitors aren't supposed to wander the campus alone. Besides, I know Gary, and I knew the kids. I can help."

"That's—"

"We don't need your help," Mira cut Ty off before he could say something she'd regret.

Gianna rested one hand on her cocked hip. "I get the PTF is its own organization and all, but you shouldn't discount local help. I know this place and these people. I also know the detectives already on this case and what they have and haven't done. Why waste time covering the same ground?"

"We don't need—"

Ty cleared his throat. "We'd be grateful for an introduction to the principal."

Mira glowered at him.

"Our goal is to find out if this is a paranatural case or not," he said. "Working with local law enforcement might get us there faster."

"Fine," Mira huffed. "You two go talk to the principal. I'll do another sweep of the campus and meet you back at the truck."

The demon tugged at their connection, clearly not pleased with the way the conversation was going. <You're going to leave Ty with Officer Hottie?>

"Are you sure?" Ty's brows knitted together. "Don't you want to hear the principal's answers firsthand?"

Not if I have to stand next to Gianna the whole time. "You can fill me in later."

Gianna shook her head. "Without a visitor's badge you really shouldn't—"

Mira waved the comment away and started walking back the way they'd come. *We'll check the practice field again. Maybe someone will feel like talking to us.*

"Don't act creepy," Gianna called after her. "I don't want any calls from freaked-out students that some crazy lady is staring at them."

Mira resisted the urge to flip Gianna the bird as she walked away. The demon, however, showed no such restraint. Her hand was halfway up before Mira realized and slapped it back to her side.

Chapter 6

TY

GIANNA EXHALED, shook her head, and turned to Ty. "Who'd you piss off to get saddled with a partner like that?"

He shrugged. "Just lucky, I guess."

"Lucky." She chuckled. "Right."

He schooled his expression and watched Mira round the distant corner. Her attitude had gone from bad to worse as the day wore on, and his patience was wearing thin. He was willing to cut her some slack because he knew she was suffering, but if she refused to open up to him, there wasn't much he could do to help.

The sooner we get out of this city, the better.

Still, this was a golden opportunity to learn more about his enigmatic new partner. He turned his gaze on Gianna. "How do you and Mira know each other?"

Gianna stiffened. "We were at school together, eighth grade. Mira transferred in partway through the year." She reached up and rubbed a hand over her neck and jaw. Her fingertips traced the scars there.

Ty had read Mira's police file cover to cover. Aside from the fire that had claimed one life and left her mother with third-degree burns over most of her body, Mira had also been involved in a middle school accident—a chemistry lab explosion. The fire chief cited a leaky gasket in a natural gas line coupled with some faulty outlet wiring as the cause of the explosion. Six kids were caught in the blast. Mira was one, and he'd bet money Gianna's name was on that list as well.

"We didn't know each other long, or very well. A couple months after she transferred, the school was closed for renovations."

More like repairs, he thought. *And probably slapped with a hefty negligence lawsuit.*

"It's weird seeing her again after all this time," Gianna said softly. "And for her to be in the PTF. . . ." She shook her head and started walking down the hall in the opposite direction as Mira. "Have you been partners for long?"

Ty matched her pace. "Not really."

She cast a sidelong glance in his direction. "Have you noticed anything . . . odd about her?"

A tingle ran down Ty's spine. "Odd?"

"She was kind of strange as a kid. Terrible social skills." She shrugged. "That doesn't seem to have changed much. But the way she vanished after . . . I don't know. I guess I've always thought there was more to her story." She turned down a side hallway. The sounds of the practicing band faded away. "She's never seemed strange to you?"

"Strange is a relative term, especially in my line of work."

She chuckled. She had an easy, infectious laugh. "Fair enough."

She opened a door partway down the next hall, led him past an empty reception desk, and knocked on the textured glass panel set into the top half of the inner door. She didn't wait for a response before pushing through. "Agent Williams, may I introduce Principal Gary Van Allen."

Ty stepped around Gianna in time to see a portly man with sun-burned cheeks and a peeling nose stand up behind a dark oak desk. He looked to be in his mid-forties. His charcoal eyes squinted through oval glasses in dark-blue frames that matched his off-the-rack suit. His brown hair was trimmed short, but sideburns trailed down his temples nearly to his jaw, and a thick mustache covered his upper lip. His ample chin was bare. Ty's attention was drawn to the built-in bookshelf behind the principal. Rather than being dominated by the kind of leather-bound dust collectors Ty normally equated with stodgy academic offices, the shelves sported row upon row of bobblehead Funko Pop dolls, grouped by theme.

"Gary," Gianna continued, "this is Agent Williams from the PTF. He's here to ask some questions about your missing students."

Ty pulled his attention away from the colorful collection and approached the desk. "Principal Van Allen." He offered his hand. "Sorry for the intrusion. I'll only take a moment of your time."

Van Allen gave Ty's hand a stiff shake then sat back down. He poked the bridge of his glasses, pushing them higher up his red nose. "PTF, you said?" He frowned. "Nothing paranatural about a few kids running off."

Ty arched an eyebrow. "You believe all four children ran away?"

"They were all good kids. Bright futures. But even the best kids stray sometimes, crack under the pressure, fall victim to unsavory influences. You know."

Ty nodded. "Can you tell me if the four students had any close connection? Shared classes or activities, that kind of thing."

Van Allen shook his head. "Detective Moretti asked me the same thing. We even printed off the kids' schedules to compare. A few had classes that overlapped, but nothing that connected all four."

"Can I get a copy of those schedules?"

He pursed his lips. "Why are you covering the same ground? If the PTF is taking jurisdiction, shouldn't you have consulted with Moretti?"

"Just give him the schedules, Gary," Gianna said from the doorway. "The inner workings of the case aren't your concern."

The principal scowled at Gianna.

"Unless you want the agent here to think you've got something to hide," she added.

Ty frowned.

Principal Van Allen's expression smoothed to a photo-worthy smile as he waved the comment away. "I was only suggesting that collaboration might be more efficient. I'm happy to assist the authorities in any way I can, of course."

He clicked a few buttons on his computer and a printer on the sideboard hummed to life.

"Has anyone on campus been acting strangely recently?" Ty asked, as they waited for the printer to spit out its job. "Changes in personality or behavior, violent outbursts, that kind of thing?"

Van Allen shook his head.

"Any staff that hasn't shown up for work?"

The principal stiffened. "Are you implying one of our teachers could be responsible?"

"I'm just checking all the angles," Ty soothed.

"Well, all the staff is accounted for, and Officer Lopez here can attest to campus security. Whatever happened to these unfortunate young people, I don't think it can be connected to this school. Certainly not if there's anything paranatural involved."

"I see." The principal's defensive tone put Ty on edge. Van Allen was clearly worried about political fallout if the school was deemed unsafe. In a Purist community, even a whiff of something paranatural might get a place closed down, but would the principal go so far as to cover up a paranatural on campus to protect his school's reputation? "Just one more question. Do you have any halfers or practitioners on campus?"

Principal Van Allen blanched.

Ty could have pulled the school's registration records from the PTF files, but that wouldn't have told him what he really wanted to know. Van Allen's reaction spoke volumes. He was scared.

"We did an iron test of the full student body at the start of the new semester," Van Allen said. "There are no fae children enrolled here."

Ty clenched his jaw. The practice of spot testing students for latent fae blood had been common practice during the Faerie Wars but was phased out in the years following the signing of the peace treaty. Unfortunately, with the recent breakdown of the treaty and rising tension between humans and fae, more people were calling for stricter identification and segregation policies. The idea of educational segregation for any reason made Ty's blood boil.

He took a breath to steady himself, then said, "Those tests don't identify practitioners."

"We don't have any relatives of identified practitioners. That's as sure as we can reasonably be." Van Allen folded his hands on the polished wood. "Children going missing is always disturbing, and I hope they're found, but I believe these disappearances to be mundane—high-achieving kids who needed to escape the pressure of expectations. It happens all the time. Detective Moretti has already confirmed as much, so I'll thank you not to spread any unfounded rumors about paranatural influence at this school."

The irony was that having fae or practitioners on campus probably would have made the school safer. Ty had been hoping there might be someone sensitive to magic who would have noticed something going on that the humans hadn't. He still wasn't convinced the runaway theory was wrong, but he couldn't see Mira letting this bone go until they found some hard evidence one way or the other.

Ty gave Principal Van Allen a stiff nod. "I'm not looking to cause any trouble for your school. I honestly hope these kids have just run away."

The principal rolled his chair to one side and lifted a few sheets of paper off the printer tray. "I'm glad to hear that." He passed the papers to Ty. "Thanks for stopping by."

Gianna opened the door as Ty approached. She waved to the principal. "See you later, Gary." She followed Ty through the main office and into the hall. "So what's next?"

Ty turned to her. "Excuse me?"

"In your investigation. Are you going to take jurisdiction for the case?"

Ty looked Gianna up and down. Her weight was all on the balls of her feet. Her hands were clasped over her abdomen. He frowned. "I haven't decided yet."

"It's just, if you *are* taking jurisdiction . . . I could help."

He frowned. "Help?"

"As a local contact. Like, I assume you'll want to talk to the victims' families. I could set that up."

"Thanks, but I'm perfectly capable of looking up names and addresses myself."

"Sure, you could find out where they live, but I've been working at this school for a while now. I know the kids that went missing. I know their families." She shifted her weight. "This is a close-knit community, and a lot of the people here don't like anything associated with magic. That includes the PTF. If you show up on their doorstep insinuating that their kids were somehow involved with magic, even if only as victims, you're going to meet resistance."

"The PTF *protects* people from magical threats."

"In theory, sure, but there's a stigma to it, too. Especially now, with the experiment in Colorado that's allowing paranaturals to serve as agents."

"Magic is the best way to fight magic."

"Maybe so, but a lot of people don't see it that way."

"You're saying you don't think these families will cooperate with my investigation?"

She set a hand against her chest. "I'm saying that, as a local these families already know, I can help ease your interactions."

He frowned, taking in the tension in her stance. "Why are you so interested?"

She jerked, eyes widening. "I just . . . want to see justice done."

He crossed his arms. Tapping a local asset was pretty standard procedure for agents in the field, but in his experience, local cops tended to resent getting saddled with that duty. They didn't volunteer. "Even if I decide to utilize a local contact, the logical choice would be the detective already working this case. Correct me if I'm wrong, but I don't think that's you."

Her smile faltered. Pink spots bloomed on her cheeks. She narrowed her eyes. Her knuckles turned white. "Look, Moretti's a great cop, don't get me wrong, but he's six weeks from retirement. The last thing he wants is a messy case. He's happy to stamp them all runaways and collect his pension. If there's something bigger going on here, he doesn't want to know about it."

"Whereas you can't wait to dive in."

"Like I said, I knew those kids. I want to see justice done."

If his interview with the principal was any indication, Gianna wasn't wrong about the resistance they were likely to encounter with the families. Having a familiar face on hand might prove useful. He also suspected there was some deeper motivation behind her wanting to work this case, and he wanted to find out what that was, but he could just imagine the fit Mira would throw if he took Gianna up on her offer. And Mira's mood wasn't the only consideration. The closer Mira worked with law enforcement, the more likely it was someone would uncover her secret, and Gianna was already too suspicious of Mira for Ty's liking. No, the best way to keep Mira safe was to keep her as far away from cops as possible. Especially if this did turn out to be her type of case.

He shook his head. "Sorry, but no." He turned away.

"But—" She took two steps after him and grabbed his sleeve.

He glared over his shoulder.

She let go. "I *can* help you."

He recognized that hungry look in her eyes—ambition. He'd seen it often enough during his time in the military, the PTF, and the police force. He'd seen it make careers. He'd also seen it drive good people to make bad decisions. Ambition could be powerful, but it could also be dangerous. He shook his head again and continued walking. "Not this time."

MIRA

"WELL, THAT WAS a total bust." Mira brooded as the colorful billboards and graffitied walls of the city slid past the window of Ty's truck. The first house they'd visited hadn't had anyone home. At the second house, they'd been greeted by a gruff, middle-aged woman who hadn't let them past the front door even after Ty identified himself as a PTF agent. They'd ended up conducting the interview on the front step . . . if the handful of terse answers they'd received could even be called an interview. After having the door all but slammed in their faces, they'd decided to regroup at the motel and save the remaining interviews for the morning in the hopes that everyone would be in a better mood.

<Maybe we shouldn't mention the whole PTF thing tomorrow,> the demon mused. <We've never had trouble getting answers before, and Ty's badge didn't make anyone more talkative.>

"I agree."

Ty glanced at Mira from the driver's seat. A crease wrinkled the space between his eyebrows. "You agree with what?"

She stiffened, embarrassed that she'd spoken out loud. "I thought having an official standing was supposed to make my job easier. That was the line you sold when I agreed to work with you as a PTF consultant." She shot him a sidelong glance. "Do all your interrogations go this poorly?"

"We're talking to the families of victims, not suspects. What would you have me do? Arrest them?"

<Ooh, yeah. Let's do that.>

She shrugged. "If it'll get this case moving. Maybe the threat of a night in holding would loosen their tongues." She waved a hand. "Obstruction of justice, or whatever."

"And where exactly would we hold them?" He turned left at a stop sign, heading toward their motel. "I haven't officially taken jurisdiction here or even contacted the local LEOs. I can't exactly show up at the precinct and say, 'Hey, would you mind locking all these people up until they feel cooperative?'."

"Then what's even the point of your badge?"

Ty was quiet for a moment, as though considering what to say. He glanced at her, then swung his eyes back to the road. "We *could* get local support. That might make the interviews go more smoothly."

She flicked a stray strand of hair out of her face. "I've never had a problem getting answers out of people on my own."

"By lying, tricking, or threatening."

<He's got you there.>

"At least I get results. And in case you've forgotten, I spend most of my time *avoiding* authority figures."

Ty sighed as he eased the truck into the parking lot of their motel and cut the engine. "I didn't forget."

"Let's take another look at those case files." Mira exited the truck. The air conditioning in the cab had cooled her sweat, but even with the long shadows stretched across the parking lot, the full force of the Florida heat coated her like a wet blanket as soon as she opened the door.

I do not miss this humidity.

The demon's chuckle rumbled through Mira's head. <That's one benefit of an incorporeal form. I never have to deal with sweaty bras.>

Mira dragged her feet over the burning pavement as she followed Ty around the gated pool and up the sidewalk to their room. She glanced at the clear water in the pool.

<I'm up for a dip if you are.> A mischievous note crept into the demon's tone. <Do you think Ty brought swim trunks?>

Mira turned her face forward and smashed her nose against the solid muscles of Ty's back. She staggered back a step, rubbing her nose. "Ouch! Why did you stop?"

He pointed a finger ahead.

Mira sidestepped to see around Ty's wide shoulders. An elderly woman was sitting on the concrete step in front of their door. She was a little on the heavy side, though she seemed to have enough light-brown skin to fit a woman twice her size. Her steel-gray hair was cut short and swept back in tidy waves. Thick, golden hoops hung from her ears, and a matching bangle wrapped her wrist. She wore white jeans, tan sandals, and a navy-blue, petal-sleeve blouse with lace trim. When she looked up, her dark-brown eyes danced with relief.

Mira snapped her mouth closed and swallowed.

Ty tipped his head toward Mira but kept his gaze on the woman climbing to her feet between them and their motel room. "Do you know her?"

Mira worked some moisture into her suddenly dry mouth. "That's my abuela."

Chapter 7

MIRA

"MIRA!" ABUELA CAME at Mira like a charging rhinoceros and wrapped her in a viselike hug that left her gasping for breath.

<How did she find us? How did she even know we were in Florida?>

Mira felt like a drunk on a carousel as thoughts spun together and blew apart in rapid succession. Then she recalled who it was that had recommended this motel, and how insistent he'd been that Mira should reconnect with her family. Betrayal twisted like a knife in her back. She shook her head. *If he wasn't a priest. . . .*

Abuela took a step back, but she kept her hands on Mira's arms. "Let me take a look at you." She twisted Mira side to side, handling her like a rag doll. She pressed her palms to Mira's cheeks, squishing her face. "You look tired. Have you been getting enough sleep? You push yourself too hard." She lifted one of Mira's arms. "You're nothing but skin and bones." She pinched the flesh over Mira's ribs.

Mira yelped and slapped a hand over the tender spot. "I'm fine, abuela. I eat and sleep plenty."

Ty chuckled.

She shot him a scathing look and switched to Spanish. "It's good to see you, abuela, but what are you doing here?"

Abuela drew herself up, which brought her to roughly one inch taller than Mira, and responded in her native tongue. "This is how you speak to your grandmother? Where have your manners gone?"

<Uh oh. I think you pissed her off.>

"*Lo siento,*" Mira apologized, continuing in Spanish. "You caught me off guard. I wasn't expecting to see you on this trip."

"Yes, in and out like a thief with no regard for the people who care about you."

"It's not like that."

<It's exactly like that.>

"I'm working a case."

"So what, you don't eat or sleep while you're working?" She clucked her tongue. "I could almost believe that after seeing the state of you."

She rolled her eyes. "I'm perfectly healthy."

Abuela waved the comment away with a flap of her hand. "You'll stay with me while you're in town."

"What? No." Mira gestured to the motel room abuela had been staking out. "We're all set here."

"Nonsense. No one should stay in a motel when they've got family nearby."

<It *would* save money.>

"I'm working." She strained the word, trying to put emphasis into it without raising her voice.

"You can work from home."

"I need to stay with Ty." She indicated him with a wild gesture that nearly turned into a backhand across his face.

He leaned out of harm's way. His eyes were wide. His gaze jumped from woman to woman with a blank look. A small crease puckered his brow.

From his lost expression and the way he was watching their rapid-fire exchange like a ping-pong game, Mira guessed he didn't know more than a word or two of Spanish.

"He's tall."

Mira turned back to her grandmother to find her scrutinizing Ty almost as closely as she'd assessed Mira.

"Nice build. Strong arms. Good features." Abuela pursed her lips. "Not Latino though. Where's he from?"

"I don't know. New England, I think."

Abuela shrugged. "Beggars can't be choosers. If you like him, I like him."

"What? No. I don't like him. I mean, I don't *not* like him. I. . . ." She shook her head, trying to get her thoughts in order.

The demon's laughter burst in her head, scattering her concentration.

<I love your grandma. We should stay with her.>

"No!"

Abuela frowned. "No what?"

Ty was laughing again, and his laughter mixed with the demon's voice inside her head. The sounds twisted together, drawing up memories of Gianna and her friends, their laughter bouncing off the polished surfaces in the chemistry lab.

Mira pressed a palm to her forehead and took a step back.

Abuela set a hand against her arm. "What's the matter?"

"Nothing."

Ty was frowning now, the mirth in his eyes replaced by worry. "Are you okay?"

"I'm fine." She spoke in English for his benefit.

Abuela clucked her tongue again. "You see, you push yourself too hard. You need a rest and a good meal."

"Maybe she's right," Ty said.

She rounded on him. "She wants me to stay at her house while I'm in town."

Ty pressed his lips into a thin line and took a deep breath through his nose as he mulled over her words. "Maybe you should. It could be good for you to reconnect with your family."

Mira rolled her eyes. "Not you, too."

Abuela shook her head. "No manners at all. What's happened to you?"

Mira cringed. Even after a decade of living on her own, her grandmother's disapproval was like ice in her veins.

"I just think maybe you should take this opportunity," Ty said. "You might not be back this way for a while."

"Then it's decided." Abuela put a hand on each of their arms. "You'll both come stay with me."

Ty stiffened as if he'd just grabbed a live wire. "Wait, I'm not coming."

"Mira says she needs you close."

It was Mira's turn to twitch. "That's not what I said."

<It's out there now. Can't deny it.>

"I just think we should stick together to, you know, discuss the case. For work."

Ty nodded. "Yeah. For work. Of course."

"We're not—" She waved a hand between them.

"Absolutely not," Ty agreed. "Strictly professional."

Abuela glanced from one of them to the other. Her lips twitched up. "I have more than one guest room."

"Thank you, really," Ty said, "but I wouldn't want to intrude." He looked at Mira. "We can coordinate on the phone."

"Nonsense," abuela said. "You're both staying with me, and that's final."

Ty looked to Mira for support.

Mira shrugged. Once abuela set her mind to something, you'd have more luck moving a mountain. "Abuela has spoken."

Ty glanced once more at abuela. He exhaled, letting his shoulders sag. "I'll get our stuff."

Abuela squinted at Ty's back as he passed into the motel room. "You're really not together?"

Mira shook her head. "Not like that."

<Not yet.> The demon gave her a mental nudge.

Abuela frowned. "Why not? What's wrong with him?"

Mira chuckled, but a pain twisted in her chest as she recalled the way Ty had recoiled from her advances in the train yard. *More like what's wrong with me.*

"We're just partners. No need to complicate things."

"Hmm." Abuela made that *cluck cluck* sound with her tongue that meant she was mulling something over.

"Look, abuela, I don't want to make a big deal about my being here, okay?"

She patted one wrinkled hand against Mira's wrist. "Sure, sure."

"I mean it. No party. No reunions. I want to keep a low profile."

"Whatever you want." Abuela smiled a big, toothy grin. "I'm just so glad to have you home."

MIRA

DIM LIGHT FILTERED through the gauzy curtains of Mira's childhood bedroom. It wasn't the golden glow of true sunrise, but rather the first pink blush that hinted at the coming day. Mira tightened the laces on her sneakers. This was her favorite time of day, when the rest of the world was still asleep and the air was filled with promise. The "simple dinner" abuela had insisted on throwing together last night was still heavy in Mira's system, giving her more than enough fuel for a pre-breakfast run.

She stood up and inhaled deeply. The scent of jasmine perfume, guava preserves, and the faint musk of cigar smoke took her back to her childhood—before Detroit and demons had entered the picture. She stretched her arms above her head, working out the tension in her shoulders. Everything in the room was just so, from the well-polished furniture, to the dust-free surfaces, to the doily-covered nightstand. She straightened the covers on the bed, pulling every seam tight.

<I see where you get your OCD.>

"There's nothing wrong with being tidy."

<It seems like an awful lot of effort when you're just going to sleep in it again tonight.>

Mira turned and gave the room one last look. The order of her abuela's house had seemed suffocating when she was young. As she'd struggled through her teenage years, she'd come to appreciate the need to exert control on the smaller, more manageable aspects of her life. Now, having that order around her was a great comfort.

I wonder if abuela feels the same way?

The demon chuffed. <You think she's compensating for the chaos of suburban life?>

"Abuela wasn't always a suburban grandma. She left behind everything she knew in Cuba when she was a teenager, paddled across the Florida Straits on a tire raft, and waded through cypress groves just to get to this country. I'll bet establishing this kind of order was her way of dealing with all the uncertainty that came before."

<I guess human kids really do grow up just like their parents . . . or grandparents, in this case.>

Mira pursed her lips. "Let's get going. We need to beat the sun if we don't want to roast."

She slipped into the hall and gently closed her door. The house was quiet. Abuela's door was closed, as was the guest bedroom where Ty had spent the night. Mira paused outside his door, but it was the solid wood on the other side of the hallway that held her attention.

She set her palm on the door frame and whispered, "*Hola, mami.*"

<You should go in.>

Mira shook her head and continued down the dark hall. She'd lost track of the number of times she'd glanced at that door during last night's dinner. Abuela had suggested she take Maria a tray, but Mira hadn't had the courage to open that door. She hadn't even peeked inside when abuela went in.

<It's been years. I'm sure she's forgiven you by now.>

Melting someone's face and driving them insane isn't the sort of thing that gets forgiven.

She slipped past the empty bathroom, dining room, and kitchen, careful to step lightly on the hard, white tiles. The bright colors of the living room walls were muted by the dim light. The front door swung inward on silent hinges. She stepped onto the stoop, sealed the house behind her, and exhaled.

"I see you had the same idea."

She swallowed a yelp as she spun to find Ty standing near the corner of the house in a T-shirt, shorts, and sneakers. One hand was braced against the pink stucco of the building, while the other pulled his foot back in a deep quad stretch that strained the cluster of pale scars on his thigh.

"What are you doing out here?"

<Um, I think that's pretty obvious,> the demon droned.

Ty shrugged and let his foot return to the ground. "Figured I could get a quick run in before the day heated up." He frowned. "Is that not what you're doing?"

"I am. I just. . . ." Mira shook her head and stepped off the porch. "I didn't expect anyone else to be up yet."

He nodded, but his gaze remained wary, as if he were dealing with a dog that might bite. He gestured up the palm tree-lined street. "I was just wondering which direction to head in. If you don't mind a little company, maybe you could show me around?"

Of course I mind your company. Mira clenched her jaw to keep her thoughts from spilling out her mouth. *This was supposed to be my quiet, relaxing time before having to deal with you, and abuela, and Lord knows what else the day is going to throw at me.*

The demon slipped into control while Mira was busy fuming and fumbling with a polite way to turn him down, plastered a big grin on her face, and said, "I'd love to."

Mira spun away from Ty. *Why would you say that?!*

<Because it sounds like fun.>

Fun? Are you insane? Now I'll have to worry about small talk, and being polite, and smelling like sweat, and—

<Relax! Everyone sweats when they run, and you meat bags always smell like *something.* As for small talk, you'll be running. I doubt he'll have a lot of extra breath. Besides, it'll be good for you two to do something besides hunt demons together.>

"Um, are you okay?"

Mira spun again to find Ty hovering near her shoulder. "Fine. Yeah. Why wouldn't I be?"

His eyes cut toward abuela's house.

She followed his gaze. "Okay, maybe I'm a little . . . I don't know. It's weird being back here. Good, but stressful."

"I get it."

Yeah, right. She eyed him incredulously. *As if anyone could.*

<Well, it's not like we know a lot about his life, certainly not where his family's concerned. Maybe he's as estranged from them as you are from yours.>

She pursed her lips. Ty hadn't volunteered much about his past beyond what she needed to know to work with him, which had steered well clear of anything personal. She would have liked to keep the same shroud over her own past, but having him read her police files had shot that option out of the water.

<Maybe we should do a little digging on Ty to even out the playing field.>

I like where you're going, but wouldn't investigating our partner come across as a lack of trust?

<Only if he catches you.>

"Look, if you don't want me tagging along on your run, just say so. I totally get it." Ty headed for the gate in the white-washed, iron fence surrounding the yard. "Just tell me which way you're running, and I'll go in the other direction."

Mira sighed. *Great, now he thinks I'm a moody bitch.*

<He's not wrong.>

"Shut up."

Ty glanced at Mira over his shoulder, one eyebrow raised.

Heat crept into her cheeks. "Sorry, not you." She joined him at the gate. "You can run with me." She stepped onto the sidewalk and gave him a mischievous smile. "If you can keep up."

She started off at an easy jog, heading east toward the river. Ty hustled to catch up then kept pace on her right, matching her stride for stride. Within a block, her skin was slick, and her hair stuck to the back of her neck. It took a few minutes for her lungs to get used to the heavy thickness of the air. Once her muscles were warm and her breathing evened out, she opened up and let loose.

Ty's sneakers pounded the sidewalk beside hers. His stride stretched. She was taking two steps for every one of his. Her arms pumped by her sides. She wasn't at full throttle yet, but she was close. Three blocks later they burst into the open air of a tree-lined plaza overlooking a river. A fresh breeze slammed into her, cooling her sweat and rustling her damp hair. She wiped her forehead. Ty staggered to a stop beside her, propped his hands on his waist, and stretched his chest wide, pulling in that blessed breeze.

"Not bad," she said.

He smiled. "I hope you're not done yet."

She chuckled. "Not by a long shot." She pointed to her right, where a wide boardwalk traced the edge of the water.

He nodded and set off to the south at a moderate jog, not straining, but enough to keep their heart rates up.

Sleeping yachts lined the edge of the river. Some were small speeders, others looked large enough to live on. The boardwalk hung out over the water, separating it from the bustle of the waking city. Restaurants and hotels with patio seating were coming alive, setting out chairs and cutlery in preparation for their first guests. The smells of fresh-baked goods, sweet fruit, and sizzling bacon wafted from kitchens. The many outdoor bars along the riverside seemed almost lonely as they waited for the return of night and the throngs that would fill them. A deep, rhythmic beat boomed from a second-story window, and Mira adjusted her footfalls to match the tempo until the music faded behind her.

"How far does this go?" Ty asked. His words came out a little breathless, which reminded Mira of the one-night stand that had brought him into her life in the first place.

"All the way to the ocean."

Diamonds danced over rippling waves as the sun finally broke the horizon, streaking the ground with long shadows and orange light. More joggers filled their path, joined by parents pushing strollers, elderly couples in tracksuits, and men and women with pin-up bodies wearing barely enough to avoid a ticket. The waterside restaurants filled with patrons, and the quiet of lapping waves and sea gull calls was replaced by overlapping conversations and the clink of silverware against porcelain. Children squealed in hotel pools, already looking for a break from the heat, as their parents nursed hangovers in lounge chairs.

The mouth of the river widened as the inland waters mixed with the salt of the sea, and the boardwalk that had carried them there curved to the right and morphed into a cobblestone sidewalk through a sprawling park. Mira slowed her pace, and Ty matched her. She moved over to one of the many benches that looked out over the water and leaned down to stretch her hamstring.

"That was a beautiful path," Ty said. "Thank you."

She smiled. Despite her concerns, running with Ty hadn't been stressful. In fact, she was feeling more relaxed than she had in days, if not weeks.

<See, you two just need to find some common ground outside of the whole hunting-paranatural-threats thing.>

Much as I hate to admit it, you might be right. He looks more relaxed, too.

The tight lines around Ty's mouth and eyes had eased, his smile wasn't forced, and his stance was easy. She hadn't even realized how tense he'd been until she saw the difference.

I'm anxious because of this trip home. What do you suppose has been bugging him?

\<Best guess? You.>

She frowned. *Have I been that bad lately?*

\<Nah. I think he's got his own baggage, but I can say from experience that partnering with you is no picnic.>

Gee, thanks.

\<Like I said before, you just need to get to know each other a little better, smooth out the rough edges. It's not like we worked like clockwork when we first met.>

"Ha!"

Ty glanced at her, his eyebrows knit together.

She waved him away, still chuckling over the idea that her partnership with the demon had been a smooth transition. *Though considering that most rifters burn out within weeks, we did pretty damn good.*

\<We did fucking awesome.>

"Yeah, we did." She glanced at Ty, who was now doing side lunges on the grass. Maybe the demon was right. Maybe she and Ty just needed a little more time to get used to each other.

Ty straightened, stared out over the water for a moment, then turned as if looking for something.

"What's up?" she asked.

"I could really go for some coffee right about now."

Mira pointed to a shop at the far end of the park, where she could just make out a sign with a stylized coffee cup above the door. "Looks like there's a café over there."

"Want to race? Loser buys."

\<Oh, it's on.>

Mira grinned, leaned down, and took off at a sprint.

"Hey!" Ty was two steps behind when he started moving, but his longer legs made up the lost ground quickly. Unlike Mira, who was dodging obstacles, he cut a straight path to the café. He hurdled a bench, vaulted a trash can, and scattered a group of geese that flapped and honked in outrage. Halfway across the park he was three steps ahead.

Mira's lungs burned. She pushed her legs harder, but Ty pulled another few inches out of reach.

\<Oh, Rift no, we are not going down that easily.>

Magic swelled through Mira as the demon poured extra energy through her system. The burn in her lungs eased. Her muscles launched her farther with each step. She started gaining ground.

Ty glanced over as she came even with him. Surprise and competitive fire flashed in his eyes. Somehow, he managed to speed up.

A couple enjoying a picnic on the grass shouted in surprise as Ty leapt their outstretched legs. Mira swerved around with a breathless, "'Scuse us."

Ty's breath hissed between clenched teeth. His lips were pulled back in a grimace. His arms and legs were a blur, but she was pulling ahead.

She hurtled across the street separating the park from the shops without looking for traffic. Ty was right on her heels. A horn blared behind them.

She reached out one hand. Ty's fingers were stretched in her peripheral vision. Her palm slammed into the bricks of the café wall, followed closely by the rest of her. Ty hit the finish line a second later.

She ricocheted, stumbled, and straightened with a grin. The demon was dancing inside her. "I win."

He pointed an accusatory finger at her and panted, "You used magic, didn't you?"

<Obviously.>

She shrugged. "You never said I couldn't."

He shook his head. Laughter danced in his eyes. "That's a cheat, and you know it."

"How is that any less fair than those stilts you call legs?"

Laughter echoed through Mira's head.

"Touché. What'll you have?"

"An iced *café con leche*."

"You want a bagel or something, too? It's my treat."

She shook her head. "Just the coffee."

"Suit yourself." He pulled open the glass door to the café and went inside.

Mira walked over to another of the many benches and sat down. Waves lapped against the park levee. Sea gulls circled over the water, calling to one another as they danced on the wind. She tugged at her shirt, pulling the damp fabric away from her skin to let more air in. Her hair was plastered to her forehead and neck, and the sun was barely above the horizon.

Ty dropped onto the seat beside her and handed her a plastic cup. Ice rattled against the sides, peeking through the brown liquid. She rolled the cup along her forehead, relishing the cold. "It's going to be another hot one."

Ty nodded, tore off a chunk of blueberry scone, popped it into his mouth, and chased it down with a sip from an iced drink a shade darker than hers. Sweat dripped down his temple and neck. His shirt clung tightly to his torso, tracing the lines of his shoulders and chest.

"I'm glad this worked out."

She blinked, pulling her gaze away from the contours of his shirt. "What?"

"The morning." He lifted his drink in salute to the sun. "Actually, I'm kind of surprised to find out you run."

She shifted on the bench. "Why shouldn't I?"

He shrugged. "It just seems like, with magic to bolster your body, you wouldn't be that concerned with more mundane upkeep."

She stared into her drink. Condensation dripped down the sides, wetting her hands. "I can't always rely on magic to save me." She recalled the feeling of waking up in a prison cell, cut off from her magic, and shivered. The demon's anxiety at that memory leaked through. Neither of them had been happy to lose the other, even temporarily. "And buffing up is easier when you've got a good starting point. If I were an out-of-shape slob that suddenly had to run for my life, I'd be in trouble no matter how much magic I pumped into my muscles."

"Fair point."

She took a sip of coffee, stretched her legs out in front of her, and leaned back with a contented sigh. "I'm glad this morning worked out, too. Turns out when you're not being a total control freak, you're actually pretty easy to get along with."

"Gee, thanks." He tore off another chunk of scone.

"Save some space. You're going to have to eat again when we get back."

"Nah, this will be enough for me." He popped the bread into his mouth.

She chuckled. "Good luck convincing abuela of that."

Chapter 8

TY

TY PULLED A PALE-pink, button-up shirt out of his suitcase and sniffed it to check for freshness. It was hard to tell over the odor of his sweaty body, but it seemed clean enough. He glanced around the fifties decor of the guest room he was in. *If we're here more than a few days, I'll need to do some laundry.*

The squeal of water rushing through the pipes in the wall suddenly went quiet. Mira had called first dibs on the shower, but it sounded like she was done. He grabbed a clean pair of boxers and jeans and stepped into the hall. The bathroom door was still closed.

He shifted his weight from foot to foot as he waited. The smells of cooking bacon and baking bread filled the house. Mira had been right. As soon as they'd returned from their run, her grandmother had insisted on making breakfast for them, ignoring his protests. *Oh well, a little extra fuel might be helpful in getting through the day.*

He leaned against the flower-patterned wallpaper in the hallway across from the bathroom door. His gaze drifted to the next door up the hallway. It had remained closed since they'd arrived last night, save one time when Mira's grandma had taken a plate of food inside. He supposed the two women had discussed whoever was hiding behind that door, but he hadn't been able to follow much of the rapid-fire conversation. He was really beginning to wish he'd taken Spanish as an elective in college.

He was intensely curious about who, or what, was behind that door, but Mira had told him in no uncertain terms that that room was off-limits. There'd been no room for misunderstandings in that part of the conversation. Still, the investigator in him itched to turn that handle.

The bathroom door opened. Ty pushed off the wall as Mira stepped into the hallway. A cloud of steam followed her out, obscuring her for a moment. When he caught a clear look at her, his heart jumped into his throat.

Her wet hair hung in loose waves that kissed her shoulders. Droplets clung to the smooth skin along her collarbone. She clutched a green, terrycloth towel over the swell of her breasts.

She looked up through damp lashes, fixing him in place with her mismatched gaze. "Your turn." She inhaled deeply, straining the fabric hiding her body. "Don't take too long. It smells like breakfast is almost ready."

He cleared his throat and nodded, not trusting his voice.

She slipped past him, so close that a few drops of water transferred from her shoulder to his arm.

He darted into the vacated bathroom and closed the door. Dropping his clothes in a pile on top of the toilet, he braced his hands against the sink. The mirror was fogged over with steam. He took a deep breath. The air smelled like Mira, slightly spicy with citrus undertones. It pressed against him like a hug.

He wiped a hand across the mirror, clearing a swath of reflection.

She's your partner, he reminded himself. *Anything more would get too complicated.*

"Besides," he told his reflection, "she isn't the only person in that body."

He turned the shower on colder than he would normally like it, stripped off his sweaty clothes, and stepped into the water. Five minutes later, his body and thoughts were scrubbed clean. He dried completely and dressed before leaving the bathroom.

Mira was sitting at the dining table while her grandmother ferried dishes back and forth from the kitchen when he joined them.

"Sit." The old woman pointed to the seat next to Mira with a wooden spoon. She had as much command in her voice as any drill sergeant Ty had worked under. "Eat."

Ty pulled out the chair and settled in. The polished oak was covered with heaping trays. Scrambled eggs, sourdough toast, a creamy rice casserole, bacon, sausage links, melon slices, and little pastries all vied for his attention. It was enough food to feed an army.

Mira's grandmother set an empty plate in front of him and started dishing. She didn't stop until every inch of porcelain was covered.

"Um, thank you."

She gave a curt nod and sat down at the head of the table, where she immediately started speaking in Spanish to Mira again.

He couldn't understand much of what they said, but the cadence of their conversation as they spoke over one another and gestured like puppeteers made him smile. Ty tucked into his meal. He understood now why Mira hadn't wanted to eat at the park. Even without a pre-breakfast scone, this would have been too much. He bit into a pastry that surprised him with a burst of guava and cream cheese in his mouth. A sudden wave of nostalgia swept over him.

These weren't the flavors or language he was used to, but they felt like home, and he found himself missing his own family. Saturday morning pancakes hot off the griddle, topped with mango salsa and slathered in syrup. His father's "kiss the cook" apron, glasses fogged with steam as he flipped the next round. His sister sitting with her knees up and a big mug of tea cradled in her hands. His mother taking a moment to relax between emergency calls from the hospital. *How long has it been since we shared a meal like that?*

He stabbed a piece of melon. *Too long.*

He glanced at Mira and her grandmother as they jabbered away. He hadn't spoken to his family since Jamal's funeral. Jamal had been more than a partner. He'd been a brother, a common feature at those Saturday morning breakfasts. His family had grieved nearly as deeply as he had, and it was the guilt of feeling responsible for that loss that kept him away. He was a coward.

Ty peeked sideways at Mira. Color flushed her cheeks as she responded to something her grandmother said. Despite her reluctance to come back here, she wore an easy smile and her eyes twinkled.

Maybe I should give my parents a call.

MIRA

MIRA NODDED ALONG as abuela caught her up on all the marriages, births, and deaths in the family over the past decade, then dove into the rumors and scandals.

"You wouldn't believe how she treats that dog." Abuela shook her head. "It's more spoiled than her children."

Mira laughed. "They're *tio* Carlos's children, too. You can't blame it all on Sophia."

<Although, from the sound of it, your Uncle Carlos doesn't have much say in . . . well, anything.>

Mira grabbed another piece of toast and slathered it with guava jam. She had missed these flavors. Guava was hard to come by in a lot of the country.

Ty pushed back his chair and stood. "If you'll excuse me."

Abuela frowned. "There's plenty more. Take seconds."

He patted his stomach, which looked as lean and flat as ever. "The food was delicious, but I couldn't take another bite." His expression was all satisfied smiles, but something about his eyes seemed sad.

Mira had been happy enough to chat with abuela in Spanish, another experience she'd missed lately, but it suddenly occurred to her that Ty had been eating quietly on his own that whole time. *Do you think he felt left out?*

<If he did, he should have said something.>

"We could talk in English, if you want," Mira said.

He waved her offer away. "I wouldn't want to intrude."

"*Psh.* You're a guest," said abuela. "I apologize. I should have been more considerate. I just got so caught up reminiscing with my grand-daughter. Please, forgive me."

"There's nothing to forgive. You've been a wonderful host, and I'm thrilled that you two are getting the chance to reconnect. I just need some time to get my thoughts together before we head to our interviews today."

Mira half rose. "Shouldn't I—"

"Stay with your grandmother." Ty set his hand on her shoulder and gently pushed her back into her seat. "You should take advantage of the time you have. We can head out when you're done."

Ty lifted his dirty plate and utensils.

Abuela flapped her hands. "Leave them. I'll take care of all that later."

He frowned. "Are you sure?"

"Yes. You're a guest. Don't worry about it."

He shrugged. "Thank you for breakfast."

Mira and abuela remained quiet until he was closed in his room, then abuela turned to her. "He's so polite. And a good appetite. I think you should keep him."

"He's not a pet, abuela."

"He likes you, I think."

"We're partners. Professionals. That's all."

She pursed her lips. The thick creases at the corners of her eyes crinkled. "I've seen more come from less."

<She's more determined to see you laid than I am.>

What she wants is for me to settle down, start a family, and have a normal life.

<You don't know that.>

That's what everyone in this family wants.

<Well, that's not gonna happen so long as I'm around.>

Mira sighed and stood up. "I should get ready, too. We've got a lot of work ahead of us."

"Have you had any luck locating Father Bembe's missing boy?"

Mira stared at her for a second, then shook herself. *Of course abuela knows about the case. Gossip moves faster than currency in a neighborhood like this.*

"Not yet."

"But you agree there is something *other* involved?" She glanced side to side as if suspecting a PTF containment team might smash through the windows and swarm her dining room at the mere mention of something paranatural.

"I don't know. Father Bembe seems convinced, and that's enough for me, but Ty needs hard evidence, and we haven't seen any of that yet. Hopefully we'll learn something useful from today's interviews."

Abuela nodded. "Father Bembe has the sense. God speaks to him."

Mira pushed in her chair.

"And He acts through you." She folded her wrinkled hands together in her lap and focused her cloudy gaze on Mira. "I have faith in you, Mira. You'll find the boy."

But will I find him alive?

She carried her dishes, as well as Ty's and abuela's, to the kitchen sink and washed them. Ty might be a guest, but Mira was family. Even after a decade away, she was family.

Abuela cleared the rest of the table, storing the leftover food and arranging it in the fridge. Once breakfast was put away, abuela settled into a rocking chair that looked out the front window of the living room. Mira headed down the hall toward her bedroom.

Her bare feet slapped the cool tiles. All of a sudden, she jerked to a halt.

She blinked a few times in confusion, trying to prompt her feet to move. She remained stuck in place.

<We should say hello.>

She glanced to the side and realized where she'd come to a stop. She was directly outside her mother's door.

What are you doing? She strained her muscles, but the demon was holding her fast.

<We're here, and we don't know when we will be again. I think we should say hello.>

Are you insane? Do you not remember what happened last time?

<Maybe she's better.>

And maybe she's not.

<There's one way to know for sure.>

You just want to satisfy your curiosity.

<What's wrong with that?>

"What's wrong is that I have to deal with the emotional fallout of your social experiments."

<Like you aren't already traumatized by the thought of her. How could it get any worse?>

"Are you speaking to me?" Abuela peeked around the corner from the front room.

"*Lo siento, abuela.* I was just thinking out loud."

She nodded, and her face disappeared behind the corner once more.

Mira clenched her jaw. *Let go.*

<No.>

You know, ever since you got those few minutes of alone time in my body in Baltimore you've been much more grabby for control.

<What can I say? I'm becoming a more independent individual.>

You can't be an independent individual. We share a body.

<Easy for you to say. You're plenty independent.>

Mira chewed her lower lip. If the demon was getting tired of their arrangement. . . .

<Relax, I'm not about to kick you to the curb and go on a suicidal rampage in your body.>

The demon's teasing tone belied the seriousness of the statement. Mira had only spent a few minutes disconnected from her physical form while the demon had taken full possession of her body, but those few minutes in limbo had seemed to stretch forever. If that's what other rifter hosts felt like all the time . . . well, she'd rather die.

If you need more body time, maybe we could arrange that.

<If I spent more time in our physical shell, we'd need to feed twice as often to hide the effects.>

Mira's teeth tore the soft skin of her lip. She winced. They had trouble finding enough rifters not to have to feed on regular humans as it was.

<Though I wouldn't complain if you listened more to my prompts and opinions. Then maybe I'd feel like I'm living a complete life even when I'm not in the driver's seat.>

Mira thought of some of the crazy impulses the demon had suggested in the past and wrinkled her nose. "I can't promise I'll *always* go along with you, but I could try to be more accommodating."

<Great. You can start now. Go say hello to your mother.>

Mira sighed. Her shoulders sagged. Memories of her mother's screaming face and accusing eyes drifted in her vision. She really, *really* didn't want to open that door. But she didn't want to risk a tug-of-war with the demon for control of her body either. Especially since she knew that was a contest she would lose. She took a deep breath and turned the doorknob.

The only light in the room leaked around the drawn curtains covering the single window. She stood on the threshold for a moment to give her eyes a chance to adjust. There was a narrow bed, nightstand, and a small dresser. A brown recliner rested on a purple-and-yellow rug that sat like a colorful island against the pale floor tiles. Mira's mother was tipped back in that chair with her feet up. A woven blanket trailed off her lap. She wore a loose, white nightgown with blue birds embroidered around the collar. She stared at the ceiling.

"Peonies would be nice." The woman's words were low, mumbled, spoken without seeming direction. "Radishes, too."

Mira swallowed and pulled the door closed behind her. She took a step forward. The near side of her mother's face was almost normal looking, but as she stepped closer she found the jagged border where the scars began. The angry red Mira remembered from the last time she'd seen her mother had faded almost to her natural pale ochre, but the texture had become even more distinct with a high contrast between the peaks and valleys. Folds of skin like melted wax rippled the surface. The lid of one eye was pulled tight, forcing a slant that wouldn't allow it to open completely. The corner of her mouth sagged in a lopsided grimace. The tendons in her neck stood out in high relief, and the skin along her collarbone resembled lumpy modeling clay. Someday Mira hoped to afford a proper skin graft for her mother, but she had trouble enough making ends meet with her freelance PI work, and abuela was on a fixed income. It had taken a church collection just to cover the initial medical bills of keeping her alive. Everything else went toward the painkillers that kept her comfortable and the sedatives that kept her calm.

A tremble shook Mira's hands. She clamped them together over the butterflies in her abdomen. Guilt and regret squeezed her chest and bubbled into her throat.

"Mami?" Her voice came out a strangled whisper. She coughed and tried again. "Mami? It's me, Mira."

The woman in the recliner continued to stare blankly at the ceiling. "Don't touch the roses. They have thorns."

<I'm not sure if this counts as better, but at least she's not screaming.> The demon seemed to slide into the background of Mira's thoughts as its curiosity faded.

Mira took another step forward. Now that she was here, she didn't want to leave without some kind of acknowledgment. She came within reach of the chair and stretched out her hand. The skin on her mother's wrist was tight and hard beneath Mira's fingertips.

"Can you hear me?"

Her mother's gaze slid away from the ceiling. She rolled her head ever so slightly in Mira's direction. Her eyes were mismatched, but not like Mira's. Hers had been paled by a milky cloud.

"Mira?" The word came out slurred through a mouth that barely moved.

"It's me, mami." Mira squeezed her wrist.

Tears shimmered in her mother's uninjured eye.

<Hey, maybe she's doing better after all. What did I tell you? Aren't you glad you came in to see her?>

Mira's mother stiffened under her grip. Her mismatched eyes grew wide, straining the stiff skin over her eyelid. Fear seeped into her expression. She yanked her arm away with more force than Mira would have believed possible from the frail-looking woman. The downturned mouth opened, and Mira's mother let out a horrified scream.

"Shh, shh, it's okay. You're okay." Mira stroked her mother's hair, trying to sooth her even as her own panic threatened to overwhelm her.

<What the heck is she screaming about?>

That first scream was followed by another and another, each gaining in pitch and volume. She flapped her arms as though warding off the fires of her memory, smacking Mira across the face and arms. Her gaze rolled wildly, losing focus.

Mira stumbled back. Her cheek stung from the slap, but it was the pain in her heart that ached most. Her chest constricted. She couldn't breathe. The room grew even dimmer as memories of smoke and flame licked at the edges of her vision. The smell of seared flesh flooded the room.

<Calm down.>

I have to get out of here. Her sweat-slicked palms fumbled the doorknob.

Maria Fuentes screamed as though she were suffering the effects of the fire all over again.

Mira finally yanked open the door and stumbled into the hallway, gasping and sweating more than she had after her morning run.

Strong hands pinned her shoulders.

"What happened?" Ty's face floated inches from Mira's. His voice was a little too high, pinched with worry, but still strong and sure. The soldier in him was looking for direction, something he could fight or fix.

Mira wished desperately that there was something to point him at, something he could protect her from. As much as she hated the idea of someone else defending her, she would have taken the offer in a second and been grateful if he could have saved her from the pain she was feeling, but a soldier wasn't any use against the anguish in her heart.

She shoved him away with all her strength and bolted down the hall to her bedroom, slamming the door behind her. Her momentum carried her to the far side of the room, where she sank to the floor and wrapped her arms around her knees.

I ran away again. Just like I did in Detroit. I hurt her and then ran away.

<You didn't hurt her. You didn't do anything to her.>

She curled tighter, pressing her forehead against her wrists, and shouted, "You don't understand anything."

The demon slunk back to the recess of her mind. Whether to give her the space she needed or to sulk, Mira neither knew nor cared. She squeezed her eyes shut and let the tears roll down her hot cheeks.

Chapter 9

TY

TY STARED AT MIRA'S closed door in dumbfounded shock. He'd never seen her so upset before. He'd watched her face down a sovereign-level demon without getting flustered. What he'd just seen in her eyes was nothing short of panic. He glanced at the closed door she'd come out of. Screams continued to emanate from the room beyond. Who, or what, was in there?

Mira's grandma shuffled down the hallway. She looked sad, her expression drawn with resignation and weariness. She did not, however, seem particularly concerned by the sounds of bloody murder pouring out of the room.

"You." She smacked Ty's upper arm with a light, open backhand, then pointed to the offending door. "Give me a hand."

Ty swallowed, nodded, and reached for his gun before he realized he wasn't wearing his holster.

Mrs. Fuentes didn't hesitate. She wrapped one wrinkled hand around the doorknob and pushed inside. The screams grew louder as the door swung open.

The light inside was dim, just enough for Ty to make out the figure thrashing in the recliner in the middle of the room. She was a middle-aged woman, petite and so slender she looked to be made of matchsticks. She'd sunk down so her back was in the seat of her chair with her bottom nearly falling off the edge. Her head rolled wildly from side to side. Her eyes were scrunched closed, but her mouth was wide open as she continued to scream. Ty caught sight of thick, rippled scars along her face and neck as she jerked. His stomach dropped, and his heart took up residence in his throat.

He knew exactly who this was, though they'd never met. He'd seen the aftermath images in a case file, read the description of those injuries. This was Maria Fuentes . . . Mira's mother.

Mrs. Fuentes trundled past her daughter, the deep creases at her eyes and mouth and the droop of her shoulders the only indicators of her despair. "Hold her down so that she does not injure herself while I prepare her medicine." She continued to a small cabinet on the far side of the room, pulled a key from her pocket, and retrieved a black, fabric case with a zipper around three sides.

Ty approached the banshee. He licked his lips, took a deep breath, and tried to scoot the distressed woman higher into her chair so she wouldn't fall out. A set of fingernails raked across his cheek. He stumbled back, one hand jumping to cover the fiery lines.

He set his jaw, pursed his lips, and moved in again. This time he was less gentle. He clamped his hands over the flailing wrists and pinned them to the armrests. The howling rose in pitch till he feared his eardrums might shatter like thin glass under the bombardment. Bones barely masked by flesh pressed into his palms as the woman strained. One wrist was soft, while the skin of the other felt like bunched leather hardened by chemicals and heat. The stale odor of sweat and tooth decay mixed with a sweet, floral perfume that couldn't quite cover the less pleasant smells wafting into his face.

"You'll need to make sure she can't move at all." Mrs. Fuentes tapped the side of the needle she'd prepared and pressed the plunger until the smallest bead of liquid formed at the tip. The needle shook from the slight tremor in her hands.

Ty shuddered. He wasn't a huge fan of needles at the best of times. Watching an elderly woman with shaky hands try to inject a raging patient in the back room of a Miami residence was like witnessing a nightmare come to life.

Mira's grandmother shuffled toward him.

Swallowing his repulsion, he dropped his weight onto the panicked woman. His shoulder pressed into her sternum, pinning her in place. Her heart beat against him like a child pounding its fists. This also, unfortunately, placed his ear right next to the shrieking hole of her mouth. He used his stomach to sandwich the nearest arm to the chair while clasping the other at the shoulder and forearm. The woman's legs kicked and slid against the rug, as though making up for the kinetic energy trapped by her imprisoned arms.

Mrs. Fuentes pushed up the sleeve of her daughter's nightgown, exposing thin, pale skin that clung to the wiry tendons and ligaments beneath like cellophane. Needle tracks to rival a heroin addict ran up the woman's arm.

How often does this happen? Ty pushed the thought away and concentrated on keeping his prisoner as still as possible while Mrs. Fuentes wiped a damp pad over the inside of the captive's elbow and touched needle to skin.

The thin metal disappeared. The plunger came down. The needle came out.

Mira's mother took a deep, shuddering breath. She relaxed under his grip. The screams subsided.

Ty remained in place for a moment more, then slowly pulled back. The woman's frantic flailing did not resume. She stared into space with wide, glazed eyes. A trail of drool trickled from the corner of her mouth. All the muscles in her face had gone slack.

Maybe it was *heroin.*

Mrs. Fuentes seemed to deflate as she exhaled. She turned away and shuffled back to the cabinet, but not before Ty caught the glint of moisture in her eyes.

He waited while she sealed the used needle in a clear bag, replaced the bottle she'd filled it from in her zippered case, and returned the case to its locked home. Then he cleared his throat. "Does this happen often?"

She lifted one shoulder. "Usually once or twice a month." She returned to her daughter's side and wiped a strand of sweat-slicked hair off her forehead.

"Perhaps she should be in a hospital."

Mrs. Fuentes narrowed her eyes. "She should be with her family."

"But in a professional facility—"

"They could do nothing for her that I can't do here, and with more love. If she was alone in some cold room, surrounded by strangers, I think she would have given up years ago."

Maybe that would be for the best. He pushed that thought aside and said instead, "How do you manage this on your own?"

She sighed. "I usually call my son, Luis, to help when she has one of her episodes. He doesn't live far away." She tucked another strand of hair behind the woman's ear and smoothed it in place. "Could you carry her over to the bed? She will rest better there, I think."

"Sure." He tucked one arm under the woman's knees and his other behind her back. She weighed almost nothing. He tried to imagine how it was possible for someone to waste away in a house where Mira's grandmother did the cooking but couldn't quite wrap his head around it. He felt as if he'd gained five pounds in the short time he'd been her guest.

Maybe she's overcompensating.

The mattress silently accepted the limp woman, sinking to accommodate the familiar form. Ty straightened and backed away.

Mrs. Fuentes arranged her daughter's hair once more and straightened the seams on her nightgown.

Ty glanced toward the door, wondering if he should leave the women alone now that his help was no longer needed.

"I'll make us some café con leche."

His attention swung back to Mrs. Fuentes. She shuffled toward the exit, and he followed her out.

The house seemed too bright, too quiet, after Maria's room. Especially in the kitchen, where sunlight streamed through the east-facing window and reflected off the polished white counters.

Ty settled at the small, round table as directed and watched Mira's grandmother bustle about, heating coffee, steaming milk, retrieving mugs. He'd already had two coffees; he wasn't sure more caffeine was a terrific idea. Interviewing families with jittery nerves seemed like trouble. Still, he couldn't bring himself to turn down his host's offer.

She set one mug down in front of him. Steam wafted off the surface.

He felt he should say something to break the silence, but his thoughts were dark and twisted. *No wonder Mira hadn't wanted to come home. To have to see her mother like that . . . to know it was her fault. . . .* He understood a thing or two about guilt. Jamal's face drifted up from his memories, smiling and laughing one moment, twisted with pain the next as the air in their own private pocket of Hell ran out and his blood turned cold. Ty had screamed as long and as hard as the woman in the bedroom when his best friend died. If someone had offered him a shot of oblivion at that moment, he'd gladly have accepted.

Mrs. Fuentes set a second mug beside his hand, making him jump and snapping his attention back to the present. "Take this one to Mira."

He stared at the hot, brown liquid. "I'm not sure—"

"She needs it." She leveled her steely gaze at him. "And so do I."

Reminding himself that the woman wasting away in the back room was this person's child, he stood, took the two coffees, and left Mrs. Fuentes to deal with her grief in private. He couldn't imagine having to watch someone he loved suffer like that day in and day out.

His gaze drifted inadvertently to the closed door of Mira's mother's prison as he walked past. He quickened his pace.

Standing outside Mira's door, his courage flagged. What could he possibly say to her?

He looked back toward the kitchen. Mrs. Fuentes was nowhere in sight.

I could just go to my own room.

His mouth turned sour at his own cowardice. His partner was hurting. He'd promised to keep her safe. Granted, ghosts from her past and overwhelming emotions weren't what he'd thought to keep her safe from, but danger came in all forms. The least he could do was offer her a warm drink and whatever support he could.

He pushed back his shoulders, lifted his chin, and faced the wooden portal like a soldier on the battlefield. Tucking one mug into the crook of his elbow, he rapped his knuckles against the door.

There was no response.

He frowned. Should he leave her alone after all? Their partnership was still new, and he didn't know her all that well. Maybe his presence would only make things worse.

What would I do if it was Jamal behind this door?

He closed his eyes and pictured his friend locked away in his bedroom after getting dumped by the girl of his dreams. He'd later married that girl, but at the time it had seemed like the end of the world.

First off, I'd be holding beers instead of coffee. He smiled. *I pushed past his barricades, and we railed at the world until there was nothing left to say, then we made a plan to get his girlfriend back.* Except there was no "get her back" in this situation. Mira's mom wasn't going to get better. Alive or not, she was gone.

The empty ache in his chest that had formed when Jamal died twisted inside him. Loss wasn't something he could fix, but it was something he could empathize with. He pushed the door open.

MIRA

THERE WAS A SOFT tap at the door.

Mira curled tighter, squeezing her knees to her chest and pressing her forehead against her arms. She sniffed. The tears had trailed off, along with mami's screams, but her head felt thick and heavy. Her face was hot. Her thoughts spiraled, but they were entirely her own. The demon continued to sulk in the dark recesses of Mira's psyche.

Mira's door made no sound, but somehow she could tell when it opened. A slight change in pressure, perhaps. Or maybe it was the feeling of being observed that made the small hairs on the back of her neck stand up. Soft footsteps came toward her, muffling further when they crossed from the tiles to the thick rug that covered most of the floor. The intrusive presence stopped beside her.

She sniffed and tipped her head enough to peek out through the curtain of her hair. A white mug of steaming liquid hovered in front of her face, suspended from dark-brown fingers. The smell of the coffee finally managed to penetrate her clogged sinuses.

She struggled for a moment, torn between accepting Ty's offering and kicking him out.

The mug continued to hover, tempting her.

Eventually she uncurled enough to reach out. Her muscles were cramped in place. Every inch felt like straightening a tightly coiled spring. The mug was warm. She brought it to her knees and cupped her second hand around it, staring into the liquid.

Ty sat down on the bed. His leg bumped her side. He sipped his coffee and sighed.

Mira gripped her cup tighter. The heat against her palms became uncomfortable. He'd seen. Of course he'd seen. Abuela would have needed help to get mami calm that quickly. He'd known before, but only from a piece of paper and crime scene photos. Now he *knew*. He'd seen with his own eyes what became of people who got too close to Mira. Even people she loved. *Especially* the people she loved.

She released the mug with one hand and traced the bulge of her Saint Jude necklace—the patron saint of hopeless causes. Despair settled over her so heavily that she couldn't even bring herself to invoke his name.

Ty cleared his throat. "Do you know what happened to my last partner?"

Mira shook her head. Between the boulder crushing her chest and the feeling that her lips had been super glued together, she didn't dare try to speak.

Ty shifted his weight. "His name was Jamal. We grew up together. We were best friends." His voice cracked, and he took a moment to sip his drink. "We were on assignment to bring in a fae halfer who'd recently come into his powers. I made the call to follow the kid into a building without waiting for backup. I was cocky. I thought we could handle him on our own." He shifted again, took another sip, and stared at the far wall as though staring into his past.

Mira watched him in her periphery vision, unwilling to risk making eye contact. The words "without waiting for backup" had pricked her interest. *So he wasn't always such a stickler for following protocol.*

He took a deep breath and let it out in an unsteady stream. "I barely made it out of that building. Jamal didn't. Not a day goes by that I don't feel the weight of that guilt."

Ty's anger in the train yard suddenly came into sharper focus as another piece of his personality clicked into place. *The plan was there to protect you.*

Guess I should cut him some slack on the whole overprotective, control freak thing.

Mira caught the inside of her lower lip between her teeth, worrying the flesh. She appreciated what Ty was trying to do by sharing his trauma, but what happened to his partner and what happened to her mother weren't the same. She cleared her throat, trying to dislodge the wad of emotions wedged there. "Maybe you made a bad call, but it wasn't you who hurt your friend. Everyone makes mistakes sometimes. You should forgive yourself."

He nodded. "So should you."

She clamped her teeth together, forcing the words between tight lips. "I didn't *make* a mistake. I *am* a mistake. That's not something that can be forgiven."

Ty's hand settled on her shoulder.

She looked away, studying the colorful weave of fabrics that made up the rug she was sitting on.

"You're not a mistake. You're amazing."

"I'm a monster, and you know it."

"You're wrong."

She twisted to face him, sloshing coffee over her hand. She ignored the burn. "I saw the look in your eyes when I fed off that rifter in the train yard. That wasn't awe or admiration. It was disgust."

Ty's brown gaze darted away. "I'm just not used to—"

"Working with a monster."

"That's not what I was going to say." His volume was climbing, showing his frustration.

Mira's anger rose to match. She grew more confident. She was comfortable with anger, unlike the emotions that had her cowering on the floor. She set her coffee aside and stood up. With Ty still sitting, she was in the rare position of looking down at him.

"Don't bother denying it. I know what I am."

He reached out with one hand. "I don't see you as a monster."

She stepped out of reach. "Then why did you reject the demon's offer that night?"

His eyes widened momentarily, confirming her suspicion.

"You're afraid of me."

He shook his head.

"And you have every reason to be." She gestured to the bedroom door. "Look what happened to my mother."

Coffee splashed across the carpet as he sprang to his feet and gripped her shoulders, giving her a little shake. "That's not why I didn't sleep with you."

"Then why?" she shouted back.

"Excuse me."

They both spun to glare at abuela standing in the open doorway with a furrowed brow and deep frown.

Ty released Mira's shoulders and took a step away from her.

Abuela pointed back down the hallway. "There's an Officer Lopez at the door."

Mira's chest seized, cutting off her air. She looked at Ty. He didn't meet her gaze, but his wrinkled brow and tight frown made her think he was as surprised by Gianna's arrival as she was.

Abuela looked from Ty to Mira. "Should I ask her to wait while you two finish your . . . conversation?"

"We're done." Ty kept his gaze down as he slipped past abuela and stomped out of sight.

Mira glowered at his retreating back. She reached out to the demon without thinking. *Can you believe the nerve of that guy? Acting all accepting after the way he rejected us?*

<Oh, am I allowed to speak again? You actually *want* my opinion now?>

Mira ground her teeth. Then she caught abuela looking at her, and her own gaze slid to the floor. Heat crept up her neck and flooded her cheeks. "Sorry you had to hear all that," she mumbled. "And about mami. I didn't mean to trigger an episode. I just went in to see how she was doing."

"I'm glad you did, even if it didn't turn out the way you hoped. Keep trying. Someday she may find her way back to us. And don't worry about the argument." She smiled and turned away. "All couples argue."

"We're not—" Mira clipped off her response. Abuela was already gone.

She grabbed the damp towel she'd worn back from her shower and scrubbed the spilled coffee out of her carpet. *Stupid Ty, leaving his mess for me to clean up.* Once she was satisfied the stain wouldn't set, she peeked into the empty hallway. Voices drifted to her from the front room.

What the hell is Gianna even doing here?

Feeling as if she'd swallowed a basketful of snakes, she slipped into the bathroom, splashed some water over her hot cheeks, and spent a moment to collect her rampaging thoughts and emotions. When she had a reasonable grasp over herself, she went out to face her childhood bully.

Gianna was seated at one end of abuela's couch, a coffee mug in one hand and a piece of toast in the other. Ty was sitting at the other end of the couch. Abuela was in her rocking chair.

"What are you doing here?" Mira asked into the silence that greeted her arrival.

"*Tsk*. Where have your manners gone?" Abuela scolded.

"I heard your interviews didn't go so well last night." Gianna said, unfazed by Mira's directness. "Mrs. Martinez went so far as to call Detective Moretti to complain." She glanced at Ty, and the two shared a look that Mira couldn't quite decipher. "I came to offer my assistance with the remaining families."

"We don't need your help." Mira said.

"You sure about that? 'Cause from what I overheard, Mrs. Martinez didn't give you squat."

Heat flared in Mira's face. "How did you even find us?"

Gianna gave her a flat look. "I'm a cop. It's not exactly rocket science to find a person's address, and you've only got so much family in the area." She gestured to abuela.

I knew we shouldn't have come here.

<Not much we can do about that now, and she's not wrong about our progress with the unhelpful Mrs. Martinez.>

Mira glanced at Ty, who was staring at Gianna with an appraising look. She shifted her gaze back to the cop. "Could you give us a minute?"

Gianna downed the last of her coffee, set the empty mug on a waiting coaster, and stood. "I'll wait outside." She saluted with her toast.

Abuela, always the attentive hostess, jumped up to show Gianna to the door, even though no one could possibly get lost in the five steps it took to reach it. Mira was only slightly surprised when abuela slipped outside as well, leaving her and Ty alone in the living room.

Mira paced the length of the room twice before facing Ty. The memory of their recent argument was still fresh in her mind, but she did her best to focus on the issue at hand. "What do you think?"

Ty braced his elbows on his knees and leaned over his clasped hands. "Working with someone the locals recognize may make this investigation more efficient, but I'm not sure it's worth the risk."

Mira nodded, relieved that Ty wasn't going to try to convince her to take Gianna's offer.

"Then again, Gianna isn't exactly following protocol here." He tapped his index fingers against his lips and fell silent.

Mira dropped into abuela's abandoned chair. "So? Not everyone plays by the book."

Ty nodded. "Could be Officer Lopez is just ambitious. She wouldn't be the first beat cop to try to jump the ranks with a big bust. But she seems particularly determined. What if her interest in this case is something more?"

"You think she's involved somehow?"

<There's a thought.> The demon rolled the idea around as though tasting a complex wine. <I didn't pick up any rifter vibes off her, but I wasn't looking very closely. Even if she's human, I guess serial killer could be a logical progression from teenage bully. She certainly has the means. Plus kicking her butt could be therapeutic for you. Okay, I'm liking this theory.>

Ty shrugged. "Maybe she's just an overzealous rookie looking to make her mark, but to show up on your grandma's doorstep after I already shot down her first attempt to join the investigation—"

"Excuse me? When did that happen?"

"After our meeting with the principal."

<I knew we shouldn't have left those two alone.>

"So you already told her to back off?"

Ty nodded.

"Yet here she is," Mira mused. "If she *is* the killer, kidnapper, whatever, she'd want to keep tabs on the investigation."

<I say we kill her.>

"That's a possibility," Ty said. "Assuming it's actually the *case* she's interested in."

Mira frowned, then stiffened as she took Ty's meaning. "You think she could be investigating *me*."

"She's definitely curious about you."

"So keep her close to see if she's our bad guy, or keep away from her to protect my secret. . . ."

<Or kill her. Killing her is still on the table.>

Mira rubbed her temples to ease the first twinge of a headache.

"And there's always a chance she really does just want to see justice done for those kids," Ty said. "She did know them, after all, and closing a case like this *would* be a big career boost."

Mira lowered her hands and drummed her fingers against her armrest. "Do you really think having a local police contact would be useful?"

"After the way yesterday went? Yeah, I do, but it doesn't have to be her. If we want the benefits of a local but decide it's too risky for you to be around Officer Lopez, I can contact the precinct and request an official liaison."

<Jeez. When he says it like *that*, it makes us sound pathetic.>

I'm letting fear of an eighth-grade bully affect my decisions.

<Okay, yeah, that does seem kinda pathetic.>

Ty spread his hands. "There are perks and pitfalls to either choice, but it's your secret that's at risk, so it's your call."

Mira took a deep breath and closed her eyes. The memory of Gianna's adult face blurred with the plump contours of the girl Mira knew as a child. A girl who'd pulled her hair and called her stupid, who'd poured milk down her back and tripped her in the hall. *Why did it have to be her?* She shook her head. *But if she can speed up this case. . . .*

Mira sighed and opened her eyes. "If there's even the smallest chance Gianna's involved with the disappearances, and we need a cop anyway, we might as well kill two birds with one stone."

<So we *are* going to kill her?>

"She can join us for the interviews." Mira held up one finger. "Just the interviews." *That should give us long enough to find out if she's involved.*

Ty nodded.

<And if it turns out she's the bad guy, *then* we kill her.>

Chapter 10

MIRA

MIRA SWAYED ON the back seat of Gianna's police cruiser as they headed toward the final house on their interview tour. Much as she hated to admit it, the interviews had gone smoother with Gianna's help. When the campus cop rang a doorbell she was greeted with smiles and nods rather than suspicion, and the families had been quick to assume Ty and Mira were regular detectives working their child's case—an error no one bothered to correct. For all that Mira was happy they were finally getting some straight answers, she was appalled at the reaction these people had to even the smallest hint of anything paranatural touching their lives.

The people in this town would lynch me as soon as look at me if they knew what I was. That realization, coupled with the way Gianna had been buddying up to Ty all morning and the awkwardness Mira felt toward him since their fight, had amplified Mira's already bitter mood, highlighting the fact that she stood apart.

Gianna said something from the driver's seat, but the words were too quiet for Mira to make out over the road noise. She leaned a little closer but was blocked by the black mesh that separated the front and back of the car.

Ty slapped his thigh and burst out laughing.

The deep sound made Mira's knees turn to rubber and flooded her abdomen with heat. The fact that she'd been left out of the joke quickly doused the warmth and replaced it with ice.

She pursed her lips and crossed her arms, leaning back against the cruiser's leather bench. The stench of nervous sweat, vomit, and industrial cleaner wafted off the fabric. She glanced at a questionable stain that darkened the cushion next to her and scooted a little farther to her right. The soles of her sneakers stuck to the floor mats. *I feel like a criminal back here.*

<It's your own fault. Ty offered you the front seat.>

She slumped further against the cracked leather. Mira had chosen the back seat because the idea of sitting next to Gianna with Ty breathing down her neck had made her skin crawl. Getting a bench to herself had seemed like the better option at the time, but after speaking through a grate and having to wait until someone opened the door for her at each stop, she was regretting her choice.

At least the forced separation had given her and her demon time to study Gianna's energy. Either there was nothing magical about her, or she was powerful enough to shield her true nature from Mira's demon. That was an unsettling thought, but one Mira couldn't discount after being tricked into befriending a sovereign-level rifter less than a month ago. She'd barely made it out of that encounter alive. She wouldn't let her guard down again.

Gianna's blue gaze found Mira in the rearview mirror.

Mira looked away, pretending to study the houses sliding past. They were in a pretty nice neighborhood. Not mansions-and-tennis-courts nice, but nice enough that most of the yards had pools.

"So, where did you end up going to high school after you left?"

Mira pretended she hadn't heard.

Gianna cleared her throat and repeated the question a little louder.

Mira sighed. "I got my GED," she lied.

"Was that hard?"

"No."

"High school was pretty tough for me." She gestured to the scars on her face and neck. "These are what's left after plastic surgery. They used to be worse."

Mira pictured her mother's ruined face and closed her eyes. *At least you could afford the surgery.*

"I'm so sorry you had to go through that." Ty's solicitous tone made Mira want to jump out of the moving car—partly to get away from this conversation and partly to avoid being reminded of the way he'd spoken to her that morning when he'd tried to console her, which in turn reminded her of their argument. It was probably a good thing her door only opened from the outside.

"Did the other kids get scarred?" The words were out of her mouth before they registered. She'd often wondered about the extent of the damage she'd inflicted in that explosion, but she'd been too much of a coward to find out.

Gianna nodded. "Carlos got the worst of it. He lost sight in one eye. Tony only got a line across his nose and a chunk taken out of his ear. I think he was actually happy with that look—it made him feel like a badass.

Luz also got plastic surgery." Again Gianna's gaze found Mira's in the mirror. "We assumed you got messed up, too—that maybe that's why you never came back to school—but you seem fine."

Ty shifted in his seat. "It's crazy how different people can come out of the same situation with such different injuries. On one of my deployments, I saw an IED go off right in the middle of a four-man squad. All four were blown off their feet. Two of the soldiers died. The other two walked away without a scratch on them."

Mira was vaguely aware that Ty was trying to shift the focus, to protect her secret, but her mind had latched onto the fact that Gianna had left someone out of her injury recap. Jennifer had been standing right next to Mira when her magic had gone haywire. Maybe that had protected her . . . or maybe it had put her at ground zero. Mira had nearly visited Jennifer at the hospital dozens of times, but she never made it past the check-in desk. She'd wanted to know how badly she'd hurt her friend, and yet she didn't. She was having the same problem now.

<It's over and done. Don't torture yourself.>

I need to know.

<You've been fine not knowing till now,> the demon pointed out.

Mira swallowed. "What about Jennifer? What happened to her?"

Gianna's reflection paled.

Mira's heart sank.

"She got a few scars, but not any worse than the rest of us."

<Great, nothing to feel guilty about.> The demon sounded almost as relieved as Mira felt.

She exhaled, feeling a weight lift from her shoulders.

"I guess maybe she just couldn't deal with them as well. Or maybe it was something else." Gianna shook her head. "I never could understand why she did it."

Mira's heart stopped dead in her chest. She licked her lips to work a little moisture into her sawdust mouth.

<Don't ask,> the demon pleaded.

"Did what?"

The silence stretched until she wondered if Gianna hadn't heard her. She'd nearly worked up the courage to ask again when Gianna said, "She killed herself freshman year."

The sound of the ocean rushed into Mira's ears. Fireworks exploded in her vision. She pictured Jennifer. Awkward, tall, quiet Jennifer who hid behind her hair and slouched so she wouldn't get called on. She pictured the bushes in the back corner of the schoolyard where the two of them swapped lunches and pretended the rest of the world didn't exist. Then she pictured Jennifer in a casket, face scarred by broken glass. Had anyone attended her funeral?

<It's not your fault.>

I should have been there.

<Dead people don't care who comes to their funeral.>

Not the funeral. Before. I should have been there for her. I should at least have said goodbye.

<Why would saying goodbye make any difference?>

It wasn't the scars. It was being alone. Jennifer always felt alone.

<Then saying goodbye doesn't seem like it would have helped.>

I could have tried to explain.

<That you're an unregistered practitioner possessed by a demon? Yeah, that would have gone over well.>

That I wasn't abandoning her. That I was still her friend.

<Can you be friends with someone you never see?>

Mira stared at her hands, limp in her lap, as she mulled over all the what-ifs that might have changed the course of Jennifer's life. Ultimately, she could come to only one conclusion. *She would have been better off if she'd never met me.*

"Mira." Ty's hand on her shoulder snapped Mira out of her spiraling thoughts. "Do you want to sit this one out?"

She blinked and looked around. Ty was standing on the sidewalk, framed by the open car door. Gianna was walking up the path of a two-story house with bougainvillea bushes on either side of the porch.

"I'm fine." She pushed off Ty's touch and stepped out, hating the way her dismissal made his eyebrows pull together and the small crease that formed at the corners of his downturned mouth.

<You should be nicer to him.>

She watched him as he closed the car door, knowing the demon was right. She opened her mouth to apologize, but nothing came out. How could she explain how coming home had affected her? The ghosts? The sense of disconnect? What could she say to fix the chasm she'd created? Every possibility felt too raw. She choked on the words. Living half her life alone had left her ill-prepared for interactions like this. She cleared her throat. *Let's just focus on the job.*

She followed Gianna, thoughts unsaid. Ty was two steps behind. The front door opened as she reached the porch.

A man with the build of a wrestler opened the door. He was at least a foot taller than Mira, with wide shoulders barely contained by his sea-green polo shirt. He wore khaki shorts and sneakers so white they must have been new. His salt-and-pepper hair was buzzed nearly as short as Ty's. That, along with his wide jaw, gave his face the appearance of an egg. A pair of thin, rectangular reading glasses perched on the bridge of his nose. He tucked his chin to look over them at his visitors.

"Mr. Miller," said Gianna. "Thank you so much for giving up part of your Saturday to meet with us."

"Anything to help with the investigation." Mr. Miller stepped back and motioned for the group to enter his home.

That house could have given abuela a run for her money in the cleanliness department. The narrow table near the entrance held a ceramic bowl full of keys and a glass vase of fresh-cut flowers, each centered on a white, lace doily to protect the polished wood beneath.

Mr. Miller closed the front door and led everyone through an arched opening into a long, rectangular room with a sectional couch and an oval coffee table. "Marcia," he called, "they're here."

A wisp of a woman with flyaway blond hair loosely contained by a large clip on the back of her head stepped into the room through another arch at the far end. She wore a pale-yellow dress dotted with tiny purple flowers. Her skin was suntanned brown, except for pale circles around her eyes that made her look like a raccoon. She had thin, pale lips to go with her spindly figure, and she assessed the visitors with tired green eyes.

"Thank you so much for coming." Mrs. Miller shook each of their hands. "We were beginning to think the police had given up." She gestured for them to sit and asked, "Would you like some tea, coffee, lemonade?"

"No, thank you," Ty said. "We'll try to make this quick."

<*I* would have liked some lemonade.>

Thinking of their earlier conversation about giving the demon's opinions more weight but not wanting to delay their interview, Mira promised, *I'll get you one when we're done here.*

Everyone sat, the Millers huddling close together at one end of the curved sofa while the three guests spread out along the rest of its length.

Ty cleared his throat. "Why don't you start by telling us a little bit about your son."

<Ugh! Why does he have to start with that question every time? We already know the basic bio.>

He's putting them at ease before slamming them with the hard stuff that might make them balk. Mira tried not to roll her eyes as she explained . . . again. She didn't care much for Ty's "good cop" approach either, but abuela had always preached that you got better results with honey. Mira often preferred the stick approach herself, but she settled back against the sky-blue fabric and let Ty take the lead.

"He's a good kid." Mr. Miller narrowed his gaze at Ty. "Not mixed up with anything... weird. He gets good grades. Has friends. Plays sports." He shook his head and repeated, "He's a good kid."

Is he trying to convince us, or himself?

<Check out the wife.>

Mira shifted her focus. Mrs. Miller was wringing her hands in her lap, staring at her pale knuckles.

Maybe she disagrees.

<Ask.>

Mira shot a glance in Ty's direction. The control freak in him wouldn't appreciate getting thrown off rhythm, but the demon was right. All three families they'd spoken with so far had started off with the "good kid" speech. Mrs. Miller was the first parent who looked like she might not believe it.

"Had his behavior changed at all recently?" she asked. "Any differences in his personality or routine?"

Mr. Miller stiffened. Mrs. Miller looked up, her eyes wide. The couple exchanged a glance.

"Thomas used to be on the track team," said Mrs. Miller. "He used to go out with his teammates after school and on weekends." Her voice caught.

Everyone waited while she took a moment to settle herself. Mira leaned forward, resting her elbows on her knees.

"About a month ago, he quit the track team. He stopped hanging out with his friends." She pressed the back of one hand against her lips.

"Did he say why?" Ty asked. "Was there some kind of altercation or falling out with a teammate?"

Mira smiled. Ty had beaten her to the question by half a second. One of the other victims had been a track star. Another had been a cheerleader. Tom being on the team would have given him a connection to both. One that hadn't shown up in his bio since he was no longer on the team.

Mr. Miller set a hand against his wife's back and said, "No, no, nothing like that. He just needed a change of pace. I'm sure he would have gone back next semester."

Parents never know the whole story.

<Speaking from experience?>

I was a kid for eleven years before I met you.

<Do you think he got possessed?>

We can't rule it out. She laced her fingers. "Around the time that Tom left the track team, did you notice him acting oddly at all? Did he seem like a different person?"

Ty met her gaze. This time she'd beaten him to the punch, but she could see in his eyes that they were on the same page. Gianna, on the other hand, seemed to be studying Mira and Ty more than the Millers, which made Mira want to squirm.

<Maybe she wants to ask Ty out and she's trying to decide if you're dating.>

Or maybe she's a serial killer who has murdered four children, and she wants to make sure we don't figure anything out here today.

<I thought you were starting to think this Tom kid might be a rifter.>

I'm keeping my options open.

"He was staying up all night, playing that stupid game." Mr. Miller's words broke into her thoughts.

"What game?" Ty asked.

"I don't know. Some online fantasy game." He snapped his mouth shut as though fearing he'd just let slip an accidental confession.

"Playing fantasy games doesn't make someone a paranatural," Gianna soothed, finally shifting her attention away from Mira. "Quite the opposite, in fact. A paranatural would have little need for that type of escapist pastime."

Both Millers seemed to relax.

<These people really don't want their son to be associated with paranaturals.>

People are scared of what they don't understand. And the human race has made a career out of refusing to understand anything that's different.

"Could we take a look at his room?" Ty asked.

They'd scoped out each of the other missing kids' rooms, with the exception of the one whose mother had slammed the door in their faces last night. So far, Mira hadn't found any trace of rifter energy.

"Detective Moretti already did," said Mr. Miller. "But if you think it will help." He gestured for them to stand. He led them up a set of polished oak stairs and through the first door on the left. He flipped on an overhead light, moved to one side, and said, "Everything is just the way he left it."

The three investigators crowded in. The carpet was pastel green. The walls were white and decorated with the types of posters you'd expect to see in any teenager's room—Tom's tastes seemed to swing toward country bands and college football. A queen-sized bed took up nearly half the room. The remaining space was halved again by a wooden dresser and a metal desk with a black top and drawers down one side. A silver laptop sat on the desk.

Ty moved to the closet and slid one panel to the side. Shirts on hangers, shoes below them, and a wicker laundry basket in the corner. A line of books ranging from calculus how-to guides to western adventure novels were arranged on the upper shelf, first by category, then by size.

<Huh. This kid's even more organized than you. Is that a Florida thing? Why is everyone here so obsessed with things looking neat and tidy?>

It's not a Florida thing . . . and definitely not normal for a teenage boy. In my experience, people keep things tidy when other aspects of their life are falling apart and they don't want anyone to notice.

Mira knelt beside the crisply made bed.

<A night on the town says we find porn underneath.>

No bet. Mira fully expected to find a stack of sticky Playboys when she peeked under the bed. What she found was a clear tub of Lego blocks, a well-worn baseball mitt with a dingy ball nestled in its webbing, and a stack of *Men's Health* magazines. The only thing out of place was a small, silver cylinder.

She turned to Gianna and said, "Evidence bag?"

Mira didn't usually bother with evidence, but since there was still the possibility of a human culprit, it couldn't hurt to follow the rules. She wrapped the clear, plastic baggy Gianna fished out of a pocket over her hand, reached under the bed, and pulled out the oddity. It was a tube of deep-red lipstick. She considered the makeup for a moment then held it up for Mr. Miller to see. "Did Tom have a girlfriend?"

Tom's father lifted the bagged tube from Mira's outstretched hand and examined it. "Not in over a year. This probably belongs to my wife. It must have fallen out of her pocket when she was in here collecting laundry or something."

<Or something . . . no way that lipstick jumped out of the woman's pocket and rolled all the way from the closet to under the bed. She was probably snooping. Humans love to snoop.>

As if demons are any better. You guys spend most of your time spying on the mortal realm.

<That's different. We're looking for a way in. Though I will admit watching the energies that fly off humans during sex is a lot like watching a fireworks display.>

"We can ask her when we go back down." Ty held out his hand, and Mr. Miller set the lipstick on his palm.

Mira braced one hand against the cotton comforter and straightened. A single step brought her to the boy's desk. "This is where he gamed?" She lifted the lid of the laptop as she spoke. There were a handful of icons on the screen, including one in the shape of a stylized dragon.

Ty and Gianna joined Mira at the desk, one towering over each shoulder.

Mira resisted the urge to squirm.

Ty pointed to the dragon icon. "If he was playing an MMO, he was probably chatting with people. If we track them down, maybe we can figure out what was going on with him before he disappeared."

Mira double-clicked to launch the game.

Mr. Miller waved his hand at the loading screen as though he could shoo the image of barbarian warriors and scantily clad mages away. "I don't understand it, but I think that stupid game might be why he took the break from track . . . to spend more time online." He sighed. "What was he thinking?"

The game finished loading and prompted Mira to enter a username and password.

She looked at Mr. Miller and asked without much hope, "Do you know his login info?"

Mr. Miller shook his head.

<Shocker.>

"We could subpoena the game company's records," Ty said. "That should give us the usernames and IPs of anyone Tom chatted with." He turned to Gianna. "Know any friendly judges?"

She darted a quick glance at Mr. Miller, then shook her head. "Not while Moretti's the lead investigator."

Is it me, or does it seem like Gianna wants Ty to claim PTF jurisdiction?

<Which would be pretty dumb if she was any kind of paranatural.>

But kinda genius if she's a regular human serial killer who's trying to throw the investigation off track. Involving the PTF would move all the suspicion to a paranatural culprit.

<And the human killer would get off scot-free.>

Mira narrowed her eyes at Gianna, who caught her gaze, frowned, and took a step back. Turning to Ty, Mira asked, "How long would a subpoena take?"

<We're not actually going to wait for paperwork, are we?>

It doesn't hurt to get more details.

"Probably a few hours, at minimum."

No. We're definitely not waiting.

<How do real cops ever get anything done? Whereas ViVi would have that system cracked wide open in under a minute.>

There's a thought. Mira chewed the inside of her cheek and considered the hacker contact who'd set up the relays and firewalls on her own computer in exchange for helping her out with a nasty gremlin infestation.

She nudged Ty in the ribs to get his attention, rose to her tiptoes, and whispered, "Clear the room."

His eyebrows drew together. The corners of his mouth turned down, but he gave an almost imperceptible nod and turned away from her. "I have just a few more questions, Mr. Miller. Why don't we go back downstairs?"

Mira pointed to the bathroom visible through the open door on the opposite side of the hallway. "You all go ahead. I'll just pop in to use the restroom before I come down." She looked at Mr. Miller. "I assume you don't mind?"

"Um, sure. Go right ahead."

Mira waited for the others to file out, then strolled over to the bathroom as they tromped downstairs. As soon as Mr. Miller turned the corner into the living room, Mira pulled the bathroom door shut and darted back into Thomas's room. She yanked out her cell phone and called ViVi.

"Come on, come on. Pick up." Mira bobbed on the balls of her feet as she waited.

"Who's this?" ViVi's voice was distorted on the line, turning the high-pitched squeak of her real voice into a rumbling baritone.

"Mira. I need a favor."

"When else do you ever call?" The raspy baritone chuckled. "What's up?"

"Can you hack into a boy's computer and tell me who he's been chatting with in an MMO called Arcane Clash?"

"No."

Mira's heart sank.

"But it looks like that game is hosted by Mahonodoa Limited. If I can get into their servers, I should be able to find your boy's IP address pretty quick and see what his logs give up."

Mira exhaled.

The demon's laughter rippled through Mira's head. <Gotta love that girl's delivery.>

"I'm in a bit of a rush," Mira said.

"Surprise, surprise. Lemme shoot a blast to my contacts and see if anyone's got a backdoor into Mahonodoa's system."

Mira paced the room, careful to keep her steps light so as not to alert those below. She half expected to hear the *click-clack* of keys over the line as ViVi worked her techno-magic, but all she found was silence.

"Aaaaand I'm in. Thank cyberspace for gaming geeks who can't stand to miss out on exclusive gear. What's your target's name and location?"

"Thomas Miller. Miami, Florida."

"Gimme a sec."

Mira stared at the ceiling, counting off the seconds. The muffled voices continued downstairs. No red flags yet.

"It looks like your boy mostly only chatted with one other player. SugarB58."

"Can you get a real name to go with that handle? And maybe an address?"

"Keep your panties on."

Mira made three more circuits of the room.

"Brian Stetler. Lives in Fort Lauderdale, Florida. Want me to send you the details?"

"Yes. And thank you. You're amazing."

"I know. You can pay me back by swinging by the next time you're in Arizona."

Mira frowned. "More gremlins?"

"Not exactly. I'll fill you in when you get here. Don't make me wait too long."

The line went dead. A second later, Mira's phone *pinged*, and a text with a Fort Lauderdale address lit the screen.

Mira made a quick stop to flush the empty toilet before heading downstairs. Mrs. Miller was standing alone in the living room, staring through the large window toward the front lawn.

"Where are the others?" Mira asked.

Mrs. Miller startled, turned, then pointed out the window.

Mira joined her.

Gianna was standing next to her cruiser with a phone pressed to her ear. Ty was on the sidewalk beside Mr. Miller. A deep scowl creased his face.

<What do you suppose is going on?>

Let's find out.

Mira let herself out. Mrs. Miller trailed along behind her, as though hoping the other woman's presence might mask her own.

Ty glanced up and moved to intercept her halfway down the sidewalk. Mr. Miller followed. He took his wife's hands when the groups came together.

"What's going on?" Mira asked.

Ty tipped his head to indicate Gianna. "Not sure. Officer Lopez got a call just a minute ago. She seemed to think it might be pertinent to our case."

Mira glanced at Gianna, fully absorbed in her phone call, then looked at the Millers. "Could you two excuse us for a sec?"

She pulled Ty away by his arm. His triceps was tight under her hand. They moved to the far edge of the lawn.

"What's up?" he asked in a low whisper.

She stepped closer, pressing against the length of Ty's arm, and stretched until her lips brushed his ear. "I found out who Thomas was talking to."

Ty turned his face to look at her. Their noses brushed. His exhale warmed her lips.

Heat flared in Mira's abdomen, racing to her extremities and back like an electric surge.

His tongue darted out to wet his lips. The bulge of his Adam's apple bobbed with an audible swallow. Then he took a step back. He moved so suddenly that Mira lost her balance and stumbled into the vacated space.

"Who?" Ty cleared his throat. His voice had come out huskier than normal. "And how?"

Mira opened her mouth, but Gianna's voice cut in before she could answer.

"We have to go, now." She was marching toward them like a woman on a mission.

"Do you have news?" Mrs. Miller called. She was clinging to her husband's arm as though he were the only thing keeping her upright. "Is it about Thomas?"

Gianna waved the Millers off. "Please go back inside."

"But—"

"We can't discuss anything at this time," she said more forcefully. "And we're in a hurry. Now go back inside."

Mr. Miller's expression seemed frozen halfway between horror and outrage. He was clearly not used to being ordered around. He took a deep breath, lifted his chin, and said, "Come on, dear. Let's let these people do their job." He emphasized the last three words and pinned each of them with a glare as if to say, "Or else." Then he led his wife back into the house.

"What's the situation?" Ty asked as soon as the front door was closed. He'd taken another step away from Mira.

"I asked a friend to call me if Moretti moved on anything that might be related to our case."

<Oh, it's *our* case now, is it? Look at this lady, muscling in on our turf.>

"He just got called to the Everglades. Some tourist stumbled across a mutilated body that might belong to one of our missing kids."

Everyone looked at the Millers' front door.

"Moretti, local PD, County, and FDLE are already there. We need to hurry if you want a crack at the scene."

"That's a lot of cops," Ty said. He shot Mira a worried look.

Mira shifted her weight. A fresh crime scene meant dealing with investigators—people trained to be suspicious and suss out secrets. People she generally did her best to avoid.

"Mira, you mentioned you had another lead to follow. Maybe we should split up for the time being . . . cover more ground."

Gratitude and anger swirled through Mira in equal parts.

<Oh, come on. He expects us to do *another* interview while he gets to examine the corpse? How is that fair?>

Try not to sound so excited about a corpse, it makes you sound insane.

<Only by human standards.>

Let's assume those are the standards I'm working with. She sighed. *Besides, he's only trying to protect me.*

<And you're okay with that?>

No. She tamped down the warm fuzzy feeling creeping its way into her heart. *But that doesn't make him wrong.*

"If we're going, let's go." Gianna walked toward her car. "They're not gonna hold the scene for us."

Mira looked between Ty and Gianna. She ground her teeth. "Drop me off at abuela's house. I've got something else to take care of." She stomped over to the cruiser, yanked open the passenger door, and slammed herself into the front seat. *Let Ty deal with the piss stains this time.*

Chapter 11

TY

TY STARED OUT the window of Gianna's cruiser, but he didn't see the scenery sliding past. He was replaying the image of Mira racing away from her grandmother's house on her motorcycle. Gianna and Mira had been all too happy to part ways, and it was probably best they spent as little time together as possible, but watching Mira leave without him had twisted his insides into knots.

She's been investigating on her own for years, he reminded himself. *She'll be fine without me.*

Somehow that thought didn't make him feel any better.

". . . this case yet, or not?"

"Hmm?" He gave himself a little shake and shifted his gaze to the driver's seat as Gianna's voice drew him back to the present. "Sorry, what did you say?"

She shot an irritated look in his direction before returning her attention to the road. "I asked if you'd decided whether or not you're going to take jurisdiction of this case."

He frowned. Enough beating around the bush. It was time to find out exactly what Gianna's angle was. "Why are you so interested?"

"I told you. I—"

"Not interested in the case, interested in my claiming jurisdiction. Do you hate Moretti that much?"

Her grip tightened on the steering wheel. "Moretti's fine. I just think it would be good to get a fresh pair of eyes on the case."

"And we're doing that. I don't need jurisdiction just to look."

"You might change your tune when we get there."

"Oh?"

"With so many departments already crawling over the scene, if you're not prepared to whip out your badge, we might as well turn around now."

Ty crossed his arms. He didn't like the direction this was headed. "I thought that was the point of letting you escort me. If I wanted to make a big splash, I could have done that on my own."

"Sure, but my influence only goes so far. I can't butt in when there are multiple agencies involved. You on the other hand. . . . The PTF would supersede them all."

He sighed. *I guess it was too much to hope that I could fly under the radar forever.*

"So? Will you take jurisdiction?"

"If I have to." He studied her expression, then said pointedly, "I might be able to get what I need simply by swapping liaisons to someone already working the official case."

She tensed her jaw. Her knuckles turned white on the wheel.

That definitely hit a trigger. Still doesn't tell me if her interest is sinister though.

After a dozen blocks of silence she said, "How long have you known your partner was a paranatural?"

The muscle in Ty's cheek twitched before he slammed his poker face into place. His pulse kicked into high gear. He calmly turned his face toward her and asked, "What's this nonsense now?"

"Don't play dumb. I know what Mira is, and I can prove it."

He resisted the urge to wipe the sweat off his palms.

"I always had my suspicions, but I didn't start digging till I saw you two at the school. Then I really started to wonder. And what do you know? I found an article about this 'angel' in Baltimore who looked an awful lot like little Mira. After that, it was just a matter of piecing the stories together. The fire in Detroit just before Ms. Fuentes came back to town all burnt and crazy. The dead girl who was killed in the church Mira attended just before Mira left town." She sat up a little straighter as she listed her findings.

Every point Gianna scored dug into Ty like a knife. He could feel the fragile partnership he'd built with Mira crumbling with every word, burying him one brick at a time under the facts he couldn't refute . . . the secrets he couldn't protect.

"I'm not sure if she's a practitioner or some kind of fae," Gianna continued, "but it doesn't really matter. Magic is magic, and that shit can get you killed around here."

"Coincidence," he said, refusing to give Gianna the confirmation she clearly wanted. "Pure speculation."

"Maybe," she said. "But enough to force a test if she's brought to the PTF's attention." She eyed him. "Unless they're all as willfully blind as you."

Two more blocks rolled by in silence. She wasn't wrong. Even an *accusation* of magic could ruin a person's life. Just look at the way the families he'd interviewed shied away from the subject.

"Why are you doing this?" His voice was dull and hollow sounding.

Gianna's gaze flicked to him, then returned to the road. "Here's the deal. You claim jurisdiction of this case, and you appoint me as your official liaison. We solve the case together, and you give me the credit I'm due. In exchange, I keep my mouth shut about Mira's dirty little secret."

"*Suspected* secret," he said stubbornly. "Basic blackmail then."

"Call it what you want. We either both get what we want, or neither of us does."

Ty dug his fingers into his thighs. His muscles were humming with the desire to spring into action. He wanted to snuff this threat to his partner so badly, he didn't trust himself not to snap her neck then and there. He took a deep breath and let it out slowly. "You're playing a dangerous game."

"So are you. Leaving someone like that loose? If word got out that the PTF was secretly deploying paranaturals outside their designated test zone, well. . . ." She shrugged. "You get the idea. And just in case you're thinking about killing me and dumping my body in the Everglades, you should know I'm not an idiot. I've made contingency plans."

"The thought never crossed my mind," he lied. "What if it turns out there's no paranormal aspect to these disappearances? The PTF doesn't investigate mundane crimes."

"It does today . . . if you want your partner's secret to stay safe. Sorry, *suspected* secret. Human, fae, or other, we find the person responsible, and I make the collar."

Ty drummed his fingers against his leg, reviewing his options. He couldn't force her silence short of killing her, and if she was telling the truth about her contingency plan, that was as good as outing Mira himself. There was no telling what Mira might do if she found out what Gianna was scheming, but he was betting it would be of the "shoot first" variety, which would trigger Gianna's fail-safe. One way or another, he had to take care of this without Mira finding out. If he accepted Gianna's terms, he'd as good as confirm her suspicions, giving her more leverage. That was a slippery slope he wasn't sure he wanted to start down.

"So? Do we have a deal or not?"

I need to find out how much she knows. The best way to do that is to play along.

"This seems like an awfully roundabout way to get assigned to a case most detectives would probably steer clear of. So what is it? Personal? Professional? Or are you just desperate for attention?"

Color flooded Gianna's cheeks. "Shut the fuck up."

That hit a nerve.

They continued in silence, save the rattle of the air conditioner, as the city gave way to wilder land. Standing water reflected the blue-and-white sky in a still strip that ran parallel to the road. Bushes and tall grass crowded close on the other side, so dense Ty couldn't see the ground. The flat expanse stretched away for miles.

After twenty minutes, Gianna turned onto a dirt road that snaked between the marshy land on a causeway of raised earth barely wider than the road itself. She followed the dry path to an island filled with a parking lot, a small building with a sign advertising airboat tours, and a wooden pier. She cut the engine and pivoted to face Ty. "What's your answer?"

Ty had spent the remainder of the drive mulling that over. Either Gianna was a kidnapper and maybe killer trying to derail the investigation, or she was a glory-seeking cop looking for a quick ticket to fame. Both were dangerous, but in either case, the only way to protect Mira was to keep Gianna close.

"Fine. You want credit for the collar, it's yours, but don't interfere with the actual investigation."

Her eyes narrowed. "I'll have you know I'm a damned good investigator."

"So good you have to resort to blackmail just to work a case?"

"Good enough to uncover Mira's secret from a handful of seemingly unrelated events."

"Facts twisted to fit your preconceptions and personal prejudice. I'm not convinced there's any actual evidence behind your claim, but true or not, an accusation like that would slow us down, and there are kids' lives at stake."

Gianna's hand moved to the scars on her neck. "I—"

"Look, I'm telling you the credit for this case is yours. That's what you wanted, right?"

She snapped her mouth shut and glared at him.

"But I have a condition of my own."

She leaned away from him. "What?"

"Mira can't know about this deal."

Gianna's eyes widened. "You think you can convince her to work with me without some kind of ultimatum?"

"Let me handle that. Do you accept my terms?"

"Don't eff up the investigation. Keep Mira in the dark. Yeah, I'm good with that." She stuck out her hand.

He looked at her open palm. "This isn't an agreement between equals." Leaving Gianna's hand where it was, he unbuckled his seat belt and peeled himself off the vinyl.

The air was heavy and carried the musky sent of rotting earth. The dirt he stood on seemed solid enough, but there wasn't much of it. Twenty feet to either side, the ground sloped away to reeds and water. A nearby bush rattled its leaves. The brown-and-black patterned scales of a snake slipped out of sight.

Ty looked down at his sneakers and wished he'd invested in some tall, thick boots for this trip.

Gianna circled around the front of the car and headed for the single structure that took up half the island. "Come on. We'll take an airboat the rest of the way."

MIRA

MIRA OPENED UP the throttle on her bike. Wind whipped her jacket and dried the sweat off her skin as she hugged the curves of the coastal road. She'd missed this lately. The speed. The isolation. The freedom. Working with Ty was all about compromise, but here there was just her and the road roaring by at sixty miles per hour.

The demon was singing in her head, calling out sights as they flashed past, but Mira was used to that. They'd been together so long that her incorporeal passenger was almost as much a part of her as she was. Sometimes she even found herself doubting the demon was real. Maybe she'd lost her mind that day her magic broke loose, and everything the demon had done since was just a manifestation of Mira's own twisted psyche. But then, the demon had had a few choice opinions to share on that theory.

Mira slowed for a group of beachgoers carrying coolers and umbrellas as they scrambled across the street in their swimsuits and sarongs. The highway would have been faster, but Mira wanted to see the ocean. Besides, with Ty and Gianna teamed up for the Everglades mission, Mira was in no rush to get back.

The thought of Ty partnering with Gianna sent a bitter ache through her chest.

Mira glanced at the people walking toward the shore. It was a group of six—three men, three women. They were all around her own age. They talked and laughed as they made their way over the hot sand. Two of the men held hands. The third had his arm around a woman's waist. They bumped shoulders as they walked.

A horn blared.

Mira snapped her attention back to the road. The light had changed. She was holding up traffic.

<If you want to go to the beach, we could—>

Mira revved her engine to drown out the offer. There was no point dreaming about a life she'd never have.

She curved inland and wound through the streets of Fort Lauderdale. Strips of patchy grass dotted with Florida elms separated narrow sidewalks from the patchwork roads. Single-family homes bordered by hedges were interspersed with condo complexes. Out-of-state plates and rental cars lined the streets. She pulled to a stop in front of a white building with sharp angles, narrow windows, and gray-rock trim and pulled out her phone to check the address.

"This looks like the place."

<It looks like a spring break flop house.>

"Maybe it is. This is Lauderdale, after all. But if ViVi says we'll find Brian Stetler here, who am I to argue?"

She killed the engine, pulled off her helmet, and climbed the central staircase to the third floor. She knocked on a blue door with a brass *3B* nailed to the front.

A moment passed. She heard rustling inside. A chain scraped. The door opened to reveal a willowy woman in a silk bathrobe.

Mira opened her mouth to ask if the woman knew Brian Stetler, but the demon's voice interrupted her thought.

<Whoa, I did not see that coming.>

What?

Mira gave the woman a second look . . . and froze as her gaze came to rest on the face framed by the long, blond hair. She had a wide jaw and high cheekbones accentuated by her makeup. Her lips were stained red. But it was her green eyes that stopped Mira dead. Those eyes belonged to Mrs. Miller, the missing boy's mother.

What the hell?

Mira pointed at the apparition before her, stripping back the image in her mind and overlaying it with the photographs from her files. "You're Thomas Miller."

The woman's eyes went wide. She tried to slam the door.

Mira bulled her way inside. "Do you have any idea what your mother is going through right now?"

"Thomas" stumbled back, looking confused and panicked, a deer on the verge of bolting. "You know my mom?"

"I'm looking into the death of her son."

The woman blanched. "She thinks I'm dead?"

Mira sighed and rubbed a hand over her forehead. "Let's take this from the top."

TY

THE WHIR OF THE airboat's massive fan made conversation difficult as the aluminum hull skimmed along the waterways of the Everglades. That was fine by Ty. He had nothing left to say to the manipulative woman who'd threatened his partner in exchange for a shot at fame. He just prayed her ambitions ended there. If Gianna decided outing a rifter acting on behalf of the PTF would get a better headline, she might change tactics in a heartbeat. If that happened, Ty would need to get Mira out of town in a hurry.

The boat skimmed through the murky water, leaving a dark trail in its wake where it cut through the layer of green scum that coated the surface. Half-rotted, lichen-covered logs floated by. Every now and then, one of the logs blinked and fixed an amber eye on the passing boat. Ty shuddered when he saw a white membrane slide horizontally across that cold, assessing orb. He scooted a little closer to the middle of the boat. This was not water he'd fancy taking a dip in.

Gianna nudged his shoulder. He glanced at her, and she pointed. They rounded a bend that revealed a collection of boats identical to theirs clustered around a swell of land. People in suits, uniforms, and what looked like fishing gaiters crammed together around something Ty couldn't make out on the ground. Several faces looked up as Ty's boat approached, some with curiosity, others with irritation. This party was already crowded, and no one else was invited.

Ty's boat bumped against the shore, knocking into another beached boat. Gianna jumped off as the boat rocked. Ty waited a moment to gather his balance, then leapt ashore. The ground sank under his heels. He stumbled forward. Water seeped into the depressions he'd left.

"Are you sure this is stable?" he asked no one in particular.

"About as stable as it gets in the Glades," said a man with dark aviator sunglasses, a wide-brimmed hat, and a badge marking him as a member of the Florida Department of Law Enforcement. "This area is off-limits to tourists right now, so who are you, and what are you doing here?" His words carried a slow drawl that made Ty impatient, but he politely waited for the man to finish before responding.

He pulled out his PTF badge and flashed it at the man, then lifted it high so those behind the welcome committee could see, and said in a loud voice, "PTF Agent Ty Williams."

Several of the gathered people shot dirty looks at Ty when they heard his credentials. A few looked relieved. One snorted and spat into the tall grass.

"And just what are *you* doing with him?" A heavyset man with graying hair, a thick gray mustache, and liver-spotted skin wedged his way to the front and pointed a finger at Gianna, who'd slunk off to one side, keeping herself apart from both Ty and the crew crowding the island. "You're supposed to be babysitting brats. You've got no business at a crime scene."

Gianna cringed. Her gaze darted to Ty, then back to her accuser. She took a deep breath and lifted her chin. "I'm serving as Agent Williams's local liaison."

The man cast Ty a sidelong glance. "Yeah, I'll bet you're giving him the full service."

A couple of uniformed cops snickered.

Color crept into Gianna's cheeks.

Ty was starting to understand why Gianna had felt it necessary to blackmail her way onto the case. Not that he had any intention of forgiving her for threatening Mira, but these assholes needed to be brought down a peg.

He stepped in front of Gianna. "I've asked Officer Lopez to assist me because she has firsthand knowledge of the missing kids. She's already helped me conduct several interviews, and her insights have been invaluable."

Gianna stood a little straighter.

"Yeah, yeah." The man waved a hand in front of his face as though he smelled something worse than the ambient rot and stagnant water. "Have her assist you all you want, but when you're ready to work, I'm the guy you'll need." He thumbed his badge. "Detective Moretti. I'm the lead on this investigation."

The man with the aviator shades who'd first intercepted Ty cleared his throat. "This case has spread beyond your local jurisdiction. At this point, FDLE should take over."

Ty waved his badge in front of their noses. "PTF takes priority. I'll take point from here on."

"Only if there's proof of paranatural involvement," Mr. Aviators said. "What's the PTF's interest in this case?"

"I'm neither required nor inclined to share that information right now. It's enough for you to know that suspicions have been raised and I've been dispatched."

"Then why didn't we get a call at the department?" Moretti asked. "Where's your paperwork to officially take jurisdiction?"

"I'd assumed, apparently wrongly, that I'd have cooperation from the local departments, but if you're that big a fan of paperwork . . . here." He reached into his wallet and pulled out a card for Director Garrett, the man who'd convinced him to renew his position with the PTF after Ty had taken his "sabbatical" to recover from the death of his friend and partner. There were other, more local contacts who'd vouch for him, even without knowing the details of the situation, but Ty was betting the title "Director" would give these chest thumpers pause.

The two local alphas looked at the card, then at each other.

Mr. Aviators backed down first. "The PTF will of course have full cooperation from the FDLE and the Sheriff's Office. I'm Special Agent Donovan, assigned to this case. I was only curious what new evidence had come to light that prompted your involvement." He lifted both hands in a placating gesture. "Though I acknowledge your right not to divulge that information."

Moretti turned up his nose at the offered card. "Sure, fine. If you want this steaming pile, it's all yours." He pivoted and bowed, inviting Ty forward with a sweeping gesture.

Ty tucked the rejected card away and walked forward. Moretti moved to follow, but Ty froze him with a glance over his shoulder. "Your services are no longer required here, Detective Moretti. Officer Lopez will continue to serve as my liaison. I expect you to afford her all professional courtesy and deliver any existing evidence reports to her as quickly as possible."

Moretti glared daggers at Gianna as she trotted to catch up to Ty. The old man's face was splotched with purple. His fists quivered at his sides.

I really hope pissing that guy off doesn't come back to bite me in the ass, Ty thought as he turned away from the slighted detective.

Chapter 12

TY

THE COPS WHO'D watched Ty's display of dominance from a distance backed up at his approach, giving Ty his first look at the body . . . if it could be called that. Strips of soggy fabric twisted around chunks of gray meat that only vaguely resembled the shape of a person. Shards of exposed bone stuck out at odd angles. Insects swarmed the area. The smell of rotting flesh smacked Ty in the face, and bile burned the back of his throat. Something stung his neck. He smacked it. His hand came away with a brown smear on his palm. He wiped it on his pants. Ty looked over the gathered people. "Which one of you is the coroner?"

"That would be me." A middle-aged woman wearing thick purple-framed glasses, a yellow T-shirt, overalls, gumboots, and a Marlins ball cap raised her hand.

Ty indicated the body. "What can you tell me?"

"Well, the gators and other scavengers have been at him pretty good, but let me show you around." She crouched and indicated he should come closer.

Ty swallowed and tried to take shallow breaths as he squatted next to the corpse.

The coroner used a thin piece of metal to point out a wide section of bone. "The pelvic bones shows your victim is male." She used the probe to lift a flap of skin and exposed a skeletal grin. "Dentition puts him in his mid-to-late teens."

Mr. Aviators tapped Ty's shoulder. He held a clear evidence bag with a tattered piece of bloody fabric inside. The cloth was thick, and heavy embroidery thread spelled out the letters "as Ma" in gold against the blue fabric. "We think this is what's left of Lucas Martinez's letter jacket. The timeline fits."

The coroner nodded. "I won't know for certain until I get him back to the morgue, but from the boy's weight and build, I'm fairly comfortable identifying the remains as Lucas Martinez."

"Can you tell me how he died?"

A woman in the uniform of Miami PD, likely one of Moretti's underlings, chuckled. "I'd think the gator-chewed bones and minced meat would be a dead giveaway."

"And I'd think any cadet would know the Glades are a great choice for a body dump," Gianna shot back.

The coroner ignored them both. "As I said before, he's pretty picked over, and he's been underwater for a while, which is normal for a gator kill. He probably washed loose from whatever log or rock a gator stuck him under."

Ty frowned. "Why would an alligator hide a corpse?"

Everyone looked at him like he was an idiot. The surly cop coughed "tourist" into her hand.

"To tenderize the meat," Gianna explained. "Makes it easier to pull apart."

Ty swallowed, caught a whiff of rotting Lucas, and gagged.

"Anyhoo," continued the coroner, "these here are gator bites." She indicated a piece of exposed femur scored by a series of deep gouges. "The teeth scrape bone as the flesh is pulled loose." She pointed to another section of bone, where smaller scratches created patterns in tight clumps. "These are from scavengers, most likely rodents." Next she peeled back a strip of water-logged cloth to expose the boy's ribcage. One side had been cracked open and caved in. Bits of muscle hung between the remaining ribs. Across the more intact side were a series of deep gouges. They were thicker and longer than the rodent bites, but closer together than the alligator teeth. "I'm not sure what made these."

The coroner then carefully lifted a collection of bones and tendons that Ty's brain took a second to identify as an arm. She turned it in her gloved hands so the underside of the wrist was visible. "And most disturbingly. . . ."

Ty squinted at the wound on the wrist. There seemed to be a curved dent in the bone.

"These were most likely made by human teeth."

Gianna gasped.

Ty held his breath in a vain attempt to block the stench as he examined the wound more closely. If the victims were being eaten, Father Bembe's insistence about paranormal involvement was looking a whole lot less far-fetched.

The coroner set the arm back down. "That's about all I can tell you right now."

"Thank you." Ty stood and took two quick steps away from the body. A fly buzzed by his ear, and he shooed it away. He cleared his throat, set his hands on his hips, and looked up at the lazy clouds drifting across the pale sky. He could practically feel his skin crisping under the afternoon sun, and the wet fabric sticking to his back made him imagine he was being cooked and tenderized for some horrific feast.

"What's our next move, boss?"

He dropped his gaze to Gianna. Agent Donovan was standing beside her. The others had gone back to bagging evidence.

Ty rubbed the back of his neck, chasing off yet another biting insect. "Let's see . . . Lucas was the second of the four kids to go missing—"

"Five," interjected Donovan.

"What?" Ty counted on his fingers. "Davis, Martinez, Miller, and Sanchez. Who else is missing?"

"A nineteen-year-old named Charlotte Hernandez. She was a college student at the University of Miami. Her roommate reported her missing last night, but apparently no one's seen her for about five days."

Ty frowned. "What took the roommate so long to report her missing?"

"College students come and go at all hours," Donovan said with a shrug, "especially this close to spring break. It's not surprising it took a while for someone to notice she wasn't coming home between parties."

Ty nodded. "Did Hernandez have any connection to the other victims? Did she graduate from their high school?"

Donovan shook his head. "She's from out of state. But the university isn't too far from the high school, and according to the roommate, they were at a party in Coral Gables the night she went missing. Chances are good there were high schoolers there too, so maybe some of your victims crossed paths."

A crackle brought everyone's attention to the walkie-talkie clipped to the cop who'd called Ty a tourist. She moved as far away from the prying eyes as the limited amount of solid ground would allow, pressed her hand to a button, and said, "Repeat, Dispatch. Did not copy."

A muffled voice drifted over the crime scene, but Ty couldn't make out any words. The other cops had turned away. They had their own jobs to take care of.

"Copy." The woman turned around. She glanced at Moretti in the boat, hesitated, then approached Ty. She cast a scathing look at Gianna, then deliberately angled her body to exclude her from the conversation.

"If you're taking point on this case, you should know that we just got a report of another missing person."

Ty's stomach sank. *That brings the total to six in just over a week.*

"Another high schooler?"

She shook her head. "A college student. Miami University. She went missing from a dance club last night."

Ty swore under his breath, looked at Gianna, then pulled out his phone and called Mira.

MIRA

MIRA HELD HER magic primed as she settled on a white love seat and watched a person she'd thought was dead pour lemonade at a kitchenette. *I can't believe you realized before me.*

<You flesh bags are so superficial. Gender is just window dressing.>

"Then he . . . *she?* . . . *they?* are one hell of a decorator," she mumbled.

"Hmm?" "Tom" paused in pouring the second cup. "Did you say something?"

"What should I call you?" Mira indicated the high-end wig and silk robe.

"Tanya. She/her." She smiled. "Thanks for asking."

Tanya brought the two cups over to the living area and handed one to Mira. "Sorry I tried to slam the door in your face. You surprised me."

"Yeah, you surprised me, too." Mira set her drink on the glass coffee table in the middle of the sitting area.

<That looks tasty. Why aren't you drinking?>

Until we know exactly how Tanya here is connected to the other missing kids, we need to keep our guard up.

<She's not a rifter.>

I'm not getting "killer" vibes off her either, but we've been wrong before.

Tanya settled into a plush blue chair at one edge of the green shag carpet that marked the sitting area as separate from the rest of the tiled apartment. She cradled her lemonade in her lap. "I knew my parents would worry, but I never imagined they'd think I was dead."

Now that she was listening for it, Mira caught the slight crack in Tanya's voice that so often plagued adolescent males.

Mira leaned back to get a better view of the room that split off from the living area. She caught sight of a dresser stacked with a dozen foam heads, each sporting a wig in a different fashion or color.

<That's a nice collection.>

Too nice for the handful of days this kid's been missing. Mira shifted her gaze back to Tanya. *The easiest way for a kidnapper to get to someone is to become their friend.*

<You're thinking our kidnapper lured Tanya here with the promise of pretty things?>

Maybe. But if we're looking at someone who's keeping kids rather than killing them, that's not likely to be a rifter.

<Could be a fae. They sometimes collect mortals.>

Mira pressed her lips together. *Or maybe that lazy cop was right about the kids just being runaways. At least in Tanya's case.*

<And the others?>

Mira studied Tanya. "What exactly do you know about Brian Stetler?"

Tanya jolted as if she'd received an electric shock. "Why do you want to know about Brian?"

"Are you aware several other teens have gone missing from your school?"

"Yeah, but. . . ." She paled. "Wait, you think Brian had something to do with that?"

"If he lured you here, he might have done something similar with the other kids."

"No. Never." She shook her head emphatically, making her blond waves dance.

<That wig is super well attached.>

Focus!

At that moment, the front door swung open.

"Hey, love. I picked up some—"

Mira sprang to her feet, compressing her magic into a fireball in her right hand.

The tall brunette who'd walked through the door froze in place. She was in her mid-to-late thirties, wearing wedge heels, a short, tight, denim skirt, and a billowy cream-colored blouse with split sleeves. Her sculpted eyebrows arched above round, blue eyes. The delicate bow of her lips formed a startled "oh." She had one hand on the keys jammed into the doorknob. A cardboard drink tray balanced in the other. Several fabric grocery bags dangled from her forearms.

"Who are you?" Mira demanded.

Tanya jumped between Mira and her target. "Stop! This is Brianne." She glanced over her shoulder, winced, then met Mira's gaze. "Brian Stetler."

Mira goggled at the woman in the doorway. From her smooth legs to the swell of her breasts, to the subtle makeup highlighting her delicate features, nothing would have made Mira think this woman wasn't female.

<That explains a thing or two.>

She makes a prettier woman than I do, Mira marveled.

<Maybe you should try harder. I bet she'd give you some pointers if you asked nicely. Look what she did for Tanya.>

That brought Mira's thoughts back to Earth. *Sense anything?*

<Not a single demonic ripple. Not even any magic potential.>

What about a fae? A succubus maybe?

<She's a totally normal human.>

Mira let her fireball dissipate, trusting that she was a match for any mere mortal, even if they did turn out to be a killer.

"Have a seat." She indicated the red lounge chair that made up the third side of the seating arrangement.

Brianne's fearful gaze darted to Tanya.

<Do you think she'll take a hostage?>

Be ready if she does.

But Brianne didn't run. She sidestepped to the designated seat and sank down. "Who are you?"

"Tanya," Mira said, "close the door."

Tanya pulled the jangling keys from the lock and swung the front door closed.

"Now we're all going to have a nice, calm conversation." Mira lowered herself slowly to the couch. She never took her eyes off Brianne.

Tanya returned to her blue chair and huddled with her knees pulled up to her chest. "You're a paranatural."

Mira was cursing herself up and down for letting her surprise manifest like that. She'd meant to stay alert, but not understanding the situation had made her jumpy. Now she had two civilians to deal with who knew at least part of her secret.

<Are we going to kill them?>

The fact that the demon could ask that question without the slightest hesitation in its tone sent shivers down Mira's spine.

<People already think Tom is dead.>

We're not going to kill them.

<Then how are we going to make sure they don't talk? You saw the way the parents we interviewed reacted to even a whisper about magic. This is not a para-friendly town.>

Brianne sniffled and asked in a quavering voice, "Are you going to kill us?"

"No! Would everyone stop asking me that?!"

Both women jerked away from her.

"Sorry." Mira raised a placating hand. "It's been a frustrating day."

"Why are you here?" Brianne asked.

"She thinks you're a kidnapper," Tanya said before Mira could frame a response.

Brianne's mouth dropped open. Her shoulders relaxed. She stared at Mira. "Is that what this is about?"

<I'm not great at human expressions, but she seems relieved.>

I agree.

<Probably not a kidnapper then.>

Not so much.

Mira cleared her throat. "I'm investigating a number of missing teens who attended Tanya's high school. Have you ever had contact of any sort with Olivia Davis, Lucas Martinez, or Ramon Sanchez?"

Brianne shook her head. "Never heard of them." She finally set her bags down on the floor and moved the drink tray she was holding to the coffee table.

<Well, shit.>

Mira turned to Tanya.

The younger woman raised her palms. "I only knew them in passing. We weren't friends or anything."

"What can you tell me about them?"

"Luke was a jerk. He was a star on the track team. Always had two or three girls on the line. I think he dated Olivia at one point. She was a cheerleader. I never really talked to Ramon. He mostly kept to himself." Tanya shrugged. "I'm sorry they're missing, but I really don't know anything."

Mira sighed and rolled her neck to ease some of the tension creeping down her shoulders.

This case sucks.

<Maybe Ty's having more luck with the dead body.>

"At least I can take your name off the victim list."

Tanya tensed. "Are you going to tell my parents where I am?"

Brianne sat up a little straighter.

Mira looked from one woman to the other. She settled her gaze on Tanya. "I won't tell them where you are . . . but you should."

Tanya exhaled and relaxed a little.

<Poor Mrs. Miller.>

Mira shifted in her seat. "Look, kid, if you want to run away and start a new life, that's your business, but your parents are super messed up right now. Just cutting them out of your life without any explanation is a pretty shitty thing to do."

<Says the girl who ran away twice.>

"I agree," Brianne said. "You should go see them."

"What? No." The panic was back in Tanya's voice. "You can tell them I'm alive, that I just ran away, but this"—she indicated her wig and the swells beneath her robe—"they won't understand."

"They might," Brianne said. She looked at Tanya with sad eyes. "You won't know unless you try."

Tanya shook her head. "My mom, maybe. But my dad? He's all about sports, and hunting, and male bonding. He loves having a son. It would break his heart to have that taken away."

Brianne crossed her arms. "You think his heart isn't breaking right now?"

"If you feel that way, why'd you invite her here?" Mira asked.

She turned her blue gaze on Mira. "Because I didn't want her sleeping on the streets." She sighed, relaxed her arms, and crossed one long leg over the other. "I know what it's like to be young and scared. I've been there." She swung her attention back to Tanya. "I wanted you to have a safe place to experiment and get your head on straight. I was hoping you'd have a little more time, but with things the way they are. . . ." She shrugged. "It's time to talk to your parents."

"What if they won't accept me?" Tanya whispered.

"Then that's on them," Brianne said. "But take it from someone with a little experience in these matters. People can be more accepting than you think if you just give them a chance. If you reject them first because of what you think *might* happen, then *you're* the asshole."

<This sounds familiar.>

Shut up. Mira coughed to clear the thick feeling at the back of her throat. "This is touching and all, but I've got three more kids to find." She stood, looked from one woman to the other, and said, "About me being . . . um—"

"We won't tell," Tanya said.

"We understand a thing or two about living a lie." Brianne walked over and set her hand on Mira's shoulder. "I hope you have someone in your life who sees and accepts you for who you are."

The thickness was back in Mira's throat, so she just nodded and let herself out.

<I like those ladies.>

Yeah. Me, too.

<If we do find a rifter to drain, I might give Brianne a call. She seems fun.>

Mira trotted down the condo stairs. Three steps from her motorcycle, the phone in her back pocket vibrated. She pulled it out, saw Ty's name, and answered.

"The body in the swamp is most likely Lucas Martinez," Ty said without preamble.

Mira pictured the school photo she'd memorized of the missing kid.

<Tanya said he was a jerk.>

That doesn't mean he deserved to die.

"You still there?" Ty's voice broke into her thoughts.

"Yeah."

"I've taken jurisdiction of the case."

"What? Why?"

"It was the only way to get access to the scene, and it's already yielded another lead. We've got two more possible victims, both college students from Miami University."

Mira rubbed her fingers over her forehead. Standing on the sidewalk in the sun, she was starting to sweat. "That would mean the kidnapper has a wider hunting ground than we thought."

"And it brings their body count up to six. Charlotte Hernandez fell off the grid five days ago, but the second girl only disappeared last night. She might still be alive. I'm heading over to the dance club where she was last seen to check it out. Care to join me?"

"Yeah," she glanced up at the third-story windows. "I've got some news of my own to share."

Ty rattled off an address.

Mira said, "See you there," hung up, and mapped out a route on her phone.

<I know you don't like carrying it around, but those doohickeys are useful.>

"Yeah, yeah." She memorized the roads and shoved the phone back into her pocket with more force than was strictly necessary.

<Something bugging you?>

No.

<Liar.>

Mira sighed. "I'm just surprised he took jurisdiction of the case without even talking to me."

<At least this means there's no reason for Gianna to tag along anymore.>

That cheered Mira up. She was almost smiling as she turned her bike back toward Miami.

Chapter 13

MIRA

CLUB ECHO WAS a three-story glass-and-steel construction in the heart of Miami. An LED billboard above the main entrance scrolled between an advertisement about free drinks for ladies every Saturday night, Salsa lessons on Wednesdays, and the headlining DJs scheduled to perform at the club. Red ropes draped between poles marked off the area in front of the doors and traced the edge of the building halfway down its facade. Mira imagined there would be lines around the block come sunset, but right now the street bustled with the normal city traffic of weekend shoppers.

Mira looked up and down the sidewalk. There was no sign of Ty or his silver truck.

We must have beat him here.

<Do you want to wait for him?>

Mira considered. She wasn't used to waiting for anyone. Ty had the badge, but Mira was confident she didn't need it. She'd been doing this kind of thing for years. *Nah.*

She approached the main entrance and gave a man standing on the far side of the glass a little finger wave. The bouncer had muscles on his muscles. He wore black cargo pants and a black T-shirt stretched so thin she figured it would burst into a shower of confetti if he flexed. He looked her up and down, opened the door a crack, and said in a polite but gruff voice, "Sorry, miss, we're not open yet."

"I'm aware." She flashed him her forged PI badge. "I'm here to talk to your boss about the woman who went missing last night."

"She's with us."

The bouncer turned, giving Mira a clear view of Gianna as she walked up to the entrance.

<Damn, this girl's harder to shake than a catchy jingle.>

"What are you doing here?" Mira demanded.

"Same as you." Gianna placed one hand against her hip. "Assisting with Agent Williams's investigation."

Mira opened her mouth, caught the look of curiosity on the door-man's face, and snapped her teeth together in a feral smile. She forced out the words, "And where exactly is Agent Williams?"

"Chatting with the manager," Gianna said. "He wanted to wait for you, but the owner's a busy man, and we weren't sure how much longer you'd take to get here."

Mira pushed between Gianna and the bouncer and stepped into the club. Mr. Muscles pulled the door shut behind her. "Where are they?"

"Ty has this interview covered," Gianna said. "He should be wrapping up any minute now."

"So it's 'Ty' now, is it?" A muscle twitched below Mira's left eye. "Just how friendly did the two of you get out there in the Glades?"

<This girl is definitely interested in your man.>

The demon's words splashed over Mira like a bucket of ice water, dousing her anger.

He's not mine. Never was, never will be. If he wants to hook up with the likes of Gianna, I have no right to interfere. The admission burned like a sub-zero wind chill across her heart.

"Relax." Gianna flipped the trailing end of her braid over her shoulder. "Ty and I are strictly business." She smirked. "Not that I wouldn't hit that if he offered."

<Let's kill her now.>

Mira stared at her adolescent rival for a long moment, reining in her less-than-civil impulses, then she turned and headed for the bar that dominated one edge of the club. "I need a drink."

For a moment, Mira was afraid Gianna might try to join her, but all that followed her was the unpleasant sensation of the other woman's gaze boring into the back of her head. She resisted the urge to rub her neck as she settled at one of the bar's empty stools.

"We're not open yet," said the blond woman in the white blouse and black apron who was cutting garnishes behind the bar.

Mira indicated the shelves of bottles displayed in front of the mirrored wall. "You're fully stocked." She reached into her wallet and slapped a twenty onto the counter. "And I've got cash. Just give me a shot of Jack."

TY

TY SHOOK HANDS with the club manager—a middle-aged Korean man with silver feathered at his temples who wore a dark-gray suit and a purple tie. "Thank you for your cooperation."

"Anything I can do to help get this matter resolved quickly."

And put an end to articles about missing girls and PTF investigations that might hurt your bottom line. Ty squeezed the man's hand a little harder than necessary, then released it, reminding himself that it didn't matter *why* Mr. Jung was cooperating, only that he was.

Mr. Jung cradled his hand slightly as he sat back down behind his polished oak desk. A filing cabinet, wall safe, and the wooden chair Ty had occupied for their interview were the only other furniture in the small office. Ty walked to the room's single door and let himself out.

A long brick hallway ran the length of the club with a break halfway down that allowed access to and from the dance floor. Doors to offices and storage rooms lined the right side. The manager's office was all the way at the back, as far from the noise of the business he managed as he could get. Ty walked down a green carpet runner that muffled his footsteps to the opening on the left, unclasped the chain blocking his path, stepped through, and reclipped it to the steel ring anchored to the wall. A sign cautioning "Employees Only" dangled from the middle of the easily bypassed deterrent.

Gianna was waiting for him at the base of the steel-grate stairs that connected the staff area to the dance floor. She hooked a thumb behind her. "Your girlfriend finally showed up."

Ty's heart fluttered oddly. He followed Gianna's gesture to the bar, where Mira perched on a stool with her back to the room. The white streak in her hair stood out like a warning against her dark brown and the black of her jacket.

"She's my partner," he said flatly. "Nothing else."

"Whatever. More importantly, she was none too happy to see me here."

He raised an eyebrow. "Can you blame her?"

Gianna shrugged. "Maybe not, but we need to make this work, and you took away my leverage with your stupid 'don't tell Mira' condition."

More like the noose you were going to hang yourself with.

"How are you going to make her cooperate?"

"I'm going to *talk* to her," Ty said. "Not every situation requires a threat."

He took a step toward the bar. When Gianna moved as if to follow, he raised a hand. "You wait here."

Mira downed a shot as Ty approached her from behind. She pulled out her wallet, slapped a bill on the counter, and held up one finger. The bartender poured dark-amber liquid into the empty glass.

Ty smiled. This was exactly how Mira had found him on the first night they met . . . drinking his worries away at a bar.

Mira reached for her refilled glass.

Ty swooped in and snatched it out from under her fingers. He tipped the burning liquid into his mouth and set the glass upside down on the counter. "It isn't healthy to drink alone."

"Not nearly as alone as I thought I would be." Her mismatched gaze darted to the side, found Gianna, then snapped back to him. "What's she doing here?"

Anger pinched her expression, but also hurt. Did she feel he had betrayed her? Somehow he needed to make this right or any trust he was building with Mira would shatter, taking their chance of a true partnership with it.

The bartender retrieved the overturned glass and moved to the far end of the counter to wash it.

Ty opened his mouth, but Mira's whispered hiss cut him off. "She was only supposed to tag along for the interviews. That was it. Then you ditch me for the Everglades lead, which"—she waggled a finger in his face—"was horse shit, by the way. And I'm still expecting details on that. Now she shows up here, and you tell me you've taken jurisdiction without even consulting me, which seemed to be what she was angling for this whole time. Just what did that hussy do to get you twisted around her finger?"

She paused for breath. Her chest heaved, drawing Ty's attention to the bulge of the Saint Jude necklace beneath her shirt—the saint of lost causes.

He set his hand over hers on the polished wood and kept his voice low and even. "Like I said before, taking jurisdiction was the only way to get access to the corpse. Since I'm point on this investigation now, it's expected I have a local intermediary. If not Gianna it would have been Moretti, and trust me, you would not have liked that asshole. Better to stick with the devil we know."

Mira clenched her jaw and said through gritted teeth, "I still don't trust her."

"Neither do I," Ty said emphatically. "All the more reason to keep her close."

A crease puckered between Mira's eyebrows. "Did something happen on your trip to the Glades?"

This time Mira's question didn't ring with accusation, but her earnest expression twisted barbs into his chest. He hated lying to his partner. He hated hiding the fact that her existence was being threatened. He hated Gianna for putting him in this position, and he hated that he couldn't trust the demon in Mira not to make the situation worse if she found out what was really going on. He squeezed Mira's hand. Somehow he would protect her from both Gianna and herself.

"Hey not-love-birds," Gianna called from across the club. "Are we doing this or what?"

Mira pulled her hand out from under Ty's. "I can't promise not to pop her head like a pimple if she keeps pissing me off."

"Please don't." Ty tried to make his voice light. "The paperwork for something like that would be a nightmare."

He waved to Gianna, who strolled over and uttered an exasperated, "Finally." She swung her gaze from one of them to the other. "We all good here?"

Mira rolled her eyes.

"Yeah," Ty lied. "We're good."

MIRA

TY PULLED OUT his phone, tapped the screen a few times, and turned the device for Mira to see. The screen displayed a young woman's face. She had hazel eyes, light-brown hair cut in a bob, and a wide smile. "This is Kendra Jackson. She and three friends from school came here last night. No one's seen her since."

Mira studied the girl's features. She was pretty in a low-key, not-trying-to-attract-attention sort of way. She didn't look like the kind of girl on the prowl for company. But then, you never could tell what people were really like behind their public faces.

"Her friends didn't see her leave?" Mira asked.

"Nope. And they insist she's not the type to hook up with strangers."

<Unlike us.>

Mira's gaze drifted to the wet ring left by the upturned glass she and

Ty had both drained. Her thoughts turned to that first night they'd met.

"The manager gave us access to the club's security footage." Ty tucked his phone away and indicated the stairs he'd come down. "Let's go check it out."

The three of them crossed the dance floor under the curious watch of the bartender, the bouncer, and a few other staff members working to get the club ready for guests. Once beyond the "Employees Only" chain at the top of the stairs, they stepped into a hallway that ran the length of the building. The doors were unmarked, but Ty seemed to know where he was going. He took them to the second-to-last door on the left, rapped his knuckles on the plain wood, and opened it without waiting for a response.

A young woman in cut-off jean shorts and a purple tank top turned to face them. Her skin was a shade darker than Ty's, and her black curls were molded to her scalp in a short Afro. She blew a bright-pink bubble that popped against her dark lips and waved them into the room. "Welcome, badges, to the nerve center. Make yourselves at home."

She sat with one slender leg tucked beneath her on a swivel chair in front of a laptop and a bank of monitors that each showed a different angle of the club, including the hallway they'd just walked down.

<No sneaking up on this one.>

"You monitor the club in real time?" Gianna asked.

The woman blew another bubble and nodded. The bubble popped. "I'm the eye in the sky, baby. Name's Tiff. I assess and identify threats before they become a problem. I also do callouts and tell crowd control where they're needed. Gotta keep the guests safe or they won't come back. An incident like last night could be the death knell for a place like this . . . if this is where it happened."

"Were you working security last night?" Ty asked.

"Yep."

Mira leaned over to examine the monitors. They seemed to cover the entire club pretty well. "You see anything suspicious?"

"Nope. A few drunks, a couple creepers. Standard Friday night."

Ty nodded. "Can you replay the footage?"

"Of the whole night?"

"The missing person report we were forwarded said the girl and her friends arrived at nine, and they lost track of her around ten thirty," Gianna said. "Let's focus there and see if we can spot her leaving with anyone."

Mira scowled at Gianna, but the suggestion was a good one, so she kept her mouth shut.

Tiff clicked her mouse and tapped a few keys on her laptop. The images displayed on the monitors changed. The emptiness of the off-hours club was suddenly crammed with people laughing, talking, and gyrating to a silent soundtrack.

"This is at nine forty-five," said their digital guide.

Mira studied the monitors as captured history crept toward the present. "There." She pointed to a cluster of people near the coat check. Kendra Jackson was shrugging into a black, knee-length jacket. She took the time to clasp each button down the front, then walked out the front door. She didn't wobble or weave, so she hadn't been drunk or drugged. Other people came and went at the same time, but she paid them no attention. She left the club alone.

"The time stamp there is nine fifty-eight."

"It doesn't look like an abduction," Gianna said, sounding disappointed, as the footage continued to stream.

Tiff reached toward her keyboard. Just before she touched it, something flashed on the monitor Mira had been watching.

"Hang on," Mira said. "Can you play that back from the moment just before Kendra walked out the door?"

Tiff moved her mouse. The scene on the monitors reset. Kendra had just buttoned her last button.

"What did you see?" Gianna asked.

Mira ignored her. She squinted at the monitor. Kendra walked out the club's door. Mira continued to watch. A full minute after Kendra, a woman with a blond updo, wearing a short black dress and strappy heels, left the club. She glanced toward the security camera for just a second, but in that moment her eyes flashed like a cat's caught in headlights. The coppery flare was there and gone in an instant.

What do you think?

<It could just be a lens flare on the recording.>

Could be. But Mira didn't think it was. Her gut was saying paranatural.

"Well?" Gianna prompted. "What did you see?"

"Can you play this video in reverse? Mira asked. "See who she interacted with before she left?"

Gianna blew out a frustrated breath. Ty waited silently, his gaze fixed on the screen.

"Sure." Tiff tapped a few more buttons, and Kendra's final moments at the club unwound on the monitor. She walked backward through the door, undid her buttons, took off her jacket, and handed it to the man working the coat check. Then she strolled backward out of the screen.

Mira shifted her attention from monitor to monitor, tracking Kendra's movements as she wove her way through the throng in reverse. Kendra started to dance. She stayed mostly in a cluster of similarly aged girls who were probably her friends. Every now and then one of them would break off, or another person would come into their area. Sometimes couples would pair off for a while, then split apart. People weren't so much dancing *with* other people as just mixing together randomly as they each did their own thing.

Mira spotted the blond woman who'd caught her attention on the security footage near the exit. She wove gracefully through the crowd, blending easily into the rhythms of the dancers. She danced with one of Kendra's companions, then time unwound further and brought the blond to Kendra. The woman leaned in, close to Kendra's ear, as though whispering a secret. The two danced together for only a few moments, then the blond moved away. She danced with another of Kendra's companions, then moved away from the group as time continued to rewind. While the others kept their eyes on Kendra as she and her friends made a trip to the bar, Mira watched the blond woman. She danced with several other people before she tipped her face directly toward a camera. A flash of bronze sparked in her eyes, caught on film like a lens flare.

Mira smiled. *Gotcha.* She let the footage stream by for a few more seconds to hide the moment of her triumph, then said, "That's enough."

"Did you find what you were looking for?" Tiff asked.

Mira straightened from her inspection of the monitors and popped her back. She shook her head.

"I didn't see anything suspicious," Gianna said.

<Amateur.>

Mira suppressed a smile. She turned and found Ty studying her.

<He knows we found something.>

He suspects, she agreed. *Hopefully he's smart enough not to say anything in front of Gianna though, because I'm sure as hell not sharing my theory while she's around.*

"So you agree that club security wasn't to blame for that lady disappearing," Tiff said. "You all saw her walk out of here on her own two feet."

"I don't see any negligence on the part of the club. Or you," Ty added. "But send me a copy of the footage as evidence." He handed her a business card.

"Will do." Tiff spread a Cheshire Cat grin. "Now if you'll excuse me,

I've got a few hours of free time I'd like to spend *not* in this room before we open tonight."

The three investigators filed out, and Ty closed the door.

"What's our next move?" Gianna asked as soon as they reached the club's main floor.

"*My* next move is to grab some grub while Ty fills me in on what you guys found in the Glades," Mira said. "But you're not invited."

Gianna's jaw clenched. The muscle under her eye spasmed. "Look, I get that you don't like me. I don't like you either. But I'm on this case, and I'm not going anywhere, so get over it."

Ty moved as though preparing to step between the two women.

"Sure," Mira said. "But as you pointed out this morning, you're better equipped to handle interactions with the locals than either of us, and someone has to tell the Millers that their kid is still alive."

Chapter 14

TY

TY MOVED TO BREAK up the fight that seemed to be brewing between Mira and Gianna. He could imagine Tiff watching them from the club's nerve center, calling in the scuffle to floor security. Then Mira's words filtered through his distracted mind. He turned to stare at her. "You found him?"

Mira wrinkled her nose, as though she wanted to say something but was holding back. "Thomas Miller ran away. That disappearance has nothing to do with our case."

"Where did you find him?" Gianna asked. "*How* did you find him?"

"That's not important. Just tell the Millers that their child is okay and should be in contact with them soon."

"You didn't bring him back?"

"I'm not a cop. Dragging home runaways isn't my job." She pivoted and started walking toward the club entrance, then glanced at Ty over her shoulder. "Do you feel more like pasta or sandwiches?"

The twinkle in Mira's eyes made Ty think the demon inside her was enjoying itself.

"Wait a sec." Gianna scrambled to get in front of Mira. "You have to give me more than 'he's alive.' The Millers will want to know where he is, why he left, how to get hold of him. . . ."

"They may want all that," Mira agreed, "but what they're going to *get* is the assurance that their child is safe. The kid can explain the rest for themselves." Mira stepped around Gianna and continued toward the exit.

"What about the footage?" Gianna spun. "You saw something, didn't you?"

"I saw Kendra Jackson walk out of this building entirely alone," Mira called over her shoulder as she continued to walk away.

"You—"

Ty grabbed Gianna's wrist, preventing her from going after Mira. "Let it go."

Gianna rounded on him, yanking her arm free. "The deal was inclusion in the investigation."

"The deal was credit," he corrected. "So go claim it. You'll be the Millers' hero when you tell them you've found their son alive."

"And when they ask me where he is?" she hissed.

He shrugged. "Make something up. Tell them he's debriefing with a trauma counselor or something."

"That'll hold as well as a bucket with no bottom."

"Mira's not going to tell you where he is."

"Do you know where she went while we were in the Glades?"

Ty kept his expression neutral. "No."

"Did she tell you what she found when we left her upstairs at the Millers?"

"No."

"Would you tell me if she did?"

"No."

She balled her fists. "Why not?"

"Because Mira said Thomas Miller has nothing to do with our case, and I believe her. So go bask in whatever glory the Millers have to offer and leave it at that."

"I know she's just trying to get me out of the way so the two of you can discuss whatever she noticed on the security footage."

"Then I guess you're not totally hopeless as a detective."

She poked him in the chest with one finger. "Just remember our deal. When you and Ms. Mysterio make a plan, you loop me in. Otherwise, I go to the press. We'll see how good she is at keeping secrets then."

Ty ground his teeth as he watched Gianna stomp away. He'd already promised her the credit for this case; why couldn't she just sit back and wait for the praise to roll in like a good little blackmailer?

Gianna shot a clipped remark at Mira as she passed. The bouncer by the door widened his eyes and watched Gianna leave. Mira said something to him that made him laugh.

Ty took a deep breath. Solving this case and finding the rest of the missing kids was priority one. He'd hold off worrying about how Gianna fit into the puzzle until he had to.

"Sandwiches," Mira said as he joined her at the exit.

"What?" He pushed open the door and held it open for her.

"You lost your vote." She turned right and strolled down the street. "I just remembered this amazing little sandwich shop that served the best cubanos." She stopped next to her Ducati Scrambler, lifted the helmet off the handlebars, and handed it to him.

"What about you?"

"My head's harder than yours. Save your worry for yourself."

If only it were that simple.

He pulled the helmet on. The inside smelled like Mira—peppery, with a sweet, citrus undercurrent. The scent made his heart race and brought back the memory of her slipping past him in the hall wearing nothing but a towel. He inhaled deeply.

"Earth to Ty."

He blinked. Mira was straddling the motorcycle.

"You coming or not?"

He swung one leg over the back and settled his weight. It wasn't a large bike. He had to press up against her to keep from sliding off.

Mira set one finger against the ignition plate. The bike rumbled to life between his legs.

"Hold on," she called over her shoulder.

There was nowhere safe to put his hands.

Mira opened the throttle, and the bike rocketed forward.

Ty slipped his hands around her waist. He could feel the heat of her skin through the thin fabric of her shirt. The vibrations of the bike moved through her and into him. He tightened his grip, molding his stomach to her back. She fit perfectly within the cage of his body. He let himself imagine for a moment what it would be like to hold her like this without the excuse, then he tucked the image away in the vault of his dreams and secrets. He'd only known Mira for a short while, but it didn't take long to realize she would fight a cage in all its forms—even a cage of love. A failed relationship would equal a failed partnership, and that was something Ty couldn't risk.

By the time Mira pulled to the curb in front of a small brick building with a red-and-white awning and plastic benches out front, Ty had his professional mask back in place. He released Mira's waist, swung his feet to the ground, and stepped away as soon as the purr of the engine stopped coursing through his body. He took one last deep breath, then pulled off Mira's helmet and handed it back to her. He turned to face their destination as she dismounted.

"My abuela used to bring me here when I was little." She looked at the facade, and her expression grew distant, as though she were seeing the shop through the eyes of her younger self. Then she grabbed the door and held it open for him. "Let's see how it compares."

While the outer tables had been empty, most of the deli's indoor tables were full, despite the odd hour. Ty chalked this up to the gust of air-conditioned breeze that greeted him when he stepped inside.

He and Mira walked up to the counter. A heavyset man with arms the size of tree trunks and a nonexistent neck wiped his hands on a white towel and asked, "What can I getcha?"

"Two cubanos, an iced café con leche, and"—Mira cast a questioning look over her shoulder—"what do you want to drink?"

"Pepsi." Ty handed the man his credit card, then glanced at Mira. "Unless your feminist sensibilities want to pay."

Mira waved a hand. "I'm broke. Gender's got nothing to do with it."

They waited at the counter until their orders came up, then took the two paper-lined baskets and their drinks back into the sweltering heat. Neither of them even suggested eating inside.

Mira took a bite of her sandwich as Ty settled onto his plastic chair. She closed her eyes and made an *Mmmmm* noise that sent an echo of the motorcycle's vibrations through Ty's system. "Just like I remember."

Ty examined his own meal—a panini-style, toasted sandwich with meat, cheese, pickles, and mustard sauce. Not a combination he'd ever tried before. He took a bite. It was tangy and tart. He nearly purred himself.

Mira took a sip of her coffee, set it down, and fixed him with her stare. "So, what did you and Officer Busybody find in the Glades?"

Ty filled his mouth with soda and swallowed. "You first. Is Thomas Miller really alive, or were you just getting rid of Gianna?"

"Yes. To both." She cocked her head slightly. Her eyes lost focus. "That's not our secret to tell."

Ty raised an eyebrow. "What isn't?"

Her gaze snapped to him like a magnet. "What?"

"You said 'That's not our secret to tell'."

She smiled. "Then I guess I can't tell you."

He leaned forward and opened his mouth.

Mira held up one hand and set the other over her heart. "Miller is alive. I promise. They ran away from home for reasons totally unrelated to our case." She took another sip of coffee and leaned back in her chair. "Now tell me about the Glades."

Ty sighed. It wasn't that he didn't believe Mira . . . he just hated that she didn't trust him enough to tell him the whole story.

Like you told her about Gianna? whispered a little voice at the back of his mind.

Ty cleared his throat. "Lucas Martinez's body was waterlogged, decomposing, and picked over by animals, but there was evidence that something with human, or at least humanesque, teeth chewed on him at some point. So either our human killer is a cannibal, or—"

"Bembe was right."

Ty nodded. "There are quite a few fae creatures that might fit the bill. As I understand it, human flesh is a bit of a delicacy for some species." He glanced down at the salty meat in his sandwich, suddenly wondering if this was the right time for this conversation. Not that there was ever really a right time to discuss eating people. . . . "I think we can discount the more animalistic species. Even if one of those had made it into the mortal realm, which isn't impossible, it seems unlikely it would target such a specific group of people. But even if we assume human-level intelligence, we're still left with a pretty long list of possibilities."

"What are your top picks?"

He tipped his chin up and studied the underside of the awning that was protecting them from the direct rays of the sun. "Setting rifters aside for the moment. . . . Wendigo eat people, and they have specific hunting grounds, but they tend to stay in colder climates. Goblins and pishachas will eat just about anything, but both are opportunistic. We're looking for a hunter, not a scavenger. Ghouls are another good choice for cannibalism, but they tend to stick to cemeteries, not marshes, and definitely not schools. Rougarous are rare, but they've been cataloged in this area before. And of course there are the werewolves, which we now know for a fact exist."

Mira shook her head. "Werewolves do a good job of containing their shit. I doubt they'd get sloppy about a rogue now. Not when the whole world is watching to see if the paranatural experiment in Colorado blows up in our faces. Still, that's a good list."

She looked impressed, but the way the corners of her mouth twitched up made him think he hadn't quite passed her little test.

"But?" he prompted.

"You're missing a very important suspect."

"A suspect with eyes that reflect light?"

She perked up. "You noticed."

"I'm PTF. We're trained to notice weird things . . . even if we don't always know what they mean."

The sandwich shop door opened. Two men in Bermuda shorts and

Hawaiian shirts walked out, chatting animatedly. Ty waited until they were half a block away. Then he leaned over his lunch and pitched his voice low. "What do *you* think the blond woman was?"

Mira also leaned in. Her smile grew. She was enjoying his not knowing. Anyone passing on the street might have mistaken them as a couple whispering sweet nothings over the table, maybe leaning in for a kiss. He doubted anyone would suspect their conversation might include cannibalism and dead children.

Mira's lips moved. Her whisper was barely more than a breath. "I think we're hunting a vampire."

Ty pulled back in surprise. He'd seen too much, both in and out of the PTF, to discount any story about a paranatural creature, no matter how far-fetched, but he'd always assumed vampire myths were based on the many fae who had similar descriptions and feeding habits. He took a moment to shift his perspective, recenter his thoughts, and come to terms with this new information. Then he fixed his gaze on Mira and said, "What can you tell me about them?"

Disappointment flickered across Mira's expression, followed closely by triumph.

Ty had gotten used to these quick reversals in his partner's moods. They were usually an indication that she was having some internal debate with her demon. He wondered if it was Mira or the demon who'd been disappointed by his reaction.

Mira took another bite of her sandwich. She studied him as she chewed. She swallowed then said, "They're strong, but their main advantage is their speed. They move fast, think fast, and heal fast. They're not fae, so your PTF-issued iron bullets won't do more than piss them off, even if you do manage to hit them. The only sure way to kill one is to take its heart and head and burn it all to ash."

Ty nodded. "So blades rather than bullets." He sighed. He'd been trained to use the iron-steel Damascus sword issued to anti-fae special forces during the war, but it had never been his first choice of weapon. *Let's hope my sword skills didn't rust too much during my time as a cop.*

"And magic before that. Vampires tend to have some level of illusion magic, so don't trust your eyes, but most of them aren't good enough to do more than basic parlor tricks. I'll do my best to shield you, but you'll need to stay close. Mind magic isn't my forte, so I'll need to touch you to snap you out of any brain fog they put you under."

Ty dropped his hand to his pocket. He didn't reach inside, but the slight bulge of the stone outlined beneath the fabric was a comfort. His mental anchor had proven useful against fae illusions. He just hoped it was as effective against a vampire. "What about silver, sunlight, holy water, garlic?"

Mira shook her head. "Sunlight is the only one of those that has any effect. That's why we need to wait until after dark to go back to the club."

He frowned. "You think she'll go back?"

"Vampires are territorial. Some are solitary hunters, but they more often live in nests of anywhere from five to fifty, and they tend to hunt in proven places. If that blond took Kendra last night, chances are good that she or one of her nestmates will be scouting the club tonight, if only to keep an eye on the fallout."

"Great. Is there any way to tell what they are besides the shiny eyes?"

She shook her head. "Don't rely too much on the eyes. It's a useful tell, but they only reflect like that when they're excited or upset. Most of the time they look totally human. More so than me, even, because their demon taint is so diluted."

"They're rifters?"

"The first one was, but not for thousands of years. The ones alive today are just copies of copies of copies." She smiled. "They make a decent snack, though."

"Is that why . . .?" He pointed first to her brown eye, then to the gold one.

She nodded. "I'd probably be shiny on the footage, too."

"Then how do you know she wasn't a full rifter?"

"The fact that she walked out of the dance club without killing anyone. That'd be like a starving man walking past a free buffet for the promise of a single biscuit later. Demons aren't that good at executive function." She made a sour face. "Present company excluded."

Ty frowned. "What about the rifter we fought when we first met? She seemed quite good at planning and deferred gratification."

Mira's expression went slack. Something like grief flickered behind her eyes. "That was a sovereign demon. Those are crazy rare. Whatever we're dealing with here isn't that clever."

Ty wished he could take the question back. He wasn't sure why talking about the rifter they'd killed in Baltimore bothered Mira so much, but the topic clearly upset her.

"So how do we hunt a vampire?" he asked, bringing the conversation back to safer ground.

She smiled and gave him an assessing look that traveled like a caress over his entire body. "With bait."

Chapter 15

MIRA

I EXPECTED HIM TO freak out more about the whole "vampires are real" thing, Mira thought as she steered her bike toward abuela's house.

<Ty's too cool for that. I imagine it would take a lot more than some fangs and cannibalism to freak out the kind of guy who'd team up with the likes of us.>

Good point. Mira took a deep breath and was momentarily distracted by the way Ty's arms tightened around her waist. His hands were warm on her skin, even through her clothes. His hips cradled hers. She had the sudden urge to lean back against him. Instead she leaned forward, hunching over the gas tank, and gripped the handlebars tighter.

She turned the corner onto abuela's street and let off the throttle. Aside from Ty's truck, Mira's van, and abuela's small sedan, the street in front of abuela's house was clogged with a red pickup, a white SUV, and a blue coupe.

<Looks like a party.>

Mira rumbled slowly down the road. It was possible the vehicles were for other houses . . . but the rest of the street was fairly clear.

If abuela has guests, maybe we should steer clear.

<You're not going to be able to blend in at the club in what you're wearing now.>

Mira pursed her lips. She rolled past the parked vehicles and squinted through the front windows of abuela's house. There were definitely people moving inside. She crinkled her nose, tucked the bike against the curb, and cut the engine.

Ty swung off the back and handed her the helmet.

Mira looked him up and down. She could get what she needed from the van that was her mobile home, but she didn't have clothes for a man in there. Unfortunately, Ty had gone for low-key professional in his choice of attire for the interviews . . . which would scream "I'm a cop" if he wore it to the club. She huffed out a sigh.

"Looks like your grandma's got company," Ty said as he stepped onto the sidewalk.

"Looks like." She climbed off the bike and studied the front of the house, frowning.

Ty glanced at her. A small line of worry folded the skin between his eyebrows. "We have a little time before dark. We could wait for them to leave and come back later."

Mira shook her head. "With this many people, it has to be family. And if it's family, they already know I'm in town. And if they know *that* . . . well, chances are they won't be leaving anytime soon." She rubbed her eyes, gave her cheeks a little slap, said, "Let's get this over with," and headed for the door.

The sounds of chatter in both English and Spanish bombarded Mira as soon as she opened the door. A dozen faces turned at her entrance. Some she recognized. Some she didn't. There was a moment of silence, as though the room were taking a breath, then Mira was surrounded by patting hands and smiling faces that babbled at her too fast for her to respond.

Ty entered behind her, and the room paused again. Glances were cast about, a few whispers drifted into the lull.

Abuela shuffled to the front of the group. "Let them in. Goodness, they'll never make it past the front door if you swarm them like that." She gripped Mira's upper arm and dragged her to the center of the living room.

Mira cast Ty an apologetic glance over her shoulder and thought, *Good luck*. The crowd closed behind her.

"Oh, little Mirana, how long has it been?" A heavyset woman with the swell of pregnancy leaned so close that her musty breath wafted into Mira's face when she spoke. She had black hair held back by a white scarf with red poppies on it and the same brown eyes Mira shared with her mother. "Do you remember me?" She continued in rapid-fire Spanish. "I'm your *tia* Marta." The stout woman wrapped her arms around Mira and squeezed her against her ample bosom. "We're all so glad that you're finally home."

Mira choked on the cloying scent of patchouli perfume and tried not to flail as she resisted the urge to shove her mother's oldest sister away.

<Wow. Friendly bunch.>

Marta abruptly gripped Mira's shoulders and pushed her to arm's length, holding her in place. "Let me look at you." She twisted Mira side to side, gripped her chin to turn her face, then pinched her arm.

"Ow!" Mira jerked away from the pawing woman.

<Not much for personal boundaries.>

"You're nothing but skin and bones," Marta said. "What have you been eating?" She waved the words away. "No matter. We'll soon have you healthy again."

"I'm plenty healthy," Mira griped.

"You look as if a stiff wind could bowl you over." This came from a portly man only slightly taller than tia Marta. Mira recognized his wide nose and the gap between his front teeth.

"*Hola, tio Carlos.*"

"Ha." He gave Marta's arm a playful smack. "Me she remembers."

"She remembers me, too," Marta said. She turned expectantly on Mira. "Don't you, dear?"

"Of course I remember you, tia."

Marta lifted her chin and stared smugly at Carlos. "There, you see?"

Another man placed one hand against Mira's back. "If you want her to eat, let her eat." He propelled her away from Carlos and Marta toward the dining room, where a smorgasbord had been laid out on the table. Mira's guide tipped his head toward her and whispered, "You looked like you could use a rescue."

Mira smiled. Quick to laugh and slow to anger, tio Luis had always been her favorite relative. "Thank you."

She picked up a plate and started loading it.

<You just had a sandwich. Are you really going to eat more?>

Hungry or not, if I don't eat I'll never hear the end of it. This is the fastest way to escape.

"So who's your beau?" Luis propped one hip against the table and crossed his arms over the thin blue fabric of his T-shirt.

Mira followed his gaze to Ty, who'd been dragged into the far corner of the living room by Marta's husband, Antonio, and Luis's husband, Rafael. Heat flooded her cheeks. "He's not my beau, he's my partner."

Luis raised an eyebrow. "Rafael is my partner."

"Not that kind of partner. A professional partner."

"Ah." Luis nodded, then frowned. "Then why is he living with you?"

"He's . . . it's complicated."

He nodded again. "Ma told me what happened this morning."

Mira glanced at the closed door halfway down the hall. She shifted her feet. "Thanks for helping abuela with my mom all these years. I know that can't have been easy."

Luis shrugged. "That's what family does."

Mira stared at the bits of food on her plate.

"Are you going to stay?" Luis asked the question so softly Mira almost convinced herself she'd imagined it.

She shook her head.

"It's not good for you to be always alone."

<What am I, chopped liver?>

The corner of Mira's mouth quirked up. "I'm not alone."

Luis looked at Ty, misinterpreting her words.

Abuela shuffled into the dining room, a wide smile on her face. "It's so good to have everyone together again." She clasped her hands. "If only Beatriz were here."

<Who's Beatriz? I don't remember meeting a Beatriz.>

My mom's youngest sister. You never met her.

<Is she dead?>

Mira shook her head. *Beatriz ran off when she was nineteen. According to my mom, she was a wild spirit who wanted to see the world. She stopped by twice before I moved to Detroit. I barely remember her, but I remember the stories she told.*

<She sounds fun. Maybe we should look her up. You seem to take after her more than this lot.>

Except she left by choice. I wasn't looking for adventure.

<But you can't deny we've got some pretty great stories.>

Mira turned to abuela. "Have you heard from her lately?"

"I got a postcard from Greece last week. She's living with a painter."

Mira smiled. Then she scowled. "Tio Luis, will you excuse us?"

He looked at the two women and backed out of the room. "I'll go introduce myself to your partner."

As soon as he turned his back, Mira hissed, "I asked you not to tell anyone I was here, and you respond by throwing a party?"

"I didn't throw a party," abuela said defensively.

Mira gestured to the crowd beyond the arched opening. "What do you call this?"

Abuela puffed her chest and lifted her chin. "Luis came to check on Maria, as he always does on Saturday morning. He asked why she was already sedated, so I told him about the incident we had. Then Marta came over for a visit, and Luis told her that you'd come home. After that, she insisted on waiting to see you, and Luis said he'd wait, too. Then Rafael came looking for Luis, and Carlos wanted me to watch the kids while Sophia was out, and—"

Mira held up her hand. "I get the idea."

"You shouldn't hide from your family," abuela chided.

"I'm not *hiding*. I'm just busy. I have a lot of work to do."

"Everyone works. You don't see the others making excuses to miss visiting. Even Beatriz stops by every once in a while."

<Ooh, snap. She's got you there.>

"Not helping," Mira hissed under her breath.

"Well, I'm sorry you don't find my advice helpful, but it's true."

Mira shook her head. "You don't understand, abuela. I. . . ." She shook her head again.

<To quote your own advice, "You won't know unless you try.">

We're not talking about a lifestyle choice here. I'm a monster.

<Says you. Maybe your family wouldn't see it that way. I don't.>

Of course you don't see it that way. You're a demon.

Abuela set her hand lightly on Mira's arm. "Whatever your reasons, you don't have to hide from us. We'll always love you. That's what family does." She squeezed Mira's arm then went back into the living room.

Mira picked at the contents of her plate and watched her relatives through the opening into the other room. They chatted and chuckled. Hands flapped in gestures that struggled to keep up with the speed of speech. Luis and Rafael stole a kiss. Antonio, Marta, and Carlos grilled Ty in the corner, but Ty didn't seem to mind. He laughed and slapped Carlos on the arm.

<He seems to be enjoying himself.>

Easy enough since he's not actually related to any of them.

<Or maybe they're just nice people if you give them a chance.>

I'm sure they are. They're *not the problem.* She bit into a buttered roll, sighed, and stepped toward the opening.

"How is she related to us?"

Mira stopped. The high-pitched voice had come from the other side of the living room wall. She leaned closer to the opening.

"Shh. Keep your voice down." This came from a lower voice, though still accented by youth.

"Mom says she's our cousin," said a third voice.

"I've never met her."

"I've never even heard of her."

"If she's a cousin, where's she been all this time?"

"I heard our dads talking earlier. I think she has something to do with why tia Maria is so messed up."

"Maybe she started the fire."

Mira's heart pounded in her ears. Her hands began to tingle.

"Then why would the grown-ups be acting so happy to see her?"

"Maybe they're afraid of her."

"I'll bet she was in prison. That's why we never met her before."

Mira took two steps toward the doorway before she realized that she wasn't the one moving her limbs. She planted her feet.

No.

<I wasn't going to hurt them, just give them a little scare.>

No, she emphasized again.

<The little shits have no idea what they're talking about.>

"Mira."

Mira's attention swung to Marta, who was walking toward her and flapping her hand in a "come here" gesture. Mira took a deep breath, fixed her expression, and stepped through the doorway.

Five children ranging in age from six to sixteen huddled together in the corner on the far side of the wall. They shrank away when her gaze fell on them.

"Let me introduce you to your cousins," Marta said as she joined them. "Loretta you remember, right?"

Mira eyed the teenage girl Marta indicated. Mira didn't recognize the girl's brown eyes, pouty lips, or long braided hair, but she recognized the name. "You're Carlos's and Sophia's oldest, right?" She held one hand parallel to the floor at hip height. "You were only about this tall the last time I saw you."

<You weren't much taller, yourself.>

"And these are her sisters, Isabel and Anna." Marta pointed to each of the younger girls, then she swung her finger toward a tall boy of about twelve. "Roberto and his sister Camila, who's at piano practice right now, belong to Luis and Rafael."

Mira's mouth twitched up in a genuine smile. *Good for them. Luis always wanted kids.*

"And lastly, my own Manuel." Marta hugged a small boy to her side. "Although he won't be the baby for much longer." She patted her rounded abdomen. "My oldest, Alejandro, is off at college, and my daughter, Caridad, should be here shortly. I told her to come over after cheerleading practice. Do you remember her?"

Mira pictured the three cousins who'd been around when she was younger. Alejandro had been close to her own age, so she'd played with him back before Detroit. Loretta had been barely more than a toddler when Mira came home after the incident with her mother, and there'd been another girl about the same age. All Mira really remembered about that one was blond pigtails. She'd had more important things on her mind at the time.

"Sure," Mira said. "She'd be what, about fifteen now?"

"She turned sixteen last month." Marta beamed.

The front door opened and a young woman in a blue-and-gold cheerleader outfit walked in.

"Speaking of my angel, here she is now." Marta waved her daughter over. "Cari, come say hello to your *prima* Mira."

Caridad crossed the room, but as she moved closer to the group her smile turned into a frown. She pointed at Mira, glanced over her shoulder at Ty, then focused back on Mira. "Didn't I see you two skulking around the athletics yard after school yesterday?"

Mira studied Caridad. Her long, blond hair was pulled into a high ponytail that tugged the skin around her brown eyes taught. She was wearing a cheerleader uniform in the high school's colors.

<Score! Let's see what she knows.>

Mira felt a little awkward bringing up her investigation in the middle of a family gathering, but a lead was a lead. She might not get a better opportunity. "I'm looking into the disappearances of some students who went there. Did you know any of them?"

The girl took a step back. Her eyes went wide. "You're a cop?"

Marta cleared her throat, shot a wide-eyed glance at Mira, then asked her daughter, "Did Ronnie drop you off? You should have invited her in."

Mira scowled at tia Marta. *She's totally trying to change the subject.*

<Maybe she has something to hide.>

Cari's gaze shifted to her mother. "I did, but she says she doesn't like coming here anymore after that incident with Maria last week." She cast a sidelong glare down the hallway. "I don't blame her."

Mira opened her mouth to ask again about the missing students but switched gears as her mind latched onto her mother's name. "What happened with Maria?"

"Oh, it was nothing." Marta waved the question away, clearly not any happier with the new topic of conversation than the old.

"She went psycho," Caridad said.

"Cari," Marta scolded.

"It's true." The girl turned on Mira. "Maria was sitting here in the living room one day when Ronnie and I stopped by to see abuela, and she totally flipped out. She started throwing things at Ronnie and screaming about monsters and demons. She cut Ronnie's forehead with a broken plate."

<So it's not just you.>

How is that better?

Cari hugged herself and muttered, "It's not right to keep someone like that in the house. She's dangerous."

"She's family," Marta said. "And family takes care of each other, no matter what."

"Yeah, but—"

"No buts. Family is family."

Cari rolled her eyes. "Whatever. Can I go home now?"

"You just got here," Marta said.

"I've got a headache."

Marta frowned. "Okay, sweetie. Go collect your father."

Cari bolted as soon as she was given the go-ahead.

Mira took a step after her, mouth open to call her back.

Marta's hand darted out to grab her arm.

Mira struggled for a moment with the instinct to hurt the person trying to restrain her. She took a deep breath. Marta was staring at her with pleading eyes. The huddle of young cousins watched the exchange with curiosity.

<Cari's getting away.> The demon's desire to act was palpable. <We need to interrogate her.>

Having my own freak-out isn't going to accomplish anything . . . except maybe convince them all that Maria isn't the only dangerously crazy person in the family.

Mira allowed tia Marta to pull her away from the children and other guests.

"So you're a policewoman now?"

Mira shook her head. "I'm a private investigator."

"And you've come home to investigate the missing children? There are crimes everywhere. Why here? Why now?"

"Father Bembe asked me to look into it. One of the missing kids goes to his church."

Marta frowned. "I see. It's good you're trying to help, but please don't ask Cari about the missing kids. It's very upsetting for her."

Mira scowled. "That's literally the whole point of my being here. If she knows something about the students who went missing—"

"Olivia was a fellow cheerleader, and Lucas was a classmate. The last boy, Ramon, invited Cari to the junior prom just before he disappeared. She's a mess. Please, if you care about this family, don't cause my daughter any more pain."

Mira winced.

Marta stared at Mira, her eyes wide and waiting.

<Don't tell me you're actually considering ignoring this lead.>

Mira gritted her teeth and nodded.

<You can't be serious.>

Marta gave Mira a tight smile and patted her arm. "It's good to see you . . . even if we aren't the reason you came." She collected her son and crossed the room to join her husband and daughter at the door.

<Family or no, we need to question Caridad.>

Mira didn't respond. The investigator in her wanted to pull this thread, but the pleading in tia Marta's eyes made her feel like a monster for even considering it.

<She knew three of the victims. She might know more.>

Let's see how tonight's hunt goes. With any luck, this will all be over tomorrow.

Chapter 16

MIRA

THE CLUB WAS entirely different from the empty space they'd visited earlier. Every inch of the main floor was filled. People danced in groups or drifted from stranger to stranger. The mingled odors of sweat, lust, and perfume were thick enough to choke on. Heat radiated off the moving bodies, slicking Mira's skin as she passed among them. The thin fabric of her dress left her back bare and plunged between her breasts in a deep V, revealing the silver Saint Jude medallion against her sternum. The rapid salsa beat of the music thrummed through Mira's bones and sang through her muscles like a siren's call. The demon swayed her hips and swung her arms as they wove their way across the floor for the fifth time since the sun set. She spun with a woman wearing a snakeskin skirt that barely covered her panties, then ricocheted into a man with golden dragons embroidered over his red silk shirt. She performed a series of *enchufla* with a *dile que no*, then spun away with a flare of her handkerchief skirt that nearly exposed the knife and phone strapped to her thigh.

<We should do this more often.>

This isn't for fun.

<That doesn't mean we can't have any.>

We're supposed to be keeping an eye out for vampires.

<We're also supposed to be blending in. You should act more drunk.>

With the way you're weaving us around this dance floor, I look plenty drunk.

<What are you talking about? I'm a terrific dancer.>

"Any sign of her?" Mira spoke at full volume as she continued to dance so her mic could pick up the words over the general noise of the club.

"No shiny eyes." Ty's reply came through the device tucked in her ear.

She joined and broke away from another partner, which brought her to the center of the room. *Let's do another sweep.*

Mira took full control of the movement of her body while the demon drew power to focus on the search. Mira had a lot of nifty magic tricks as a practitioner, but there were some things the demon was just better at.

The room around her faded to mist. The music became muted. The odors dropped away. The walls, floor, and ceiling of the club became hazy darkness layered with pinpricks of light, as though Mira was looking at an out-of-focus night sky. The people around her were pale clouds in roughly human shapes that blurred and blended as they moved among each other. Distorted faces peeked out of the darkness, there and gone like the flicker of a strobe. The citizens of the Rift couldn't reach the physical plane without a host, but they often spied on the shadows of life through the veil that separated the realms. That veil peeled away the superfluous layers of reality like gender and appearance. Only the core of a being was potent enough to make an impact.

Mira danced with the hazy shapes that fluttered around her. None carried the darkness that would give it shape in this in-between place. She spread her awareness to the edges of the room. Only the pale ghosts of humans surrounded her.

The demon released its magic. The people around Mira came back into focus, contained once again by skin, hair, and clothes. She swayed to a stop and took a deep breath. Her heart was racing.

"You're a terrific dancer." Ty's words made Mira jump.

She glanced at a security camera mounted near the stairs that led up to the small room where Ty was watching the club . . . watching her. Heat flared in her cheeks.

"Next time, you should join me." The words came out while Mira was distracted.

What the hell! Why did you say that?

<Because you wish he was dancing with you.>

No I don't.

<You forget, I share your body. I know *exactly* what's going on in here.>

"I'm not much of a dancer." Ty's response doused Mira's heat.

See, he isn't even interested.

<That's not what he said. Maybe he really isn't a good dancer. Offer to give him a private lesson.>

"No."

"No, what?"

"We could—Shut up!" Mira shouted the word to stop the demon from speaking. Several nearby dancers gave her curious looks.

"Is everything okay?" Ty's voice was laced with worry.

"We're fine."

<Speak for yourself,> the demon sulked.

"I'm fine," Mira amended. "Just forget it."

She picked up the rhythm of the music again and eased back into the crowd that had momentarily distanced itself from her. She kept her movements restrained.

<You're not going to tempt a vampire with moves like that. You're not gonna tempt *anyone*.>

She glanced toward the nearest security camera, then quickly away. *Just do another scan.*

<I just did one.>

So? Do another. That's the whole reason we're here.

<If we do this too much, it'll wear you out.>

I'm fine.

<And if you start showing puppet lines?>

Mira glanced involuntarily at her fingers to check for black lines spreading from her nails—the first symptom of the demon using up too much of Mira's life force. Her nails were short and clean, with white crescents at the tops. Her skin was light brown and free of magical disease.

<Vampires are an okay snack, but they don't have the lasting power of a real rifter.>

I said I'm fine. Do another sweep.

<Whatever. Don't whine to me when you start looking like a zombie.>

Mira continued to circulate among the dancers as her demon swept the room for demonic signatures other than their own. Luckily, vampires didn't have direct access to their demonic abilities, watered down as they were, so they wouldn't have any way of telling what Mira was until it was too late.

Cloud figures danced around her, flittering lights in the roiling mist. She spun and scanned. People poured through the front door in staggered clusters as the bouncer who'd let Ty and Mira through controlled the flow of traffic. A dense crowd jostled for space at the bar.

<There.>

Mira zeroed in on a man in a ribbed blue T-shirt and black leather pants with loops and straps dangling from the belt. A thick gold chain hung around his neck. He had a spray-on tan, side-swept brown hair, and eyes the color of algae flecked with gold. He was still a little fuzzed around the edges, but he stood out like an island among the sea of clouds.

"Got you," she whispered.

The world snapped back into focus. Suddenly there was an ocean of people between Mira and her target.

"Check out the guy at the bar in the blue shirt and bondage pants," she said as she danced her way toward the edge of the floor.

"I see him," came Ty's reply.

"That's our man."

"His eyes aren't glowing."

"I told you they might not."

"Are you sure?"

"Trust me." Mira broke free of the gyrating crowd and wound her way to the bar.

The vampire was chatting with a twentysomething woman in a glittery white halter top and blue jean shorts. He ordered from the bartender and handed the woman a drink. They laughed. He leaned in and whispered something. The woman shook her head. Her dark curls brushed her bare shoulders.

"Is he doing something to her?" Repressed anxiety tightened Ty's voice.

"He's not killing her," she said lightly.

"I can see that. Is he using magic?"

Do you sense anything?

The demon was quiet for a moment. Vampires used a strange hybrid of magic that was neither demonic nor fae, and was therefore harder to detect. <No.>

"Not that I can tell, but that doesn't mean he isn't."

"Comforting."

She shot a dirty look at the security camera above the bar. "Do you want to switch jobs?"

The vampire and his maybe-target finished their drinks. They exchanged a few more words, then both left the bar. The woman headed for the bathroom. The man went straight to the dance floor.

"Who do you want to follow?" Ty asked.

"The primary target." She strolled after the vampire. "Keep an eye on the woman."

"There are no cameras in the bathroom," he reminded her.

"Just let me know when she comes out. We can't risk losing this guy."

Mira stayed just close enough to the vampire that she could track him, but not so close that she was in any danger of coming face-to-face with him. He danced with a dozen women. Some he traded out right away. Some he stuck with for a while. Occasionally, he would lean in to say something to them. Sometimes they would nod. Sometimes they would laugh.

"The girl from the bar is headed for the exit," Ty said. "Should I have the bouncer stop her while our suspect is distracted?"

"We need to see if he follows her out."

"If the vampire magicked her to leave, he may assume she's gone out even if we intercept," Ty said. "We should secure the woman's safety."

<He might be tracking her movements in some way we can't detect,> the demon countered.

Either way, stopping her could make a scene. "We can't risk tipping him off."

"I don't like the idea of using an innocent as bait."

"You agreed to this plan."

"That doesn't mean I like it," he said. "If anything happens to her. . . ."

"I won't let it," she promised.

<He's going to hold you to that.>

So will I.

<You sure? This plan is risky. If he decides to drain her on the street instead of taking her back to the nest. . . .>

No other bodies have turned up besides Lucas, and that was in the Glades. They must be taking them back to a nest.

"He's moving."

Mira kept pace with the vampire as he danced his way closer to the exit. He walked by the coat check without stopping.

"Looks like we have a winner," Mira said as she followed the vampire past the bouncer and into the night. "Get your ass down here."

TY

"KEEP YOUR DISTANCE," Ty said into the microphone plugged into Tiff's laptop. The crackle of static told him Mira had already left the building and the reach of its communications network. He released the mic button, stood, and cast a quick glance at Tiff. "Thanks for the assist."

"Anything to clear the club. Just make sure no more patrons go missing." She waved him toward the door.

Ty checked the unbuttoned, blue silk shirt he was wearing over his white T-shirt, making sure it covered both the shoulder holster for his Glock and the belt sheath nestled at the small of his back that held his K-

Bar. He and Mira had decided discretion was more important than reach for this particular mission, and swords weren't exactly concealable. Ty was better with a knife anyway.

He let himself out of the tech room, hustled down the stairs to the main floor, and skirted the dancers. The beat of the music had been muffled in the security room. Here it was a mallet to the head that hammered him down to his bones. He passed behind one woman just as she misted herself with a cloud of perfume that made his nose sting and his eyes water with its potency. The bouncer gave him a nod as he reached the exit and hooked a thumb to the left, indicating the direction Mira had turned after leaving. Ty nodded. He scanned the street. A sizable crowd was waiting to get into the club. Groups of people mingled on the sidewalks or wandered in and out of the various bars and restaurants that lined the streets. There was no sign of Mira or the man she was following.

Ty pulled out his cell phone as he started walking in the direction the bouncer had indicated. He brought up the app he'd installed to track Mira's phone. She'd wailed like a banshee about the tracking app when he'd first suggested it, but it was the easiest and least disruptive way for him to follow her while she kept their target in sight. The yellow pulse on the app's map showed Mira four blocks away already. She was moving fast. Ty's gaze flicked between the phone screen and the area around him as he jogged to catch up, dodging the many pedestrians out enjoying the Miami night life.

Seven blocks from the club, Mira's marker stopped. Ty slowed with a block between them. An alleyway opened just beyond the Nordstrom Rack clothing store he was walking past. The alley had a wide mouth that created a break in the line of cars parked along the street. The shop on the far side was a jewelry boutique with a white stucco exterior. Headlights flashed across the mouth of the alley like strobes as Miami's traffic flowed by. A group of chatty twentysomethings argued over prices two doors up, in front of a Vietnamese restaurant. Ty's heartbeat was a rapid-march snare drum hammering in his ears.

He tucked his phone away, slunk along the Nordstrom's large display windows, and peeked around the corner. The red bricks of the clothing shop were rough under his palm. The aromas of cooking food and diesel exhaust filled the alley. Puddles reflected the lights from the street in streaks of color. A fire escape clung to the stucco side of the boutique shop; there were balconies in front of the second- and third-story windows, but the street-level ladder was pulled up out of reach. A large, green, metal dumpster was tucked against the near wall about halfway up the alley, and Mira was crouched behind it. The far end of the alley didn't connect to the street on the other side of the block. Instead it split into a T that cut behind the buildings. At the intersection point, the man Mira had IDed as their vampire was talking to an Asian woman with pale skin and long black hair. She was wearing black jeans, black boots, and a black leather jacket that complemented her companion's strapped pants. The woman the vampire had been talking to at the bar stood between them. She was frowning but didn't seem otherwise distressed.

Moving slowly so as not to draw attention, Ty crouched low and inched his way along the Nordstrom's wall toward Mira and the cover of the garbage bin.

Mira pivoted to watch him approach. She pressed a finger to her lips . . . as if he didn't know to stay quiet. When he joined her behind the dumpster, she set one hand on his shoulder and leaned in until her lips brushed his ear.

"The new girl's a vampire, too." Her voice was barely more than a breath that warmed his skin.

She pulled back, and the chill of her sudden absence made him shiver in the warm night.

Ty peeked around the corner of the painted metal that shielded them. Rust flaked under his hand. The savory aromas of the Vietnamese restaurant down the street were replaced by the rancid scent of decay. The female vampire had grabbed the woman from the club by the upper arms. She was speaking to her in a low tone that Ty couldn't hear. The woman, for her part, seemed stoned. She nodded her head lazily and tipped her head back.

Ty choked back a curse. They'd been counting on the vampire taking his meal home, not a dine-and-dash scenario. He shifted. Mira gripped the sleeve of this shirt.

"We follow the plan," she hissed.

Ty turned on her, keeping his voice low. "They're going to do it here. We have to stop them."

"The goal is to find the nest. If Kendra Jackson is alive, that's where she'll be. And if she's dead, at least we can take all the bloodsucking bastards out at once."

"You promised we wouldn't let anything happen to the bait," he growled through clenched teeth.

"I promised I wouldn't let her die," she corrected. "Maybe they just want a quick sip before they take her home to share. Or maybe they'll make a meal here but leave her alive. A lot of smart vampires do. As long as they stop before she's dead, we can keep our cover and follow them back to their nest."

Ty stared into the cool detachment of Mira's expression.

"Miami PD, freeze!"

Ty and Mira both twisted toward the mouth of the alley. Gianna stood on the sidewalk with her gun raised. She was staring at the far end of the alley, where the vampires were about to have dinner. Her gaze flicked to Ty's hiding spot but returned quickly to her target. Still, he'd caught the triumph in her eyes.

Shit. How did she find us?

"Get down on your stomachs, now." Gianna took a step into the alley. Her black sneakers squeaked against the pale concrete. "I said—"

A streak of darkness flashed past the dumpster. One second, Gianna was backlit by the streetlamps at the mouth of the alley. The next, she was flying through the air. The male vampire in the blue shirt and bondage pants was standing in her place. Gianna slammed into the stucco wall just below the fire escape with a shudder-inducing *crack*, then dropped to the ground in a limp heap.

The vampire followed her movements. When she landed, he moved toward her. Not in a flash this time, but with the slow stalk of a predator enjoying the hunt.

As Ty straightened from his hiding place, he emptied the entire clip of his Glock into the vampire's back. Sure, it wouldn't kill him, or even slow him down, but it was enough to draw his attention away from Gianna. The man jerked with each impact. His blue shirt turned the purple of a deep bruise.

Ty ignored Mira's soft curse behind him as he holstered the empty gun and pulled out the seven-inch blade sheathed at his belt. This was exactly the kind of foolhardy heroism he'd warned her not to do, but he couldn't let Gianna get killed. He couldn't just sit back and watch the monsters have their fun. He charged full tilt at the bloody man who'd turned to face him. The eyes that locked onto him were wide with surprise, but they shimmered with liquid gold that matched Mira's when her demon was in the driver's seat.

Staring into those eyes, he bellowed a challenge and brought the tip of his knife down with all of his might. Muscle parted between the man's neck and shoulder. The edge of the blade bit into his clavicle, and still the tip burrowed deeper. The vampire shrieked. A metallic stench flecked with spittle flew into Ty's face. The man's jaw stretched beyond logic.

Dagger-like teeth erupted from his gums. His skin grew translucent, traced with pale-blue veins, and his face lost any semblance of humanity.

I've got one shot.

Ty twisted the blade and dragged it sideways toward the vampire's throat. But the vampire's surprise had been replaced by rage. It jerked away. The knife pulled out of Ty's hand, still embedded in the vampire's neck. Ty stumbled as he lost the connection.

The vampire reached across his chest and pulled the blade free. The bloodied metal clattered to the concrete. The stained shirt, shredded by the exit of Ty's bullets, stretched with each heaving breath. The skin beneath those tears, while smeared with blood, seemed intact. Even as Ty watched, the knife wound in the vampire's neck began to close.

Well shit. Ty settled into a fighting stance and raised his arms to a guard position. *My odds of survival just went from slim to snowball in Hell.*

Chapter 17

TY

THE WORLD AROUND Ty suddenly plunged into darkness. Not the dark of night in the city, not the dark in the long shadows of the alley, but the darkness of a burial shroud wrapped tightly over his eyes. The walls of the alley, the vampire he faced, even the ground beneath his feet faded to nothingness. He was standing at the center of a universe in which the last lights of creation had winked out.

He blinked, rubbed the back of one wrist across his blind eyes, and blinked again. The inky blackness persisted. He took a deep breath. The smell of the garbage he'd huddled behind was gone. He strained his ears. Only the rapid-fire beat of his own heart echoed through the darkness. Something sliced his forearm. Wetness trickled out of the gash. The sensation was almost a relief in the emptiness. At least he could still feel his body.

A second slash split open the side of his thigh. A third slashed his back, gluing the fabric of his shirt to his skin. He spun at each new wound, throwing wild punches, but his attacker was nowhere to be found. He was being played with.

Taking another deep breath, Ty dropped his useless guard and sank his hand into his pocket. He half expected to feel his exposed vitals ripped to shreds by his unseen attacker, but the vampire could have killed him a dozen times over if it had wanted to.

It probably wants to make me suffer for putting all those holes in it earlier.

Ty needed to break the hold of the illusion blinding him before the vampire lost interest in this game and decided to finish it. He closed his eyes against the emptiness and focused on the feel of the river rock in his pocket. He rubbed his thumb over the smooth contours of its familiar oblong form and traced the scratch that ran along one side with his nail. He marked every curve, every dimple.

A hot flash of pain lanced his cheek. Blood ran to his chin. He kept his eyes closed.

"Focus on the present." He whispered the words, but they shattered the silence encasing him like a bullet through a pane of glass. He shifted his feet. The soles of his shoes rubbed against the surface of the concrete. He inhaled and rejoiced at the smell of day-old noodles left to bake in a metal box. He continued to trace his anchor as he opened his eyes. The alley was back, but a translucent fog clung to it, blurring the edges of the world.

The vampire closed for another strike, a shadowy figure darting out of the mist.

Ty forced himself not to react until the blow landed and a new cut tore through his calf, then he yelped and staggered away, spinning as though searching for the source of his pain. The vampire danced away. Its movements were fast and fluid but not untraceable as it circled him.

Ty kept his gaze unfocused, trusting his periphery to find what he needed.

The vampire darted in again. Ty turned just enough to take the hit on his shoulder instead of his neck, then flailed and stumbled back toward the reflective object he'd spotted on the ground. He pretended to fall, catching himself awkwardly on his elbows. His fingers closed around the handle of the bloody knife the vampire had discarded earlier. Ty swung his head from side to side as though searching the black for the next attack, careful never to look directly at the vampire as it closed in on him.

Behind the vampire, other shapes moved through the mist—Mira dealing with the second vampire.

Ty held his breath. He waited until the vampire was nearly on top of him. The man drew back for a slash with elongated fingers tipped with claws. Ty lunged.

Metal flashed. The tip of the K-Bar arced toward the side of the vampire's neck. Golden eyes went wide. The vampire's momentum was carrying him straight into the blade. Then, at the last possible second, and too fast for Ty to properly register, the vampire changed direction. He arched away from the knife, aborting his attack. The blade sliced along the front of his neck. Crimson liquid spilled down his chest, but the majority of his neck was intact.

Ty reversed his grip on the knife and went for a follow-up, but he'd lost the element of surprise. The vampire wasn't underestimating him anymore. One pale palm slammed into the side of Ty's wrist. The blade dropped from his suddenly numb fingers as a wave of tingling raced up his arm like an army of ants. The vampire's other hand slammed against Ty's sternum.

His breath left in a noisy rush as he skidded twelve feet across the concrete. What had seemed like smooth ground was suddenly sandpaper against his skin as he tried to stop himself. He tumbled and rolled out the mouth of the alley and into the gutter of the adjoining street. Light from the street lamps danced on water as he splashed through the city's runoff, soaking one sleeve of his shirt and the side of his pants.

The world was spinning. He took a labored breath, finally able to force air into his battered lungs. The sounds of traffic and pedestrian chatter drifted to him through the fog in his mind. No one was screaming. No horns blared as cars barreled past.

They must be using an illusion to mask our fight. Ty wasn't sure if that realization was frightening or a relief. If he and Mira succeeded in taking out the vampires, it would mean an easier cover-up and a lot less paperwork. If they failed, no one would ever know what happened to them . . . just like all those missing kids.

The vampire was stalking toward him out of the mouth of the alley. The space behind him suddenly lit up like the Fourth of July. Ty winced as the bright light silhouetting the vampire stabbed into his eyes. Heat seared Ty's exposed skin. A rumble like the deep bass of the dance club's music rattled the nearby windows. The vampire glanced over his shoulder.

Ty scraped together what energy he could and charged the distracted vampire like a linebacker. His shoulder connected with the blood-soaked shirt over the man's rock-hard abdomen. He continued to plow forward.

The vampire took one step back, then planted his heel. Ty might as well have been shoving against a mountain.

Clawed fingers grabbed the back of Ty's shirt, tearing skin and fabric alike as he was flung away. He bounced once against the pavement, then the vampire was on him again. Hands like steel vises gripped his upper arms and lifted him clear off the ground with no more effort than raising a feather. The vampire sneered in his face, and a guttural snarl reverberated in its throat, but the golden gaze drifted to something over his shoulder.

"Bah."

The vampire's utterance wafted a breath of stale blood over Ty's face that made his stomach turn. He was outmatched, exhausted, and out of ideas, but he wasn't about to make this easy. He jerked his knee up as hard as he could and winced in sympathy at the crushing contact.

The vampire grunted and staggered. Ty's feet touched the ground, but only for a moment. The vampire yanked open the trunk of a green sedan parked near the mouth of the alley. The car's alarm blared. Its taillights flashed. The vampire flipped Ty headfirst into the open trunk.

Panic surged as Ty dropped toward that cramped space. He threw out his hands to stop his descent, but his weight and momentum carried him forward. His fear erupted in a throat-rending yell. His shoulder and the side of his head hit the felted surface, followed by the crushing weight of the rest of his body. He swiveled toward the opening just in time to see the lid of the trunk come down. There was a screech of twisting metal. The top of the trunk pressed against his hip. His legs were wedged against the sides. He twisted to relieve the pressure on his broad shoulders.

There should be a latch. There has to be a latch. All trunks are supposed to have a latch. He groped along the sides of the trunk, squirming as best he could to reach every surface, every corner. His heart was racing. His breath was hot and stale as the toxins of his own body suffocated him. He squeezed his eyes closed and plunged his hand into his pocket once more.

Memories of rubble, and blood, and screaming himself hoarse in a small dark space bombarded him. The face of Jamal, his last partner, his lost friend, drifted in his vision. The sensation of Jamal's blood coursing over his hands was amplified by the metallic smell of his own injuries. Muffled sounds drifted out of the darkness, too indistinct to pinpoint. A rescue crew come to dig him out of the rubble? Or Mira fighting to survive two vampires? The past and present swirled together in a dizzying nightmare as Ty's breaths came faster.

He traced the scratch on the surface of his anchor, desperately trying to remember where he was and what he was supposed to be doing, but the ghosts of his past would not release him. He sucked in a mouthful of hot, humid air and screamed.

MIRA

MIRA'S FINGERTIPS brushed the cloth of Ty's pant leg but closed on empty air. The *crack, crack* of gunshots echoed off the alley walls.

She swore under her breath as he drew his knife and charged the male vampire who'd sent Gianna flying. Beyond Ty and his target, the interfering cop lay crumpled beneath the fire escape.

<What was she even doing here?>

"Screwing up our plans," Mira growled. She swung her attention to the second vampire and the victim from the dance club. The plan had been for Ty and her to *follow* the vampire at a discrete distance. If they'd been forced to engage to protect the woman, Mira was supposed to take point with Ty close by so she could protect him with her magic. Now Ty was running in the wrong direction. *Freaking hypocrite, always going on about how important it is to follow the plan so no one gets hurt.*

<Should we support him?>

Mira glared at Ty's back. The knife he'd drawn was arcing toward the male vampire. Even with surprise and luck, a mortal against a vampire was long odds. Still, Ty was a trained PTF agent, and he'd made the choice to engage. The woman they'd used as bait was an innocent civilian. Now that the plan had gone sideways, the vampires wouldn't hesitate to kill her.

Mira drew in her magic, concentrated it into what basically amounted to a molasses bomb, and launched it past Ty's shoulder with the force of a baseball in a batting cage. It hit the male vampire in the arm. *That should slow him down enough to give Ty a chance.* Then she amplified her speed and strength, shielded her mind against illusions, and charged out from behind the dumpster in the opposite direction as Ty.

<Let's do this!>

The female vampire had looked up from her meal at Gianna's arrival. Blood stained her mouth and dribbled down her chin. She had one hand tangled in her victim's dark curls. The woman from the club was whimpering. She clutched at the hand supporting her by her hair as her knees buckled. Tears coursed over her cheeks. Blood flowed from the side of her neck, where the vampire's abrupt change in position had torn flesh. The edge of her halter top absorbed the liquid, transitioning from ruby to blush to the original glittery white.

Upon seeing Mira charging her, the vampire whipped her arm forward, propelling the bleeding woman into Mira's path.

<Incoming!>

The woman collided with Mira, who braced against the impact. The woman clawed at Mira's chest and arms, groping for support. She smelled of sweat, blood, and urine. Snot coated her upper lip. She bawled and burbled, "Please, help me. I don't want to die."

"Get off me!"

Mira lost precious seconds trying to disentangle herself. By the time she shoved the woman away, the vampire's follow-up was already too close to dodge. Mira took the full force of the hook right across her jaw. Lights exploded in her vision. Even with magic coursing through her body, a vampire's strength was enough to ring her bell.

She staggered several steps, nearly tripping over the woman who was now dragging herself across the concrete in an attempt to get away.

<Block right!> The demon's energy surged in Mira as it pushed her body to act despite the jangling effect of that first punch. Her right hand

circled back in a butterfly block that trailed a shimmer of bluish magic through the air like an afterimage.

The vampire's fist connected with the blue shimmer with a bone-splitting *crack*. She shrieked and retreated a few steps, cradling the shattered fingers of her right hand.

Mira straightened and drew a dagger the length of her forearm from the sheath strapped under her skirt. She gripped the blade in her left hand, concentrated her magic into her right, and faced off against the vampire. "Let's try this again."

The vampire shook and stretched her injured hand. Her split skin had already sealed over the glint of bone Mira had seen. Her nails thickened and elongated. Her jaw stretched. Her dark eyes seemed to sink. Her skin clung to the skeletal frame of her face. A smirk twisted her thin lips. She ran at Mira with all the speed of a pissed-off vampire.

Mira barely got her blade up in time to parry the opening swipe. She spun and recentered in time to throw her own magic-amplified punch, but the woman knocked it aside. Clawed fingertips snagged the fabric of Mira's dress, ripping it to ribbons, but she managed to keep her flesh intact as she spun again and landed a kick against the vampire's knee, cracking bone.

The vampire howled.

The demon laughed. <Must be a baby. Nothing over two hundred years is this slow.>

She's still faster than us. Mira grunted as she blocked one punch only to take another to the ribs.

<I could fix that.>

Not without ruining my complexion.

Mira shot a charge of magic at the vampire's face in the form of a burst of lightning, then closed with her dagger to sever the tendons in the vampire's remaining knee.

Her opponent dropped but brought her taloned fingers around in a slash that raked Mira's arm and left four bloody gashes.

<Take her head!>

Mira's arm raised her dagger in response to the demon's command.

No. She shifted trajectory. The knife sliced through the vampire's chest, leaving a deep furrow between her breasts that exposed her sternum for the split second before the wound started healing.

<What are you playing at?> the demon demanded.

We need to take her alive if we want to find the nest.

<We need to kill her before she can report back that we're hunting

them. Then they'll scatter, and we'll lose any chance of finding them.>

The vampire rolled to the side while Mira and her demon struggled for control of the dagger.

<Shit. See what you did?>

"You're the one who got all stabby," Mira grumbled. "*My* plan was to snap her neck. That'd buy plenty of time to secure her."

<Sure. Except for the other one kicking Ty's ass over there.>

Mira's gaze flicked to the mouth of the alley, where Ty was down on his butt and elbows. His eyes darted from side to side as though he couldn't see what was right in front of him, which in this case was a vampire closing in on him.

Coño!

<We only need *one* vampire, right?>

Fine. We'll take this one out and catch that one. Mira bit her lower lip. *Hopefully before he kills Ty.*

The Asian woman stood up. She limped slightly, but her leg was holding her. Her lips peeled back in a snarl that exposed her fangs.

Let's end this quickly.

The energy swirling over Mira's right palm turned to flame, The flame spread like wildfire up her arm as she let it grow, then shrank back to her palm as she compressed it. She pictured in her mind exactly what she wanted the spell to do, then extended her arm as though she were throwing a baseball. The tightly packed bomb of magic made a whistling noise as it soared through the air.

The vampire dodged—not surprising; even an injured vampire had great reflexes—but Mira hadn't been aiming for the vampire.

The magical missile impacted the stucco wall on the far side of the alley and burst apart. A wash of flames shot at the vampire's back like a volcanic eruption. Her lustrous black hair sizzled and curled, filling the air with the acrid scent of char. She flapped and flailed and tore off the black leather jacket that had taken the brunt of the explosion and was now turning her into a dancing candle.

Mira closed with her dagger, but the vampire whipped the flaming jacket between them like a matador's cape. Embers scattered from the jacket like fireflies. Mira lunged. The vampire mirrored her.

Mira's dagger sank into the vampire's heart at the same time as the vampire's clawed fingers knifed through Mira's skin and muscle, burrowing between her ribs.

Mira coughed. Blood filled her mouth. She couldn't quite catch her breath.

The vampire smiled. Blood stained her elongated teeth and thin lips. "I can survive this." She leaned in. "Can you?"

Mira took a wheezing breath and smiled back, though her lungs felt as if they were full of acid. "I can now."

The demon surged within her, filling her like a vessel. The anchors that bound them together burned with energy. The skin around Mira's nails cracked and blackened. The magic that had been contained in Mira's right hand flared and flowed over her, coating her from head to toe in white light. Bolts of black lightning crackled in that glow, and flecks of molten gold put the fading embers of the earlier fire to shame.

"This one's barely enough to bother with," the demon complained with Mira's voice.

A car alarm sounded at the mouth of the alley. Mira spotted Ty at the edge of her peripheral vision. It looked as though the vampire he'd been fighting was trying to shove him in the car's trunk.

"Just get it over with," she said.

"With pleasure." The purr in Mira's voice made her shiver.

The demon's energy pulled in on itself, calling out the energy in the vampire. Black tendrils formed like smoke around the hand protruding from Mira's side.

Panic flickered across the vampire's expression. "What are you doing?" She pulled her hand away. It made a wet sucking sound as it exposed the gaping wound in Mira's side.

Mira gasped, gagged, and coughed up another mouthful of blood. *We definitely have a collapsed lung.*

"No problem." Mira's free hand, now controlled by the demon, darted out. Her fingers wrapped around the vampire's wrist, stopping its retreat. She twisted the dagger.

The vampire jerked against Mira's hold, but she couldn't break free. Trails of black smoke tinged with bronze now bound them together, as energy flowed out of one and into the other.

The Asian woman sagged, just as the woman from the club had in her grip. Her eyes rolled in a vain attempt to focus on Mira. "What *are* you?"

Mira grinned. "The victor."

The vampire's skin tightened around her bones until she looked like a bag of vacuum-sealed leftovers. Then her vellum skin began to crack. The bronze sheen in the woman's eyes faded, leaving them black for a moment before the haze of death clouded them. The last trickle of smoky energy sank into the glow surrounding Mira. She pulled out her dagger and released the vampire, whose dried husk hit the pavement with a dull *thud*.

Mira licked her lips—the demon savoring its meal—small though it was. She inhaled deeply, relishing the feel of full lungs. The skin, bones, and muscle along her ribs had reknit.

We need to help Ty.

"Right." The demon turned toward the mouth of the alley.

The second vampire was staring, open-mouthed, at his companion. His gaze shifted to Mira. Then he turned and bolted up the street.

"Shit." Mira raced to the mouth of the alley.

The vampire was careening through pedestrians, barely more than a blur at his current speed. The people he ran into cursed and looked around, some in the direction he'd run, some back toward her.

Double shit. The illusion's gone. People are going to notice us.

"I can catch him." Mira slipped her dagger back into its sheath and braced in a runner's position.

A terrified but muffled scream came from the trunk of the car next to her. The frame of the trunk had been buckled, the metal folded over at the edges to prevent it from opening.

Ty doesn't like small spaces.

The vampire skidded around the corner at the next intersection.

The demon sprang into motion. Mira made it three steps, then tripped herself and fell flat on her face in front of a group of teenagers blocking the sidewalk.

"Are you all right?" asked a nervous-looking girl with long brown braids.

Mira rolled onto her back and sprang to her feet. "What the Rift was that?" She spun and looked past the teens to the corner where the vampire had vanished. "You let him get away!"

The teenagers stepped back, exchanging confused glances.

"We have to help Ty," Mira insisted.

She, or rather the demon, gestured up the street. "That fang face was our only lead. Now he's going to tell the others we're onto them."

"I know," she snapped. "But we can't just leave him."

The teenagers continued to back away as they stared at the blood-smeared crazy lady arguing with herself on the sidewalk until a curly-haired redhead finally said, "You're nuts." The group scattered and ran.

Mira turned back toward the alley. "We're drawing too much attention."

"Whose fault is that?" the demon huffed.

She pulled a curtain of power around her shoulders like a cape, relaxing a little as the cool tingle of the perception filter settled over her. The eyes of the onlookers skittered away from her as she marched back to the alley. Anyone who looked too long would start to feel queasy and get a massive headache.

Mira lifted one hand, as though checking her manicure. The black puppet lines that formed when the demon took control were gone, thanks to the extra boost of energy she'd gotten from the vampire. Unfortunately, that also put the demon dangerously close to the surface. "We need to secure the scene before somebody calls the cops."

"Isn't Ty in charge of the cops now?"

"Do you really want to test that with a mummified vampire corpse?" she countered.

Ty's screams were still coming from the crumpled trunk, mingling with the blare of the car alarm. Mira twisted some of her magic into a crackle of electricity that danced over her fingertips. She set her hand on the hood of the car and fried the electronics underneath. The alarm spluttered and died. The car's lights went dark. The few people who'd bothered to glance at the noisy car when the vampire's illusion collapsed turned away.

<What's even the point of a car alarm?>

Who knows?

She channeled all her magic into her fingertips and grabbed the folded edges of the trunk. Her fingers sank into the metal. "One, two, three." She yanked with a superhuman burst of strength that tore the steel trunk open like an aluminum can.

As the effort faded, Mira felt the demon settle back. Their energy was still a little lopsided, with the demon closer to the surface than was really comfortable, but they weren't in danger of sprouting more puppet lines anytime soon.

Ty's scream became louder, then cut off, as the metal trapping him peeled away. He was sweat-soaked and panting. His chest rose and fell in rapid gasps. The streetlights reflected off the whites of his wide eyes.

"Mira?" His voice was scratchy and hoarse. "Is that you?" He pulled his hand out of his pocket and reached out to her.

"Yeah, it's me." She gripped his wrist and helped him sit up. "Mostly."

He looked around. So did she. Some people were looking in their direction again. Mira's spell kept them from focusing too closely, but she couldn't cover the fact that the back of this car had bloomed like a mangled metal flower with a man at its center. No one was getting too close, but cell phones were out—maybe to call the authorities, maybe to record the excitement. Either was bad news for her.

"We need to get out of here." She tucked an arm under his shoulder and supported his weight as he climbed free of his metal tomb.

"This is going to be a bitch to explain to the locals," he grumbled. Then he jerked to a stop, turned toward the alley, and said, "Speaking of locals . . . how's Gianna? And what happened to the girl from the club?"

Mira grew suddenly cold, then hot. She'd completely forgotten about the mortals in the alley.

Do you think they saw what we did to that vampire?

The demon shrugged. <Let's hope Gianna did. That would give us the perfect excuse to kill her.>

Ty lifted his arm off Mira's shoulder. "I'm all right now."

She eyed several patches of spreading blood that decorated his body. "You sure?"

He nodded and continued into the alley. Gianna was still on her side where she'd landed, a crumpled pile under the fire escape. The woman from the club was face down on the opposite side of the alley. Apparently, she hadn't managed to crawl very far.

Ty pointed to the woman. "You check on the civilian. I'll take Gianna."

"Find out how much of the fight she saw. Specifically—"

"If she saw you use magic." He limped toward Gianna.

Mira walked over to the prone woman who'd clung so desperately to her earlier, pausing halfway to pick up Ty's K-Bar. The woman smelled like urine, and the tattered ends of her cut-off shorts were wet. Mira crouched, brushed the woman's dark curls away from the side of her neck not covered in blood, and pressed two fingers to her cool skin. A steady but sluggish pulse beat under Mira's hand. "Probably passed out from blood loss and fear."

<We don't know how much she saw. If the police question her. . . .>

I know.

<We should take her out, now, quick and clean.>

We're not killing an innocent girl.

<A girl who may have seen us drain a vampire.>

Not gonna happen.

<And if she exposes us?>

We'll find another way.

"Hey." Ty's hand on Mira's shoulder made her jump. He knelt beside her. "How is she?"

"Alive but unconscious." She handed him his knife. "Gianna?"

He sheathed the blade and glanced over his shoulder. "Not good. She's awake, but she can't move, or even feel her legs. I'm worried that impact might have broken her back. She needs an ambulance."

Mira winced. For all that she didn't like Gianna, the thought that the foolhardy officer might be paralyzed was a sucker punch to the gut. She studied Gianna's prone form. From this angle she could only see her back and the top of her head. "If she's awake. . . ."

"She didn't see the fight," he said. "She told me the alley was empty when she came to, other than the corpse. Apparently, she can't even move enough to see over here."

Mira shifted her attention to the mummified corpse of the vampire she'd killed, yet more evidence of what she was. She rubbed her temples. "This was supposed to be a simple tail; follow the vampire back to its nest. Instead we end up with this steaming hot mess."

"Do vampire corpses fade like fae, or . . .?"

She shook her head. "They're mostly human. They leave physical bodies."

"And you're sure it's dead? Like, all the way dead?"

"I'm sure. And it's obvious she was killed by magic. We can't let the police see that body."

"Crap."

"I can get rid of the corpse, but—" She tipped her chin toward Gianna.

"I'll distract her while you do your thing, then we can call this in. We'll spin it that the assailants were fae, hence no corpse."

"There's still the matter of *this* witness." She gestured to the unconscious woman on the ground beside her. "I don't know how much she saw before she passed out. If the police question her. . . ."

Ty frowned at the woman. "Can you, I don't know, wipe her memory?"

"Not without doing serious damage."

<What if we just move her till we know what she knows and decide then?>

Mira snapped her fingers. "If Gianna hasn't seen her, we can tell the police she ran off during the fight. I can take her to Father Bembe's church until she wakes up. That'll give me a chance to find out what she remembers, and bonus, I can avoid interacting with the police."

"Except she needs medical attention," Ty countered. "And enough people saw you that if you're not here when the police arrive, it's going to look suspicious."

<If she hasn't died yet, she probably won't.>

Mira sighed. *We can't risk it.*

<But possible exposure? That's a risk you want to take?>

That's a risk we take every time we use our magic. Besides, Ty's right about it looking suspicious if I bolt. Too many people could place me near this alley. To Ty she said, "Distract Gianna. I'll get rid of the corpse."

Mira waited for Ty to return to Gianna, then walked over to the corpse. She knelt beside the Asian woman who'd become a monster. Her dark eyes stared sightlessly toward the heavens. A familiar ache hitched in Mira's chest.

<We had no choice. It was kill or be killed.>

Mira crossed herself, tucked her chin, and recited, "Hail Mary, full of grace. Pray for us poor sinners, now and at the hour of our death." She closed the woman's eyes. Her skin crinkled like parchment under her fingers.

She pressed her palms to the corpse's chest and channeled her magic. Vampires started out human; their bodies were basically the same once you stripped away the magic that made them special, which Mira had already done. All that was left was a meat sack of bound molecules. Mira pushed energy into those bonds, and, one by one, they popped like grapes. The resistance under her hands collapsed into a pile of gray ash. She called up a gust of wind that whipped her hair around her face and dried the sweat on her skin.

Mira rested her fingertips against her Saint Jude pendant as she watched what was left of her latest victim be scattered along the alley like so much dust. The ache in her chest grew stronger.

<She was a monster, a killer.>

And what does that make us?

Chapter 18

MIRA

MIRA STRAIGHTENED from the empty patch of alley where the woman she'd killed had been lying and walked toward Ty and Gianna. Ty was sitting in front of Gianna, blocking her view. His cell phone was pressed to his ear. He seemed to be talking to a dispatcher. He named the nearest cross streets and told them to hurry.

Mira touched his back.

He swiveled and looked up at her.

She nodded.

He stood and said, "An ambulance is on its way. Stay with Gianna while I flag them down." He cast a quick glance at the bare concrete where the vampire had died, then trotted to the mouth of the alley.

Mira looked at Gianna, whose narrowed brown eyes were boring into her. Granted, the malice coming from the other woman might be attributed to their past, or to the fact that Mira had intentionally excluded her from this operation, or to Gianna dealing with the possibility that she might be paralyzed. But it could also mean that Gianna had lied to Ty about seeing Mira perform magic . . . that she had watched Mira drain the life from a woman who clearly wasn't human.

We need to know what she knows.

<You think she pulled one over on Ty?>

She glanced at Ty. He was pacing back and forth at the mouth of the alley. He held his phone pressed to one ear and used his free hand to wave away gawkers and curious citizens. She turned her attention back to Gianna's hostile stare.

Lowering into a deep squat, she wrapped her arms wrapped around her knees and asked in an offhand tone, "How much do you remember?"

Gianna's gaze darted side to side. Now that Mira was right in her face, she seemed to be having trouble looking at her directly. "Not much." She licked her lips. "Nothing after hitting the wall."

<She's lying.>

No shit. "How did you even find us?"

Gianna laughed, then winced. Her eyes teared up. "I'm not an idiot." Her voice was thready. She had to pause for breath. "It was obvious you found a lead this morning, and just as obvious you had no intention of telling me what it was, so I followed you."

Mira clenched her jaw. "You nearly got us all killed. Because of you, our plan got shot to hell, and we lost our best chance at stopping these disappearances."

"If Ty had held up his end of the bargain, I wouldn't have screwed up your stupid plan."

<Bargain?>

Gianna clamped her mouth shut with a grimace, though whether from pain or because she'd said more than she intended, Mira couldn't tell. Gianna seemed to be barely holding it together as she sucked shallow breaths through her gritted teeth.

Mira waited for Gianna's expression to ease, then leaned close and said, "What bargain?"

Gianna's eyes went wide. "What? Nothing, just . . . you know . . . partners exchange information."

"Except you're not a partner," she said. "At least, you shouldn't be." She glanced toward the mouth of the alley. Ty was standing farther out now, waiting for the sirens Mira could hear in the distance. *Did he really believe her shitty acting, or does he know she saw me kill the vampire and lied to my face?* The fluttering warmth that so often filled Mira when she thought about her new partner suddenly felt more like needles than the brush of butterfly wings.

<She knows you're a practitioner. We should finish her off while Ty is distracted, before the cops arrive.>

First we need to find out what kind of deal she made with Ty that had him wrapped around her pinky.

<Want to poke around in her brain?>

I'm not very good at that kind of delicate magic, and you're even worse. We'd probably end up lobotomizing her before we found any answers.

<That'd be one way to deal with her.>

But it wouldn't tell us why Ty's covering for her. Mira thought for a moment. If Gianna knew Mira was a practitioner, maybe it could work in her favor. *Maybe we should explain her options.*

Mira smiled. Or maybe it was the demon. It was hard to tell. Either way, the expression made Gianna shrink away from her. Not that she could get very far in her current condition. Mira leaned in as close as she could without lying down next to Gianna and whispered, "You saw what I did, didn't you?"

Gianna's mouth opened and closed, but her pain-dulled brain seemed to have trouble coming up with a convincing response.

Mira waved a dismissive hand. "I know you did. So the question is really: What to do with you now?"

Gianna tipped her head, as though trying to catch a glimpse of the mouth of the alley behind Mira's looming figure. She opened her mouth.

Mira clamped her hand over the other woman's lips. "Make a fuss, and we're going to have a problem." She waited for Gianna to nod, then pulled her hand away. "I'm going to give you one chance to come clean. Tell me what your deal with Ty was, and why you wanted so badly to be on this case."

Gianna spat a blood-speckled spray onto the concrete, decorating the practical black Mary Janes Mira had worn to the club. "You're going to kill me anyway."

"Not necessarily." She lifted a hand between them, channeled her magic, and waggled her fingers. Ribbons of black, white, and gold drifted off her skin in a mini version of the aura that surrounded her when she was in full rifter mode.

Gianna's eyes grew wide as saucers, but the look in them was fear, not surprise.

"I can get what I want without consent," Mira said, "but I prefer to be civil. Digging through memories gets messy. It won't necessarily kill you, but—"

"You're a monster."

"Maybe." Mira gave a small shrug, as though the words held no meaning for her, but inside they were a bullet to her heart.

<She doesn't know what she's talking about.>

She watched us suck the life out of a woman, and now we're threatening her. How much more monstery can you get?

<Okay, yes, but she doesn't know the whole story. We have reasons.>

Everybody has reasons.

<Those sirens are getting close. Are we doing this, or not?>

"So what's it going to be? Words? Or thoughts?"

Gianna twitched as though trying to move, but her body didn't respond. Tears welled in the corners of her eyes, but her scathing glare marked their cause as anger more than pain.

"Fine," she gritted. "I already suspected you were a freak, so I did a little digging and found evidence that would expose you. The deal was that I got credit for the collar in the missing kids case in exchange for keeping my mouth shut about you."

Mira sat back. "Ty agreed to that?"

"With the added stipulation that you be kept in the dark."

He doesn't trust me.

<He was probably just trying to protect you. Again. Although, I agree he went about it all wrong. If he'd told us about Gianna from the beginning, we could have taken care of her right away. No more threat. No more blackmail. Easy peasy.>

That's probably why he didn't *tell us.* Mira shoved aside her disappointment at Ty's assessment of her character. She wasn't even sure which one of them she was most upset with—Ty, Gianna, or herself. She looked at the woman. "Why are you so eager to solve this case?"

Gianna rested her head on the damp concrete. "This case is big. Like, make-or-break-a-career kind of big."

"And you were hoping it'd make yours." Mira settled onto her butt and crossed her legs to ease the numbing tingle spreading through her feet. "There have got to be easier ways to get assigned to a case."

"Not for me." Gianna closed her eyes. "My career got seriously derailed a few months back when I made the catastrophic mistake of dating a coworker. He had more seniority, but he recognized my deductive skills, so when he got tossed a big case that had him stumped, he asked for my insights." Once Gianna started talking, it was like a dam had burst. Words tumbled over one another in a rush to get out. "We teased out the details of his case over candlelit dinners and between the sheets after making love. Then one morning, I had an insight that cracked the case wide open. He was over the moon, and so was I." Her already closed eyes crinkled as she scrunched them tighter.

"He took the credit," Mira guessed.

<People suck.>

"He was all too happy to share my bed, but when it came to sharing credit. . . ." Gianna bunched her fist against the concrete, scraping her knuckles. "We were both looking to fill the open detective position when Moretti retires, and closing a case like that would go a long way. He became the department's poster boy. When I tried to tell our supervisor about the part I'd played, my ex claimed I was just a jilted lover trying to get back at him for breaking up with me, which he claimed to have done *before* cracking the case. That was bullshit, of course. I dumped him when I realized what a backstabbing asshole he was. But the supervisor took his side, and my ex made sure everybody in the department heard his version of the story. I became a pariah. The other cops saw me as some emotionally unhinged bimbo trying to sleep her way to success. No one would take my ideas seriously. No one wanted to work with me. A week later I was reassigned to babysitting duty at the high school." She took a shuddering breath.

I get the feeling this is the first time Gianna's unloaded like this.

<Don't tell me you actually feel sorry for her?>

As though sensing Mira's reaction, Gianna's eyes snapped open. She fixed Mira with her dark stare. "I'm not looking for pity."

Mira stiffened and lifted her chin. "I wasn't planning on giving any."

"This case is my chance to prove I'm a damn good detective and rub it in the chauvinistic noses of everyone who doubted me."

<I know she's your teenage nemesis and all, but I'm kinda starting to like her. She's got spunk.>

"There's more than one way to get recognition." Mira caught Gianna's gaze, trying to see past the hostile surface to the woman within. "You knew, or at least suspected, what I am. Why not just expose me and get your accolades that way?"

"Because as much as I might resent you for what happened all those years ago, you aren't my target. Moretti and the other detectives who ridiculed me have seriously screwed the pooch on this investigation. Showing them up, showing the world how incompetent they are. . . ." She lifted one shoulder. "Exposing you wasn't worth missing that opportunity."

"What about now?" Mira asked. "Do you still want that opportunity?"

<What are you thinking?>

That she can keep her mouth shut when it suits her, and I no longer think she's a kidnapper-slash-killer.

<You don't want to kill her.>

I never wanted to kill her.

The demon sighed.

Gianna searched Mira's face. Her forehead puckered. "You're not going to kill me?"

Mira shrugged. "I want to get justice for the missing kids, but I'd prefer to avoid fame for obvious reasons. It seems to me that we can help each other out." She extended her hand.

<Wow. I seriously can't believe you're offering to work with her, considering the way she tormented you back in school.>

I'm not thirteen anymore, and neither is she. We both deserve a second chance.

Gianna stared at Mira's outstretched hand, inches from her own, for a long moment, then she gripped Mira's fingers. She winced and gasped at the movement.

Mira glanced at Gianna's unmoving legs. "The ambulance should be here any minute."

"Yeah." Gianna's voice was strained. She set her hand back on the concrete.

<Even if she arrests the killer, gets an award from the mayor, and proves she's better than every other detective in the city . . . her career may be over if that vampire broke her back.>

"Are you in much pain?"

"Parts of me are. Others are just numb."

Mira pinched her lower lip between her thumb and forefinger and gave it a tug. *Do you think we can fix her?*

<Healing magic is right up there with mental magic on our list of skills.>

You heal me.

<That's different. We share energy. I don't have to think about it.>

So what if we gave her some of our energy? We've got a bit to spare right now.

<We might need it later.>

She needs it now.

The demon groaned.

"What's the matter?" Gianna asked, looking confused.

"Nothing, I just . . . had a thought." *Well?*

<Fine. But I can't promise it will heal her.>

The people we share energy with get faster, stronger, more energized. . . . It can't hurt.

<I said *fine* already.>

Mira stared into Gianna's wary expression. "I want to try something that might be able to help you."

"Help me with what?"

She gestured to Gianna's limp legs.

Gianna perked up. "Seriously?"

"I said *might*. I don't know if it will work."

"I'll take it. Whatever it is, I'll take it." Gianna was practically vibrating with desperation.

Mira adjusted her position so she was on her knees. She braced her hands on the ground and leaned down.

"What are you doing?" Gianna's whisper was filled with panic.

"Trust me." Mira sank until her lips met Gianna's. There was a moment of resistance, then Gianna relaxed. Energy flowed from Mira into Gianna—healthy, vibrant energy. As their energies mingled, Mira could sense Gianna's body. She was no doctor. She couldn't tell what was what, but she could feel the damage. Broken bones, torn tissue, blood in places it shouldn't be. She'd survived her fair share of fights. She knew what it felt like to be battered.

As the kiss continued and the surplus energy the demon had drained from the vampire seeped into Gianna's wounds, her body began to mend. It wasn't as fast as when Mira healed, but there was definite progress. The demon sank further into Mira's subconscious as their balance shifted, and Mira regained full control.

<That's enough.>

A little more.

<You've already used up all the extra.>

There's still a lot of damage.

"What's this about?"

Mira pulled back to find a startled-looking Ty and two people wearing EMT uniforms looking down at her. She stood up and brushed the front of her dress as she stepped away from Gianna. The EMTs—a short man with a thick blond beard, and a brunette woman who looked as if she could bench press a city bus—quickly moved into position. The man lowered a rolling stretcher beside Gianna while the woman started checking her vitals and asking her questions. A third EMT—a trim man with a graying ponytail—was crouched over the woman on the far side of the alley.

Ty caught Mira's elbow and pulled her a few steps farther from the flashing red and blue lights near the mouth of the alley. "What were you doing to Gianna?"

"Not killing her." Mira yanked her arm away. "I can't believe you still don't trust me."

He froze. A look of confusion crossed his face, followed almost immediately by realization. He glanced at the activity around Gianna.

"Did you really think she'd keep your secret when threatened?"

He turned back to her. "You threatened her?" He slapped a hand to his forehead. "Geez, Mira. And you wonder why I didn't tell you? I knew you'd lose your shit if you found out about the blackmail."

"Oh, you knew that, did you? Because you know me so well after all of what, a month?"

He glanced again at the medics and dropped his voice to a strained whisper. "I know you're afraid of your secret getting out."

"And that I'm a murderer."

"I don't think that."

He reached out, but she backed away.

"You don't trust me."

"I *do* trust you," he said. "But you're not the only one in there."

<Oh sure, blame the demon.>

"I had the situation under control," Ty continued. "There was no reason to risk—"

"Being honest."

"Worrying you. You've been under a lot of stress, what with coming back to Miami, seeing your family, facing Gianna . . . I was just trying to save you more turmoil."

"Maybe. But the fact remains, you didn't think I'd be able to control myself"—she dropped her voice—"or my demon, if you told me the truth."

Ty rubbed the back of his neck. "I'm sorry I didn't tell you about my deal with Gianna."

<More like sorry he got caught. I can't believe he's blaming this on me.>

To be fair, you did *want to kill her.*

<So? She's still alive.>

Mira sighed. Two squad cars and a second ambulance pulled up at the mouth of the alley. Gianna had been moved onto the gurney, and the EMTs were wheeling her toward the first ambulance. Ty was about to have his hands full feeding the locals their cover story, but Mira needed to get this off her chest first. She set one hand against his shoulder. His muscles were rock hard under her palm. "If you trust me, trust me. All of me. All the time. Otherwise, we're done."

Ty opened his mouth, but a shout from a man who looked to have a fuzzy gray caterpillar clinging to his upper lip ended the conversation.

Chapter 19

TY

"FANCY FINDING you here," Moretti said as he came to a stop in front of Ty and Mira.

Ty shot a glance at Mira, who dropped her hand to her side. He wished he could take more time to fix the strain he'd created by keeping his deal with Gianna a secret, but that would have to wait. He just hoped she'd give him the chance to explain once they had some privacy. He tamped down his frustration, rounded on the portly cop, and said, "What are you doing here, Moretti? This isn't your case anymore."

Moretti raised his hands. "I just heard the call of 'officer down' over the radio and happened to be in the area." He glanced at Gianna as she was lifted into the first ambulance. "Besides, it looks like you could use a new liaison."

Ty pinched the bridge of his nose. As irritating as he found Moretti, he did need a local to process the scene and disseminate their cover story. "Fine. We tracked a suspect from the night club where Kendra Jackson went missing."

"We?" Moretti cast a questioning look at Mira.

"This is Mira," Ty said, "a PTF consultant."

"Quite the harem you've got."

Mira stiffened, hands closing to fists at her sides.

Ty quickly went on, "We followed the suspect to this alley, where a second person was waiting to ambush a woman the first had lured from the club."

"A tag-team hit."

"Exactly. Once we confirmed their intent to harm the woman, we stepped in. We took one down. The other got away."

Moretti made a show of looking around the alley. "I see an injured woman and an injured cop. What happened to your suspect?"

"She was fae," Ty said. "As any cop who's cleared the academy should know, fae bodies disappear when they die."

Moretti pressed his lips together and grunted. "I assume Officer Lopez can corroborate your story?"

"The beginning," Ty said. "She was injured early in the fight, and unconscious for most of it."

"And the club girl?" Moretti indicated the woman being loaded into the second ambulance.

"Also unconscious for most of the fight, and most likely bewitched by the fae who led her here before that. It's unlikely she'll have any useful insights, but I'll chat with her once she wakes up."

Moretti stared into the middle distance. "Guess this proves your claim of paranatural involvement." He shifted his focus to Mira, eyeing her up and down like a horse trader unimpressed by what was on offer, then turned back to Ty. "How'd you take him down?"

Good, Ty thought. *Let him dismiss her.* "That's why my badge reads 'PTF agent'," he said. "I'm trained for situations like this."

Mira shifted beside him.

Probably laughing at that last bit. Ty set his hand on Moretti's shoulder and turned him toward the mouth of the alley. "Now that you're up to speed, I need you to process this scene. Collect the names and contact info of any potential witnesses. I'll handle the interviews myself. There's a damaged car over there." He pointed to the mangled trunk. "The owner will need to be contacted."

"Shouldn't we start by setting up a perimeter? Canvas the area for your second perp?"

"He's long gone."

"But—"

"He's also more than your officers are equipped to handle. What you *can* do is prevent this incident from creating a panic. Your job tonight is damage control. Leave the fae to me."

A medic approached. She gestured to Ty and Mira. "We should get you two checked out."

Mira waved the woman away. "I'm fine."

The medic eyed the blood decorating Mira's dress and skin but turned to Ty.

"I'll be right there." Ty waited until she retreated, long black ponytail swishing behind her, then held one finger in front of Moretti's nose. "No mention of fae or the missing kids case to the press. For the time being, this was a botched mugging that Officer Lopez happened to notice. She saved the woman's life at risk of her own."

"A real hero," Moretti said dryly.

Mira opened her mouth, closed it, then said, "I'll meet you back at the truck."

She stalked away before Ty could respond, not that he had any idea what to say to her at the moment.

Moretti snorted. "Your *consultant* seems pretty full of herself."

"Get to work," Ty said. He hobbled after the raven-haired medic. Now that his adrenaline was wearing off, every inch of his body ached, and he was pretty sure the bone-deep cold he felt was due to blood loss. He might not have suffered any life-threatening injuries, but he had more than a few stitch-worthy lacerations from his bout with the vampire, not to mention the enervating exhaustion and emotional drain that followed his PTSD episode in the trunk. He perched on the back bumper of the third and final ambulance to arrive and rubbed his eyes. He felt as if he could sleep for a week.

Moretti was barking orders at the uniforms, relaying Ty's instructions while making it seem as though he were the one in charge. That suited Ty just fine. *Let the guy get off on his authority if it means less work for me.*

Once the witnesses were rounded up and identified, he was going to have to interview each and every one to find out what they saw, and more importantly, what they recorded. He'd also need to head to the hospital to talk to their club victim when she woke up. It was bad enough that Gianna had gotten firsthand confirmation of what Mira could do. If anyone else had seen. . . . Thinking of Gianna reminded Ty of the fact that Mira now knew he'd been lying to her. He groaned and ran his hands over his hair.

"Were you going for death by a thousand cuts?" asked the ponytailed EMT as she wrapped a pressure cuff around his arm.

"Something like that."

"You should go to the hospital," she said as she stuck a butterfly bandage on a gash over his eye. "Some of these are pretty deep."

He looked to the south. Mira was probably back at the club already. If he'd been thinking clearly, he would have given her the keys to his truck so she didn't have to wait in the cold. "Just patch me up as best you can."

"You need stitches."

"I'll be fine."

She stared at him for a moment, then muttered, "Your funeral." Her tone said she'd worked on enough headstrong hotshots to know when to save her breath.

Ty bounced his leg while she bandaged his various cuts, scrapes, and puncture wounds. He was dead tired but too antsy to sit still.

A familiar rumble drew his attention to the street, past the yellow tape Moretti's officers had used to mark off the area. His silver pickup idled by the sidewalk just beyond the police line.

"Are we done here?" he asked the EMT.

"If you're sure I can't convince you to take a ride to the hospital," she said.

"I'm sure."

"Get rest." She pushed a felted gray blanket into his arms. "Lots of it."

Ty nodded, wrapped the welcome warmth of the blanket around his shoulders, and shuffled toward his truck. He climbed into the passenger seat. Between the weight of his eyelids and the floaty feeling in his head, he was perfectly content to let Mira drive. He didn't even bother to ask how she'd gotten it started without a key.

TY

"WAKEY WAKEY, sunshine."

Ty groaned and tried to roll over. His forehead connected with something smooth and cold. He opened his eyes and stared through the passenger window of his truck at Mira's grandmother's house. The house wasn't all that far from the club. He must have fallen asleep almost immediately after climbing into the cab.

The driver's side door slammed, making him jump. Mira circled around the hood and opened his door. "Get some sleep. We'll check on the girl at the hospital first thing in the morning."

"Mmm." He rubbed a hand over his face and slid onto the sidewalk. Mira closed the truck door behind him. He took a dozen steps, each one easier than the last, as the night air cleared the cobwebs from his mind. He reached the front step. A metallic clatter made him turn. Mira had opened the back of her van.

"You're not coming in?"

"I'll be along shortly. You go ahead." She climbed inside and pulled the door closed behind her.

Ty climbed the steps and set his hand on the doorknob, then he paused. *I should talk to her.* He looked back at the van parked on the quiet road. No light escaped the back. Mira was completely cocooned inside. The last thing he wanted was to have an emotionally wrought argument with his partner about why he'd chosen to keep her in the dark concerning Gianna's motivations and the deal he'd made to keep her safe. But after a shower and a quick nap, they were going to be back in the thick of it. He needed to clear the air while he had the chance.

He gave his cheeks a light slap to sharpen his focus, turned around, and walked back down the path to the street. Quiet muttering came from the back of the van. Ty shuddered. He tried not to let it freak him out that Mira had a second personality inside her, but it was kinda hard to ignore when she had conversations with herself. He reached out and pulled the van's back door open.

Mira jerked, startled. She was sitting on the truck bed floor with her back propped against the cabinets set in one wall and her feet against the cabinets on the opposite side. She had tears in her eyes. One hand was wrapped around her Saint Jude medallion, the other held a razor blade. The angle of her legs had pooled her dress in her lap, exposing her muscular legs, and there on her thigh, in line with the parallel scars that marred her skin, was a fresh cut.

"What the hell are you doing?" Ty bellowed. He climbed into the truck bed, pulled the door closed behind him, and grabbed the razor out of Mira's hand.

"Me?" Mira shouted back. "You're the one barging in uninvited."

Ty tossed the blade onto the counter and picked up a pad of gauze waiting by Mira's hip.

Mira started to move away, but Ty grabbed her inner thigh with one hand and pressed the gauze to her wound with the other, pinning her in place.

"Why would you do this to yourself?" His voice was tight with emotion. He was angry at Mira for what she was doing, and scared about what it could mean, but he was also angry with himself. He'd seen these scars the first night they met, when they slept together. He'd wondered about them then but hadn't cared enough to ask. Now he wished he had.

"I'm fine." She tried to push his hands away, but he held firm. She sighed and tipped her head back until it thumped the cabinet. "Don't be such a drama queen. It's just a little cut."

"Because you didn't get beat up enough by the vampire? You felt you needed a little more?"

Mira's eyes flashed gold. "It's her penance."

Ty stiffened. Mira's tone had changed subtly.

"Shut up," Mira growled.

Ty took a moment to collect himself. He peeled back the gauze to check the wound. The bleeding had nearly stopped. He picked up a clean piece of gauze and pressed it against her thigh, only then realizing the position they were in. His knee was tucked under her leg, wedging it up. His right hand was high on her inner thigh, and he had a clear view of the exposed black satin of her panties. Heat filled Ty's abdomen and crept into his face. He licked his lips and took a deep breath. His thumb moved against the smooth surface of her skin as though it had a mind of its own.

Mira opened the box of Steri-Strips on the floor beside her and pulled out two small bandages. "That's enough with the gauze."

Ty gave himself a mental shake. *She's your partner. Get your mind out of the gutter.* He pulled his hand away. Crimson drops stained the white fabric, but the bleeding seemed to have stopped.

She pinched the cut closed and attached the adhesive strips.

"You really shouldn't do this," he whispered.

"It's none of your business."

"How does that even work? I've seen you take way more damage than this and heal without a scar."

"She won't let me—I said shut up!" Mira gritted her teeth. "Look, I get that you're trying to help, but seriously, back off."

"I—" Ty's phone buzzed in his pocket. He ignored the first two rings. He wanted to explain to Mira how upset seeing her hurt made him, but every phrase he came up with made him sound like a stalker with a hero complex.

"Are you going to answer that?" Mira tipped her chin to indicate his pants.

He reluctantly took his remaining hand away from Mira's leg, breaking their skin-to-skin contact, and pulled out his phone. "Williams here."

"Ty," Father Bembe's voice was strained. "They—"

"Mister PTF, I presume?" Bembe was interrupted by a new voice— the rough alto of a woman.

"Who is this?" Ty asked.

"Father Bembe requires your presence at his church," the voice said. "Yours *and* your soul-sucking friend's. You have ten minutes. Then the good padre starts losing body parts." The line went dead.

Ty lowered the phone. The lingering fatigue that had survived the emotional jolt of seeing Mira bleeding was burned away by a burst of adrenaline. He stared into Mira's anxious expression. "We need to get to Bembe's church, now."

Chapter 20

MIRA

"HOW THE HELL did they even know to go after Bembe?" Mira growled as she tugged on the pair of black cargo pants she'd pulled from the narrow wardrobe tucked in her truck's back corner. Her hip bumped a counter as she maneuvered in the small space. "It has to be the vampires." She yanked her sweaty, bloody dress over her head. "The timing's too much of a coincidence for anything else. But how did they find him? We haven't been in contact since our first day in town. They couldn't have been keeping tabs on us at that point." She spun and pointed at Ty with the dress bunched in her hand. "Maybe they were watching *him*. He was already poking into the missing kids, looking for Ramon. They must have seen us when we arrived, and tonight they just put two and two together."

Ty stared at her for a moment as she blurted her thoughts. Then his eyes darted away as though repelled by a magnet. He cleared his throat and turned to examine the first aid products on her counter.

Mira looked down. Her Saint Jude pendant nestled between her exposed breasts. The flat planes of her abdomen were bare to the waist of her pants. Between this and the earlier show, Ty had seen every inch of her tonight, save what was hidden by underwear. He'd seen, and he'd turned away. Just as he'd turned away at the train depot in Georgia after watching her feed.

I repulse him.

<His loss, 'cause this body's got it going on.>

It's not our body that bothers him. She threw the bunched-up dress into her hamper, yanked open a drawer, grabbed a black T-shirt, and tugged it over her head hard enough to strain the seams when it hit her shoulders. She sighed. *It's what's inside.*

<Then he's an idiot. You're awesome. I'm awesome. What's not to like?>

Mira chuckled, and the ghost of a smile tugged at her lips. She squashed the feeling. *Bembe needs us. That's all that matters right now.*

"If you're done being a prude. . . ." Mira said as she pulled open another drawer. This one held an assortment of knives, guns, and miscellaneous weapons.

Ty peeked over his shoulder, as though worried she might be trying to trick him into seeing her naked, then turned fully around to assess the available arsenal.

"This is for sure an ambush." Mira kept her focus on the weapons. "Stock up."

Ty strapped a nine-inch Bowie knife to his thigh, slipped a four-inch blade in an ankle holster, and pulled out a .44 Smith and Wesson to wear opposite his Glock. "Just let me grab my sword from the house, and I'm ready to roll."

Mira watched Ty exit the van, then turned back to the armory drawer to make her own selections. She strapped her kukri to her thigh in place of the dagger she'd used earlier, since she was no longer trying to be discrete, tucked a pair of camp knives in a belt sheath at the small of her back, one in each direction, and slipped on a shoulder holster with six throwing knives.

<How many vampires do you think are at the church?>

Mira shrugged. *No way to know.*

<Should we bring the grenades?>

Mira looked at the metallic canisters. She shook her head. "They've got a hostage."

<Poo. At least we don't have to hold back on killing them this time, right?>

"Finding the nest would still be good, but rescuing Bembe is the priority. If you get a clean shot, take it."

<Heck yeah, I will.>

"Mira!"

She spun to find Ty at the back entrance of the van, hands gripping the metal frame. His sword was strapped to his waist, so he'd finished his errand, but his rich, brown complexion was disturbingly pale.

"I just got a call from Moretti. The woman from the club never reached the hospital."

"What?!"

<Where did she go?>

"How should I know?"

"What?" Ty stared at her in confusion.

"Not you," Mira said, wishing for the millionth time that everyone could hear the demon in her head instead of just her.

He nodded. "The ambulance driver says their passenger woke up, refused treatment, and demanded they let her out. I honestly can't believe she was in any condition to walk away, but the EMTs insist she was fine when she exited the vehicle. Moretti sent a unit to pick her up, but there was no sign of her when they arrived."

"They let the witness to a crime just . . . walk away?"

"They're medics, not cops. It's not like they could hold her against her will."

<Sure they could. She was injured. It wouldn't have been hard.>

He means legally.

<Oh.>

"I told Moretti to send an officer to the woman's house," Ty said. "Hopefully she just called a ride to take her home and we can intercept her there."

Mira strapped a boot knife to her ankle, closed the drawer, and put on her sneakers. "We'll worry about her later. Bembe's our priority right now."

MIRA

THE NEIGHBORHOOD around the church was quiet. This was not the type of place that had parties raging into the wee hours of the morning. This neighborhood's residents were tucked soundly in their beds, resting up for Sunday Mass. Mira pictured parishioners filing into Bembe's church, all decked out in their Sunday best, only to find their priest dead on the nave floor. She glanced at the dashboard clock. Nine minutes had passed since Ty's phone rang. As though feeling her urgency, Ty edged the gas pedal closer to the floor. His silver pickup raced down the empty streets.

"We should park around back and scope the place out," he said.

Mira shook her head. "We don't have time, and even if we did, the church will be full of vampires on high alert. It's possible to sneak up on a vampire if it doesn't know you're coming. If it does. . . ." She shook her head again. "Besides, we don't want to do anything that will get Bembe killed."

"So what's the plan here? Just walk in through the front door?"

"That's right."

"That's suicide."

"One way or another, this will likely turn into an all-out brawl. My goal is to get close to Bembe before that happens. Then you get him to safety while I cover your exit."

Ty twisted to stare at her, open-mouthed. "You expect me to leave you in a church full of vampires?" He turned his attention back to the road and squeezed the wheel. "Not gonna happen."

"Father Bembe will be a weight around my neck, and frankly you'd be in the way, too. I'd have to split my attention between fighting them and protecting you."

"I held my own okay against that vampire in the alley."

"You mean the one who used you as a scratching post even after I slowed him down for you?"

He stiffened. "You what?"

"The one who got away, because I had to save your ass from a car trunk?"

<Harsh, but fair.>

"Fine," Ty said. "Point taken. I'll get Bembe and stay out of your way."

Ty pulled to the curb across the street from the church and cut the engine. They were parked in front of a pink adobe one-story with decorative white rocks in place of a yard and a wrought-iron fence around the property. The churchyard was dark. The pictures in the stained glass were lost in flat shadows. Bembe's manicured bushes hunkered on either side of the front steps like sleeping soldiers who'd failed their guard duty.

We need to keep the fighting contained until Ty can get to Bembe.

<They're going to be on us as soon as we step inside.>

Then we'll use that to draw them in. The more they're focused on us, the easier it will be for Ty to do his job.

<What if Bembe isn't in there?>

Then we let loose and force them to tell us where he is. She climbed out of the truck and joined Ty on the path to the church's front door. "This is going to get messy." She cracked her knuckles. "You ready?"

He drew the Smith and Wesson with his left hand and pulled the sword from its sheath. He took a deep breath. "If we don't survive this—"

"Oh, I'm going to survive."

"Fine. Well, if *I* don't survive this . . . I just want you to know—"

"Don't."

"You're amazing."

<Hell yeah, we are.>

Mira fought to ignore the fluttering warmth in her chest. *He's just saying that 'cause he thinks we're gonna die.*

<Who cares? It's still true. Take the compliment.>

"Come on." Mira drew her kukri and headed up the path.

<I think the appropriate human response is "Thank you." Or maybe, "So are you.">

Ty was a silent shadow at her side as they approached the door.

<You really suck at having friends.>

Focus, or you won't have to worry about how much I suck at anything anymore, because I'll be dead and you'll be back in the Rift.

<As if I'd let that happen.>

Mira paused on the front step. She took a deep breath, collected her energy, and called the demon forward. *What do you see?*

The church seemed to melt, a structure made of smoke that could no longer hold its shape. Beyond the doors, shapes moved through the mist. Two at the far end of the church. Four spread to either side. Two more at the very edge of her awareness.

"There are eight people inside," she whispered.

"If we assume one is Bembe, that means seven vampires," Ty said.

"Don't assume anything." She blinked. The solid walls of the church were back. She wrapped her hand around the cool brass of the door handle. "Get ready."

<I'm always ready.>

Ty settled his stance and blew out a long, steady breath. "Ready."

Mira pulled open the church door and crossed the narthex.

The nave was dark save for the flickering light of a single votive on a shelf near the altar. The ceiling was all but invisible. The pews created a path straight to the front of the church, but anything could be hiding in the deep shadows between them. On the slightly raised area where Father Bembe would stand to give his sermon, the same place where Mira had once killed a demon-possessed little girl, were two people. The candlelight reflected off Bembe's sweat-slicked skin and the whites of his eyes. He was wearing green pajamas. Beside him stood a woman whose head came to his jaw, though the fluff of her curly black hair made her seem taller. Her skin and clothes were so dark she faded into the night.

"Right on time." The woman's voice was low with a slight Creole accent—the voice from the phone. She smiled, and the candlelight revealed pearl-white teeth tapered to points.

"Let him go," Mira said.

"In good time. First, put away y'all's weapons."

"Not gonna happen."

The woman raised a hand to Bembe's throat. She set one claw-like nail against his skin. "Y'all came in the front door. That tells me you want to save this man. Do you really think you can reach me before I kill him?"

<Let's rush her.>

"If he dies, so do you," Mira growled.

"No doubt," she said. "But my goal here is to ensure no one else dies tonight."

"You've got a funny way of showing it," Ty said.

The woman shrugged. "Considering what y'all did to Seo-yoon, I felt it best to take out some insurance." She tapped her fingernail against Bembe's neck. "Now, would y'all like to have a seat, or shall we have this conversation standing up?"

We need to get closer to Bembe.

<If we move away from this door, the other vampires will be able to circle around and box us in.>

Mira scanned the pews and far aisles. Her night vision was pretty damn good, way better than a human's, but she couldn't make out any of the vampires she knew were hiding nearby. *If we don't get closer, Ty will have no chance of reaching Bembe when the fighting starts.*

Ty moved forward, walking cautiously up the central aisle. He held his gun toward the side shadows and kept his sword in front of him.

<Guess he came to the same conclusion.>

Mira hustled to catch up to Ty, then matched his pace as they crept up the aisle. Nothing moved in the shadows.

"That's close enough." The woman indicated the pews with her chin. "Take a seat."

"How about you call your backup out of the shadows?" Mira gestured with her blade.

The corner of the woman's mouth twitched up. "I can see this conversation is going to be a slog." She glanced toward the windows. "But we don't have all night, so let me explain the situation. If you attack, I will kill this man." She nodded toward Bembe. "If you somehow manage to kill me, my companions will kill you. Even if you somehow manage to kill all of us and survive, the woman you saved earlier tonight will die."

A bowling ball dropped into Mira's stomach.

Ty took a step toward the woman, but Mira grabbed his arm.

"You took her from the ambulance," Mira said.

<Damn, I should have guessed that! But how did they get to her so fast?>

Mira played back the fight in the alley. "The one who got away. Once he was clear, he circled back."

"We couldn't very well risk exposure, now could we?" the woman said.

"No witnesses is sort of the vampire mantra." She smiled. "Thank you, by the way, for taking care of Seo-yoon's corpse. One less mess for me to clean up."

Mira once again scanned the shadows. She could feel eyes on her. Had the male vampire been watching her in the alley? She stiffened. *That's how they found out about Bembe. He heard me talking about bringing the witness here.* She nearly slapped her palm to her head, but that would have given off the wrong vibe for the current situation.

<It's not your fault.>

It is, actually.

<Okay, maybe it's a little your fault, but that doesn't change the situation. We just need to kill them all and save the hostages.>

Except the girl's probably back at their nest, and we still don't know where that is.

"Here's the deal," said the woman beside Bembe. "You are clearly a dangerous person, and I'd like to convince you to leave us alone. The good father here has seen fit to explain that y'all are investigating the missing kids in this area. I assume you think we're to blame. You're wrong."

"So the fact that two people vanished from the club we tracked your friend from is just a coincidence?" Ty's voice was pinched. His muscles were practically vibrating beneath Mira's hand with the strain of holding still.

"One person," the woman corrected. "A terrible accident, and nothing to do with your case."

"Yeah right," Ty growled.

"The club is a fertile hunting ground. Why would we draw attention to that fact?"

"Because you're bloodsuckers ruled by your hunger," Mira supplied.

The woman sighed. "The woman yesterday was a mistake. We hunt in pairs, with one vampire sending the mark out to a rendezvous spot and the other lying in wait. Usually, the two each drain a set amount, barely more than a sip apiece. Then the target is sent back to the club, slightly anemic and a bit hung over, but very much alive."

Mira tightened her grip on her knife. "Vampires are monsters. You really expect me to believe you're not killing people?"

"Our nest has roughly twenty members. If we killed a person every time we fed, it wouldn't take long for someone to find us. At the very least, the club where we find most of our meals would be closed due to all the deaths and disappearances. Correct me if I'm wrong, but that girl the other night was the first loss reported from that club. And as I said, her death was an accident." She nodded toward the shadows on her right.

A middle-aged man stepped forward. He had pale, nearly translucent skin and crew-cut, light-brown hair. He wore a dark-blue blazer over a gray shirt and black slacks. His gaze was down and his shoulders hunched, as though he was ashamed to be seen.

"This is Daryl," said the woman. "He killed your club victim."

Mira looked the man up and down. He wasn't the same vampire she'd followed tonight. "And you're just handing him over?"

"Not at all," said the woman. "But if I'm going to convince you not to eradicate my nest, I thought it prudent to explain the situation. Daryl here is a baby. He was turned barely a year ago. He was supposed to have backup in the alley when the mark arrived, but his watcher was . . . distracted. When the woman from the club arrived, Daryl lost control. By the time his partner showed up, the girl was drained beyond the point of recovery."

Daryl shrank in on himself. If there had been a large enough rock handy, Mira got the impression he would have crawled under it.

Mira sneered. "That's supposed to convince me you should be allowed to live?"

"It's supposed to convince you that what happened to the woman from the club was a mistake," she said. "We don't kill indiscriminately. This town has lost what, four, five children in the past week? Vampires are required to keep a low profile. If we had stolen those human youths for food, why would we be so sloppy about it?"

That gave Mira pause. A vampire's survival revolved around remaining hidden. Their very existence was a closely guarded secret. *Well, shit.*

"None of this changes the fact that you killed a person," Ty said.

"So did you," the lead vampire said.

"The girl from the club was an innocent," he countered. "The vampire we put down was trying to kill us."

"In self-defense," she said. "As Liam describes it, you attacked first."

"She was draining a human."

"Seo-yoon was a vampire for thirty-one years. She never killed anyone . . . ever."

Ice shot down Mira's spine and numbed her limbs. The face of the vampire whose energy she'd consumed filled her vision.

<She's clearly lying,> the demon said. <Who ever heard of a good vampire?>

Mira licked her lips and whispered, "Who ever heard of a good demon?"

The vampire at the altar narrowed her gaze at Mira. "We're not demons," she said. "And we're not the monsters y'all make us out to be. We're only doing what we must to survive."

She never killed anyone. . . . I'm *the monster.* The thought circled Mira's mind like a wasp, distracting her with its buzz and the threat of its repeated sting.

"Hey." Ty bumped her shoulder. "Snap out of it."

The woman at the altar lifted her hands away from Bembe and stepped forward with her empty palms raised. "As I see it, our nest has already paid for the death of the woman at the club. A life for a life." She took another step forward. "What I propose is a truce." She fixed her gaze on Mira. "Liam told me how Seo-yoon died. I don't know what you are, but I want no part in fighting you. Swear to me that you'll leave my nest in peace. In exchange, I'll release both hostages and share all we know about the missing children."

Chapter 21

TY

TY GLANCED AT MIRA, then quickly back to the vampire woman beside Bembe. Mira seemed distracted, staring into the middle distance. He wished he could ask her a few more questions about vampires, like whether they're bound to tell the truth like fae or how likely they were to keep their word. Barring that, he'd just have to go with his gut, which was telling him the woman standing in front of him did not want to fight. Of course, his gut had been wrong before . . . and the results had been catastrophic.

He looked at Mira again. This time she met his gaze. Her lips were drawn into a compressed line, and a crease folded the skin between her eyebrows, but she gave a single, subtle nod. She was on board. Child-killer info trumped vampire slaughter.

"Deal." Ty's voice rang through the empty church louder than he'd intended. The vampires definitely had him on edge.

"Good." The lead vampire smiled, but it didn't warm her expression. She focused her gaze on Mira. "Swear that you will not come after our nest."

Mira's jaw tightened. "I swear I won't hunt you so long as you aren't killing anyone." Her gaze flicked to the man who'd *accidentally* murdered Kendra Jackson. "Starting now."

The vampire woman huffed. "Good enough." She waved her hand, and another vampire stepped out of the shadows. It was the blond from the club's surveillance footage—the one who'd enthralled Kendra Jackson and sent her to her death. "Ava, tell them what you saw."

Ava shifted her feet and lifted her chin. She wore loose black pants and a tight navy-blue tank top. Her hair was tucked into a messy bun. Her pale skin practically glowed in the candlelight, and copper swirled in her hazel eyes. "I was sent to look into the cause of the missing kids after the second one was reported. We thought maybe someone was poaching in our territory. And we were right, but it wasn't another vampire." She rested her hands on her hips. "Since the first two victims hung in the same crowd, I tracked other members of that group, which led me to a house party in Coral Gables."

A chill rippled through Ty. "Charlotte Hernandez."

Ava pinned him with her copper-green gaze. "There was a fae stalking the party that night."

"What kind of fae?"

She shook her head. "I didn't stick around to find out."

"Fae hate vampires," Mira clarified. "They'll kill them on sight."

"Once we knew a fae was involved," said the woman beside Bembe, "we backed off. We did our best to stay out of its way so we wouldn't cross paths again."

"Can you tell us what they looked like?" Ty asked.

"Female," Ava said. "Long dark hair. That's about all I got before I bolted."

Ty looked at Mira. "Back to square one."

Mira let out a long, slow exhale. She pointed at Bembe with her blade. "Release the hostages."

"Once my people are clear," said the lead vampire. She nodded to Ava, who walked to the door that led to Bembe's office, opened it, and stuck her head inside. The vampire Ty had tussled with in the alley stepped out. His hand was wrapped around the upper arm of the woman from the club, who trailed him in a daze.

"How much does she remember?" Mira asked. Her voice was almost even, but Ty caught the slight hitch. She was worried about her secret.

"Nothing." The vampire leading her came to a stop at the edge of the pews. "We've erased everything after leaving the club. She thinks she got drunk and stumbled into the night on her own."

"We'll put her to bed," said the lead vampire. "The police can find her there in the morning, but they won't get anything useful out of her." She turned to Bembe. "We'll clear this one as well." She raised a hand.

"Stop." Mira stepped forward.

The vampire turned. She raised one eyebrow. "He knows us," she said. "This cannot be allowed."

"He's a priest," said Mira. "He keeps secrets all the time. He knows my secret and has kept it all my life. He can be trusted."

"By you, maybe. I don't have that luxury."

"It's all right, Mira." Bembe's voice was smooth and sure. "If my ignorance is what they require, so be it."

Mira shook her head. "He's the reason I'm here investigating in the first place. He has a right to know what's going on."

"Then by all means, tell him," said the vampire. "Just leave us out of it."

Mira took another step forward. "But—"

"Enough." Bembe raised a hand to forestall her. He met the vampire's gaze and nodded. "Do what you must."

The woman frowned, then nodded. "Thank you for understanding." She placed her fingertips against the priest's temple.

Father Bembe slumped to the floor. The woman caught his pajamas as he fell and lowered him the last few inches, so he didn't crack his head.

Ty's attention traveled from the unconscious priest to Mira. Her fists were clenched at her sides. Her blade shook. Her whole body vibrated with angry tension.

The vampire leader eyed Ty. Mellow bronze swirled in her gaze, pulling him in. "By all rights, we should wipe this one, too."

"Don't push your luck." Mira's words were a fierce growl that slashed at Ty's attention.

He blinked, clearing the fog that had been slowly filling his mind, only then realizing that the women were talking about him.

"He's mortal, and PTF to boot."

"He's my partner. Wipe him and our deal is off."

The vampire leader pursed her lips. "If he slips, the blood will be on your hands."

"I'll take that risk."

"Then on your head be it," said the woman. "We shall take our leave now. Make no move to follow."

Ty's gaze skipped between Mira and the vampires filing out of the church. *Please let this end smoothly.*

The male vampire from the club dragged his hostage, stumbling, out of the building. The leader was the last to leave. She waited until every one of her people was clear of the church before stepping off the altar. She circled around the side of the pews, giving Mira and Ty a wide berth, and kept her attention on Mira the entire time.

Mira turned to watch the woman leave, never exposing her back. Ty turned as well. He didn't really think the vampire would try anything at this point, but he wasn't sure if Mira's demon would take the shift in numbers as an invitation to attack, and he couldn't be certain how much sway the demon actually held. He tightened his grip on his weapons as his palms grew slick.

The vampire paused at the front door. "Good luck on your hunt. Here's hoping we never meet again." She stepped backward and pulled the heavy oak doors closed, sealing Ty and Mira inside the church.

Mira spun with the sound of the door hitting the jamb still echoing through the church and raced up the aisle to Bembe. The light from the flickering candle intensified, brightening the room, as though the presence of the vampires had held it in check up to that point. Ty recalled the unnatural blackness he'd faced in the alley and shivered.

He sheathed his sword, holstered his gun, and walked up the aisle.

Mira cradled Bembe's head on her arm. She had one fist twisted into the collar of his pajamas, as though she intended to shake him.

Ty knelt on Bembe's opposite side. The urge to console Mira was strong, but he didn't know what to say. He had no idea how a vampire mind-wipe worked, or what its effects might be. He dug his fingers into his thighs and festered in his silent inadequacy.

Bembe gasped and shuddered. He jerked in Mira's arms as though waking from a nightmare. His wide eyes rolled until his gaze settled on Mira. "What are you doing here?" He sat up and looked around the room, taking in the single burning candle, empty pews, and dark windows. "What am *I* doing here?" He touched his head, glanced at Ty, then twisted to look at Mira again. "What's going on?"

"What's the last thing you remember?" Mira's voice was pinched, but Ty couldn't tell if it was from worry or anger. At least the singsong lilt that only seemed to come out when the demon was running the show was absent.

"I locked up the church and rectory, got ready for bed, and went to sleep. Then I woke up here."

Ty cleared his throat. "Some bad people used you to get our undivided attention."

"Bad people?" A deep crease formed between Bembe's eyebrows. "Why can't I remember?"

"They cast a spell on you," said Mira. "They were practitioners."

Ty's gaze jumped to Mira as the lie left her lips. She glared at him as though daring him to contradict her. He swallowed.

"Are they responsible for the missing children?" Bembe asked.

Mira shook her head.

"But they did give us a new lead," added Ty.

Bembe swung his attention to Ty. His eyes were narrowed with focus. "What lead?"

Ty shot Mira a quick glance, but she was staring at her empty hands. Her expression was unreadable.

"The perpetrator is a fae."

"According to these practitioners you say are 'bad people?' And you believe them?"

Again Ty looked to Mira for help, but she seemed totally absorbed in her own thoughts. *How the hell am I supposed to explain this if we aren't going to tell Bembe about the vampires?*

"Well, we thought these people might have been responsible at first . . ." Ty shifted his position, taking the opportunity to look away from the piercing gaze of the priest. ". . . but they convinced us otherwise."

Bembe frowned, clearly underwhelmed by Ty's explanation, but he shifted his focus back to Mira. His frown grew deeper. He set a hand on her knee. "What troubles you, child?"

Mira closed her eyes. "I'm fine."

The tightness in her voice was gone, replaced by a hollow apathy that worried Ty even more. He was used to her irritation, her defensiveness, even her occasional playfulness. He'd never heard her sound empty.

"Is it these practitioners who have you upset?" Bembe asked, no more convinced by Mira's words than Ty was. "I know such encounters are hard on you." His gaze wandered the room, as though taking stock, before settling back on Mira. "Did you fight with them?"

"Some of them," Mira whispered. "But not here."

Bembe took a long inhale and let it out slowly. "Do you wish to make a confession?"

She shook her head, eyes still closed.

"If you took a life, I'm sure it was justified."

She crumpled even tighter. A tear glittered at the corner of her scrunched eye.

"You did what had to be done, Mira." Ty hadn't intended to speak, but seeing her in pain broke him. "That woman might not have been the one who"—he glanced at Bembe—"pulled the trigger, but the whole group was culpable. You saved the woman from the club. You saved me. You saved Gianna. We all would have died if you hadn't intervened."

"Except I was wrong. No one would have died. They weren't the monsters I assumed they were. The only murderer in that alley . . . was me."

"Maybe they didn't plan to kill anyone, but once they'd been found out, do you really think they would have hesitated to kill every one of us to cover their tracks? If you have to blame someone, blame me for charging in like an idiot."

"You were just covering Gianna's stupid ass." Mira finally opened her eyes. A little heat crept back into her voice. "Although, she wouldn't have been playing secret hero in the first place if not for you and your deal. So yeah, you can take the blame on that." She sat up a little straighter. "And after all your whining about teamwork and communication, you go charging in half-cocked and shoot our plan all to hell."

Ty shrugged, happy to take the verbal lashing if it got Mira back to her usual self. "What can I say? I'm a hypocrite."

She smiled. The candlelight glinted in her golden eye and flashed briefly across her teeth. Then her expression collapsed like the melting sides of the candle. "Reasons or no, I still killed her." She dropped her hand to her thigh and whispered, "Seo-yoon."

Ty pictured the thin line of blood under that hand, hidden by clothes and bandages. He recalled the metallic scent when he'd opened the truck door and interrupted her twisted little ritual. *What had the demon called it? Her penance.*

Mira was shutting down again, wallowing in her guilt. *Yeah, I know that path.* He gritted his teeth, recalling his own recent spiral into self-loathing. He knew from experience that comforting words and platitudes couldn't puncture that barrier, but anger . . . anger could burn through all manner of walls. "If you're so concerned about your sins, why not take the father here up on his offer? It would be a hell of a lot safer than the self-mutilation you've been inflicting. Or are you proud of your tallies?"

Heat flashed in her eyes. "How dare you?"

Bembe glanced from one to the other of them. "What are you talking about?"

"Go ahead and show him, Mira."

He reached toward her, and she slapped his hand away. "Back off!"

"What's the matter? Memorials are meant to be seen, right? To honor the dead? Otherwise, what's the point?" He lifted his palms. "Well? If you're not offering a memorial, why are you doing it?"

Mira twisted to the side and snarled, "You stay out of this."

Looks like the demon agrees with me. That thought made him a bit uncomfortable, but he pressed on. Mira wasn't looking pitiful anymore. She looked as if she wanted to rip out his beating heart and stomp it into the ground. *One last push should do it.*

"You know who else keeps tallies like that? Psychopaths and serial killers. They like to keep mementos of their work, like badges of honor. So which is it? Are they memorials or mementos?"

She sprang to her feet. "Neither."

He rose to meet her. "Then what are they?"

"None of your damned business, is what they are."

"What are they?" he pressed.

She took a step backward, shaking her head.

He closed the distance between them and grabbed her arms, giving her a little shake for emphasis, and shouted, "What are they?"

"They're my punishment!" She screamed the words into his face, and as she did, flames erupted from her skin.

Ty snatched his hands away, but not before the hair on his wrists was singed off. He smacked his smoking palms against his thighs with a curse. *Maybe I pushed a little too hard.*

"Mira!" Bembe's voice was smooth and cold as polished marble.

"I'm sorry." Mira took two stumbling steps away from the altar. She bumped a pew and reached out to steady herself, which left a semicircle of char on its edge. Tears streamed from her eyes but evaporated halfway down her cheeks. She took fast, labored breaths.

"Calm down." Bembe's words radiated authority despite his being in his pajamas.

All at once, Mira froze. Color leached out of her hair, widening the white stripe that was always there. The flames shrank, then died away completely. Wisps of steam rose off her clothes. When she looked up, both her eyes were solid gold.

"Sorry, Mira needs a minute." The lyrical purr of the demon accented Mira's voice.

"You're Mira's demon?" Bembe asked, his tone faltering for the first time.

Mira's nose scrunched. "When you say it like that, it sounds like she owns me. Let's just say I'm the being sharing her body."

"Do you have a name?"

She shook her head. "Names are a mortal concept."

Bembe frowned. "Then how do demons refer to each other?"

She tipped her head to one side and looked up, considering. "For those strong enough to have a sense of self within the Rift, it's more of a *me* versus *not me* scenario." She lowered her gaze back to the priest. "It's not like we have block parties to gossip about the neighbors."

This was the most Ty had ever heard the demon speak without Mira interjecting, save right after a feeding, when the surge of new energy made the demon stronger. He cleared his throat. "What's going on here? What have you done with Mira?"

The narrowed golden gaze settled on him. She put her hands on her hips. "Mira's fine, but while I've got uncontested control of the mouth, there are a few things I'd like to clear up, starting with your obvious discrimination against me."

"What?" Ty stiffened at the accusation. "I never—"

"You consistently blame me when shit goes sideways. Granted, I may not be the most stabilizing of influences, but Mira's got plenty of impulse control issues all on her own." She pointed to the char on the pew. "Case and point. So stop assuming every bad decision she makes is my fault."

"Sorry," Ty said, flabbergasted. "I hadn't realized you were offended."

"Secondly," the demon went on, steamrollering over Ty's apology, "What's with you suddenly refusing to sleep with us?"

Ty shot a glance at Bembe, then looked away. Heat crept into his cheeks. "I really don't think this is—"

"You were happy enough with our performance the first time, I could tell. But now you're all grossed out when we ask, so what gives?"

"Um . . . have you discussed this with Mira?"

"Yeah. She told me to stop asking, but I can tell she's into you, so I figure it's because she feels shitty when you shoot us down."

Guilt and elation did a little dance in Ty's chest. He hated that he'd hurt her with his rejection, but the news that Mira was attracted to him flamed the foolish spark of desire that he'd been unable to extinguish despite all logic screaming that a romantic relationship with his partner was a bad idea.

"If you're not interested, you're not interested. But if you're just chickening out because we're too much for you, you should at least have the balls to say so rather than acting all nice and caring, then shooting us down when we reciprocate. You're really feeding into Mira's whole 'I'm a monster, and nobody loves me' thing."

That last line, even spoken in the demon's mocking tone, stabbed an icepick through Ty's heart. "She's not a monster."

The demon crossed her arms, cocked her head, and glared at Ty. Dark lines were beginning to form beneath her eyes, spiderwebbing down her cheeks like black fractals. If the demon stayed in control much longer without a boost of outside power, Mira's physical body would deteriorate. He had to convince Mira to stop hiding behind her demon before the damage grew more severe.

"Neither of you are monsters," Ty amended.

"I tried to explain this to Mira when she was a child," Bembe said. "While her actions may seem evil when viewed in isolation, she is actually creating good in the world. She is serving God's will. The lives she takes are to protect the innocent, or at the very least, to set them free."

The golden gaze closed for a moment. Her weight shifted, as though she were listening. "Mira says, 'Not this time'."

Ty stepped forward, but stayed just out of reach, fearing the damage Mira or her demon might do if he pressed too hard again. "Killing that"— he caught himself just in time—"that person in the alley was no different than killing the rifter at the train yard. You stopped a dangerous person before they could hurt more people."

Mira's eyes opened. They were still gold. The puppet lines marking her possession were growing thicker. She gestured toward the space where the vampire leader had stood. Dark lines traced her fingernails. "Not according to tonight's visitor."

Ty took a deep breath and exhaled. If they believed that the vampire Mira had killed in the alley had never murdered anyone, then Mira was right . . . she'd killed an innocent woman. But that vampire *had* been draining the woman from the club, and her companion had flung Gianna hard enough to kill. There was no way Mira, or anyone, would have believed that situation to be anything but a fight to the death. How could he convince her that her actions in the alley didn't make her a monster?

"Do you think I'm a monster?" he whispered.

Mira set her hand against her chest. "I don't really use that word."

"I'm talking to Mira."

"Oh." She paused. "No. She doesn't."

"I've killed."

The golden gaze didn't waver.

Of course the demon wouldn't think much of killing. He just hoped Mira was listening. "I killed during the war, and they called me a soldier. I killed for the PTF, and they called me an agent. I killed as a cop, and they called me a hero. But the titles don't erase the blood on my hands. If you're a monster . . . so am I."

Bembe stepped shoulder to shoulder with Ty. "I encouraged you to walk this path. I set young Maritza in your sights. I aimed and fired you like a gun right here in this very church. The stain may be gone, but I see it every day. Her death is on my conscience as much as yours. Perhaps more. So if you are a monster for your actions . . . so am I."

"In the end, it doesn't matter what you call yourself. All that matters is how you live with yourself. If you truly believe what you're doing is evil, stop. But I agree with Father Bembe. I believe you're a force of good in this world. That's why I wanted to work with you."

Mira's eyes fluttered. When she met his gaze, her right eye was brown.

The white in her hair faded back to a thin stripe. "I didn't even hesitate when I killed that woman in the alley."

"I would have made the same call in your position," Ty said. "Maybe we made a mistake. We're human. It's bound to happen sometimes. You can't let it define you."

A tear streaked Mira's cheek, flowing down the black lightning paths of her puppet lines. "How much good balances out how much bad? When a normal person makes a mistake, they apologize or pay a fine. When I make a mistake, people die. Even when I do the *right* thing people die. How can that not define me?"

"The night we first met, I was drinking alone at a bar. You took the second drink on the counter. That drink was meant for my friend, my partner, Jamal. It would have been his birthday, but he wasn't there to drink with me, and that's my fault. I made a mistake. He died." Saying those words out loud was like ripping the scab off a still-healing wound and pouring salt inside.

"You made a bad call," she said, "but you didn't kill him."

He looked at Bembe, recalling his earlier words of solidarity. "I didn't pull the trigger, but I aimed the gun. None of us exists in isolation. Every outcome is a mess of too many variables to count, too many choices leading to a single moment in time. So how can one person be responsible?"

"Are you telling me you don't feel guilty about Jamal's death?"

He shook his head. "The guilt doesn't go away. I just found a way to move past it."

She raised an eyebrow.

"Jamal's dream was to help people who couldn't help themselves. I want to help as many people as I can."

"His dream became your dream."

"Something like that. And working with you, I know I can help a lot of people."

"I've been telling myself all along that the lives I take are for the greater good . . . but sometimes those words lose all meaning." She set her hand over her chest, pinching the medallion beneath the fabric.

"I've never thought that particular saint appropriate for you," Bembe said. "You are not a lost cause."

The corner of her mouth lifted. "And yet . . . hopeless seems the task."

"Wanna know what helps?" said Ty.

She met his gaze and nodded.

"It's a cliché, but talking to someone who understands will help." He glanced at Bembe and shrugged. "I may not be a priest, but I know what it's like to carry a heavy past."

"I'll think about it." She looked away. "And thanks."

Ty shifted his weight, thinking back to the demon's challenge that he clarify his feelings toward Mira. *If only they were clearer to me . . . but I do owe her, owe both of them, an explanation.* "About what the demon said earlier—"

Mira raised a hand to stop him, her posture sagged with fatigue. "Not tonight. Let's just clear this case and see where we stand."

He nodded. "At least we've figured out who our culprit *isn't*. That's something. And we've verified that this is a paranatural crime."

She rubbed her temples. "So not *quite* square one."

"You look totally wiped," Ty said. "And is there anything we can do about your. . . ." He indicated the black around her fingernails.

Mira spread her fingers and stared as though seeing them for the first time. "*Coño.*"

"This has happened before." Ty did his best to sound reasonable. "How did you get rid of them then?"

She looked at him. Panic danced in her eyes. "That's not gonna fly."

He frowned. "Why not?"

"Feeding." She lowered her hands. "Feeding is how I get rid of them. I dumped too much energy into Gianna. Now the demon doesn't have enough fuel to heal me without an influx from somewhere other than my own body."

Ty started to recoil but stopped himself. *Showing my disgust will only strengthen Mira's messed-up self-image of being less than human.*

Mira turned away, her shoulders slumping. "I can wear gloves and glasses. Lots of rifters do that to pass for human."

Shit. He'd been too slow to hide his reaction. Squashing the mental image of Mira sucking the life out the rifter at the train yard, Ty took a step forward. "If you need energy—"

Bembe grabbed Ty's arm and stepped in front of him. "Take it from me."

"What?" Ty and Mira spoke in unison, staring at the priest.

"You both need to be at the top of your game if you're going to get to the bottom of Ramon's disappearance. That means you need energy, Mira." He glanced at Ty. "And Ty looks as if he's already been beaten half to death. I'm the logical choice."

Relief surged through Ty at the priest's logic, followed closely by a wave of shame at his own cowardice. *I've seen what the rifters we track look like when she's done with them. I know she wouldn't go that far, but still. . . .* A second wave of shame washed over him. *No wonder she thinks I don't trust her. She's right.*

"You don't have to do this," Mira said.

"I'm well aware, but I want to. I can't find Ramon's killers or bring them to justice. But this I *can* do, so let me do it."

She nodded. "Then you'd better sit down."

Bembe settled on the charred pew. "Will it hurt?" To his credit, his voice was as sure as ever.

"I'm not sure," she admitted. "I've never talked to anyone after doing this. Best scenario, you'll probably feel like you've got the flu for a few days."

Ty sat on the bench across the aisle from Bembe, close enough to watch the show, but not so close as to be a part of it.

Mira knelt in front of the priest and placed her palm against his cheek. She took a deep breath and let it out slowly. Bembe shuddered.

Ty squinted. Nothing seemed to be happening.

Bembe's breath came quicker. He gritted his teeth.

Mira took another deep breath. The puppet lines under her eyes withdrew like a lightning strike played in reverse, racing back to its source.

Bembe grunted.

The tips of Mira's fingers returned to their natural color—pale brown around trimmed nails.

Bembe's eyes fluttered closed. He slumped forward. Mira caught him before he could fall off his seat. Sweat slicked Bembe's skin, which had taken on a chalky pallor, and his breathing was labored.

Mira hugged him. "Thank you."

Ty studied Bembe's sickly features. "This is what you did to the guards when you escaped custody in Baltimore, isn't it?"

Mira nodded.

He'd been present but unconscious at that time. Both men had ended up in the hospital with a serious case of anemia, and Ty had hated her for harming them during her escape, but they'd both made full recoveries. *Bembe will be fine.* He let out a breath he hadn't realized he'd been holding. "Should we take him to a hospital?"

Mira shook her head. "I didn't take that much. Let's just put him in bed. He'll be fine after a bit of rest." She nestled under Bembe's arm and straightened to lift the limp priest.

Ty positioned himself under Bembe's other arm, sharing the weight. "We should get some rest, too, for whatever's left of the night. We can pick up the fae thread tomorrow."

Chapter 22

MIRA

THE POUNDING ON her door matched the pounding in her head as Mira startled awake. She threw off her comforter and rolled out of bed. Her knees hit the floor at the same time as her feet. Her hands were a second behind. She sat back and rubbed one hand across her sleep-crusted eyes. The bedroom door burst open.

Mira's right hand slipped under her pillow by instinct, clutching the hilt of her kukri and drawing the blade in one smooth motion. She barely managed to stop the arc of the blade before it bit into the side of her tia Marta's neck.

Marta's eyes went wide. She stumbled back, colliding with a small wooden dresser to the side of the door.

"Put that away." Abuela flapped a hand at Mira from the open door-way.

Mira sheepishly lowered her knife to the floor.

"And you. . . ." Abuela turned on Marta, somehow managing to look severe despite the large curlers wobbling in her hair. "I told you not to barge in like that. Honestly, it's like no one in this house has any manners these days." She crossed herself over the pink paisley of her nightgown, apparently taking the lack of manners in her household as a far worse transgression than the near decapitation of her eldest daughter.

<Ha! I love your family.> The demon chortled. <Stuff like this never happens when we stay in motels.>

Mira rose to her feet. "Sorry, tia, you startled me."

"Who sleeps with a knife under their pillow?"

<Who doesn't?>

Marta waved the words away as soon as she said them. "It doesn't matter." She strode forward and grabbed Mira's arms, giving her a little shake.

This close, Mira could see that Marta's eyes were red-rimmed. She wore no makeup, and her hair was tousled. *No self-respecting woman raised by abuela would leave the house in such a state unless something was seriously wrong.*

<So the possession of practical protection is looked down on, but lack of face paint is a cause for concern? Talk about backward.>

"You're a detective now, right?" Marta gave Mira another little shake.

<Seriously, with all the craziness that happens in this world, shouldn't everyone sleep with a knife?>

Let it go.

"You have to help me." Marta shouted the words into Mira face.

<I'll bet Ty sleeps with a knife.>

"Drop it!" Mira brought her hands up in impotent defense from the verbal onslaught, knocking Marta away in the process.

Marta stiffened, her bloodshot eyes going wide again.

<Fine, whatever. But makeup over knife seems like skewed priorities. That's all I'm saying.>

Abuela crossed herself again and opened her mouth, probably with another comment on the lack of manners being shown in her house, but Mira beat her to the punch.

"Sorry, tia." Mira rubbed her arms. The older woman's grip had been tight enough to bruise. "Please, just calm down and tell me what's going on. What do you need help with?"

"It's Caridad." She wrung her hands into the bunched fabric of her cream-colored blouse. "She's missing."

Abuela gasped.

Dread washed through Mira, clearing some of the cobwebs from her brain.

The demon perked up. <I told you we should have questioned her before.>

Not now! To Marta she said, "Since when?"

"She wasn't in her bed this morning, and the window was open. Someone must have come in and taken her." Marta twisted the fabric of her shirt as though trying to wring water from it. "Do you think it's the same person who took the other children from her school? It must be, right? Tell me you know who it is. Tell me you know where they took my daughter." Marta's voice gained in pitch and tempo as she spoke. The final word came out as a breathy squeak.

<She's losing it,> the demon said flatly.

Her daughter's missing. Of course she's upset.

<You should smack her.>

Mira recoiled. *What? Why?*

<That's what they do in movies when people get hysterical. Give her a good smack. She'll thank you.>

No, she most definitely would not, and abuela would probably disown me. She shook her head. "What else can you tell me about the scene?" Mira asked. "Were there signs of a struggle? Was anything missing?"

Marta shook her head. "Everything was tidy. Clothes in the hamper. Books on the desk. Her bed was made."

<Wait. Her bed was made? What kind of kidnapper makes their victim's bed after snatching them?>

"I didn't see her purse," Marta continued. "Maybe whoever took her took that, too."

Mira winced, a picture forming in her mind. "What's outside Caridad's window?"

"It leads onto the roof."

"And how tall is your house?"

Marta shrugged. "A single story."

<Teenage girl, Saturday night. . . .>

Yeah. Mira set a hand on her aunt's shoulder, her earlier panic easing. "Is it possible Caridad just went out . . . on her own?"

Confusion flitted across Marta's features, then her expression twisted with anger as the accusation sank in. She shook Mira's hand off. "Cari is a *good* girl. *She* would never do anything to hurt her family."

The demon rippled through Mira's awareness like a stone tossed in a pool. <That was low.>

Mira took a breath, forcing her own anger aside, but she couldn't entirely dislodge the image of her mother that Marta's words had conjured. "Maybe not intentionally, but—"

"No." Marta straightened to her full height, which wasn't all that impressive, since her swollen stomach made her appear almost as wide as she was tall. "Cari was taken. She had to have been."

"Come to the table, Marta." Abuela took her daughter by the shoulders and steered her out the door. "We'll discuss this over breakfast."

<What are you gonna do?>

Mira pinched the bridge of her nose. The pounding in her head had grown worse with her aunt's yelling. Based on what Marta described, the most likely scenario was that Cari had snuck out on her own. But with so many kids going missing and a fae on the loose, Mira couldn't discount the possibility of foul play. *We'll look into it.*

<You don't actually think the teenager with the tidy bed and missing purse was kidnapped, do you?>

Probably not, but there's no harm in checking. We can grab Ty and discuss ways to flush out our fae culprit while we track Cari. If she just slipped out for a night with friends, she shouldn't be too hard to find. Hell, she might come home on her own by the time we finish breakfast. In the meantime, we'll do what we can to calm Marta.

Mira pulled on a pair of jeans and a clean shirt and followed the older women down the hall. She glanced at Ty's closed door.

How did that commotion not wake him up?

<Maybe he *is* awake and wisely decided to hide in his room from the noisy women outside.>

Well it's time to come out. I don't want to have to go over all this again when I explain why we're visiting my aunt's house this morning. She rapped her knuckles against the door.

"He's out," abuela called over her shoulder. "He left first thing this morning. Said to tell you he'd gone to the hospital to check on Gianna."

<So much for that plan.>

Mira shuffled the rest of the way down the hall, trying to order her thoughts. The throbbing ache behind her eyes made it hard to think. The energy she'd taken from Father Bembe had been enough to erase the visible marks of her possession, but she hadn't dared take any more. Which meant no extra energy to waste on things like headaches or sleep deprivation. She dropped into one of the wooden chairs, propped her elbows on the table, and rested her head in her hands.

"Sit up straight," abuela chided as she settled Marta in another chair and headed for the kitchen.

Mira suppressed a groan, but straightened in her seat.

<What is this mortal obsession with sitting straight? Is it a status symbol or something?>

Mira chuckled. *Or something.*

"*Aqui tienes, amor.* This will help." Abuela set a steaming mug of café con leche on the table in front of Mira and patted her shoulder.

"*Gracias.*"

She set another in front of Marta, then took her seat. "Now, Marta, why don't you tell us exactly what happened with Cari."

Marta took a long, slow sip of her coffee. The tension in her shoulders eased a bit, and her expression softened, though the lines of worry around her mouth and eyes didn't smooth. "Cari went to bed a bit early last night. She said she wasn't feeling well. I checked her temperature, which was fine, so I assumed it was from all the emotional strain she's been dealing with lately." She stared into the mug cradled between her fingers. "This morning, I popped my head in early to see how she was doing and ask if she wanted me to make waffles, but her bed was empty." Her knuckles turned white on the coffee mug.

Abuela reached out to pat Marta's arm. "Mira will find her."

<Excuse me? Says who?>

I was going to do it anyway, Mira reminded.

<But we haven't even discussed pricing for this job yet.>

She's family.

<So we'll give her a discount. We still gotta eat.>

No, you don't.

<Fine. *You* have to eat.>

Abuela's been giving us free room and board.

<For now. Once we leave, we'll have practical concerns again. You can't afford to keep doing jobs pro bono.>

Mira shook her head. *We've been watching too many courtroom dramas.*

<I'm just saying, your grandma shouldn't go volunteering us without asking. We set our own terms. That's the whole point of being a freelance investigator.>

I'm going to look for Caridad for free. Those are the terms. Happy?

<Now that we've discussed it among ourselves, yes.>

Mira chuckled. When she looked up, she found both her relatives staring at her. Heat crept up her neck. *Was I talking out loud?*

<How should I know?>

She cleared her throat and took a drink to cover her discomfort.

"Well?" Marta prompted.

Mira looked from one woman to the other. "Well, what?"

Marta frowned. "Will you find my Caridad?"

"Oh, yeah," Mira said. "I mean, I'll do my best."

Marta clasped her hands together over her ample bosom and looked up as though sending a silent prayer. She returned her gaze to Mira. "Thank you."

Mira shifted in her seat. "I know you don't think Cari left on her own." Marta stiffened, and Mira rushed on. "But we need to actually eliminate that possibility first. Is there anywhere Cari might go, a friend she might contact?"

Marta's gaze slid down and to the side. "I called her best friend as soon as I discovered Cari was gone."

<So she *did* suspect teenage rebellion.> The demon's words carried an air of satisfaction, and it was all Mira could do to keep the expression from showing.

"No one answered," Marta continued. "But that's not terribly odd. They're probably getting ready for church."

<Or pretending not to hear the phone ring because they're harboring a runaway and didn't want to face Mom's wrath.>

The reminder that it was Sunday brought to mind an image of Father Bembe, sweating and shivering, as she and Ty tucked him into bed last night. *I hope he's got someone who can deliver this morning's sermon in his place.*

<Stubborn as he is, he'll probably have someone prop him against the lectern and do it himself.>

"Does Cari's friend live near you?" Mira asked.

Marta nodded. "A few blocks away."

"Then we'll swing by their house on the way to yours, see if we can catch them before they leave for church. Once we know for sure Cari isn't out with friends, I'll see what I can learn from her room."

Marta pushed back her chair and rose.

"I'll whip together a couple breakfast sandwiches for you to take," abuela said. "To keep your strength up while you investigate."

Marta's forehead crinkled as she looked back and forth between her niece and mother, clearly torn between worry for her daughter and fear of suggesting Mira skip breakfast.

"Just toast is fine," Mira said, rising from her seat.

Marta exhaled in relief.

Abuela shuffled into the kitchen, shaking her head and muttering about proper eating habits. She toasted two slices of bread and slathered them with butter and guava jelly. When she handed the plate to Mira, she leveled her brown stare at her granddaughter and said, "Bring Cari home safe."

"I will," Mira promised.

Abuela glanced at Marta and pitched her voice lower. "If she *is* out with friends, she's going to get a piece of my mind for making us worry so."

I hope that's all this is. Mira downed the remainder of her coffee, traded the mug for the plate, grabbed her shoes, and followed Marta out the door.

Dark-gray clouds hung low in the sky, blotting out the morning sun. The air was heavy with the threat of rain. Mira settled into the passenger seat of Marta's white SUV and worked on her toast while they headed to Caridad's friend's house.

Despite the lack of red flags and her sincere hope that Cari's absence was a simple case of teenage thoughtlessness, worry over her cousin's disappearance strengthened with each passing block. Was Cari's connection to the missing kids just a coincidence, the natural effect of a small, close-knit community . . . or had Mira overlooked something? The thought made her insides squirm like a bait bucket as doubt plucked at her heart.

<There was no sign of a struggle,> the demon reminded her, picking up on her thoughts.

We don't know how the kids are being taken yet. What if it's not a physical kidnapping? What if it's a mental thing? A strong fae could trick a person into walking right into their arms. We saw that at the club with the vampires. Maybe this fae is hunting in a similar way. She watched the single-story houses slide past her window, each trimmed yard and painted fence promising that nothing bad could ever happen in such a pleasant community. *I won't be like Detective Moretti, assuming all those missing kids are just runaways.*

She turned her attention to Marta. "Tell me a little more about Cari," she said around a bite of toast. "You mentioned emotional strain."

Marta's grip tightened on the wheel. "She was scared."

"In general, or did she have a specific reason to be afraid?"

Marta shot her an incredulous look. "Children from her school are disappearing. Isn't that reason enough?"

"You said she was supposed to go to a dance with Ramon, right? So they must have known each other pretty well. Had you met him?"

"We knew him from church. He's a good boy."

"Do you recall him acting strange or being afraid before he went missing?"

Marta shook her head. "He seemed happy. Well, as happy as he could be in his situation. His mother is ill, you see, and he doesn't have much family nearby. I know Father Bembe had taken an interest, bless him."

Mira nodded. "He's the one who asked me to come."

"That makes sense. He's always watched over our community. Although I'm surprised he knew you were a detective now."

<"Detective" makes you sound like a cop.>

"How did he even get in touch with you?"

<Detective Fuentes,> the demon said in a mock-British accent. <Ooh, I kinda like that.>

Mira rubbed her forehead. "He sent me an email."

"Why does Father Bembe have your email address when I don't? Does abuela have it?" Marta shot her an accusatory look. "Does Luis?"

"Abuela was the only one who had it, just in case of emergencies. Father Bembe got it from her."

Marta settled back, seemingly placated.

Mira finished her toast and licked her fingers clean. She set the empty plate on the floor. Marta would get it back to abuela. "Did Cari know the other victims well?"

Marta shrugged. "Olivia was on the cheerleading team, but she never came around the house or anything. I don't think they were particularly good friends. Ronnie is the only person Cari really hangs out with." Marta glanced at Mira. "Ronnie's short for Veronica. She's the friend we're going to see."

Mira nodded. "And the other one? The track star?"

Marta shook her head. "I never met him, but from the way Cari talked about him sometimes, I think she might have had a bit of a crush. Ronnie would know."

<Doesn't seem like there's much to tie your cousin to the other victims other than attending the same school. I'm still betting on a wild night out with friends. She's probably at Ronnie's with a hangover right now.>

That gave Mira another thought. "Did Cari ever go to parties? Specifically, did she go to one about a week ago in Coral Gables?"

Marta narrowed her eyes. She eased to a stop at a traffic light and looked at Mira. "She and Ronnie went out last weekend. They said they were going to meet some teammates at a pizza parlor, but when I did laundry the next day, Cari's shirt smelled like alcohol."

"Did you ask her about it?"

Marta's gaze turned sad and returned to the road. "No. Like I said, she's been having a rough time lately. I just thought. . . ."

<Teenage rebellion.>

"We're here." Marta pulled to the curb in front of a palm tree-lined yard. The grass was shaggy compared to its neighbors, and the hedges were growing through the bars of the iron fence that ringed the property. The house itself was a squat, blue box with yellow shutters. White curtains blocked any view inside.

Mira unsnapped her seat belt and climbed out. *Please, please, please be here, Cari.* She squinted up at the gray sky, then followed Marta, who was already lifting the latch on the property gate. The hinge elicited a high-pitched screech of metal rubbing on metal.

Marta frowned. "Amelia, Ronnie's mother, is having a hard time maintaining this place on her own," she said apologetically, as though the squeaky gate somehow reflected on her by association.

"She's a single mom?" Mira asked.

"She is now." Marta crossed herself as she walked up the path. "Her husband died not long ago. And poor Ronnie, she was there when it happened." She stepped onto the concrete porch and rang the doorbell, then smoothed her hair as though just realizing the state of her appearance. "This town has had too many tragedies lately. It's almost as if we're cursed." She shuddered and crossed herself again.

Mira waited beside her aunt for a full minute. "Could they be at church already?"

Marta glanced over her shoulder. She pointed to a small red Jetta. "That's Amelia's car, there."

"Does Ronnie have a car?"

Marta shook her head and pressed the doorbell button again. "Amelia?" She knocked on the white door.

Mira tried to peek into the front window, but the curtains were closed tight. Even this close she couldn't find a gap. She gently pushed Marta aside and wiggled the doorknob.

<Should we break a window?>

Let's try to handle this with a little more care. If the poor woman just got a ride to church, I don't want her to come home to property damage.

She knelt and pulled out two of the straight pins jammed into the sole of her sneaker near the heel.

"What are those doing there?" Marta asked, as Mira bent one of the pins.

"Hiding." Mira slipped the pins into the lock.

"Are you . . .?" Marta covered her abdomen as though protecting her unborn child from this criminal influence. She turned, swiveling her head to look up and down the street, seemingly convinced the police would come tearing around the corner, sirens blaring, to arrest her at any moment.

The lock popped. Mira straightened the pins, pushed them back into the soft rubber under her heel, and turned the knob. She set a hand on Marta's shoulder.

The older woman jumped. She spun and stared wide-eyed at the open door. Her expression wavered between horrified and impressed. "Do you do this a lot?"

"Only when necessary," Mira assured her.

<Yeah. Breaking windows is much faster.>

Mira stepped inside. The front room was smaller than abuela's, but it felt welcoming, with two armchairs, three end tables, and a loveseat. A grandfather clock ticked in one corner, marking the seconds with a brass pendulum. Dust coated the glass.

<You smell that?>

She sniffed. Stale air tickled her nose. *Mildew and . . . oh no.*

Marta pushed in behind Mira. "Hello? Amelia? Are you here? It's Marta."

Mira turned to her aunt. "Maybe you should wait outside."

Marta waved her off and moved deeper into the house. "If anyone *is* here, it will be better if they see me first. Me, they know. You . . . not so much."

Mira bit her lower lip and hurried after her aunt.

<Something died here.>

I smell it.

<Recently.>

"I know," Mira snapped.

Marta frowned at her. "Don't you get short with me just because you've made yourself a stranger. Whose fault is that?"

Mira stepped in front of Marta, blocking the path to the kitchen with her body. "I need to examine the scene. Please, stay here."

"Examine for what? Cari isn't here. Just like I said she wouldn't be." She waved her arms. "Nobody's here. And we shouldn't be either. We should be out looking for Cari, like I said from the start."

"Please, tia, just trust me. Wait here while I look around."

Marta pursed her lips. "I don't like the idea of you poking through Amelia's things while she's out. And that smell!" She waved a hand in front of her nose. "She must have forgotten to take out the garbage. She'll be mortified to have us see her home in such a state."

"I think she'll forgive me," said Mira, grateful that her aunt didn't have the experience to recognize the putrid odor as more than old trash.

Marta crossed her arms, using her stomach as a shelf. "Fine. But be quick, and don't mess anything up."

Mira waited for her aunt to settle into one of the armchairs before turning to the kitchen. The sink was stacked with food-crusted dishes. Take-out boxes and Styrofoam containers propped open the lid of the trash. Flies buzzed around a few pieces of browning fruit in a bowl on the table.

<I take back every bad thing I ever said about your obsessive cleaning.>

I can't imagine anyone tia Marta is friends with letting their house go like this, grieving or not.

<Unless she's the source of the rot. Being dead is a pretty good excuse for falling behind on housework.>

Mira caught a whiff of moldy banana as she passed the table. She wrinkled her nose. "She'd have to have been gone a while for things to get this bad. And what about Ronnie? Cari said the girl dropped her off at abuela's house yesterday, so clearly *she's* still around."

"Are you speaking to me, dear?" Marta called from the other room.

"No, tia. Just thinking out loud."

"Be careful, dear. People might think you're . . . well. . . ."

Mira balled her fists. "Like my mother?"

The silence from the front room was deafening.

Mira continued her inspection. The back of the kitchen led into a dining room. The large table had only three chairs around one end. Dust clouded the polished surface. The dining room led into a central hallway with three other doors. Mira tipped her chin and sniffed again. She turned toward the scent of decay.

She set one hand over her Saint Jude pendant. *Please let it not be Cari.*

She grabbed the doorknob for the room at the end of the hall and twisted.

The curtains in the master bedroom did an admirable job of blocking out the daylight, dim as it was. Mira flipped on the light switch and scanned the room. A queen-sized bed. A dresser. A night stand. A wardrobe. A desk. One door, most likely leading to an attached bathroom.

No obvious dead body.

<But this is definitely where the dead smell is coming from.>

Agreed. Mira circled the room, looking for any signs of violence.

<There.> The demon nudged Mira's awareness, drawing her attention to what looked like a dead mouse near one of the bedposts.

Mira crouched. She took a pen off the desk and flipped the furry mass over.

<That's not a mouse.>

Mira choked back her gag reflex.

<It's hair.>

Mira looked at the bloody, gray-black hair.

<Still attached to a bit of scalp.>

Please stop describing it.

<I'm cataloging evidence. Isn't that what we're supposed to be doing?>

Mira stood up with a sigh. *Since this is the mom's room, and there's gray mixed with the black, I think it's safe to say that's Amelia's hair.*

<What do you suppose happened to the rest of her?>

Mira opened the door to the bathroom. The smell of decay was overwhelmed by the stinging scent of bleach. Mira wrinkled her nose and glared at the shiny, white porcelain tub. "Looks like we're dealing with a tidy criminal after all."

Mira walked back through the bedroom and into the hall.

<But the mom would have been older. She doesn't fit the pattern.>

Maybe the killer came after Ronnie, and her mom got in the way.

<Do you think the daughter is dead, too?>

Pushing down her dread, Mira opened the next door. Colorful posters of indie bands covered the walls. A fuzzy purple chair shaped like half an egg suspended by macrame hung in one corner. The desk was a mess of books and papers, and Mira was weirdly relieved to see the crumpled covers on the bed.

There were two picture frames on the nightstand. One was silver trimmed with pink flowers, the other was face down, as though the room's occupant hadn't wanted to see the picture but was unwilling to actually get rid of it. The upright frame held a photo of Cari and a dark-haired girl of about the same age. Both wore cheerleader uniforms. They had their arms around each other and looked to be laughing. Mira squinted at the second girl. She'd seen her on the athletic field when she and Ty had visited the school. The nagging itch she'd felt in her mind that day came back. "Does she look familiar to you?"

The demon shrugged. <We saw her two days ago, so yeah.>

Mira rolled her eyes and lifted the second frame. This one held a family portrait—a middle-aged man and woman with a dark-haired child of about twelve between them.

<Is that . . .?>

Mira darted out of the room, the photo clutched in her hand.

Marta was sitting where Mira had left her, softly humming to herself. She startled when Mira ran into the room.

Mira thrust the photo at Marta. "Is that Ronnie with her parents?"

Marta looked at the picture. "When she was younger, but yes."

Mira pointed to the man. "Her father was eaten by alligators in the Everglades two weeks ago. All they recovered was his arm."

Marta nodded, a deep frown marring her features.

"And Ronnie was there when it happened."

Again, Marta nodded.

Mira twisted the picture to look at it dead-on. It was the exact image used in the news article she'd read . . . and dismissed as unrelated. But what if she was wrong?

Mira's thoughts were a storm in her mind. The human-like bite marks

Ty had described on Lucas's body alongside those of an alligator. Ronnie's missing mother, who'd let her house go to pot, and seemed to be the victim of foul play despite not fitting the kidnapper's profile. The vampire's description of the fae at the party where the college girl went missing—a woman with long, dark hair. Cari's seeming connection to so many victims. Too many coincidences . . . all centered around Ronnie.

"I'm sorry, tia, but you were right to be worried. I don't think Cari and Ronnie are just goofing off, and I don't think Amelia is at church." Still staring at the picture, Mira pulled the cell phone from her back pocket and called Ty.

He picked up on the second ring. "Hey, Mi—"

"Where are you?"

"At the hospital. Didn't your grandma give you my message?"

"Get back to the house, now." Mira was having trouble keeping her voice even. "We're going hunting."

Chapter 23

MIRA

CARS LINED THE STREET in front of abuela's property, forcing Marta to park three houses up.

<Looks like your grandma's throwing another party.>

I have a bad feeling about this.

As soon as Marta pulled to the curb, Mira jumped out and jogged up the street, leaving her aunt to waddle after. The storm clouds had turned mid-morning to twilight. As Mira raced back to the house, the first fat drop of rain splashed against her wrist. Another landed on her head. She shivered as the cold liquid found its way through her hair to tickle her scalp. By the time she reached abuela's porch, a handful of dark polka dots had blossomed on the sidewalk. The noise of conversation drifted through an open window in the front room, but all the voices stopped when Mira opened the door. Then they came down on her like an avalanche.

"Did you find her?" abuela demanded.

"Why didn't you tell us you were hunting the kidnapper?" Carlos asked.

"Where's Marta?" said Luis.

Rafael wrung his hands. "Should we call the police?"

Ignoring the bombardment of overlapping questions, Mira zeroed in on her grandmother, who'd touched up her hair and makeup and was now wearing a lace-trimmed teal dress fit for church. "Why did you call them?"

"A family member is missing." Abuela lifted her chin. "They have a right to know."

"We came to help," said Rafael.

"Sophia took all the kids to Marta's," said Carlos. "She and Tony will look after them and be there in case Cari comes home or calls."

"The rest of us will help look for Caridad," finished tio Luis.

Marta pushed in behind Mira, huffing and puffing, one hand clutched to her abdomen, the other holding an umbrella she'd taken the time to unfurl. Luis hurried forward as Marta folded and hung the damp umbrella. He guided his sister to a chair.

Everyone looked at Mira, as though expecting her to start handing out assignments. "Look, I understand you're all worried about Cari, but this is a serious investigation that could, and probably will, get very dangerous. Ty and I will handle it. You should all go home."

There was a moment of silence as the group took a collective breath, then Mira was bombarded by arguments that blurred and blended into a wall of white noise loud enough to drown out the mounting patter of rain against the roof.

Mira covered her ears.

Abuela turned on her children and made a *hush* gesture. The room fell instantly silent. She faced Mira. "We want to help."

Mira ran a hand over her frizzed hair and let out an exasperated breath. "I understand, but I've got a better chance of saving Cari on my own."

"Except you're not on your own. Cari is family, and so are you."

"Which is why you need to trust that I'll take care of her."

"And you need to trust us to help. Family is stronger together."

<I see where you get your stubborn streak.>

Mira groaned. *How can I convince them to stay out of this?*

<Maybe if you told them you're a kick-ass rifter who does this kind of stuff all the time. . . .>

Not helpful. Out loud she said, "I don't want any of you getting hurt."

"I feel the same," said abuela. "And that includes you." She stared at her granddaughter for a full minute while Mira fought the urge to look away from her scrutiny. The matriarch glanced at her children, then nodded as though coming to some kind of decision. "I know why you think you must do this on your own, why you've always believed that, but you're wrong." She stepped forward and set her palm against Mira's cheek. "Don't you think it's time you stop hiding from your family?"

A peal of thunder shook the house. The patter of rain upon the roof became a drumroll as the storm cut loose. Mira took a step back. "What are you—"

"I'm no fool, Mira. I hear what Maria screams in her nightmares. I saw how you were changed when you came back to us after Detroit. Then there was the incident at your school, and. . . ." She shook her head. "When you ran away at thirteen, did you think I just shrugged my shoulders and said, 'Who cares where she went or why she left?'"

Mira looked down, ashamed of the worry she'd caused. She'd been ashamed even as she caused it, but there'd been no other way. *I did it to keep them safe.*

"I had the entire family out looking for you. I was ready to turn this whole city upside down. It was Father Bembe who convinced me not to involve the police. He told me you'd been called upon by God. That, as difficult as it was, I must let you walk the path laid out before you and have faith that you would someday come back to me." She gave Mira a sad smile. "I had hoped you would eventually choose to confide in me yourself, but with Cari in danger, there's no more time for delicacy." She took both Mira's hands in hers. "I know you're a paranatural."

Mira was torn between the impulse to yank her hands away and a desire to grip her grandmother tighter, as ice and fire raged through her body and the ground dropped out from under her.

<Does she know about me, too?>

Mira's mind had gone blank, overwhelmed by mixed emotions, the most potent of which were dread and relief. The thing she'd feared most since coming home had happened. Now all she could do was face the consequences.

Abuela squeezed her hands. "You're family, no matter what."

<Aww. What was it Brianne said? "People can be more accepting than you think if you just give them a chance.">

Luis moved so he was shoulder to shoulder with his mother. Marta stood and positioned herself on abuela's other side. Carlos and Rafael completed the line.

<Ooh, they're showing *fidelity*. Ten points for me.>

Pressure built behind Mira's eyes. She coughed to dislodge the tightness in her throat. "You all knew?"

"I didn't," said Rafael. "But I can't say I'm surprised."

"I am," said Marta. "I always knew you were a little strange, but I hadn't realized you were . . . um . . . what exactly are you?"

Luis scowled at his sister. "Weren't you paying attention? She's a paranatural."

"I know *that*," Marta shot back. "But what kind?"

Mira swallowed. "I'm a practitioner." The words grated like sandpaper in her mouth, yet she felt a lightening as well, as though a weight had been lifted off her shoulders.

<Oh, come on. Seriously? You're gonna hold out on them *now*? What about me?>

Baby steps. Let's see how they handle this before we drop the whole "I've got a soul-sucking demon sharing my body" bombshell.

Marta clapped her hands. "Our very own superhero. This is even better than having a detective in the family. You'll find Cari for sure. And don't worry. Your secret identity is safe with us."

"I'm not. . . ." Mira pinched the bridge of her nose. "Never mind."

<Oh, I like that. We should come up with a hero name, like Demon Sucker, or Rift Mistress.>

Those sound more like porn stars than superheroes.

The demon's energy eddied in Mira's mind. She got the impression it was trying to blow a raspberry. <So, what now, Chaos Hunter?>

Please stop.

"Didn't Ty say yesterday that he works for the PTF though?" said Luis. "Are you part of their new paranatural agent program?"

"I thought they weren't allowed to work outside of Colorado," said Rafael.

"They aren't," said Mira. "And I'm not. At least, not officially." She shook her head. "It's complicated, but the PTF doesn't know about me."

The front door swung open, causing everyone to jump as though they were children caught misbehaving.

A rather soggy Ty came in holding his jacket over the head of a very pale Gianna. The policewoman's lips were the same washed-out color as her skin, and her hair hung in limp strands. She clung to Ty's side as they wedged through the door, then transferred her grip to the doorframe as Ty turned to shake the water off his jacket.

Mira stared at the woman she'd thought might never walk again.

<At least we know our healing worked. Although I still think you shouldn't have given her quite so much energy.>

Any less wouldn't have done much good, though I didn't expect to see her up and about so soon.

"It's really coming down out there," Ty said, closing the door behind him.

Carlos peered out the window as though noticing the weather for the first time. "You should see the storms we get in August."

Gianna took a wobbly step toward the couch.

Mira hurried to her side, offering an arm for support. As she helped the other woman across the room she whispered, "What are you doing here?"

"It sounded like you got a lead."

"You should have stayed at the hospital."

Gianna chuckled. "That's what the doctor said."

Mira helped Gianna lower herself onto the couch cushions, then knelt beside her leg. She looked the injured woman up and down. "What else did they say?"

"That I'll live." The corner of Gianna's lips curved up. "And that I'm some kind of miracle. The EMT insisted I had a broken back when he checked me in the alley. The ER doctor accused him of misdiagnosing me at first, but then I kept getting better all night. When the doctor first looked at me, he said I'd need several surgeries and be in rehab for months. This morning, I walked out of the hospital on my own two feet." Tears glistened in Gianna's eyes. She set her hand on Mira's shoulder. "Truly, thank you."

Mira stiffened, painfully aware that her family was listening.

<Let them hear. Now that they know you've got magic, it'll be good for them to see what you can do.>

That's gonna take some getting used to. Although, they're not the ones I'm most concerned about right now. Mira was glad the energy she'd shared with Gianna had prevented her from becoming paralyzed, but having a crippled woman walk out of the hospital was bound to raise a few red flags, and Mira did not want to draw that kind of attention.

<Maybe you should have thought of that before you healed her.>

I had no idea she'd heal this well, or this quickly.

"They tested her with iron," Ty said, correctly interpreting Mira's underlying concern. "They thought she must be fae to heal like that, but obviously she isn't. The hospital will report her to the local PTF branch, where she'll be taken for more thorough testing once the paperwork clears." Mira opened her mouth, but he lifted a placating hand. "It's standard procedure when something odd happens. They'll do their tests, establish that she's not a paranatural, and be forced to let her go."

Mira scoffed. "Surely they'll wonder how she healed."

"Of course they'll wonder," Ty said, "but so long as Gianna can't remember what happened that night"—he gave Gianna a meaningful look—"wonder is all they can do."

Gianna met Mira's gaze. "The whole night's a blur. I stepped into that alley and . . . nothing."

<Looks like our deal's still intact.>

Mira nodded. "I'm glad you're doing better, but seeing as you were at death's door yesterday, you should probably sit this next part out."

Gianna snorted. "Yeah, right."

"I'm serious. We're going after a fae. That's not a fight for a"—Mira stopped shy of saying *human*—"an injured person."

"That's not a fight for *any* person," Carlos muttered. He pointed at Ty. "You're PTF, right? Shouldn't you be calling in the cavalry?"

Mira shook her head. "Mobilizing units would take too long." *And the last thing I need is a bunch of PTF agents breathing down my neck.* "We need to find Cari *now*."

"Cari?" Ty lifted an eyebrow.

"My cousin," Mira said. "She's been taken."

"We can't find her friend Ronnie or her mother either. They appear to be missing as well," piped Marta. "At least Mira thinks so. The house . . . well, Mira thinks so."

A wave of chatter erupted as Mira's family latched onto this new piece of information and offered advice that ranged from driving around town to look for the missing women as though they were stray dogs, to calling in the National Guard.

Ty whistled, a sharp piercing needle of sound that made everyone cringe and cover their ears. Once he had everyone's undivided attention, he said, "Too many cooks in the kitchen. Mira and I will take it from here."

Abuela placed her hands on her hips and planted herself in front of Ty as though intending to hold her ground in the face of an oncoming tsunami. "A family member is missing."

Ty stared as though waiting for her to continue, but Mira knew abuela felt that single statement was all the explanation any decent person should need.

<Poor guy's got no idea who he's up against.>

Mira walked over to Ty and patted him on the shoulder. "I've been down this road already. You're not going to budge her, and arguing just wastes time."

He frowned. "But—"

"Let's go over what we know. We can decide who does what, if anything, later." She pulled the folded picture she'd stolen from Ronnie's bedside frame out of her back pocket and handed it to Ty. "I found this when tia Marta and I visited Cari's friend's house."

Ty looked at the photo then passed it to Gianna.

"So?" Gianna asked.

"This guy"—Mira pointed to the man—"was reported eaten by alligators in the Glades a little over two weeks ago. I found evidence that the woman"—she pointed to Amelia—"was killed in her bedroom, probably within the last few days."

"Killed? Not missing?" Marta gasped, no doubt wondering what gruesome sight Mira might have found while she sat waiting in the front room.

"What about the girl?" Ty asked.

"There's a chance she's another victim, but. . . ." She pressed her lips together.

"You think she's the fae," Ty finished.

"Except I saw her at the school when we were looking for clues and didn't notice anything strange."

Ty glanced at the assembled Fuentes clan and frowned. "And the . . . consultant . . . that you had follow up? Could they have missed something?"

<Consultant?>

He means you.

<Aaaand we're back to blaming the demon.>

Is it possible?

<That a fae was standing right in front of me while I was actively looking for the presence of magic, and I didn't notice?> Contempt dripped from the demon's words.

"Unlikely," Mira said.

Abuela frowned. "Is that something—" She glanced at Ty. "Um, you know someone who can identify a fae just by looking at them?"

Mira looked back and forth from abuela to Ty. *They're both trying not to spill my secret to the other.*

<That would be sweet if it wasn't so pointless. Should we put them out of their misery?>

We'll never get anywhere if they keep talking in circles. Mira sighed. "I'm a practitioner." She shivered. *I'm never gonna get used to saying that out loud.* She waved her hands to indicate all the gathered people. "He knows. She knows. They know. Everybody knows." She let her hands fall with a shake of her head.

There was a moment of stunned silence. Then Luis blurted, "You said the PTF didn't know about you," at the same time as Ty asked, "When did this happen?"

"Okay, not *everybody*," Mira corrected. "Just everyone in this room." She hesitated. "And Father Bembe. That's everyone who knows, and it's very important that you don't tell anyone else." She met the gaze of each of her relatives. "Ever."

"The priest, I get," said Carlos, "but why her?" He indicated Gianna.

"Is it because you healed her?" Marta asked. "That was you, wasn't it? The miracle?"

Mira rolled her eyes. "It doesn't matter. You all know I have magic. Now let's just focus on finding Cari and stopping this fae."

<Of course, we're not all on *quite* the same page yet.>

Close enough.

"Right. Well . . . now that everyone knows Mira's secret. . . ." Ty looked at Mira.

She gave a subtle shake of her head.

<Clever boy.>

Ty cleared his throat. "Step one is to identify what kind of fae Ronnie is."

Abuela shook her head. "I still can't believe she is one. I've known Ronnie her entire life." She spread her arms. "We all have. Her family attends our church. Until recently, she and Cari would visit me almost every day after school. How could she possibly have been a fae without any of us noticing?"

Mira frowned and glanced over her shoulder to the closed door partway down the hall, recalling why Ronnie had stopped those after-school visits. *Maybe someone* did *notice, and you all just didn't understand why she was making a fuss.* "Did she ever meet my mom before the incident last week, with the yelling and throwing things?"

Abuela nodded. "Lots of times. Maria usually sits in the living room for a good part of each day."

Cold fingers of guilt twisted in Mira's chest. *She can't come out right now because I'm here.*

"Is it common for mami to get that upset?"

"No," abuela said. "She's usually pretty calm around people she knows. Well, except. . . ." She gave Mira an apologetic look.

Except me.

Ty bumped her shoulder with his. "What are you thinking?"

Mira shook her head. "I just thought there might be some connection between the way mami reacted to Ronnie and the way she flips out when she looks at me, as if she can somehow tell that I'm . . . wrong."

"Is that even possible?" Carlos asked.

Ty waffled his head back and forth. "Mira's a practitioner. That had to come from somewhere. And low-level powers often manifest as psychic abilities—not full-on practitioners, but people who are sensitive to magic."

<Like Bembe.>

Exactly. Someone who can sense magical energy but can't quite use it. Mira's excitement flagged. "But if she only started reacting to Ronnie recently, that can't be right."

"Unless she's not the real Ronnie anymore," Gianna suggested. "Maybe she's a fae impostor. Some kind of shape-changer?"

Ty snapped his fingers. "Not a shape-changer. A species-changer. I think I know what we're up against."

Chapter 24

TY

EVERYONE IN THE ROOM looked at him blankly.

Ty cleared his throat. "One of the possible fae species I considered earlier was a rougarou."

"That sounds like some kind of sauce," said Mrs. Fuentes.

Mira gave him a quizzical look. "Never heard of it."

"I'm not surprised. They're exceedingly rare."

"What makes you think that's what we're facing?" asked Gianna.

Ty counted off the facts on his fingers. "Eats people. Lives in warm, moist climates. Passes for human."

"About that," Gianna interjected. "Principal Gary had the whole student body tested. If Ronnie's a fae, how did she pass the test?"

"Rougarous are born from mortals. Their fae half is sealed in a sort of time bomb until they begin their transformation, which in this case seems to have started about two weeks ago. Before that, she would have registered as completely human."

Carlos brought his hands together in a time-out gesture. "What do you mean by 'born from mortals'?"

Ty licked his lips, dredging up memories from his PTF training days. Rougarous had relatively little written about them, as opposed to the histories, strengths, and weaknesses recorded about the more prolific fae, but what little was known about the rougarou was plenty memorable. "Have you ever heard of those wasps that lay their eggs inside other insects?"

Carlos wrinkled his nose. Marta looked as if she were trying not to gag. Rafael and Luis exchanged a confused glance. Mira just crossed her arms and continued to stare at him.

"They inject their eggs into a host body. Eventually, when the eggs hatch, the offspring eat the host. Rougarous are similar. A mature male rougarou will mate with a female mortal to create offspring. The child grows up human, with their fae genes dormant. Eventually, usually sometime around puberty, the fae genes activate. Then the fae . . . host . . . person starts craving what the rougarou needs to mature." Ty swallowed, hating the next words even as he said them. "They eat humans."

Mira closed her eyes. Her chest swelled as she took a deep breath.

Ty wanted to go to her, to comfort her as she came to the same realization he had—*If I'm right . . . all the missing kids are dead. Including Bembe's friend and Mira's cousin*—but there was no need. She let out a controlled exhale and steadily met his gaze with understanding and cool determination. *She would have made an excellent agent.*

One by one, the import of Ty's words sank into the other people in the room.

Luis buried his face against his husband's shoulder, and Rafael wrapped his arms around the shorter man.

Gianna locked her jaw and stared forward, gripping the armrest of the couch.

Carlos covered his mouth and turned away.

Marta crossed herself. "So Ronnie has turned into one of these rougeries?"

"Rougarou," Ty corrected. "I think so."

Mrs. Fuentes fixed her steely gaze on Ty. "How can we save her?"

Ty's insides twisted. "We can't."

The elderly woman took a threatening step toward Ty. "There must be some—"

"There isn't," he cut her off. *Better to be straight with them now than have to dash their hopes later.* "Once a host begins the transformation process, there's no way to reverse it. Either she'll ingest the required amount of human flesh to survive the final metamorphosis—in which case she'll absorb her mortal body and become fully fae—or she'll come up short on energy reserves and die."

"How close is she?" Mira asked.

"Rougarous need to eat about twenty people in order to survive the final change."

Mrs. Fuentes turned on Mira. "You can save Ronnie." She pointed at Gianna. "Like you saved her."

Gianna shrank a little in her seat, as though her recovery were something to be ashamed of.

"It's not that simple, abuela. Ty's the expert on fae. If he says she can't be saved, then. . . ."

"How do we know she's not just another victim?" Rafael interrupted. "Before we condemn her, shouldn't we be sure she actually is turning into one of these roogy monsters?"

"Both her parents dead and connections to every other victim?" Mira said. "That's way too many coincidences."

"And parents *are* usually among the first victims when a rougarou becomes active. They strike out on instinct, at whoever's nearest to them."

"That's sick," said Carlos, shaking his head. "This whole situation is just . . . sick."

"But it's what we're faced with," Mira said. "If you don't want to see the nasty truth of the world, maybe don't insist on sticking around for the discussion next time."

"Don't you speak to your tio like that, young lady." Mrs. Fuentes waved her finger in Mira's face.

Mira blew out a frustrated exhale.

"What about Cari?" Marta's voice broke through the argument, choked with emotion. Tears streaked her plump cheeks. "I'm sorry about Ronnie, I am, but what about my Caridad? Is she . . . is there any chance . . .?" Her knees buckled, and it was only Carlos's quick grab that saved his sister from a trip to the floor. He and Luis cradled the pregnant woman between them and ushered her to a chair.

"How long has she been missing?" Ty asked.

"Since sometime last night," Mira said. "Not sure when, exactly."

Ty rubbed one hand over the back of his neck and exhaled. "Rougarous usually have a specific, secluded place for feeding. A den, if you will. If she can, she'll take her victims there before—"

Marta's sob cut him off.

"If she was taken within the last few hours, there's a chance she's still alive."

The entire Fuentes family perked up, save Mira. Either she'd heard the doubt in his voice, or she was wise enough to know how slim that chance really was.

"But you shouldn't get your hopes up," he finished. "It's going to take time for us to find her."

A flash of lightning turned the curtains in the front window momentarily transparent, and the *crack* of thunder that followed rattled the glass.

"Especially in this weather," he mumbled.

"The Everglades," Mira said. "That's where you found the track star's body, and the article said Ronnie and her dad were birdwatching there when he was attacked by the 'alligator'." She put the word in air quotes.

"The Glades are huge," said Gianna. "Even if we mobilized every organization, it'd take days to search."

Marta covered her face with her hands. Carlos patted her shoulder.

Mira focused on Ty, trying to block out her aunt's distress. "You said Lucas's remains had alligator and scavenger bite marks as well as the ones we're assuming the fae made. How far could animals have dragged the body from the initial kill site?" Mira asked.

"Alligators are territorial," said Rafael. "They usually won't travel more than two square miles."

Everyone looked at Rafael.

Luis slapped his husband on the back. "Raf here is a tour operator in the Glades. He knows them like the back of his hand."

Ty nodded. "So we just need to search within two miles of where we found Lucas Martinez's body." *Maybe we have a chance of finding the rougarou's den before Caridad dies after all.* "Do you have a map?"

"In my truck." Rafael grabbed Marta's umbrella off its hook and bolted out the door.

Ty turned to Gianna. "Where was the dad killed?"

Gianna twisted her lips and looked at the ceiling. "I think they were hiking the Long Pine North Trail, but his arm was found north of Ingrahan Highway. The rest of him was never recovered."

"Is that near where we found Lucas's remains?"

She shook her head. "He was much farther north."

Rafael returned and spread his map on the coffee table in front of the couch. Everyone crowded around.

Gianna leaned forward and pointed to a road near the southern end of the Glades. "This is where the dad went missing." She moved her finger a little farther north. "This is about where his arm was found." She continued north. "Lucas was found in this area."

Ty nodded. "If we assume the father was her first kill, she wouldn't have had a den yet. She would have eaten some, then carried the rest of the body to a secluded area for a more leisurely meal."

Luis scrunched his nose, and Mrs. Fuentes covered her mouth.

"A lot of the Glades is pretty exposed," said Rafael. "If I wanted privacy, I'd head for the cypress groves." He placed his finger on the map. "Here."

Mrs. Fuentes indicated the distance from the dad's disappearance to the cypress grove. "Ronnie's not a large girl. Do you really think she could carry a full-grown man that far?"

"Rougarous are strong. Even a young one could easily lift and carry a man many miles."

"So we're looking at the cypress groves within two miles of Lucas's remains." Mira turned to Rafael. "Do you have a boat we can use?"

He nodded.

Mira looked out at the storm. Sheets of rain were pelting the street as lightning strobed overhead. "At least this weather should keep the tourists out of the Glades."

Ty tapped Gianna on the arm. "Contact the local authorities. Have them muster here." He pointed to a spot on the map just off Highway 41. "No one goes in until I give the word. We want to put a noose around her neck, not to back her into a corner. If the rougarou feels threatened before we're ready, we'll likely lose a lot of people trying to put her down. Once we have eyes on the target, we'll spring the trap."

"And what exactly is 'the trap'?" Mira asked.

He met her gaze. "You."

Mira stiffened. "Excuse me?"

Ty hated putting all the pressure on Mira, but humans would be no match against a rougarou. "Rougarous are strong, their skin is tough enough to make most weapons ineffective, and they're resistant to most magic." He glanced around the room. Mira might have told her family about being a practitioner, but he was willing to bet that little headshake earlier meant they didn't know about the demon. And he was sure Gianna didn't. He looked at Mira, hoping she'd understand his meaning. "But it shouldn't have any defense against what you can do."

Mrs. Fuentes made a choking sound. "I won't pretend to know the limits of what Mira can do, but magic doesn't make a person invincible, and if this rougy-thingy is resistant . . . how can you send her against it alone?"

"I won't send her in alone." He gripped Mira's shoulder, trying to convey his resolve, to let her know that whatever they faced he would be right there beside her. "I'll go in first to provide a distraction. You ambush her while she's focused on me."

Mira scrunched her nose and pulled away from him. "That won't work."

Ty frowned. "Why not?"

She ran a hand through her hair, fluffing the white stripe. "There's a reason I generally avoid close contact with fae." She glanced around the room, hugged herself, then focused on Ty. "For starters, they can sometimes sense me well before they can see, hear, or smell me, so I might not be able to ambush her unless she's one hundred percent focused on something else."

"Then it's my job to keep her focused," Ty said.

"And I can't just jump in and . . . take her out."

She definitely didn't tell them everything.

Ty fixed his gaze on her. "If your hesitation is about her being a kid, or a family friend. . . ." He shook his head. "We can't save her." He hated how cold his words sounded, but they couldn't afford to see the rougarou as a girl. "Once the change starts, the host is as good as dead. There's no coming back."

The gathered Fuentes family shifted their weight and glanced at one another as though wondering if anyone would argue the point.

Mira shook her head. "That's not the problem." She glanced at her family, then grabbed Ty by the elbow and pulled him a few steps away from the group and whispered, "I tried once to drain a nasty pixie halfer wreaking havoc in New Hampshire when I was younger. Not only did I not gain any energy from the exchange, I was sick for nearly a month after."

Ty's chest clenched. "Why?"

Her eyes flashed gold. "We were poisoned."

She blinked, and her right iris returned to its natural color. "As I understand it, fae and rifters have similar but opposite energy. It all works about the same, but it doesn't mesh together." She interlaced her fingers. "After that hard-learned lesson, I've done my best to stay away from fae whenever possible. I can still kill them the old-fashioned way when the situation calls for it, but it'll take a lot longer than just jumping on her back and yanking out her soul."

"So we're looking at a drawn-out battle." Ty compressed his lips and placed his hands on his hips. "That's exactly what I was hoping to avoid."

The Fuentes clan, all of whom had been straining toward them but had held their places, exchanged troubled looks at this suddenly audible pronouncement.

Mira gave him an apologetic frown, as though she'd somehow let him down by exposing this weakness in her abilities.

It's not her fault. I just have to come up with a plan that doesn't rely on her fast-acting demon powers.

He paced the length of the room, thinking back on his training. He'd never fought a rougarou in person. He didn't even know anyone who had. There were only a dozen or so recorded encounters with the species in all of the PTF's databanks.

He turned and paced back to his starting point, wracking his brain for every usable detail from his memory. *Rougarous have heightened senses.*

When threatened, they act more like animals than people, shutting off thought in favor of instinct. So if I were fighting a tiger, what would I do? He looked up. Everyone was staring at him. *You're the expert here. They're counting on you to come up with a plan.* He focused on Mira. *A plan that doesn't get anybody killed.* He cleared his throat. "I'll need to swing by the local PTF office to pick up some supplies."

Chapter 25

MIRA

THE AIRBOAT BUMPED and jolted beneath Mira as it raced through the Everglades under tio Rafael's guidance. Rain fell in curtains from the slate-gray sky. Dense stands of cypress choked off the grassy fields that had, at first, stretched to the horizon. The waterways narrowed, forcing the boat to slow. The increasing canopy caught a portion of the rain, but heavy drops continued to pelt the boat's passengers. Dead wood and creeper vines laced the tree roots, creating walls. Alligators floated like driftwood just beneath the agitated surface of the water. The air, still thick and warm despite the rain, gusted in Mira's face and tangled her wet hair. She took a deep breath and pressed her palms to the vibrating metal surface on either side of her crossed legs.

Time to work.

Another breath and she let herself slide away, deeper into her subconscious. The demon swelled to fill the vacated space. Mira could still feel the hum of the metal under her hands and hear the roar of the fan propelling them forward. She could taste the briny air and smell the musty scent of rotting wood and algae. But everything was filtered by an imperceptible distance, as though she were living in a memory. She took another breath and let herself sink further. The demon's energy filled her body, taking over. Mira drifted at the end of a tether.

"Whoa, what the heck is happening with your hair?" tio Luis shouted.

The anxiety his question stirred nearly jarred Mira out of her meditative state.

"It happens sometimes when she uses magic." Ty's voice was a rock in the storm, soothing both her and Luis as he assured her uncle such oddities were of no concern.

The trees, water, and flotsam blurred and blended, turning to blue-gray smoke around her. A long, thin shape of swirling blue drew her attention to the side—the denser energy of an alligator draped over a log. Another swirl of concentrated energy streaked overhead—a bird. Beside her, Ty was an electrical storm in the shape of a person. Gianna and tio Luis sat behind her, and farther back still was Rafael at the tiller. The four people sharing her boat were hazy human shapes marked only by the dancing energy that swirled inside them. They bore no distinction from one another, yet the pulse of Ty's energy felt different somehow, more familiar.

<Everyone resonates a little differently,> the demon confirmed.

The few times Mira had seen the world through the demon's eyes she hadn't noticed any difference between the amorphous blobs of electric potential that denoted a human presence. *Can you tell individual people apart when you see them through the Rift?*

<I've never bothered to try. Generally, demons are only interested in identifying people with special powers, and those are easy enough to spot. The rest are just white noise.>

The space around Mira suddenly expanded like an explosion in her mind. She could see beyond the trees and shrubs walling her in. The misty world of the Rift stretched out around her like a monochrome kaleidoscope. Every animal, every insect, was a burst of lightning. A frog splashed into the water ahead. A mother bird sat on three eggs in a nest, the unborn chicks a flurry of light beneath her. A cluster of ibis waded through shallows on spindly legs. Dragonflies zipped between branches like jet planes. Centipedes crawled through the rotted center of a nearby log. A family of opossums dozed in a tree off to the left. Geckos clung to tree trunks. Snakes slithered through the sawgrass. There was even a large cat lounging in the high branches of a tree far to the right. Where there was life, lightning danced through the Rift, mimicking the storm overhead.

Wow. Mira had peeked through the Rift before, usually when tracking someone or trying to lose a tail, but she'd never sunk quite so deep or seen quite so far. Handing the reins over to the demon to this extent came with risks, but they had no choice if they wanted to avoid scouring every square foot of their search area manually.

She shifted her gaze side to side, taking it all in. She was flying through a cloud with lightning flashes all around her. Dark faces drifted in the mist—other demons biding their time in the space between spaces. If Mira had been on her own, she wouldn't have been safe. Practitioners shone like beacons in the Rift, a neon sign begging for possession. But the demon riding Mira's body was no small fry, and there was no one cocky enough to challenge them here.

"There." Mira's finger rose, directed by the demon. She pointed to an area off to the right. "About half a mile ahead." The fog there was denser, darker, lacking the sparks of life that illuminated the rest of the area. "The wildlife is avoiding that place."

"Maybe because a bigger, badder predator moved in," said Rafael. He wound the boat between trees, angling as best he could in the direction Mira indicated.

The demon kept its eyes on the dark space, twisting as the boat moved. When they'd halved the distance, Mira saw a flicker of light near the center of the vacant zone. Too big for a bird. Too vertical for an alligator. "There's someone there."

Ty leaned closer, bumping her shoulder with his. From Mira's perspective, it seemed as if a nebula were colliding with her. Ty's features came into focus when they touched. His eyes were narrowed, staring into the distance as though his gaze could pierce the underbrush. "Is it Ronnie?"

"I'm not sure." Mira's voice carried the sultry purr the demon preferred. "They're too far away to make out any details, but considering the quarantine around them, I'd say the odds are in our favor. If we get much closer, and it *is* Ronnie. . . ."

"She'll know we're coming."

The demon nodded.

"Then it's time to split up." Ty raised one fist in the air.

The airboat slowed, then stopped, as Rafael heeded the silent command. Ripples radiated from the boat, mingling with the speckles created by the rain.

"Take the most direct route you can," Ty said. "We'll circle around so I can come in from the other side." He wrapped a hand around her upper arm and gave it a squeeze. "You'll have to keep her distracted long enough for me to get in place and set the trap."

"You think I can't?"

He shook his head. "I know you can. Just . . . be careful. Rougarous can be a handful, and you won't have any backup until I get there." His thumb worked a small circle against her skin, seemingly without his notice.

Warmth spread through Mira, starting from that point of contact and swelling like a rising wave to crash against her heart.

The demon smiled. "I'll take care of her." She patted his hand, then pulled her arm free and stood. The boat rocked, but she kept her balance on the swaying surface. <Do you want to handle the next part, or shall I?>

Mira was riding a little closer to the surface now, drawn in by Ty's warmth and worry like a moth to flame, but if she took over control they'd lose the long-range perception that would keep them on track. She glanced down at the backs of her hands. Dark shadows outlined her fingernails but hadn't yet started to travel up her fingers. *I'm worried about holding this balance too long, but we can't risk losing track of our target. Just get us there quickly. Then I'll take over.*

<Roger that.> The demon took a step toward the edge of the boat. *Wait.*

Mira's body jerked to a halt.

<What's the matter?>

Give me a second. Mira struggled to the surface just enough to take momentary control. She turned to the people gathered behind her. Luis was holding Rafael's hand. He'd refused to let his love go into danger alone, but he'd be worse than useless if Rafael came under attack. *I wish we hadn't had to bring either one of them.* "If shit goes sideways . . . you get the heck out of here. Leave us behind."

"We're not going anywhere without you," Luis said.

Mira caught Rafael's dark gaze. The crow's feet at the corners of his eyes pinched. The sides of his mouth turned down. His attention shifted to Luis then back to her. He gave a nearly imperceptible nod. He'd save Luis if it came to that, even if it meant abandoning the rest of them.

She shifted her focus to Gianna. She wouldn't be much good against a fae either, which was why she'd be staying with the boys in the boat until Ty gave the all clear, but at least she had a gun and a bit of combat training.

Mira leaned forward.

Gianna's brown eyes widened. The pale scars on the side of her face stretched. "Why are you looking at me like that?"

Mira pointed at her uncles. "Keep them safe, whatever it takes. I'm trusting you."

Gianna licked her pink lips and nodded. "I will."

She glanced at Ty, but there was nothing more to say. She'd see him soon enough. *Okay, let's go.*

She and the demon turned as one and approached the edge of the boat. They glanced toward their destination—the hazy glow of a presence near the center of a seeming no-man's-land—then down at the uneven surface of the rain-rippled water. They might need the demon's magic to track their target, but they'd need Mira's to reach it.

<We're going to have to get the balance just right.>

I know. Mira pulled energy into her body—a strange sensation when she wasn't entirely seated in said body—and began channeling her magic. She could feel the current of energy coming from the Rift and the demons who resided there; at the same time, she was aware of the constant drain of the demon pulling energy from her own physical body. If one pulled too hard, they could accidentally kill the other, or at the very least, break the balance between them. If they were in sync, Mira's hair would be split down the middle, half white, half brown, but both her eyes would be glowing gold, since the demon was directing.

Mira squatted down, braced one hand against the side of the boat, and stepped over the edge. Her foot touched the surface of the water . . . and stopped. She transferred her weight and set her second foot next to her first.

Gianna gasped. Luis muttered something about miracles.

Mira let go of the boat. She bobbed slightly on the surface of the murky liquid. She smiled, turned to face her destination, and started running.

Snakes, alligators, and anything else that might pose a threat were easy enough to avoid with her Rift-vision active. Inanimate objects were a bit more of a challenge with both the rain and the cloudy overlay of the Rift hindering her sight. She stumbled over rotting logs and massive roots as she wove between tree trunks wrapped in climbing vines. She slipped repeatedly on the slick film that seemed to coat almost every surface, dunking a knee or a hand. Her jeans grew heavy with caked mud, and her sneakers developed a greenish sheen, but the splash and crash of her passage through the underbrush was masked by the rain and the distant rumble of thunder as the storm continued its journey across the sky.

Her sides were heaving within moments. It seemed she was drinking, more than breathing, the thick air of the Glades. Her muscles grew warm despite the damp. She kept her pace to a fast jog—push too hard and she'd be in poor condition for the fight waiting for her at the finish line.

She thought back to the morning run Ty had crashed, and the question he'd asked her. *This is why I still run despite having magic.* She smiled, picturing their race. Somewhere out there, Ty was hurrying to the same destination, but she had to reach it first.

A dozen yards out from their target, she slowed. Rather than crashing through the underbrush, she carefully pushed aside vines and branches to climb through the tree roots.

Has she noticed us?

<I don't think so.>

She continued to creep forward until a single waterway stood between her and the person she desperately hoped was Ronnie. Occasional orange sparks flashed through the bluish blob of concentrated energy ahead.

What is that?

<What I didn't see at the high school. Fae magic.>

A relieved tingle raced through Mira's body, and a sudden bout of lightheadedness burst over her. *We found her.*

<It's sporadic and not very strong. I'd say her fae nature is still buried pretty deep. It's no wonder I didn't notice before.>

Feeling a touch defensive?

<Just saying, it's not my fault we missed it.>

The shape ahead moved, splitting in two.

What the . . .?

<Damn, looks like there's another.>

Two rougarous?

She squinted at the shapes. Both were human in form, but only one carried the occasional bright flashes magic.

<I think the one on the ground is human.>

Hope squeezed Mira's heart. *Caridad.*

<Or another victim.>

This changes things.

<Does it?>

We can't charge in, fireballs blazing, if there's a hostage.

<So what do you suggest? Ty will be here any minute, and if we don't have this fae's full attention, he's gonna be a sitting duck.>

Mira crept forward, carefully slipping between the bushes that blocked her final destination. She wiped a strand of wet hair away from her eyes. *We're close enough. You can hang back now.*

Mira's awareness rose to the surface as the demon sank further into Mira's subconscious. She glanced at her hands on the slick bark of the tree roots she was lying on. Black lines cracked her cuticles.

We're going to need a real meal soon.

<Too bad this one turned out to be a fae instead of a rifter.>

Moving slowly, she crept onto a downed cypress trunk half submerged in the water. Ronnie was standing on a midsized hummock ringed with tufts of chest-high sawgrass. She was wearing pink sweatpants caked with mud and a black tank top with a glittery golden heart stitched across the front. Her long, black hair was slicked into a high ponytail that swished side to side with each movement, flinging raindrops from the wet ends. She mumbled to herself and rubbed her hands together as she paced the hummock, seemingly oblivious to the sting of sticks and prickers on her bare feet.

Off to one side, near the edge of the solid patch of ground, lay an-other girl—Cari. She was on her side with her eyes closed, maybe unconscious. Mira couldn't tell. Her unbound blond hair, bare legs, gray shorts, sky-blue shirt, and white hoodie were all splattered with dark mud.

Mira held onto the image in her mind of the second figure's energy firing in the Rift. *Why hasn't she killed Cari yet?*

<Who knows? And who cares? Isn't it enough that she's alive? Your aunt will be overjoyed.>

It's great that she's alive . . . but weird. If the rougarou took her because it was hungry, she should be mincemeat by now.

<So?>

So maybe Ronnie isn't as far gone as Ty thought.

<She still killed her parents and a bunch of other kids.>

Maybe she couldn't help it. Maybe she lost control. She could still be trying to fight the change that's happening to her.

<You're thinking you might be able to save her?>

I don't know, but I do know that it's possible to hurt the people around you without meaning to.

<She's not you.>

I know.

<See that you remember.>

Mira nodded. *I'm going to talk to her.*

The demon groaned.

Mira pulled her legs under her, preparing to stand.

Ronnie spun, her dark eyes wide and searching. "I know you're there." She shouted the words, half threat, half question. "I can smell you."

<Took her long enough.>

The rain hid us.

Mira stood, raising her hands as though in surrender. "I just want to talk."

Ronnie took a step away from Mira. Her gaze shifted to Cari, then back.

"I can help you." Mira stepped off her log. She didn't bother to funnel energy into walking on water for the handful of steps to Ronnie's island. There were no alligators here, and it wasn't like she could get any wetter. The water was cool, but not cold. Sediment swirled around her sneaker.

Ronnie laughed. Not a relaxed, cheerful sound. More like the panicked chuckle of someone convinced the rest of the world had gone mad, so she might as well join in. "No one can help me. And who says I need help? Or want it? I'm fine. Better than fine. I'm amazing."

"You're sick." Mira took another slow step forward. "You're hurting people."

Again Ronnie's attention swung to Cari. "I wouldn't."

"You hurt your father."

Ronnie shook her head. "That was an alligator. One second he was there on the path behind me, then he was gone. I never even saw it."

A cold knot clenched in Mira's chest. *Is it possible she doesn't realize what's been happening?*

<How can you eat people and not know it?>

Split personality? Mental repression? Who knows?

"What about your classmates?" Mira pressed. "The ones who went missing."

Ronnie wrinkled her nose and lifted her chin. "Classmates? Those weren't classmates. They were jerks. Obstacles. I'm glad they're gone."

Something moved in the grass behind Ronnie. It could have been an animal—with her demon-vision turned off, there was no way to be sure—but there hadn't been any living things that close to Ronnie when she'd scouted the area. *It has to be Ty.*

Ronnie started to turn, as though she too had heard the rustling.

<Throw a fireball!>

"Olivia was an obstacle?" Mira asked instead.

"She was a bully," Ronnie shrieked, zeroing in on Mira once more. She clenched her fists at her sides, quivering with anger. "She thought she could do whatever she wanted just because she was cheer captain, and Cari actually wanted to be *friends* with her!"

Ronnie was jealous. Mira nodded to herself as the idea took root. "And she was going to go to the dance with Ramon, but maybe he wasn't the first to ask. Maybe Lucas was interested in Cari, too."

Ronnie scoffed. "Lucas only loved himself. Just ask any of the girls he's been with. I tried to tell Cari that, but she still swooned every time he smiled at her. He would have ruined her, eventually."

<I'm starting to see a pattern here.>

No kidding.

Another patch of grass rustled, this time off to Mira's right. Mira took another step forward. "But why the college student at the party? Was she hitting on Cari?"

Color bloomed on Ronnie's cheeks. She tucked her chin, looking to the side and down.

Mira changed course. "Was she hitting on you?"

Ronnie's expression fell, turning cold.

"You hit on her." Mira completed her slow trek across the water. One more step would put her on solid ground. "But she wasn't interested."

"She was . . . at first, but. . . ." She shook her head. "It doesn't matter. I have Cari. And she has me. We have each other. That's all we need."

Mira glanced at Caridad. "If you stay as you are, Cari will end up dead."

Ronnie stiffened and shook her head so vehemently her whole body rocked back and forth. "I would never hurt Cari."

"Did you mean to hurt those other kids?"

"Not Cari." She continued to swing her head from side to side. "Never Cari."

Mira stepped onto the hummock. Sawgrass caught at her pants. "Did you mean to hurt your mother?"

Ronnie froze mid-denial. Her eyes went wide. "That was an accident," she whispered. "I . . . I told her to behave. If she'd just behaved. . . ." Ronnie's breathing sped up. Her ribs heaved with each gasping inhale. She gripped the sides of her skull, digging her fingers into her hair. A low growl reverberated from her chest.

<What's happening here?>

I'm not sure. Mira pulled more energy into her body and held it ready in anticipation.

Ronnie screamed.

Cari jolted on the ground as though startling awake from a dream.

Ronnie spread her arms wide, threw back her head, and howled at the sky. Bulges rippled under her skin like burrowing insects. The sound of bones popping echoed over the water. Ronnie's arms stretched like taffy. She curled in on herself, screaming and writhing. Then all at once, the terrible sounds cut off. Ronnie straightened. She was a good foot taller than she had been, and thinner, as though her skeleton had grown and the rest of her had been spread thin to cover it. But the biggest change was in her face. Her jaw was longer and wider than before, with great hollows beneath her cheek bones. Her eyes were sunken below a thick brow, and her ears were tapered to points and coated with fur.

<I guess that's a rougarou.>

Ronnie—the rougarou—launched herself at Mira, who barely had time to bring her magic to bear before the first strike hit. Three-inch claws of glistening black tore through the shimmering shield Mira had erected and sliced open her forearm.

Mira circled to the side, boosting her reflexes and strengthening her muscles. "So much for talking."

Chapter 26

TY

TY SLUNK THROUGH the tall grass of the Everglades, having left Gianna and Mira's uncles on the airboat nearly half a mile back. He moved carefully through the water, trying not to picture what might be hiding beneath its murky surface as he crept closer to the rougarou's den. Mira had said there was no wildlife in the area around their target; it had been scared off by a larger predator. He hoped she was right.

Unseen sticks and rocks scraped his ankles. Ripples spread from his passage, slow though it was. Between the rain and a few deep holes that had nearly dunked him, only the waterproof pack on his back remained dry. His shoes squelched with each step, as the viscous mud of the marsh threatened to steal them right off his feet. *I must be getting close by now.*

He'd expected lightning strikes and flaming infernos to help him zero in on his destination as Mira engaged the rougarou's full attention, but the only lightning was contained within the roiling gray clouds overhead. The only sounds were those of his own passage and the rumble of thunder as the storm mustered one final hurrah.

He resisted the urge to slap the back of his neck as something tickled him there. A distinct splash sounded among the patter of raindrops, but noises echoed strangely through the looming trees, and he couldn't tell from which direction it had come. Turning, he mistook a slimy stick that brushed his arm for a snake and lurched sideways with a shudder. *I hate this place.*

Faint voices drifted to him. He paused, tilting his head first one way, then the other, trying to pinpoint their direction and distance. *Is that Mira? It must be. No one else should be out here. But who is there to talk to except the rougarou? And why would she speak to that?*

"I'm a monster." The memory of Mira's self-loathing bit deep, and suddenly Ty knew why Mira might approach the rougarou with words rather than magic despite his warnings. *She's going to try to save Ronnie.* He clenched his fists and moved a little faster. *She's going to get herself killed.*

He followed the voices as best he could. There were definitely two, distinct and conversing. If it was the rougarou Mira had found, she'd managed to get it talking. *Not quite the distraction I was planning on, but I'll take it.*

He parted a section of sawgrass and froze. In front of him was a raised hillock of muddy ground ringed by tall grass and surrounded by trees that would mask the island from any casual observer passing by boat. It was a perfect hiding spot.

Mira stood in the water just shy of the solid ground, facing down a young woman with a long, black ponytail and mud-spattered sweatpants. *That must be Ronnie.*

The girl began to turn in his direction. Ty hunkered lower in the grass for fear she would see him, but he dared not retreat lest the motion draw even more attention. Then Mira said something, and the girl spun with an angry shout of, "She was a bully!"

Ty exhaled in relief. He was about to pull back when something yellow caught his eye. He leaned forward another few inches.

Not yellow . . . blond.

Mira's cousin, Caridad, was on her side on the ground. Her back was to him, so he couldn't tell what condition she was in, or even if she was still alive, but the mud smeared over her spoke of a less-than-pleasant trip through the swamp.

Ty's gaze swung back to Mira. *Maybe that's why she didn't attack as we'd planned. She didn't want to risk her cousin becoming collateral damage.*

He pulled back so the tall grass once more blocked him from view and rubbed a damp hand over his face, then cringed and used the back of his arm to wipe off the stinky muck he'd just transferred to his skin.

The plan doesn't change. We've got one shot at taking this rougarou down before it eats anyone else. I'll just have to choose my angle of attack a little more carefully. He slipped his fingers into his pocket. The smooth stone he always carried was a comforting weight. He traced the thin gouge across its surface with his thumbnail and whispered, "Watch over her, Jamal. I don't need any more deaths on my conscience."

He moved to a nearby stand of trees, slipped the pack off his back, and set the first charge. Mira's and Ronnie's voices carried like birdsong, a rhythmic back and forth that faded into the ambient noise of the Everglades and the patter of rain filtering through the trees. He continued around the perimeter of the little island, careful to stay well back from sight. He placed the second charge.

A sudden scream shattered the afternoon.

Ty pulled the third charge from his pack and crept forward, ready to throw it.

Ronnie was crumpled in on herself, crouched down, arms wrapped around her head. When she straightened, it was no longer a girl who stood before Mira. The rougarou howled, stretching wide its exaggerated limbs tipped with dark claws. The pink sweatpants now stopped several inches short of her ankles, and her black shirt left a wide swath of abdomen exposed.

She's transforming. But despite the drastic alterations, there was still a human quality to her shape. He licked sweat off his upper lip and squinted at the half-changed rougarou. *Not all the way. Not yet.*

Ronnie the rougarou lunged forward, slicing at Mira with knife-like claws.

Ty tensed, raising the charge in his hand like a pitcher winding up.

There are too many gaps in the net. If we spring the trap before it's set, we'll only chase her off.

Light flashed as Mira spun to the side. Three thin stripes of crimson showed on her forearm, but she drew her kukri, settled into a fighting stance, and braced for the next attack.

This was always the plan, Ty reminded himself. *Mira fights while I lay the trap.* His fingers cramped around the flash grenade. *So why do I wish our roles were reversed?*

The rougarou lunged again. Mira slashed with her knife as she danced aside, but when the blade made contact with the rougarou's arm, the steel snapped in half. Mira stared at the useless hilt in her hand for a split second, then dropped the broken blade and swung her empty hand as if wielding a sword. An arc of bluish lightning slammed into the rougarou's side.

The scent of burnt flesh overpowered the rest of the swamp smells, but the rougarou barely stumbled, shaking off the wound as though it were nothing more than a paper cut.

Ty hesitated, gripping the canister so tightly his hand shook. He wanted to step in, to plant himself between Mira and the terrible creature that used to be a teenage girl but now had four-inch teeth that glinted like polished steel. He shook his head, fighting the urge screaming that his partner was in danger and he needed to protect her. *Trust her.* He lowered his hand. *Do your job, and trust that she'll do the same.*

He moved back to the trees and set the third charge.

The sounds of combat continued behind the curtain of grass, punctuated by the bursts of heat and light he'd been looking for earlier.

He willed himself to move faster as he set the fourth charge, the fifth, the sixth, and finally circled back toward his starting point.

He reached into his pack and retrieved two foam plugs, which he stuffed into his ears, and a remote detonator. Then he pulled a telescoping metal tube about three inches in diameter from his pack and hooked the mostly empty bag on a stub of broken branch. The slick, olive-green fabric swayed like a limp flag just above the water.

Ty inched forward, carefully pushing aside the sharp-edged grass hiding the hummock. Mira was delivering a volley of blows to the rougarou, each one making the fae stumble and retreat as though the fists pummeling her hit with the force of a wrecking ball. One pink-clad knee dropped to the ground with a muddy splash. Mira slipped on a slick patch, stumbled, and righted herself, but the instant of reprieve was enough for the rougarou to regain its feet. The massive force of Mira's blows might have been enough to keep it pinned, but Ty didn't see any actual damage. *Damned thick hide.*

The rougarou went on the offensive, swiping with claws and snapping with teeth.

Mira did her best to hold her ground, but she was forced back to the edge of the water.

Six feet to his right, Cari was sitting up. Her wide eyes glazed with shock like a doe caught in headlights. She seemed unhurt beyond bruises and scratches from her passage through the underbrush, but she didn't try to move. She just sat and stared, shaking slightly.

Ty bolted from his hiding place. He'd originally planned to spring the trap from cover, but Cari was a civilian; he needed to protect her. He skidded to a stop at her side and whispered, "I'm here to help." He covered the teenager's frightened gaze with his arm, scrunched his eyes shut, let out a high-pitched whistle, and pressed the detonator.

MIRA

A HIGH-PITCHED whistle pierced the air. *The signal.*

Mira fought every instinct that told her to keep her focus on the creature attacking her, brought her arms up in a blind block that both protected her head and covered her ears, and closed her eyes.

White light flared, brighter than anything the storm had produced. Her eyelids turned to stained glass. A thunderous *crack*, deep enough to shake her bones to dust, sounded from everywhere at once.

The rougarou screamed, a strange cross between a human wail and the cry of a wounded animal. Something bumped Mira's shoulder and bounced away.

Even forewarned and protected as she was, the flash and bang of the grenades were disorienting. She couldn't imagine how much worse it would be for the rougarou with its heightened senses.

<That's kinda the point,> the demon reminded her.

Let's just hope this gives us enough of an advantage to bring it down.

The demon grumbled. Despite Ty's warnings about tough skin and magic resistance, they'd both been surprised by how little impact their attacks had had on the rougarou. It had brushed aside lightning strikes and fireballs like flies and shattered Mira's favorite blade. Even her heaviest punches, amplified by magic, were barely enough to keep it in check.

Mira chanced a peek as the light and sound faded. The smell of spent fireworks enveloped her. Tears leaked from the corners of her eyes, distorting the scene. She blinked a few times. The rougarou was stumbling in circles in front of her, slashing out blindly with its claws. Beyond the rougarou, crouched beside Cari, Ty raised a long metal cylinder to his shoulder, squinted down the barrel, and pulled the trigger. A shimmering net launched from the end of the tube, expanding as it flew.

That had been the prize for which they'd made the detour to the PTF office. While flash bombs and concussion grenades might be found in any precinct armory, a net woven of twisted iron threads was a little more specialized. The Miami PTF office was small and understaffed, which worked in their favor. Ty had had no trouble convincing the manager—an analyst with no desire to see action—that he had the situation under control and there was no reason to contact the regional field office for backup. He'd requisitioned some choice anti-fae paraphernalia, promised to file a report when all was said and done, and walked out the door. Mira had to admit, the freedom and authority granted to PTF special agents wasn't without appeal. It almost made her wish she could have a badge herself.

Smoke wafted off the rougarou where the fine mesh of the iron net touched skin. The beast thrashed and flailed, blinded, deafened, its nose thwarted by the overpowering smell of used gunpowder. Mira almost felt sorry for it.

<Now's our chance.>

Mira funneled all her magic into her fists. With the rougarou weakened by the iron, and Mira not having to divert so much energy for defense, she should be able to crush bones with each hit. She stepped forward, clasped her hands together, and brought them down in a swinging arc that had the full force of her body's momentum behind it.

Her blow landed on the rougarou's head, though it turned at the last second, avoiding a top-down impact. Bone snapped under her fists. The rougarou's cheek and jaw shattered. Its howl became garbled and choked as it fell heavily to one knee.

Mira pulled back, readying a second strike, but froze as she noticed the net slip sideways. She glanced to the side and saw that one corner of the iron weave had caught on a splintered tree branch.

<Shit!>

Mira hesitated a fraction of a second, torn between hitting the rougarou again and freeing the net to ensure the creature stayed bound.

The rougarou dropped fully to the ground, still reeling from Mira's anvil-like attack.

The net slipped further.

Mira started her downward arc.

<Faster!> The demon's energy pushed Mira's muscles to their limit.

The rougarou rolled.

The net pulled taut, strained, then sloughed off the rougarou as it continued to roll.

Mira dropped her weight as her hands touched flesh.

The rougarou's foot sprang out, catching Mira just under the ribs. Her feet left the ground as the air left her lungs. She hung weightless for a moment, then she fell back into the tall grass, razor edges slicing her face and arms. She rolled over twice then splashed into the marsh.

She lifted her head, gasping. Her lungs were frozen, barely moving as she struggled for breath. She clutched her abdomen and held her chin just high enough not to drown as she focused on sucking in as much air as she could.

Her vision swam, but past the crumpled weeds she'd rolled through she saw the rougarou turn. It wasn't coming to finish her off. It was headed for Ty and Cari.

No. Mira struggled to move.

<Get up.>

I'm trying. Mira winced as she finally managed to take a full breath. Her ribs were at least cracked, if not broken.

<I'll work on these. You get over there.> The demon's energy was like a cold compress on Mira's aching ribs. A soothing numbness spread through her.

She pushed onto her hands and knees and started crawling. The sharp grass snatched at her clothes and dug into her palms like shattered glass. Mud squished between her fingers and weighed down her clothes.

The rougarou took a step toward Ty and Caridad, but as it moved, it changed. As before, Ronnie's limbs stretched like taffy on a pull. Her arms distorted until they nearly reached the ground. Her lower legs seemed to develop an extra joint. Her spine extended, curving to form hunched shoulders. The hanging portion of her dislocated jaw clicked back into place as her features extended into a doglike muzzle. Her already emaciated appearance grew even more pronounced, and the suppleness of her skin turned to hard leather. A light coating of pale fur covered her exposed extremities and the six-inch gap from the bottom of her tattered tank top to the waist of her sagging sweats where her elongated abdomen was framed by sharp hip bones and jutting ribs.

<Is this the final change Ty was talking about?>

How the hell should I know? Mira gritted her teeth and tried to crawl faster, to get between Ty and the rougarou before it fully adjusted to this new evolution.

<I thought she had to eat, like, ten more people before she could change all the way.>

Mira's breath was coming a little easier, but her muscles were on fire. She'd pushed her body as hard as she could with her magic, and now it was letting her know. *Just a little bit more. Then we can sleep for a week.*

The rougarou gave itself a shake, then stalked toward Ty and Cari.

Mira stretched out her hand. She wasn't going to make it. She focused a burst of energy, tapered to a dagger point, and let it fly. The spell distorted the air, soaring like the ripple of a heat shimmer toward the rougarou's exposed back. Raindrops scattered in its wake.

The spell hit . . . and burst apart on the thick hide. The rougarou didn't even slow.

Ty was pushing a frantic Cari toward the water while brandishing his K-Bar at the approaching rougarou. He looked like a child with a paper sword facing down the inevitability of an oncoming train.

Mira infused more power into her muscles. She had to move faster. Tendons tore. Fiber ripped. The demon's magic trailed behind Mira's, shoring up the damage she was doing as she pushed her overtaxed body harder.

Suddenly Cari slipped under Ty's arm. She dropped to her knees in front of the rougarou and threw her arms wide, as though she meant to hug the thing. Her wet hair molded to the shape of her skull. Tears mixed with the rain on her cheeks. Her eyelashes fluttered as the sky continued to weep. "Please, Ronnie, I know you're still in there. Just stop. I'll go with you. We'll run far, far away. We'll be together. Just stop." Caridad's plea came out in a series of halting sobs.

The rougarou hesitated. Then it swung one massively distorted arm, not so much in attack but as though clearing debris from its path. The back of its hand connected with Cari's side. The teenager tumbled like a rag doll tossed aside by a bored child who'd found something more interesting to play with.

Ty shouted and thrust his K-Bar into the underside of the rougarou's exposed ribs. The tip stopped dead against the leathery flesh. His grip hit the guard. His gaze flicked up, and a look of acceptance slacked his features. The train was on top of the child, and his paper sword had failed him. There was nothing more he could do.

The rougarou's claws slashed through the air, tearing into Ty's shoulder and forming four parallel tears diagonally to his opposite hip.

Mira cried out as if the wound were her own.

Ty grunted and fell onto his back.

The rougarou's jaws opened wide. Saliva dripped from four-inch curved teeth.

Dear God, she means to eat him.

<No doubt she means to eat us all.>

Only half a dozen feet separated Mira from the rougarou, but there might as well have been a canyon between them for all that Mira felt able to move any farther. *Even if I reach her . . . what then? My magic has no effect. I was barely holding my own against her physically before she changed again. Now she's stronger and I'm weaker. I can't win this fight.*

<So that's it? We're just giving up?>

She took a deep breath and let her chin fall to her chest. Rain trickled over her neck and down her arms. Saint Jude dangled below her, swinging on his silver chain. The medallion must have pulled loose during her tumble.

When hopeless seems the cause. . . . She scrunched her eyes closed and bunched her fingers in the mud. *There's one more thing we can try . . . but you're not going to like it.*

<Anything's better than being that thing's next meal.>

Mira would have chuckled if she had any energy to spare. As it was, she couldn't even smile. *Remember you said that.* She focused her waning power into her legs. They still felt shaky. *Give me a boost, will you?*

The demon's energy mingled with her own, blending and balancing.

The straining muscles the demon had been holding together began to fray in earnest.

One more push.

She took a deep breath, sent a silent prayer to the saint winking at her from around her neck, and launched herself forward.

Chapter 27

MIRA

MIRA BELLYFLOPPED onto the mucky grass, taking the full impact of her landing across her battered ribs. She didn't even try to catch herself. She needed those precious few inches that her fully extended arms had given her. She laced her fingers around the rougarou's rough-skinned, hairy ankle and breathed a sigh of relief that she hadn't come up short.

Drain her.

<You sure about this?>

Better than being her next meal, right? Just get it over with before I lose my grip.

White-and-black swirls flecked with ribbons of gold eddied around Mira as the demon gathered its power.

The rougarou stumbled slightly and twisted to see where it was caught. Mira stared straight down the maw of the beast, a crimson cave lined with glistening stalactites. The rougarou's long, black tongue lashed back and forth. The ankle trapped between Mira's hands pulled away, but she squeezed tighter, willing more strength into her fingers. She slid over the slick mud.

The demon's energy swelled within her, filling her. Mira didn't retreat into the background this time. She rode the currents like a surfer as the demon poured its energy into the rougarou, found what it was looking for, and pulled back like a wave returning to the sea. As the twisted light of the demon's magic flowed back into Mira, streamers of rose and burnt-orange trailed the golden threads, caught in their wake. The tangled weave wrapped around Mira's extended arms and sank into her.

The rougarou screamed, sending a shower of spittle into Mira's face and hair. It swiped at Mira, its claws raking her back and tearing her shirt, but the rougarou could not twist far enough to strike directly behind it. Straightening, it kicked the leg that Mira held like a cat shaking water off a wet paw.

Mira clenched her jaw and tightened her grip as she was jerked back and forth, flopping against the ground. She was lifted again and again only to slam back down. Mud got in her eyes, her nose, her mouth, as her body scattered puddles to find the packed earth beneath. She alternately tried tensing and going slack, but neither protected her from the bruises she was collecting. All the while she chanted to herself, *Hold on.*

The rougarou lost its balance during its one-legged dance and toppled sideways. Twigs, pebbles, and stiff grass blades grated Mira's stomach as she skidded forward, dragged along by the vise of her numb hands. The first flu-like symptoms of the fae magic were scratching at the edge of her awareness. An ache in her bones that had nothing to do with the beating she was taking. A tightness in her chest that went beyond the strain of exertion.

The rougarou rolled onto its back and propped up on its elbows to glower down the length of its body at the human still attached to its ankle. Rain coursed over its distorted features, creating clear trails through the mud. Its chest heaved, sending heavy, hot gusts that carried the scent of blood rolling over Mira's upturned face. Its lips were pulled well back, twisting its expression into a grimace, but its eyes lost focus. It shook its head as though fighting sleep.

<Almost there.> The demon's voice was strained and airy. Being the conduit, it was feeling the taint of the fae magic they were absorbing much more acutely.

Snarling, the rougarou lifted its free leg and kicked at Mira, who ducked her head and hunched her shoulders to take the hit. Hard bone connected with her shoulder. She winced and grunted. The impact was less than during their earlier battle.

It's getting weaker.

Blow after blow battered Mira's arms and shoulders. The rougarou even tried slamming its heel into Mira's hands, smashing her fingers against the bones in its ankle. Along with the outer assault, the poison coursing through Mira's system from the absorbed fae magic was turning her insides to acid. Her muscles were so cramped she didn't think she could release the rougarou now even if she tried. Whimpers escaped Mira's throat; sweat, tears, and mud coated her face as she tried to block out the pain, both inside and out.

Just hold on. She scrunched her eyes shut and panted into the wet ground.

The flow of energy coming from the rougarou lessened. The grunting growls, yips, and snarls turned into human screams.

Mira opened her eyes. It took three tries for her to lift her face enough to see what was happening. The rougarou's limbs were shrinking, pressing together like an accordion, thickening as they compressed. The long stretch of exposed abdomen compacted until the ragged hem of Ronnie's tank top met the stained pink fabric of her sweatpants. Short, coarse hair littered the ground. The leg under Mira's bloody knuckles turned to smooth, human skin.

Ronnie lay gasping and panting, her back arched, the soles of her feet pressed into the mud. Her whole body quivered with strain as the last of her breath left her. Her scream became silent but no less intense.

Mira stared in wonder, her exhausted thoughts tumbling like marbles through her mind. *She changed back.*

<There's not much left.>

Mira blinked, taking in the girl's once more human features. *Is the fae part gone?*

<I think so.> If a being without a body could be out of breath, that's how the demon sounded now. <Since the fae was manifested . . . when we started . . . that's what got . . . pulled out first.> The demon's voice grew more strained as it spoke, choked with pain. <Almost done.>

Stop. Mira was surprised by her own command. She could feel the demon's question, though it didn't put words to it. *If the fae is out of her, she's no longer a threat.*

<We've taken so much . . . she might not live anyway.>

Then at least she'll die human.

<And if she lives? She'll know what you are.>

I won't kill a child if there's a chance she can be saved. Mira tried to convey her feelings to the demon, her need to save rather than kill if there was even the slightest possibility of success, especially since the toxin swirling through her meant this might well be the last choice she ever made. *Please, let me have this.*

The flow of energy between Ronnie and Mira trickled away. The glow around Mira faded. Ronnie collapsed to the ground as all the tension left her body.

<If even a drop of fae magic is left in her . . . she may still change.>

But if we got it all . . . if she lives . . . we'll have saved her.

Mira tried to release Ronnie's ankle, but she couldn't. It was taking everything she had just to keep her eyes open. Nausea twisted her stomach, and bile burned her throat.

Ronnie's head lifted. She looked toward Cari's limp form. "I'm so sorry." Her arm twitched. Her open hand flopped a little but failed to move as intended. She looked down, over the length of her once more human body, and met Mira's gaze. Her skin was stretched tight over her bones, making her wide eyes look twice as large in their sunken sockets. Her lips were pale and cracked. Her eyelids fluttered.

"Thank you . . ."—her words, a bare whisper, floated to Mira on a cool breeze that had found its way in among the trees—". . . for stopping me."

Mira wanted to reply, but her mouth had stopped working as surely as her hands.

Ronnie's head fell back against the ground with a soft *thud*. She didn't move again.

Mira's gaze traveled over the still forms of Caridad and Ty. She knew she should be worried, she should try to do *something* to help them, but she couldn't concentrate beyond the terrible fire in her veins. Her muscles spasmed and twitched; she thrashed against the ground until she felt she might break apart at any moment. Her chest vibrated like the beat of a hummingbird's wings with sharp, shallow breaths that carried to her the damp smell of the Glades, the sharp tang of blood and bile, and the acrid scent of Ty's spent grenades. She let her eyes close. A few drops or rain found their way through the canopy to splash against her cheek, but the worst of the storm was over.

If we don't survive this, I want you to know—

<There's a chance . . .>—the demon's voice was little more than a buzz at the back of Mira's brain—<. . . I could save you . . . if we separate.>

It seemed to take eons for the demon's words to make sense. When they did, Mira jerked with more than muscle tremors. She tried to sort through her confusion, hope, and fear to create a clear response, but her thoughts slipped away like eels in the ocean of her pain.

<I can take it with me,> said the demon. <If I'm gone . . . you have a better chance of surviving.>

No. Mira's vehemence surprised her, but the realization of what the demon was suggesting finally cut through her pain-induced haze. *My energy is the only thing keeping you together right now. You'd be destroyed.*

<If I stay, we may both be.>

But we don't know for sure. We've never been this sick, but that doesn't mean we can't recover.

<If you die, you *die*. I'll just be reabsorbed by the Rift.>

But you wouldn't be you *anymore. You'd cease to exist.*

<I don't want you to die for me.>

Same.

The demon writhed at the edge of Mira's awareness, struggling both with the pain of the fae infection and the strain of the conversation. <Why would you go so far . . . for a demon?>

Mira thought about that for a moment. She hadn't asked the demon to possess her, and for a while after it happened she'd railed against the invasion. Even after they struck their deal, they didn't always agree, but the demon had been with her through every major event in her life, good and bad. It had protected her, comforted her, and scolded her. She didn't always enjoy having the demon with her, but it took up such a large space in her heart that to lose it might kill her simply by the hole it left. She'd often wondered what the demon was to her. A partner? A friend? A protector? A parasite?

A sense of clarity filled her. She finally had an answer. *Because family takes care of one another.*

A swell of warmth filled her, briefly overwhelming the pain. The demon's emotions were a kaleidoscope of happiness, confusion, concern, and hope. Mira had never felt such strong emotions from the demon before.

Whatever happens, promise me you'll be here when I wake up.

The demon hesitated. <What if you don't?>

Then you'll still have kept your promise.

The fire in Mira's veins spread from lines of pain to an even blanket from which there was no escape. Every molecule in her body seemed to be pulling itself apart.

Promise me.

The haze that had briefly been held back by the surprising strength of the demon's emotions swept over Mira's mind, twice as strong as before.

<I promise.>

She was washed away in the current.

TY

TY'S EYELIDS FLUTTERED open. Raindrops sparkled like diamonds on leaves and branches that framed a patch of blue so pale it was almost white. Something hard and sharp dug into the small of his back. He groaned and tried to shift position. Fire seared his chest. He hissed and looked down. Blood soaked the ragged strips of fabric that had once been his shirt. His flesh hadn't fared much better. His stomach heaved at the sight.

"Don't move."

He shifted his attention to the side with monumental effort. It seemed to take his mind a few extra seconds to catch up to what he was seeing. Mira's cousin was kneeling near his shoulder, ripping strips off a mud-splattered piece of once-white fabric. Bloody smears darkened her hair and coated one side of her face. A memory drifted out of the darkness in his mind—Caridad sailing through the air . . . right before the rougarou reached for him.

Ty hissed as pain brought him back to the present.

Caridad had pressed several pieces of wadded fabric against his shoulder and was attempting to wrap a long strip under his armpit to hold it all in place. "You need an ambulance." Her voice was faint, hollow-sounding, as though she were half-asleep. "We all do."

"Mira!" He tried to sit up, but she pushed him back as though restraining a child.

"Let me tie this."

"Where is she? And the rougarou?" Scattered images skittered through his mind, but the moments before he blacked out were all jumbled. He remembered springing their trap. The grenades had done their work. He'd fired the net. But then the rougarou had attacked. Had he missed? *No. I'm sure I hit it. How did it get free?* Then Caridad was in front of him. Then she wasn't. The rougarou's claws had been too fast to dodge. He'd thrown himself backward to lessen the blow, but it wasn't enough to save his skin entirely. Then those teeth, that gaping maw, coming for him as pain and fear tumbled him into oblivion.

He reached up with the arm Caridad wasn't fussing over and touched the back of his head. The sticky wetness he found there could have been from rolling in the mud, but the tenderness that made him wince when his fingertips touched his scalp convinced him his head had found a stone when he'd fallen away from the rougarou's attack.

Caridad yanked the ends of her makeshift bandage. Ty gritted his teeth to keep from crying out. The girl wiped a hand over her forehead, smearing it with more blood. "That's the best I can do." She turned her face to the side. In profile, the steep hook of her nose made her look like a bird. "I can't do anything for the others . . . besides pray."

This time she didn't try to stop him when Ty shifted to get a better look around. Mira and Ronnie—once more looking like a teenage girl in a tank top and sweat pants—were both on the ground not ten feet away. Ronnie was on her back, one hand draped over her stomach as if she were only sleeping. Mira was half on her side, half on her stomach. Her face was blocked from view, but her hair seemed to be completely white. Her arms were extended, hands wrapped around one of Ronnie's ankles. Her fingers were black. Thick, jagged lines of darkness trailed over the backs of her hands and up her wrists. Ty swallowed hard. He'd never seen the puppet lines stretch so far. Not even when she'd been nearly overwhelmed by her demon.

He scrambled onto his knees and crawled forward, cradling his injured arm across the already blood-soaked bandages on his chest. When he reached Mira's side, he sat on his ankles and rolled her over.

Caridad, who'd followed him, peered over his shoulder and whispered, "What's wrong with her face?"

Beneath the splatter of mud and blood, black skin circled Mira's eyes and bled across her cheeks as though her veins were filled with ink. Her lips were purple.

"No." The word came out more as a breath than a sound as Ty's chin dropped to his chest. *I've failed another.*

Mira's eyes popped open.

Caridad shrieked and jumped back.

Ty met Mira's gaze, but none of the warm brown of her eyes was present. They were gold through and through.

Ty twisted just enough to point behind him. "There's a bag with a phone inside hanging in the branches just beyond that grass. Bring it here."

Caridad glanced at the grass, then back at Mira.

"Hurry," Ty bellowed. The force of his command sent a new wave of pain through his chest, but at least it got Caridad moving. He turned back to Mira and cradled one side of her face with his usable hand. His gaze shifted to Ronnie—this close he could see her chest rise and fall—then back to the demon staring at him through Mira's eyes. "What did you do?"

"What we had to." The slight slur of the demon's accent was present, but the playfulness he was growing used to was gone. "I'm sorry I couldn't protect her."

Ty frowned and glanced in the direction he'd sent Caridad.

Mira shook her head. The movement was barely noticeable, except that her cheek rubbed against his calloused palm. The contact sent shivers through him.

"Mira," the demon whispered.

"You absorbed the rougarou's magic," Ty said as realization set in. "Even though you knew it would poison you." Ty frowned and glanced again at the shallow rise and fall of Ronnie's chest. "But she's still alive."

"Mira thought we'd . . . taken enough . . . to turn her fully human."

Ty stared in wide-eyed wonder. "Do you agree?"

"I wouldn't have taken the chance." She smiled. "But Mira wanted . . . to go out a hero."

Ty stiffened. "But you'll recover, right? Fae magic just makes you sick. You'll both recover." The last came out more command than question as Ty tried to chase away his doubts.

"I don't know." The demon's words were barely audible. "We've never taken . . . this much."

"You just need more energy. Like at the church." He pictured Father Bembe's anemic pallor when they'd carried him to his bed, then he glanced again at Ronnie. *She can control herself when she wants to . . . but that's when Mira was calling the shots.* He brushed a strand of white hair away from her eyes and noticed a finger-thick clump of brown near Mira's temple. *She's still in there.* He peeled Mira's fingers away from Ronnie's ankle and lifted one of her hands to his chest, pressing it just to the side of his wound. "Take it from me." Ty held the demon's gaze. "I trust you."

The corner of Mira's mouth twitched. "Nice as that is to hear . . . it's not enough." Sadness filled her gaze. "You're injured. Even taking a little would kill you, and Mira wouldn't want that."

"I don't care what Mira wants." Ty gave her a little shake. "I'm not letting another partner die in my arms."

"You're not enough. Even healthy you wouldn't be enough. Not to fight the poison and win."

Ty shook his head, searching for a solution. "How much do you need?"

"Without killing the donors? At least five. Maybe more."

Splashing drew Ty's attention to the edge of the grass, where Caridad was climbing back onto solid land with his backpack in one hand and his phone in the other. "The screen is locked," she said, thrusting the phone into his outstretched hand.

"We'll get you out of this yet," he said to Mira as he struggled to unlock the phone with his one working hand. "Just hang on."

Chapter 28

TY

"MIRA IS NOT GOING TO LIKE THIS." The demon's eyes were closed. Its voice was a thready whisper.

"I don't care if Mira hates me for the rest of her life. At least she'll be alive." He squeezed Mira's limp fingers, then rested her hand on her abdomen. "Just you behave yourself till she wakes up."

The corner of Mira's mouth twitched.

Ty stood to meet the boat as it bumped against the shore, flattening the surrounding grass. Cari, who'd spent their wait beside the unmoving Ronnie, rose to join him.

Rafael, Luis, and Gianna were rain soaked and tense with worry, but they were in infinitely better condition than the ragged group on the island.

"Caridad!" Luis splashed through ankle-deep mud to wrap the girl in a tight embrace.

Gianna stepped down more gingerly, careful of her footing. "What's the sitrep?"

"Contained but critical." Ty grabbed Luis's arm, pulling him away from Caridad. "Mira told you she was practitioner, right?"

Luis's eyes widened in surprised confusion. He nodded.

"Well, that's not all she is." He gestured to where Mira was lying in the mud. "Long story short, Mira is possessed by a demon who is, at the moment, struggling to keep her alive, and they need to absorb energy from a healthy human in order to survive." He turned back to the stunned expressions of those around him and focused on Luis. There was no time for tact. "That eliminates everyone but you and Rafael, and he needs to drive the boat."

Luis scrunched his nose. "Wait, you want me to do what now?" He looked past Ty to Mira. "What do you mean she's possessed? When did that happen?"

Ty ignored his questions. "Right now I need a simple yes or no." He forced Luis to meet his gaze. "Do you want your niece to live?"

Luis jerked as though Ty had slapped him full across the face. "Of course I do!"

"Then take her hand." He shoved Luis toward Mira.

Luis knelt in the mud and lifted Mira's hand between both of his. "What should I—?" His words cut off as his body went rigid. He began to tremble. Then he slumped to one side, collapsing into the mud with a wet slap.

Rafael was out of the boat in an instant, kneeling at his husband's side and cradling his head. He glared at Ty. "What did you do?"

"He'll be fine," Ty promised, then added silently, *Please let him be fine.* "You need to take Mira and Luis back to your family. Mira needs energy from at least four more people. I'm counting on you to convince the rest of your family to volunteer."

Rafael scowled but nodded. He carried first Luis then Mira to the boat, strapping them each into a seat. Ty's vision flickered as he watched the process. Dark and light spots exploded like bursts of glitter thrown in his face. He lowered himself carefully to the mud to keep from falling over and pressed his arm tighter against his seeping wound.

Gianna grabbed the first aid kit from Rafael's boat and started reworking Ty's bandages with cleaner cloth.

Rafael moved toward Ronnie, but Ty held up a hand to stop him. "Just them. Go now."

Rafael frowned. "You all look like you could use a hospital."

"But we need a believable scene when the authorities arrive if we're going to sell this story and keep Mira out of it." He looked at Ronnie. *And maybe it wouldn't be the worst thing if this one never wakes up.* He hated himself as soon as the thought formed, but he couldn't deny a part of him was sure Mira was being overly optimistic about saving the girl. *She wants so badly not to be a killer that she's willing to risk something I told her was impossible.* He sighed and rubbed his face. *But Mira's pulled off impossible before.*

He ached all over, his chest and shoulder were ribbons of fire, and he was so tired he was swaying where he sat. "Get out of here. Gianna and I will handle the rest."

Rafael grumbled and shook his head, but he got back into his boat and started the engine.

Ty watched the airboat whisk Mira away over the water. He just hoped what the demon had taken from Luis would be enough to see her home, and that Rafael would follow his instructions despite seeing his husband drained half to death. *I should be with her,* said a persistent voice at the back of his head. But there was nothing he could do to help her heal that he hadn't already done. What he *could* do was clean up this mess and make sure no one had any reason to go looking for alternate explanations.

It took only a moment for Raphael's craft to be lost to view among the dense trees. The ripples of its wake were longer in fading, and the rumbling hum—like that of a massive bumblebee—took longer still.

He looked at Gianna, who was tying off his fresh bandages. "Time to call in the cavalry."

"How long until the police arrive?" Caridad was staring at him with her wide, brown eyes—nearly the same shade as Mira's when she wasn't possessed. She returned to Ronnie's side, gripping one of the unconscious girl's hands in both of hers.

Gianna studied the unconscious teenager, looking as if she'd just swallowed a lemon.

"About five minutes," Ty said. "Assuming they're where I told them to be."

Gianna nodded, a stiff, jerky movement, but didn't take her eyes off Ronnie. "You said she couldn't be saved."

"Mira pulled all the magic out of her," Ty said. "I didn't know she could do that."

Gianna frowned. "Are you sure she's safe now?"

No. Out loud he said, "No more magic should mean no more rougarou."

"*Should* mean." Gianna shifted her weight. "Why didn't she just kill it?"

Caridad made an angry noise, almost like a growl, and leaned over Ronnie protectively, as though fearing Gianna might try to finish the job.

Gianna lifted her hands. "I'm just saying. She killed people. I'd rather be sure she can't do it again. I mean, what are we supposed to do? Put her in a human prison? Send her to the fae? What even is she?"

Ty kept his expression neutral to hide his own doubts. "We're going to pretend she was another victim, but we'll keep her under PTF observation. Call it a safety precaution in case there are any complications from her 'abduction'." Ty made finger quotes around the word.

Gianna gave him a skeptical look.

Ty stared at Ronnie, small and helpless, and tried not to see the terrible creature she'd become. The urge to neutralize that threat made his fingers twitch. He wasn't thrilled about releasing the maybe-cured rougarou either. And he was even less thrilled that, if she did survive, Ronnie would know Mira's secret. But Mira had chosen to try to save the girl. He wouldn't undo her efforts. *Especially since it may well turn out to be the last thing she ever does.* He shook his head and wiped at an itch near the corner of his eye. *Can't think like that. She'll be fine.*

"For now. . . ." He turned to Gianna. "Let's get you up to speed." He looked her up and down. "And a little more dirty."

Ty, Gianna, and Cari rehearsed their story while Gianna splashed through the grass and splattered herself with mud—to make her role more believable—until the heavy buzz of airboat engines returned, this time as a swarm. Ripples slapped the shore of their little island. The first boat to come into view had six officers in the passenger seats. Moretti's walrus mustache and bright-red Hawaiian shirt made him easy to spot near the front. Agent Donovan was sitting next to him in his aviator sunglasses and a smart gray suit that made no concession to the heat or the damp. Two more boats were close behind, each with a collection of passengers in uniforms from the Miami PD, FDLE, Parks Services, Sheriff's Department, and emergency medical staff. Ty shaded his eyes from the sun, which had returned at full force with the dissipation of the storm and mixed with the damp from the rain to turn the Glades into a muggy sauna.

Moretti's boots splashed down before his boat fully stopped. He barely glanced at the two teenagers and Gianna as he stomped over to Ty, who was still sitting in the mud. "What's the situation?" He shouted to be heard over the whir of the boats.

Ty bristled at the assumed authority in the older man's tone, but he kept his expression even. He waited for the engines to be shut off so he didn't have to yell, which had the added benefit of irritating Moretti. Once the chatter and motion of the disembarking men was the only noise he had to contend with, Ty said, "The threat has been neutralized." He waved down a woman in an EMT uniform and pointed to the girls behind him. "They need to be taken to the hospital."

"So do you, by the looks of you," Agent Donovan said as he strolled up beside Moretti.

Ty nodded. "I'll be headed that way as soon as we're done here."

Two EMTs went to the girls, but the third—a young man with thick glasses and floppy blond hair in need of a trim—came over to him. He peeled back Ty's bandages, which were once again red, and peered at the wound across his chest. "That's gonna need a lot of stitches."

"Like I said, I'll head to the hospital once I'm done here."

The EMT made a *tut-tut* noise with his tongue, but opened his medical kit and started cleaning the long gashes across Ty's chest.

Moretti crossed his arms over his red-and-yellow shirt. Damp crescents darkened the fabric under his arms. "If you're finally ready to share . . . what the hell happened out here?"

"It was the fae who escaped from the alley yesterday. Apparently when we thwarted its attempt to abduct the woman from the club, it went after another meal." He nodded to the girls. "They were having a sleepover. The fae broke in, killed the mother, and took both girls. It was just starting on that one"—he pointed at Ronnie—"when Officer Lopez and I arrived." He raised his voice so the EMTs around Caridad and Ronnie could hear him. "She seems to have been put into some kind of magically induced coma. You'll need to keep her under close observation at the hospital, and I'll inform the local PTF office to assign her a detail until we're sure she's not suffering any lingering effects."

The EMTs froze in their work, both looking down at the unconscious girl as though she might suddenly wake up and attack them.

Better to keep them wary.

"So what was it?" Donovan asked.

Ty frowned.

"The fae. What kind was it?"

"It was a ghoul." That had been the closest possibility Ty could come up with that wouldn't leave the PTF wondering about a human host. "Nasty buggers with a taste for human flesh."

Donovan's mouth tightened. Moretti's skin blanched.

"And you were able to take it down alone?" Moretti sounded resentfully impressed. "Not bad."

"Actually," Ty said. "I was incapacitated." He tipped his head toward Gianna, who'd come to stand at Ty's shoulder. "She took it down."

Moretti's eyes grew to the size of saucers and nearly bugged out of his head.

Ty smiled at Gianna. *Now's your time to shine.*

"You killed the fae?" Moretti spluttered. He looked her up and down. "You don't look like you were in a fight."

Gianna lifted her chin. "Brains over brawn. I placed flash-bang grenades around the perimeter while Agent Williams very bravely, but rather foolishly, leapt in to rescue the girls the fae was about to eat."

Moretti and Donovan looked at Ty as if to confirm this story. Ty did his best to look both sheepish and proud.

"Once the charges were in place," Gianna continued, "I set them off to disorient the fae. Then I was able to target it with the iron net." She indicated the loose net on the ground nearby. "Once it was restrained, it wasn't hard to finish it off with a few iron shots to the head and heart, courtesy of Agent Williams's gun, which he'd dropped during his fight with the fae."

Okay, enough with the incompliant agent details. Ty cleared his throat. "I came to as she was taking the final shots."

"And the body . . .?" Donovan looked around the trampled area.

"Dissipated," Ty said. "As all fae bodies do once they're dead."

Moretti nodded as though this were common knowledge he felt Donovan should be embarrassed to have asked about.

Ty stifled a chuckle, turning it into a cough, which set his wounds to burning again. He groaned. "If you'll excuse me. I think I'll take that trip to the hospital now."

The EMT, who'd just finished wrapping Ty's chest and shoulder with fresh bandages, nodded encouragingly and began packing his medical kit.

"I'll go with you," Gianna said. She gave Moretti a superior smile. "I'm sure these two can finish the cleanup."

Moretti narrowed his eyes and growled like a bear woken early from hibernation.

Donovan tipped down his aviators to peer over the top and said, "Good work, Officer Lopez. The community will sleep better tonight knowing their children are safe."

Gianna and the EMT helped Ty onto one of the two remaining boats by the shore. The first was already speeding away with the two girls and their EMT escorts. Half the seats were empty when Ty's boat pulled back from the sawgrass, since most of the uniforms were staying to secure the scene and argue over who had to file which paperwork.

Ty shifted on his hard chair, trying to find a comfortable position.

"She saved those girls." Gianna leaned close against Ty's non-bandaged shoulder so she could be heard above the roar of the engine without shouting loud enough for the EMT or driver to hear. "And who knows how many others that might have been targeted before the end." She was looking at the bustle they were backing away from, but her stare was focused on the middle distance as though watching some other scene. "And no one will ever know."

Ty let his mind wander to Mira as the boat turned and picked up speed. The corners of his mouth turned up. "She doesn't do it for the fame."

Gianna snorted softly. "I should think not, considering." They watched the scenery slide by in silence for a moment. "Still, I can see how doing something like this might be satisfying even without the recognition."

Ty glanced at Gianna's profile. "Tired of the spotlight already?"

She chuckled. "Hell, no. I'm going to lord this over those jerks at the department for as long as I can." Her smile faded. "I'm just saying, maybe I was a little too caught up in getting credit. I totally got shafted when my ex took the credit for all my effort on that other case. . . ." She shifted in her seat. "Like how I'm taking Mira's credit for this one . . . but my contributions on that case helped saved lives, credit or no." She looked down at her hands, and her voice grew fainter. "I was so angry at being undervalued, I never really thought about the good I'd done."

Ty yawned. The rocking of the boat coupled with exhaustion and blood loss was making him sleepy. "We all do this job for our own reasons. You just need to figure out what yours are."

Cypress trees and climbing vines blurred past. Something Ty had taken for a rotting log at the edge of the water suddenly moved. A reflective orange eye blinked at him. The wind created by the speed of their passage finally dried his hair and turned the mud on his skin to flaky powder, but his shoes still sloshed. His eyelids grew heavy.

"She really is a hero." Gianna had been quiet so long that Ty jerked when her voice startled him from the edge of sleep. "Do you think she'll be all right?"

Ty couldn't respond at first. An invisible fist seemed to squeeze his heart. After a moment, he managed to take a full breath. "I hope so."

Chapter 29

MIRA

WARM, PINK LIGHT FILTERED into Mira's awareness. Her body felt heavy, her muscles liquid. An ambient ache filled her, as though every cell had been pulled out, beaten like a dusty rug, then stitched back in place. Fragmented thoughts swirled through her mind. Tia Marta telling her Caridad was missing. Her mother screaming. The photograph on Ronnie's nightstand. Her youngest cousins gossiping in the hall. Rafael's tour boat speeding through the Everglades. A vampire with chocolate skin and midnight hair who smiled without showing her fangs. A shining net caught on a broken tree branch. The first bite of a Cuban sandwich that was every bit as good as she remembered. A twisted shape with long, skinny limbs covered in thick hide and coarse hair. Father Bembe handing her a folder. Acid in her veins.

Her eyes sprang open. Gauzy curtains embroidered with pansies drifted on the slight breeze that snaked through the open window on the far side of the room. Mira was lying on the narrow bed in abuela's back room—the room that used to be hers, once upon a time.

<'Bout time you woke up.>

Mira started, then relaxed as more memories came back. Relief flooded her. "You stayed with me."

<Well, yeah. You told me to, didn't you?>

Mira wiped an errant tear from her cheek. "You don't always listen."

<Whatever. How are you feeling?>

"Like I got run over by a steamroller. How are you?"

<Alive.>

Mira shifted to her side, swung her legs over the edge of the bed, and pushed up to a sitting position. Her arms shook with the effort. "How long was I out?"

<About three days.>

She turned her face toward the door. The ambient noises dancing at the edge of her awareness resolved into voices. The smell of cooking meat reached her nose. She took a deep sniff. Her stomach growled. She smiled. "It's good to know we can recover from even that much fae magic." A swell of pain behind her eyes made her wince. "Not that I'm eager to push that particular boundary ever again."

<Well, we couldn't have done it on our own.>

Mira froze with her hand halfway to her forehead. "What do you mean?" Faces flashed though her imagination. Her throat grew thick, and her hands went cold. "Who did you drain?"

<No one. Well, not in the way you mean. Although I am pleased to report that Ty offered himself.>

An image of Ty, unmoving, with a terrible gash splitting him from shoulder to hip, floated to the surface. *As injured as he was.* . . . Mira gripped the edge of the bed and narrowed her eyes at nothing. "Tell me you didn't—"

<Of course not. I'm just saying, he offered, and it wasn't for my sake. That boy really likes you.>

Mira let her breath tumble out in a noisy exhale and tried to ignore the flutter of warmth the demon's words had stirred in her chest. "So how'd we survive?"

<Well, we started with your tio Luis.>

"You—" Mira covered her mouth. She felt as if she'd swallowed a handful of thumbtacks.

<Just a little, don't worry. I made sure not to do any permanent damage. And let me just tell you, that kind of restraint should earn me a Nobel Peace Prize. That was like . . . I don't even know. Something really freaking hard.>

The unsettled feeling eased. She lowered her hand. "Thank you for not killing my favorite uncle."

<Right, well, Luis didn't get us very far. Luckily, Carlos and your abuela were still here at the house, and Rafael didn't have to drive anymore, so he was fair game."

The queasy feeling came back. "You took energy from my abuela?" She cradled her head in her hands and groaned.

<Marta was still here, too, but of course I couldn't take anything from her without hurting the baby. But she called her husband, Tony, and told him to leave the kids with Sophia and get his butt over here, which he did. That gave me just enough *oomph* to burn the last of the fae magic out of your system.>

Mira's head was spinning. "I don't remember any of that."

<Not surprising. You were way gone. Even I couldn't find you.>

"So now everyone . . . they all saw you. Us. What we do. How we survive." She shook her head slowly from side to side.

<They weren't nearly as freaked out as you might think.>

Mira lifted her head.

<Well, okay, I won't lie. They were pretty freaked out at first. But they all volunteered.>

Mira snorted. "More like abuela made them."

<She might have offered a few words of encouragement about family, and responsibility, and whatnot. But I honestly think they all wanted to help you.>

Talk of family and responsibility brought her thoughts back to Caridad and the reason she'd been half-dead with fae poison to begin with. "What about Cari?" she asked. "And Ronnie? Did she survive? Did what we did work? How did Ty explain her to the cops?"

<What am I, a psychic? I haven't been out of this room in three days, and most of that time I was busy trying to keep your meat sack from rotting and making sure you didn't pee yourself. If you want to know more, you should ask Ty. He's probably around here somewhere. He's been checking in on you regularly.>

Mira pushed aside the light blanket that had been covering her legs and looked down. She was wearing a loose purple T-shirt with a bouquet of white calla lilies printed on the breast and a pair of sky-blue shorts. She reached up and touched her hair. It was tangled from sleep but seemed pretty clean, all things considered. She imagined abuela and Marta scrubbing all the sweat, blood, and mud off her. *At least, I hope it was tia and abuela.*

She stood, holding the bed for support. Her legs were unsteady and seemed to weigh a ton apiece, but she managed to shuffle over to the mirror above the dresser. Her face was pale, with pink circles on her cheeks and dark bags under her eyes, but there were no puppet lines. She touched her fingers to the saint medallion hanging against her sternum and said a silent, *Thank you.*

<Maybe we're not so hopeless, after all.>

She smiled at her reflection. "Maybe not."

She dragged her fingers through her hair—brown with a white stripe—which only served to aggravate the static frizz of her wavy locks. Taking a deep breath, she straightened her shoulders and left the room. She paused for a moment in front of her mother's door, tracing the smooth wood with her fingers, but the sound of voices and the tantalizing smells of food coming from the front of the house propelled her onward.

Tio Luis was sitting in one of the plush armchairs in the front room, chatting animatedly with Father Bembe. Luis wore a purple polo shirt, tan Bermuda shorts, and suede loafers. Father Bembe had on a short-sleeve, black clerical shirt and collar, black pants, and polished shoes. Both looked well-groomed and healthy, if a little pale.

Luis's face brightened like a lighthouse when he saw Mira. He jumped to his feet and called, "Mami, she's up!"

Bembe stood as well, though more slowly. A wide grin split his stately features.

Abuela came shuffling out of the kitchen like a freight train barreling down on Mira. "*Gracias a Dios.*" She crossed herself with her spatula. "Finally, you're awake." She wrapped Mira in a strong hug, then pushed her to arm's length and looked her up and down.

Mira glanced at the greasy spatula now uncomfortably close to her face. "Sorry I worried you."

Abuela stiffened and stepped back. "Worry is not knowing where you were sleeping for these past ten years." She pointed an arthritis-swollen finger at Mira. "You scared us half to death with your"—she gestured to her own face—"black . . . yuck. Who ever heard of such a thing?"

The demon chuckled. <Yeah, they were all screaming about a plague when Rafael carried you in.>

It's not funny.

<It's a little funny. All those hands flapping in the air. If you'd seen it, you'd laugh too.>

"I'm sorry," she said again. "But I'm all right now." She took a deep breath. "I hear I have you and the rest of the family to thank for that."

Abuela nodded, as though having someone suck the life out of her were the most natural thing in the world.

Mira studied the brightly colored carpet between her feet. "I really can't thank you enough. I know it must have been . . . terrible . . . to see me like that."

"*Psh.*" Abuela waved the comment away. "You are who you are."

Luis stepped forward and patted Mira on the back. His hand was warm and firm. "You're family."

<I told you they could handle it.>

Abuela nodded approvingly. "Though I do hope this is the last of the secrets you've been keeping."

<Yeah, your grandma wasn't thrilled to find out you'd only told them half the truth before.>

Tears blurred the carpet. Mira sniffed. "That's everything." She cleared her throat and turned to Father Bembe. "I'm sorry I couldn't bring you better news about Ramon."

He nodded sadly. His expression grew distant. "He is with God now, and thanks to you, no more children will meet his fate." His gaze refocused. He pointed to the pendant around Mira's neck. "May I?"

Mira mumbled, "Of course," and slipped the necklace over her head.

Father Bembe cradled the medallion reverently in his hands. "I have been thinking about you and your connection to Saint Jude a great deal lately." He bounced the medallion on his palm, as though testing its weight. "Saint Jude is an important figure, and he's served you well all these years, but I believe another patron would suit you better." He slipped the pendant into his left pocket, then reached into his right and pulled out a second necklace. He held it out to Mira. "Take it."

She looked at the silver medallion swinging on its chain. It bore a sword-wielding angel with a serpent under his foot. Mira's eyes widened. "The archangel Michael?"

Father Bembe nodded. "God's greatest warrior and champion of justice."

"But I'm not . . . I couldn't. . . ." Mira stammered.

"As it says in the prayer of Saint Michael, 'By the power of God, cast into Hell all the evil spirits who prowl about the world seeking the ruin of souls'." Bembe smiled. "I can think of no better description for what you do."

He unlatched the clasp, reached around Mira's neck, and fastened the necklace in place. The heavy metal thudded against her sternum with the weight of an oath. She looked down at the inverted saint.

<A guardian angel. That's us. Doing good works and smiting evil.>

She touched the metal, warm from Bembe's pocket, and whispered, "Do you really think it's His work I do?"

Bembe gripped her shoulders and met her gaze. "I believe it to be true."

She smiled down at the saint. "A guardian then; a warrior against the darkness." She nodded. "I can live with that."

Her stomach ruined the mood by choosing that moment to growl loudly.

"Enough of this," said abuela. "You must be starving."

"Indeed," Bembe said. "I'll take my leave now." He smiled at Mira. "But I'm always here if you need me."

Luis patted the priest on the shoulder. "I'll be heading out as well. Take care, Mira."

Mira smiled. "Thank you both."

Abuela wasted no time waiting for the two men to leave. She braced her hand against the small of Mira's back and steered her toward the dining room.

Mira plopped down in front of a mountain of serving platters and took a deep breath. Grilled tostadas, fried plantains, arroz con pollo, and pastelitos stuffed with cream cheese and guava fought for her attention. Her stomach grumbled like an angry beast, and saliva filled her mouth. Mira started shoveling food onto her plate. Abuela disappeared into the kitchen and returned a moment later to set a steaming mug of café con leche next to Mira's plate.

She stuffed a whole pastelito into her mouth and moaned with pleasure. Then indicated the feast on the table. "Did you make all this for me?"

Abuela scrunched her nose. "You've picked up such bad habits."

Mira forced herself to swallow the pastelito. "*Lo siento, abuela.* I'm just surprised you made all this, since you didn't know when I would wake up."

"I've been cooking nonstop since you came back from the Everglades." She looked aside. "Well, I suppose Marta did most of the cooking that first day."

Realization settled over Mira like a wet blanket. "You all needed to replenish your energy." She stabbed her fork into a piece of chicken thigh. "To replace what I took."

"Everyone's been stopping by at least once a day to see how you're doing, so I've been keeping a rolling buffet going for anyone who comes."

<I think they've been coming for the food more than to see if you'd woken up,> the demon said, then quickly followed up with, <but sometimes they peeked into the back room.>

Mira smiled. *I don't mind coming in second to abuela's cooking.*

She continued to decimate the food in front of her. When her plate was clear, she loaded it up again and started over.

"You're gonna make yourself sick if you keep going like that," said a deep voice.

Mira looked up, a skewered plantain halfway to her mouth, and found Ty standing in the doorway, smiling at her. He was wearing jean shorts and a loose white shirt with the top buttons undone. Bandages peeked from the V of his collar, and his left arm was in a sling.

"It's good to see you up and about." He pulled out the seat opposite her and sat down. "Abuela was worried."

Heat flooded her cheeks, and not just from getting caught stuffing her face. Ty had never used abuela's Spanish title before. Just how comfortable had he become with her family while she was out? Butterflies and snakes vied for space inside her, twisting her lunch into a queasy tangle. She cut her gaze to the kitchen, where her abuela had disappeared again.

Ty picked up a pastelito and tore it into chunks, letting the bread fall to his otherwise empty plate. "How are you feeling?"

Mira tipped her chin, indicating the crumbs. "Don't you dare waste that."

Ty started and stared at the bread chunks as though wondering where they'd come from.

Mira made her voice a little softer. "The last time I saw you"—she licked her lips and swallowed—"I thought you might be dead."

He nodded. "Same." He met her gaze. "You, not me. Even after Luis gave you what he could. . . ." He shook his head. "I wasn't sure you'd make it back here. Or that you'd get what you needed even if you did." His gaze drifted to the kitchen.

"Honestly, I'm surprised they agreed." She shifted in her seat and pushed a spoonful of seasoned rice around her plate. "Was it your idea to sic the demon on them?"

"I'm sorry I betrayed your trust, but you were dying. If I could have given you what you needed myself, I would have."

"The demon told me you offered."

He laughed. It was a bitter sound. "I finally worked up the nerve only to be told I was no good."

"Still," she whispered, "I appreciate it." She took another bite, swallowed, and asked, "What happened to Ronnie?"

He lightly flicked one of the torn pieces of bread. It tumbled across his plate. "She's alive. Still in the hospital but awake." He met her gaze. "She says she doesn't remember anything about . . . any of it." He shrugged. "Which might be true."

"For her sake, I hope it is." Mira set her fork to the side. "Living with the deaths of others on your hands isn't easy . . . especially people you care about."

Ty nodded, and for a moment they both sat wrapped in the silence of their own thoughts.

Ty cleared his throat. "Gianna got a medal from the mayor."

Mira snorted. "Finally got the recognition she was craving, huh?" She grew somber. "I assume she saw. . . ." She swallowed. "What does she plan to do now?"

"About you and your passenger?" He shook his head. "Nothing." A small smile curved his lips. "If anything, I think you've gained an admirer. And you'll be happy to hear she passed all the tests the PTF could throw at her. Her healing was officially a miracle."

Mira exhaled. "So that's it then." She lifted her napkin, wiped her mouth, and set the cloth over her fork. "Case closed."

"What with this hunt taking more than it gave, I figured you'd wake up hungry, even after your family's generous donations." He clearly wasn't talking about the food on the table between them. "So I went digging for suspicious activity. I found some promising leads."

The demon made a lip-smacking sound in Mira's head. <Let's just hope the next one is a proper rifter. No more of this fae bullshit.>

Ty leaned back in his chair and folded his arms. "Other than the few things left in your sickroom, the truck is packed. I'm good to go whenever you are."

Mira stared at the smears and crumbs left on her plate. She'd avoided coming back to this place for so long, hiding from her past as though that would somehow make her memories less real, but now that she'd been forced to face it all . . . *it was good to come home.*

She pushed back her chair and stood. "There's just one more thing I need to do."

MIRA

MIRA PRESSED HER forehead to the smooth wood of her mother's door. "If you stay even a little, this experiment won't work."

<I can only pull back to the edge of the anchors,> the demon griped. <We don't have enough energy to reset those if they come loose.>

"Fine."

<I'll see you soon.>

Mira waited, the wood grain pressing into her skin, as the demon fell away from her consciousness. Where usually it felt as if the other entity was hovering right behind her eyes, now it felt as if a plug had been pulled in Mira's heel and all the "other" was draining out of her like bathwater. She shuddered at the hollow feeling left behind by the demon's absence, the endless silence of her own head. She prodded the anchors that tethered the demon to her. They were still intact. The demon would wait in the Rift until Mira was done, then follow the anchors back like a lifeline.

Please let this work.

Taking a deep breath, Mira twisted the doorknob and stepped into her mother's room.

Maria sat in her recliner, face turned toward the window. Shafts of afternoon light slanted across her features. A soft smile curved her lips, made uneven by the damaged skin on one side. Her eyes were closed. She was humming.

As Mira approached, she recognized the tune her mother and grandmother had each sung to her when she was a child. Her throat thickened with emotion. *What if I'm wrong? What if it's not the demon she's been reacting to? What if it's just me she can't stand?*

No response came.

Mira straightened her shoulders and continued forward. *Only one way to find out.*

She knelt in front of Maria's knees, covered by a bright patch quilt, and set her hands over her mother's thin fingers. "Mami?"

Maria's eyes sprang open. She seemed to stare through Mira for a moment before her gaze finally came into focus. She lifted a hand and set her palm against Mira's cheek. The patches of scarred skin felt like hard wax. Tears shone in Maria's brown eyes. "My baby."

Mira pressed her lips together for a moment, unable to speak.

Maria frowned and narrowed her eyes. "Are you a dream?"

Mira shook her head. "No, mami. I'm real."

"That's what you always say." She looked side to side, as if searching. "Where is the shadow?"

"It's okay, mami. The shadow's not here right now."

Maria's gaze settled on Mira once more. "Where have you been? You were a child yesterday."

Mira had to clear her throat twice before she could respond. "I've been traveling. I've seen a lot." She smiled. "I would like to tell you about it someday."

Maria patted Mira's hand. "You're home now. I'll bake some cookies, and you can tell me all about school before Steve gets back."

Another wash of emotion—guilt, regret, shame—nearly stole Mira's ability to speak. "I can't stay, mami." She set her hand over the medallion of Saint Michael that Father Bembe had given her and was filled with a sense of purpose. "There's work I must do. Important work."

"Let someone else do it."

Mira shook her head. "There's no one else who can."

"Stay," Maria insisted. "You should not be alone."

Mira smiled, thinking of Ty and her demon, of Father Bembe, abuela, and the rest of her family who'd kept her alive even when she'd given up hope. "I'm not alone, mami."

Maria frowned, then looked around as if she expected to see more people. "It's quiet today." Her focus came to rest on Mira. She gave a little start. "It's nearly time for school. You don't want to be late."

Tears leaked from the corners of Mira's eyes. "I was just leaving." She sniffed, wiped her nose with the back of her wrist, and straightened. Even that short period of kneeling had made her thighs burn. Ty was right; she needed to find proper sustenance soon so her body could fully recover.

Maria nodded. She settled back in her chair and closed her eyes. "Be a good girl."

"I'm trying." She leaned forward and pressed a kiss to her mother's cheek. "I love you, mami. I promise to visit again soon."

Maria began to hum, her lopsided smile in place once more.

Mira crossed the bright rug, opened the door, took one last look at her mother, and stepped into the hall. She exhaled and leaned back against the closed door. The granite fingers squeezing her heart to pulp began to loosen. She fingered her pendant and looked at the ceiling. *Important work.*

She gave a mental tug against the anchor pinned near her heart. The demon came rushing into her, filling her. The anchors flared, then settled as their power balanced out.

<So? Did it work?>

Mira smiled. *It did.*

A sense of excitement mixed with sorrow washed over her. <What did you guys talk about?> Mira had never heard the demon so uncertain.

She pushed away from the door and headed to her bedroom to collect the last of her things. "I told her that my friends and I have work to do."

Want more?
Continue the adventure with
A Demon Faerie Tale
Book 3 of the Rifter series.

Acknowledgments

First and foremost, I want to thank my family and friends for all their support and encouragement. My husband, who lets me bounce ideas off him and helps me untangle plot knots, tells me to keep going even when I doubt my talents, and reminds me to breathe when I get too stressed to function properly. My daughter, who sacrifices our together-time when I'm under a deadline, pitches my books to her teachers on her own initiative, and happily spent "take your child to work day" writing short stories with me. My mom, with whom I can chat endlessly about "what-ifs" and who celebrates my successes with more enthusiasm than anyone. My dad, who isn't much of a fiction reader but buys every one of my books anyway. Connie, who reads every book before it goes to print to help me make them as clean as possible. David and Jeannette, who've treated me like a daughter since the day I met them. Jillayne and Andrea for accepting me just as I am and still being my friends despite my many quirks. All the wonderful folks I've met through Rocky Mountain Fiction Writers and Colorado Authors League who've cheered my successes and commiserated with my struggles.

A special thanks to Mercy for sharing her Cuban heritage with me, to Adam for answering my cop questions, and to J. Victor Duran for providing his insights on this book. Thank you to everyone who answered my social media requests to share their memories of the Everglades and Miami with me so I could make the environment believable. Thanks to Debra Dixon for having my back with these stories and making them stronger, Teri Sullivan-Elmore for tidying them up, and the team at Bell Bridge Books for their continued support.

Finally, a hearty thanks to all my readers and followers: Your comments and reviews keep me going when those inevitable whispers of doubt creep in. Thank you all so much!

About the Author
L. R. Braden

L.R. Braden is a bestselling, multi-award-winning author of dark-yet-hopeful urban fantasy stories. Her published works include the *Magicsmith* series, the *Rifter* series, and several works of shorter fiction. A bit of a recluse, she enjoys collecting skills that may (or may not) prove useful in the event that she is suddenly transported to an inhospitable alternate reality. Since that hasn't happened yet, she mostly spends her days weaving fantastic tales, playing with her family, and getting lost on purpose. Her writing has won many awards, including the Eric Hoffer Book Award for Sci-fi/Fantasy, the Next Generation Indie Book Award for Paranormal Fiction, and the Imadjinn Award for Best Urban Fantasy.

Connect with her online at lrbraden.com